# Love in the Cupboard

## Mari Jane Law

**FUCHSIA**

Copyright © 2023 Mari Jane Law

First edition 2023

The right of Mari Jane Law to be identified as the Author of this Work has been asserted by her in accordance with the Copyright, Designs and Patents Act, 1988.

All rights reserved. No part of this book may be reproduced in any form, or by any electronic or mechanical means – except for the inclusion of brief quotations in articles or reviews – without written permission from the author and publisher.

This novel is a work of fiction. All characters and events in this publication, other than those clearly in the public domain, are fictitious and any resemblance to actual persons, living or dead, is purely coincidental.

Published by Fuchsia Publishing

ISBN: 9798373616942

Cover design: www.publishingbuddy.co.uk

## The Love & Mishaps Series

***Love & Pollination:*** Love & Mishaps Book 1
***Love in the Cupboard:*** Love & Mishaps Book 2

What Amazon readers have said about **Love & Pollination**:

★★★★★ Delightfully quirky

★★★★★ Absolutely brilliant

★★★★★ It gave me the most unexpected giggles

★★★★★ Amusing and lovely rom-com

★★★★★ A hidden gem of a read!

★★★★★ Events just keep getting funnier and funnier

★★★★★ A brilliant and quirky romantic comedy

★★★★★ A must-read for romantics everywhere

★★★★★ Twists and turns roll in hilarious fast-paced action

★★★★★ Anyone who loves Bridget Jones will love this book

For more information:
https://amzn.to/3385a5c
www.marijanelaw.com

Here are some comments from ARC readers of *Love in the Cupboard:*

"I absolutely loved this book… the ensuing shenanigans made me laugh out loud in places."

"If you are looking for something light, funny and in the genre of the classic British farce, then look no further."

"It was unique and not the regular boy meets girl story."

"…it was an excellent story; funny, poignant, sensitive and very readable. Who would have thought that a priest in a cupboard would have so much fun!"

"What a tangled web of entertainment this is. Packed with quirky characters that are so closely interlinked it makes for a humorous and delightful read. Great representation seen in the ensemble of characters too."

"If you are looking for something light, funny and in the genre of the classic British farce, then look no further. This book will have you giggling and laughing like a schoolchild with all its goings on."

"Love in the Cupboard is a delight; gentle and quirky – occasionally bordering on hilarious farce."

"I read the entire book with a smile on my face (apart from when I was snorting, chuckling, or making other noises that showed my enjoyment). This is a cracker."

For everyone living with any kind of disability or long-term chronic illness and the people who care for them.

I'm grateful to family and friends, Cambridge Writers, members of our romance writers' group and The Romantic Novelists' Association's New Writers' Scheme for all the support and encouragement I've been given in writing this book. Also thanks to Paul Burridge who designed a great cover and set up the formatting and Lisa Woodford who proofread my work. Any remaining errors are mine.

Mari Jane Law, January 2023

# Prologue

Early March

Overwhelmed by the changes in his life, Father Thomas Sheridan had sought refuge at the back of an L-shaped cleaning cupboard. He'd welcomed the dark, and he'd welcomed the presence of a bucket he could upturn and sit on. But he was no longer seated and neither was his surprise companion with whom he'd swapped places. She'd asked him to kiss her and had stood up when he'd agreed. He wanted a wife and somehow Fate—or God—had brought Faith to him.

He couldn't see her, but he could feel her femininity as she leaned against him and placed soft lips on his, a gentle hand behind his head. A floral scent filled his nostrils, and he inhaled deeply. His heart was pounding so much, he couldn't do otherwise, and it was making him quite lightheaded. Her breathing had deepened too. Nerves were zinging, legs were threatening to fold under him and blood was rushing downwards as he experienced his first romantic encounter. He hoped there'd be many more.

Of course, it had to come to an end. Lunch hours were like that. But this... this had been the most enjoyable lunch hour of his entire life.

After they'd whispered goodbye and Faith was gone, Tom was alone again. His fingers touched his lips as though to bring back the memory of those magical kisses. Was it possible to fall in love with someone you'd just met and had never seen? She had a generous heart—and she'd surely captured his.

If only he'd been brave enough to confide at the outset, without putting on that silly accent. If only he'd not allowed the misunderstandings to ride.

Perhaps if he shaved every morning and never sat in the cupboard again, she might not connect him to the mess he'd just created and would like him afresh. Yes, why not? Or perhaps he could explain what had happened to him, reveal his big secret, and she'd forgive him. She'd been so kind-hearted...

He wondered if there might be a third possible scenario but when no ideas came, he dismissed the notion.

# 1

Two weeks earlier

Faith Goddard had completed her outfit for another evening out with her boyfriend, Andy. She bounded into the living room of the two-bedroom flat in Clifton, Bristol, arms outstretched. Then she spun around in front of her younger sister, Hope, who lay sprawled on the upholstered yellow-gold sofa. 'So, how do I look?'

There was a brief rustle of paper as Hope stuffed something into a gap between the cushions. Her loosely bound, deep-pink dressing gown fell open to reveal white pyjamas with pink hearts. Light-brown slippers with white rabbit ears lay abandoned on the carpet. Faith raised her eyebrows enquiringly at the rustling sound but Hope raised hers too as though to say mind your own business. Best stick to the agenda then, Faith thought. No time for an argument before Andy called for her.

'Well, what do you think?' Faith gestured to her tight, red jeans, high-heeled boots and chiffon blouse over a camisole top. Her black hair was loose, falling way behind her shoulders, and she'd given her eyes a smoky look. The whole ensemble had taken ages to put together as she'd been indecisive. It could be a make-or-break evening, and she'd decided to load the dice her way by making the best of her appearance, given the biting weather. She'd sort out her bedroom—which looked like it had been searched by a frantic burglar—when she got back. But would that be tonight or tomorrow? Being Friday, she didn't have to be up early for work in the morning but it wasn't set in stone that she went to Andy's place—and there was no way she wanted him to see her bedroom the way she'd left it.

Hope zapped the TV with the remote and it went silent. 'You know damn well how you look. Gorgeous. And I wish I could look half as good.' Hope's lips downturned.

Faith crouched by the sofa and patted her sister's arm. 'You do. Just not when you're in your nightclothes and haven't showered for a few days.'

'Hey, I have a shower every day now. Haven't you noticed?'

Faith sniffed. 'You're right. The air does smell sweeter.'

'Ha ha.'

'Anyway, who looks great in pyjamas? When you get better, you'll look great all the time. Your hair is so pretty. I'd love to have hair like yours.' Fondly, Faith stroked a lock of Hope's soft hair.

'Really?'

'Yes. Really. Who doesn't want to be blonde? As for the curls...'

Hope's brow furrowed. 'I thought you liked straight hair.'

Faith eased herself up into a standing position. 'I have to say that as mine's dead straight. It would get offended if it thought I wasn't happy with it. A girl's best friend is her hair; I have to keep on the best side of mine. And yours is lovely. Chocolate box lovely.'

'Are you for real?'

'Dead serious.' Faith flopped into the armchair and raised her legs to admire her seventy per cent off boots from Bristol town centre.

Hope leaned on one elbow. 'What's this with death all the time? Bet you've been spending too much time with Gavin.'

Gavin lived in the flat opposite with his partner, Luke. Faith shook her head. 'Nope. Don't see that much of him. And don't you worry. You've been making great improvement over the past few months. It won't be long before you're doing more.'

'But when will that be?' Hope moaned.

Faith arranged her arms at the back of her head. 'These things take time. And patience. See how much progress you've already made?'

Catching glandular fever in her teens had been the end of a normal life for Hope as her fatigue and shopping list of other symptoms had been confirmed as ME. She'd been so terribly, terribly unwell and she'd made no secret of the fact that she hadn't wanted to be among the land of the living anymore, tearing at Faith's heart. She'd taken her sister in and had made loads of promises that were becoming increasingly hard to keep.

'It's piddling compared to how I used to be.'

Hope used to go running with her every once in a while, and race her at the local pool. They'd both belonged to the same swimming club when they were younger, had trained before school every day and had taken part in swimming galas. Looking at Hope's pasty face now, Faith couldn't discern any hint of her sister's former physical prowess.

'I know it's piddling to how you were. But you're so much better now. Focus on where you're going to rather than on where you're coming from.'

Hope aimed miserable eyes at her. 'That hill is such a mighty one to climb.'

'Steady and slow and all that. Remember what Confucius said: "A journey of a thousand miles begins with a single step."' Faith finished the sentence with a rallying sideways punch to the air.

'Yeah,' Hope agreed unconvincingly. 'But I bet he didn't have to keep resting between steps.'

'Have some hope, Hope.'

'Hmph.'

Faith spied the two mugs on the coffee table. 'Did you have company while I was at work?'

'Mm?'

Faith pointed to the mugs and then let her hands dangle either side of the arms of the chair, wiggling her fingers to get the blood flowing through again. She shouldn't have had her arms behind her head for so long.

'Oh. Yes. Luke popped round.'

'Luke?'

'That's what I said.'

Luke's name had been cropping up a lot lately, and all to do with times Faith had not been at home. 'How often does he come? He never used to. What's going on?'

Hope bristled. 'There's nothing "going on".'

'So why was he here?'

Hope shrugged. 'I get lonely on my own. Perdita's not around anymore. He pops in every now and then.'

Had Luke been coming around for... what would it be now? Two years? Surely not? 'I don't remember you saying Luke came round to visit after Perdita left.' Perdita used to live in the flat above Luke and Gavin. 'In fact,' Faith added suspiciously, 'you never volunteer the fact that he's been round at all. You only admit it when I spot evidence of a guest. That's suspicious behaviour.'

'No, it's not suspicious behaviour. I'm not a child, and I don't have to give you a blow-by-blow account of my time away from you. I don't pry into your private life.'

Faith snorted: Hope was one of the nosiest people she knew. 'So, there's nothing going on?'

'No.'

'Does Gavin know Luke comes round?'

Hope glared at her. 'I've no idea. But we're doing nothing wrong so just mind your own business. I don't need a grilling from you.' She sat up, transferring her feet to the pouffe. 'So, where's Andy taking you tonight?'

'Meal,' Faith said tersely, sure that Hope had deliberately changed the subject to put her off whatever scent of whatever was going on. And sitting up had been a psychological ploy to switch her attention away from Luke. But Faith wouldn't forget that there was something fishy going on. She'd put the mystery on the back-burner to solve at a later date. With that other mystery of the scrunched-up paper hidden in the sofa.

'Is he taking you for an Italian?' Hope asked. Probably because she knew that Faith had raved about the last Italian meal she'd had out with Andy.

'No. A pub meal.' At least it wasn't at The Lion—the last time they were there, she and Andy had been having a cosy chat when Ryan and Ashish had waltzed through the doors. *Again.* Quickly, she'd put her hand up to shield her face in the hope that they wouldn't notice Andy and her. Looking fixedly at Andy, she'd longed for the danger to pass.

'Hi guys. Mind if we join you?' Ryan had asked.

'Of course not.' Andy's tone couldn't have been more welcoming. 'You don't mind, do you, Faith?' Andy had shifted his seat across to make room for Ashish without even glancing her way. Why couldn't he have seen the guys when he wasn't with her?

The conversation had become entrenched in the world of football, and she'd zoned out.

Faith said, 'We're not going to The Lion tonight. Do you know his mates have been joining us there?'

'What?'

'I asked Andy if he told them where he would be. He said he didn't, but they do seem to know exactly when to go there.'

'So, you think he lied to you?' Concern filled Hope's eyes.

'I don't know. But surely he'd want to see me on my own if he was in love with me?'

'Perhaps it's because you've been together so long, he sees you as part of all of his life, to be shared with friends?'

Faith slowly rocked her head from side to side, mirroring her wavering thoughts on the matter. 'I'm thinking about asking him outright how he feels.'

Hope tilted her head. 'Do men like questions like that?'

'I don't know, but I need to know whether this is heading towards marriage or a dead-end.'

A furrow appeared on Hope's brow. 'Have you gone to all the trouble of looking gorgeous because you're scared you're going to lose him?'

Faith pressed her lips together and squeezed her eyes shut before she gave a little nod.

'If you ask him and he feels cornered, he might make a rash decision. You'll be lonely if it goes badly. I know my company isn't enough for you and that you're not living the life you should be. Because of me. And I'm sorry about that. Being with Andy gives you some kind of life outside home—and me. You've shared lots of experiences. He has to love you to stay with you.'

Faith covered her eyes with her hands. Was Hope encouraging her to keep the status quo because she felt guilty about the life Faith had been forced to live, the things she'd sacrificed? That wasn't a good reason to not question Andy. But the thought of not having Andy in her life was too dreadful to contemplate. She'd come to rely on him for so much, and she did truly love him.

'What is it?' Hope asked. 'You're frowning.'

'I can't imagine my life without him in it.'

'You really are obsessed with death.'

'No, I'm not.'

Hope grinned. 'Shout out the first word you think of after I say a word. Okay?'

'Yes.'

'Name?'

'Faith.'

'Age?'

'Do hyphenated words count as one?'

'Yes. Age?'

'Twenty-six.'

'Gavin.'

'Coffin.'

Hope pointed a finger at her. 'There you are then. Back to death.'

'But that wasn't fair,' Faith protested. 'You can't use that against me. Anyone who knows Gavin would say coffin.'

'No, they wouldn't. He is many things besides being an undertaker.'

'Such as?'

Hope waved a hand in the air. 'Gay comes to mind. As does fit, hunky, sexy, neighbour, Luke—'

Faith sighed. 'Okay, okay. You're right. Perhaps I am a bit depressed.' It was the uncertainty, the insecurity of late...

'Perhaps you are. Don't rock the boat when you feel like this. Just go out and have a lovely evening with the man you love. Don't worry about whether he loves you back—he's there for you and that's what counts, isn't it?'

The entry phone buzzed.

Picking up the intercom handset that was mounted on the living room wall, Faith said, 'Hi' and pressed the door release button. Then she turned to Hope. 'See you later.'

Andy's timely arrival meant that she didn't have to respond to her sister's comments. Hope had never had a relationship—what did she know about how strongly Faith felt about the importance of being with a man who truly loved her, would be there for her not for just now but long into the future too?

'I'll be in bed. See you tomorrow.' Hope flicked off the TV, stuck in her in-ear headphones and shut her eyes.

Faith grabbed her shoulder bag and thick wool coat from the hook on the wall in the hallway while mustering a fixed, happy smile; she was pleased to be seeing him, it was her unwelcome fears that were the problem. She opened the door to the outside corridor. 'Hi. I'm ready to go.'

Andy must have found time to visit a barber that week. His blond hair was neatly clipped and his fringe now allowed his thick eyebrows to be easily visible. So, she wasn't the only one who'd made an effort. In fact, he was looking smarter and crisper all round. And she didn't remember seeing that black jacket before. Had he splashed out for her? Then he *did* love her.

'You look beautiful as always.' Andy took in her appearance appreciatively but there was a strange hint of regret behind his eyes. What was that about? Was he feeling guilty that he hadn't been making much effort lately? Well, damn right he ought to be feeling guilty.

Her heart lightened. 'Thanks.'

His kiss was gentle, tender. 'Shall we go then? I'm starving.'

# 2

Warmed by the comforting heat of the fire she was sitting next to, Faith put down her cutlery and removed her coat. The movement caught Andy's attention and his gaze lingered over her top before meeting her eyes with an expression she couldn't interpret. Indecision? Uncertainty? Was regret still there?

Occasional spits from the fire wafted smoke into the dining area, irritating her nose. She bet her hair and clothes would smell like she'd spent the evening at a barbecue. Andy, who was sitting opposite her, was digging enthusiastically into fish and chips as though it was his first meal that day while she toyed with her steak as though she'd just come from a banquet. It wasn't usually how she ate in The Horse and Groom. Instead of being as hungry as one of the many horses the original inn might have once stabled, she was as hungry as one of the mice that might have lodged in its perhaps once thatched roof; her stomach may as well have been shrink-wrapped. She tucked a lock of her long hair behind her ear and sipped her dry white wine—perhaps for the courage to confront him. She knew it was against Hope's advice but she sensed something unsettling running under the surface of Andy's demeanour.

'Andy?'

'Mm?'

'The last three times we've been to The Lion, when your mates joined us, did you ask them to come?'

She was sure he used to cherish having her to himself, and now he didn't seem to notice there was any difference between being alone together or in a group—he'd paid his beer mat more attention than her. Was she being unreasonable, minding that their precious Friday evenings together were being hijacked by his football-loving friends since she and Andy often spent time at her place with Hope? Did the two situations cancel each other out?

But Andy's recent lack of interest had given her a suffocating vision of herself in the future if the path they were on was ever long enough to lead to marriage; her at home with a baby while he and his pals were getting ratted down the pub, or round theirs getting ratted while watching the footie. The images were grey and dull; there wasn't a hint of colour, and it had nothing to do with the fact that it had, so far, been an overcast, drizzly February. It would be like living her life in black and white when she longed for glorious Technicolor.

Andy used to be very attentive, making her feel fulfilled and content when he'd stroked the inside of her wrist as he asked about her day, holding her gaze with intense interest. But this evening, he rarely flicked his gaze towards her and was intent on clearing his plate as though he'd win points if he were the first to finish. He hadn't seemed to notice she'd barely touched her food. Right now, she was neither fulfilled nor content.

Not so long ago, they'd discuss plans for the weekend on a Friday evening. To go for walks or drive out of the city to a country pub, perhaps do some shopping, have dinner out or cook together at hers so that Hope wouldn't be left out. Saturday evenings, they might catch the latest thriller at the cinema or just snuggle on the sofa after Hope had gone to bed, watching a TV drama or crime series on Netflix. Then they'd make love. Sometimes she stayed over at Andy's and then their love-making would be more spontaneous as they didn't have to worry about Hope walking in on them or hearing them.

But for the past few weeks, it was as though foreplay had gone out of fashion, and Andy was in a hurry to get the deed done so that he could lie back sated and get some shut-eye—while she'd lain awake in the dark, blinking at the murky ceiling, wondering whether his rushed determination was significant or whether a lack of consideration in sex was something that happened to all long-standing couples.

She also wondered whether all sleeping men grunted like a pig. Dreams had taken a new turn as life on a farm became a regular theme; she was often feeding baskets of corn on the cob to a pen of noisy hogs or watching someone else tip vegetables or fruit into a trough—or the pigs would escape or she'd somehow have fallen asleep amongst them. Once, the vet had come to vaccinate them, and she'd tried to call out that she wasn't a pig but the man was still coming towards her in gumboots, carrying a long stick syringe ending in a terrifying shiny needle—and then she'd woken up to find Andy grunting into her ear.

She didn't have to wait long for Andy's answer about his mates coming to The Lion.

'Not that again. I told you before. No, I didn't ask them to join me.'

'So it is just coincidence?'

'Yes. Why are you so insecure?' But he didn't look up; he was concentrating on cutting up the last few mouthfuls of fish.

Memories of when they'd first met played in her mind, and she recalled his keenness for her company, texting her throughout the day when his driving and work commitments as a loss adjuster allowed. This week, the single text she'd got from him had been to cancel their Tuesday date and to say how busy he was with suspected dodgy insurance claims. When they'd finally got to speak, it had been only to arrange going out tonight.

With her gaze resting on his newly-cut blond hair and his new black jacket, the unease that niggled her wouldn't leave her alone, nudging her to speak out; he'd even tidied up his monobrow. She suspected him of being as dodgy as the law-breaking clients. But would he just repeat that she was insecure? And was she or did she have a good reason to distrust him? Or had she got it all wrong and he just had problems at work?

Andy's blue eyes caught her gaze. 'Are you getting tired of me? Is that why you're picking an argument?'

Her stomach lurched as though she'd swallowed something rotten. 'No! What do you mean?' Panic clutched her insides. Didn't he know how she felt about him? 'You know I—'

As though the words were sticking in his throat, he swallowed hard and then coughed. 'Actually, I... er... wanted to see you tonight because we need to talk.' Andy put down his cutlery and wiped his mouth.

Her heart flipped, and the heat from the fire seemed to suck all the air from her lungs. 'Oh?' It came out like a strangled cry. She cleared her throat as though to excuse the sound.

'There's no easy way to say this, and I'm very sorry, but we've reached the end of the road. I realise this might be a shock...'

So much for the loaded dice—and her fears had been grounded, yet he'd called her insecure! As she gripped her napkin under the table, she composed her face as she'd often had to do to cover up her heartbreak over Hope's suffering.

Had Andy been leading Faith along, using her while

it was convenient? Had he found someone else?

'How long have you felt like this?' She dug her nails hard into her wrist, regretting trimming them the night before, until the physical pain had an anaesthetising effect on the deep, hollow ache inside her.

'A while. But there's no point in talking about it. There's nothing you can do to change things.'

Faith bridled. She'd been seeing Andy for two years but now her romantic life was reset to zero like one of those computer games that her sister played in the lonely hours when Faith was at work, and he wasn't prepared to give a reason.

'Please explain why there's no point in talking about it.' Faith gave a good imitation of a woman in control of her emotions with barely a wobble in her voice.

He gave a remorseful smile that explained the regret she'd suspected to be lurking in his eyes earlier. 'Let's face it. How many times have you had to cancel because of Hope? How many times have I sat at your place because you didn't want to leave her on her own too much? Left the film halfway through at the cinema because she called and you were worried she'd top herself? Have you leave my place in the middle of the night because Hope was in tears, feeling so ill she was afraid to be alone? You never switched your phone off; even when it was on vibrate, you kept checking.'

It was all true. Every word. Faith's heart thumped hard against the walls of her chest, a wave of dizziness washing over her. She squeezed her eyes shut against the fear of shattered dreams forever.

'This is all about... Hope? But she's out of that terrible relapse. She's stronger and not so depressed now.'

'She has been doing better,' Andy said gently. 'But it's no good. We're like an old married couple who have no fun or excitement in our lives. It's boring; *we're* boring.'

Faith flinched. 'I thought you didn't mind.'

To cite Hope as the reason for the split was like adding an accelerant to an already fiercely burning fire of agony. But a resilience from her years of caring for Hope welled up, anger gathering in the pit of her stomach. Faith promised herself she would rise again from the ashes like a beautiful phoenix and find a man so much better than Andy. Then he'd know she'd been one loss he shouldn't have written off.

'Well, I do. Any man would mind.'

Would they? Visions of the Technicolor future she'd hoped for dimmed to a bare glimmer and the monochrome existence she'd feared came into view in stark contrast. If Andy was right, no man would want to be saddled with Hope as part of the package, so where did that leave Faith? *She'd be single forever.*

Her throat swelled as she fought the gulping sobs welling up inside her. Perhaps there was more she could do to help increase Hope's independence. Whatever her sister needed, Faith would do her utmost to oblige. For both their sakes, because there was no one else to take care of her sister—and, right now, the thought terrified Faith.

'I've packed your things,' Andy said. 'They're in the boot.' He couldn't meet her eye.

Well, now she knew which bed she'd be sleeping in tonight and she'd likely never set eyes on him again. Would the farm dreams stop too? She steeled herself to give him a measured look, taking in his crisp blond hair and his black jacket.

'So, there's no one else? It's just because of Hope?' The tips of her fingers strangled the leg of the table as her tension became unbearable. Was the break-up only to do with Hope or was that an excuse because Andy didn't want to say that the real problem was that Faith just wasn't good enough?

He shook his head. 'Loss adjusters are on the road so much, there isn't time for anything other than work. I've been seeing you when I've been in Bristol.'

'I've seen far less of you than I used to.'

'I know. Partly cutbacks—I've got a bigger patch to cover now, so I'm not around as much—and partly because I knew you and Hope needed space. I didn't want you to feel pressured.'

Faith frowned. By her not feeling 'pressured', he'd bowed out of the relationship. Made her feel... insignificant. 'So, there isn't anyone else?'

Andy shook his head. 'If there was, I'd tell you. You know how I like to be straight about things. That's why it's better to have a clean break now. You'll thank me later for not hanging around, preventing you from meeting new people.'

'Is that what you're going to do? Meet new people?'

He paused. 'Yes, but I'm not ready to get stuck into another serious relationship so soon. I need to get you out of my system first.' He had the grace to look chastened as though realising how mean he'd sounded.

'Sounds like a power flush—cleaning out the gunk from the radiators before you have a new boiler fitted.' The landlord had changed the boiler in the flat last October, so she knew all about it.

Andy pulled his lips downwards as he tipped his head to one side. 'Mm. Sounds like a good analogy. I'll have to remember that.'

'For the next time you give a girl the elbow?' The sharp retort took her by surprise, but he deserved it.

An unattractive blush pervaded his face. 'I'll take you home. If you've finished?'

Faith had barely eaten half of her meal, but Andy had eaten every scrap of his. 'Yes, I've finished.'

She hesitated before rising. Just for a moment—a long moment—she was tempted to empty her plate onto his jacket. The way he'd ended their relationship, and in public, made her want to hit back. But she knew that would be childish and that she'd regret it. So she calmly followed him into the street.

# 3

It was Friday evening, and Father Thomas Sheridan's inner voice had become so powerful, so insistent that he couldn't ignore it another day, and he worried he'd start screaming from the torment of what it was telling him to do. If his hair had been long enough, he'd have been tugging at the ends to try to mask the wrenching of his guts.

Instead, he'd knelt under the wooden crucifix attached to the magnolia wall above his bed in the presbytery. He'd bought the early twentieth-century wooden cross with the copper image of Christ in Le Puy-en-Velay in Southern France—a destination once popular with pilgrims in the Middle Ages—when he'd holidayed with a friend before his ordination. The banner above Christ's head read INRI. It stood for Iesus Nazarenus Rex Iudaeorum: Jesus of Nazareth, King of the Jews.

As he'd stared at the brown, dulled-copper depiction of Jesus, Tom recalled how he'd bought the crucifix before he'd given up his freedom. But now... now he wanted it back. Would God ever forgive him?

With intertwined fingers, he'd petitioned God for guidance and for permission to go his own way in place of his usual prayers: for being faithful to his commitments, for the grace to safeguard his chastity and for devoting his entire life to the ministry. He'd implored the Lord for help, guidance and the strength to make a decision and never waver thereafter.

When the prayers hadn't seemed to work, he'd done

a series of press-ups on the multi-coloured rug next to his bed until his muscles had burned and his heart had been close to bursting. Exhausted, he'd lain flat on his back and had wallowed in misery. When he'd had the strength to move again, he'd tiptoed down the stairs in his running clothes, let himself out quietly through the front door to avoid the other Fathers, whose murmurings he'd heard from the other side of the living room door and had begun to run through the streets of Marrow in Bleakset, a diocese in the south east of England. He'd hoped that the activity would exorcise him of his current life and his current angst.

He hadn't got very far before he'd had to turn back or he'd not make it home. Giddiness had grown as panic mushroomed inside him, and he'd craved the safety of his room. Before long, he'd managed to tiptoe back up the stairs and lock himself in.

The Church had been one vocation in Tom's life, but this second calling had grown stronger and that other inner voice would not be silenced; he wanted—no, needed—a wife.

The longing that ate away at his innards was so sharp, he sometimes became paralysed by the tight knot in his stomach screaming at him that he'd wasted his life, taunting him with how he could have had a wonderful family by now. It was like grieving for people he'd never known, experiencing a loss that wasn't real. *But it felt real.*

The moment of his epiphany had been during a baptism. It had been quite ordinary, no different to the multitude of baptisms that had gone before it, except for one remarkable event.

The four-month-old baby, whose black-haired head had been about to receive three lots of holy water, had looked into his eyes, and she'd smiled trustingly at him.

Then, she'd reached out a little brown hand with tiny fingers and had touched his wrist, her attention caught by his late father's watch. Her fingertips had danced between his skin and the watch face, and he'd been instantly smitten. Glancing up, he'd seen the love the proud parents had for each other and their child, and the shattering realisation that he was no longer happy living his life alone had slammed him so hard, he'd almost lost his balance.

Usually, babies cried when he poured holy water over their heads, but Sovi had just pinched her dark-brown eyes shut, curling into herself. When he'd anointed her with the oil of chrism, she hadn't tried to pull away, she'd just stared at him, and he'd wished she was his.

From then on, he'd frequently recalled Sovi's tender, tentative touches on his wrist, forcing him to face what he'd been missing out on, what he'd sacrificed. Seeing families together at Mass had had new meaning. Parties and events he'd been invited to had become excruciating, the sadness of his aloneness pushing him to break free.

Imagining life outside of the Church, a different kind of grief engulfed him now as he visualised being in the world alone, without his fellow priests and parishioners. He was torn, conflicted, and a battle raged inside him unknown to all, including the Bishop.

Insomnia had plagued him intermittently for years but the past twelve months had been a trial to get through, he'd been so sleep-deprived. He'd hardly touched his evening meal and even now, nausea welled up as he summoned the courage to call up the contacts list on his phone. His Excellency, The Right Reverend Brendon Costello, Bishop of Bleakset, wasn't going to like what Tom had to say so he was going to save the reason for his request for a private audience until they were face-to-face. Tom wondered how His Excellency would react—or how everyone else would react. In fact, Tom wasn't sure, once he'd smashed apart the only adult life he'd known, how he himself would react. He'd made his decision—*but was it the right one?*

His fingers trembled as he pressed the green call button.

# 4

On the drive home from The Horse and Groom, Faith saw them pass the top entrance to Clifton Rocks Railway that was now only sometimes open to tours—the funicular had stopped taking passengers to and from the bottom of the Avon gorge in 1934. After, the site had been used as an air-raid shelter and a BBC backup room and perhaps other things. Despite the ongoing restoration, she'd heard that the railway itself would never operate like it used to again. She and Andy had planned to go on a tour together, but that wouldn't happen now. Her relationship with him was as defunct as the railway. She flicked a tear away and turned her gaze to Clifton Suspension Bridge, sweeping across the top of the gorge.

When they were back outside her building, Andy switched off the engine. 'I'll give you a hand carrying your things in.'

'There's no need.' Faith fumbled for the door handle, finding his proximity uncomfortable. She was desperate to be alone.

He appraised her. 'As you like.'

But when he opened his car boot and revealed its contents, she blinked. How had so much stuff accumulated at his place? She'd only stayed over the odd night. She tried to recall just what had ended up in his flat. There were toiletries, of course. Oh, and a duck-feather pillow as she hadn't liked the one Andy had provided. Spare clothes and a dressing gown. Joggers and a pair of old trainers. Jack Reacher novels. Baking tins she'd taken for making Hope a birthday cake in secret. And the piping bag for the icing...

'Actually, could you help me put the bags in my car?' She'd noticed that her flat was in darkness. She didn't want to risk disturbing Hope in case the baking tins clanged against each other or the drawers in the hallway. It would be a tight squeeze with this lot. 'I'll take them in tomorrow.'

'Okay.'

Faith sensed he was in a hurry to be off. Irked that it was so easy for him to do the walking away, she stomped to her Honda Jazz—which was no mean feat in her heels—so that Andy could help load the boot of her car.

'Right. I'll be off then. And, for what it's worth... I'm really sorry.' He surprised her by stepping forward and giving her a quick hug. He pulled back, his expression remorseful, and then he raised a hand and swiftly turned on his heel.

As she watched his car tail-lights dim, hot tears tickling her cheeks, Faith wondered about those three magic words he used to say to her. She should have listened to her gut instincts and pinned him down over what he'd truly felt. She'd been stupid—and determined that no man would make a fool of her again.

Faith sat in her car and bawled, recalling tender moments with Andy. Then she remembered how he'd reassured her, time and again, that he understood her commitments to Hope. How he'd helped Faith with grocery shopping, picking up Hope's prescriptions, getting her watch a new battery, putting up a blackout blind for her and a multitude of other things. He'd seemed ideal, accommodating, understanding and caring. But now... now it had probably been a mirage of sorts, a dream that was not real. He'd played a persona he could not sustain, exhausted his tolerance.

Would this happen again? Why wouldn't it? It was

hard enough for Faith to cope with the tie that held her life on a short leash that was reeled in at a moment's notice. How could she expect any other man to react differently to Andy?

Her life was over, owned by Hope. Faith squeezed her eyes shut and keened quietly, rocking back and forth in the driver's seat. Her resentment released the pent-up guilt she had from feeling like this and, at times, she could have screamed with the injustice of it. Other people were free to live their lives as they pleased, and she'd not had a chance. How many years would this go on for? How many years could she stick it without cracking up herself?

Was she cracking up? Was this the last straw that would break her back, crack her open, and then the ugly resentment that was ballooning out of her would be there for everyone else to see? And they wouldn't understand. Was she selfish for wanting more freedom? If Andy had been the one for her, and she'd had that freedom, would they have made a happy life together?

Scared at the intensity of emotions that were coursing through her, barely in control, and the negative thinking, Faith dredged up an inner resource she'd come to rely on and said, internally, *Stop. Stop it right now!*

She took a deep breath and accepted she'd never watch another episode of any Scandinavian crime series again to remove the risk of association with Andy. She'd develop new viewing habits and would find things to fill her weekends and evenings.

She examined her streaked face and swollen eyes in the driving mirror. A fringe might have hidden some of the redness in her blue eyes but without one, her entire face was open to scrutiny. If it had been Halloween, she might have got away with looking so scary. She decided to stay in the car until her skin appeared less inflamed.

She patted her cheeks dry and centred herself by imagining finding a much better man than Andy—someone she could depend on, who'd prove his love for her. She turned the radio on and switched to a phone-in channel to help distract her.

The next time she checked her image, it seemed sufficiently restored to risk being seen without giving children nightmares.

# 5

Craving company and distraction, Faith headed for her neighbours' flat as their living room lights were still on. When the door opened to the sound of the bell, she saw that Gavin's black hair was wet as though he'd recently stepped out of the shower. He was also wearing a grey bathrobe over sky-blue pyjamas.

'Hi, Faith.' He blocked the gap. Despite his slim stature, he was strong—and needed to be to take his share of the weight as a pallbearer in his job as an undertaker.

Normally, the combination of seeing Gavin in his nightclothes and his obstruction of the entrance would have sent her retreating into her flat opposite. But she was desperate for someone to talk to even if that meant interrupting Gavin's "alone time" with Luke.

She forced a smile. 'Can I come in? Please?'

'Ye-s. Yes, of course.' Gavin's guarded tone suggested she might not be welcome, and she hesitated before passing him when he stepped back from the doorway. He'd understand when she told him that she'd been dumped, was not wanted, was not good enough...

The living room was lit by three IKEA floor lamps. The use of black, red and cream was softened by the indirect lighting. Perhaps a change in her own décor could help give her and Hope a brighter and more interesting life? Should she buy some throws in primary colours and revamp their living room with rugs and lampshades?

Luke, broad and muscly, suiting his job as a personal

trainer, was sitting in an armchair cuddling his angelic-looking godchild who was wearing pyjamas decorated with footballs.

'Hi, Luke,' Faith said breezily, even though she didn't feel cheerful at all. But it was either put on an act or burst into tears again, and she preferred the former.

Before she could greet Petal too, Luke whispered, 'Shh. She's just dropping off.'

He stood up, crooning over their mutual friend Perdita's child who could have been mistaken for his despite having hair much lighter in tone than Petal's dark-blonde waves. He carried her out, closing the door behind him. It must have been because of Petal that Gavin had been reluctant to let Faith in, knowing that Luke was trying to get her to sleep.

Faith's knees gave way against the sofa, and she collapsed onto the soft cushions, shutting her eyes for a moment. She took in a deep breath and let it out slowly as at that moment, it was the only thing in her life she had control over. She'd coped better with caring for Hope when she'd had Andy. Even when he wasn't doing something to help out, she'd had him for emotional support. Now she'd have to fly solo again and didn't know if she'd ever have another boyfriend.

Gavin joined her on the sofa.

'I didn't know Petal was staying over,' she whispered, welcoming the distraction of the activity here.

When Perdita had lived in the flat above Luke and Gavin's, she'd often invited them all for meals as she'd had no family of her own, being an orphan brought up by nuns. She was married now to Saul and lived in Westbridge, a small town about a twenty-minute drive out of Bristol. Saul had adopted Petal, and now he and Perdita were having a baby of their own. Faith wished she could have such a happy ending and find a good man like Saul to marry.

'Luke can't get enough of her. We're going on trips to the zoo now, the pools, parks, playgrounds. He even watches the footie with her, and he's teaching her how to kick a ball about in the garden.'

Wasn't that sweet of him? The building had a small communal garden at the back. In warm weather, Faith would sit outside with Hope. Well, Faith would sit, and Hope would lie on a blanket.

Gavin leaned in. 'Did you see her football pyjamas?'

'Yes.'

'He's even bought her a Man United T-shirt with shorts and the special socks.'

'I take it you're not into Petal in the same way?'

Gavin shook his head from side to side.

Faith mouthed a big 'O'. 'Have you spoken to Luke about this?'

'I've tried, but he's hell-bent on spending spare time with Petal. It's going to be worse now that Perdita's pregnant again. She's tired and is glad of all the breaks on offer.'

It seemed as though Luke and Gavin had a third person—Petal—in their relationship and Faith wondered if Andy had felt as bad about having Hope around as Gavin did about having Petal in his life so much. Why hadn't Andy been honest with her?

'You don't like children?'

'No,' Gavin said with feeling.

'Why don't you mention it to Perdita?'

'Luke would go ballistic. I've never seen him so angry and protective if something gets in the way of his spending time with Petal. Even when we went skiing the day after Boxing Day, all he could talk about was what she got for Christmas and whether she liked the football he'd got her—and the toy figures of players.' Gavin shifted further towards Faith, tears in his eyes. 'This is between you and me. Okay?'

'Yes.'

'Luke wants a child of his own.'

Faith's lips parted and her eyes widened. She wasn't the only one with troubles and disappointments. There was a hissing sound. She noticed a gadget with a green light plugged into the wall. Gavin sprang back to his original position on the sofa.

Luke appeared. 'She's asleep. She woke up because she had a bad dream, so I've had to put her to bed twice. And she's got another tooth coming through.'

Faith nodded understandingly, but her knowledge of children was scant. She'd never even babysat for a neighbour. Luke was so available that Perdita had never needed to look elsewhere for a break, which was something that Faith was grateful for because of the amount of support Hope needed.

Luke sniffed the air. 'Have you taken up smoking?'

'No. Wood smoke from the log fire I was sitting next to.'

'It's just as well Petal's gone to bed. Second-hand smoke—'

'I know. I'm sorry. I'll scrub myself clean before I come round again. Then I won't pollute—'

'There's no need to take offence—'

'Sorry. Of course, you should be concerned for Petal.'

'So, what have you been talking about?' Luke sank back onto his chair.

Gavin turned desperate, appealing eyes towards Faith, and she found herself staring back. He picked up his mug for the first time since she'd arrived and began to take sips, the implied message being that she'd have to answer Luke.

'I was just telling Gavin,' she said, concentrating on keeping her voice steady, 'that Andy's chucked me.'

Gavin spluttered into his mug.

Luke glanced at Gavin. 'I thought you already knew.'

'I led up to it very subtly,' she said, taking out a tissue from the small packet in her bag. 'So subtly in fact that perhaps Gavin hadn't quite understood.' She dabbed at her stinging eyes.

'I'm so sorry. Poor you.' Gavin placed a sympathetic hand on hers. 'I thought you were just complaining about the evening?' His gaze was steeped with purpose; she was to follow his lead.

'Didn't I get to the crux of the matter?'

Gavin shook his head. 'Come here and let me give you a hug.'

She shifted towards him as he put his arm around her and squeezed her shoulder. 'Well, that's how it ended. He finished with me.'

'That's terrible,' Gavin said.

'Yes. How come?' Luke asked.

The sound of a cough came from the baby monitor and Luke held up his hand. 'Let me just check on Petal.'

As soon as he left, Gavin whispered, 'I'm sorry I didn't give you time when you came in to tell us what brought you here.'

'I understand. It's probably good for me not to wallow too deeply in my troubles and it seems you have plenty of your own.'

'It's getting so I can't stand it. You see what he's like? Even when she's asleep, his mind's on her. We can't watch a whole film without him getting up. He even unplugs the landline and puts his mobile to vibrate and makes me silence my phone too.'

Luke returned. 'It's okay. Maybe some saliva caught in her throat and that's what made her cough. There's no need to worry.'

'We weren't.' Gavin's tone was dry.

'Well,' Faith said briskly to distract Luke from Gavin's remark, 'the reason Andy gave me the elbow was because of—would you believe—Hope.' When Hope had been at her most unwell and depressed, Marion, their mum, had been diagnosed with bowel cancer on top of her existing osteoporosis so her parents couldn't help out. And so the years of providing care and support had started.

'Does he fancy Hope instead?' Gavin asked.

'You obviously weren't listening at all properly before.' Faith threw Gavin a hard look, and he raised his eyebrows in recognition of his blunder.

'Why don't you start again from the beginning?' Luke said.

'Andy finished with me because he said that he can't cope with me needing to consider Hope all the time. Why hadn't he told me that spending time at my place was such a problem?'

'But Hope's so much better now,' Luke said. 'She doesn't need you like she used to.'

'Seems like you're helping out there,' Faith muttered, recalling the two mugs on the coffee table.

Gavin glanced between Faith and Luke with keen eyes. 'What do you mean? Luke's spending time with Hope?'

'Oh,' Faith said. 'I didn't know it was a secret...'

Luke tapped his fingers against the arm of his chair. 'It isn't a secret. I just hadn't mentioned it.'

'Why not?' Gavin asked. 'I tell you how I spend my time away from you. I tell you who I get to see.'

'It's not a secret. I just wanted to—'

'Hope says he's company for her now that Perdita's not around much. It's only for a mug of coffee or tea.'

Faith wanted to help Luke out and to retain focus on her problem. 'What if Hope is unwell forever and all men have the same issue with me spending so much time with her? Mum and Dad only went to Australia for a break because Mum got the all-clear, but her osteoporosis isn't going to improve. And she might end up needing more chemo. Dad can't take on any more, and I promised Hope a home with me.'

Faith wanted to be a good daughter and a good sister, yet was the price of losing her own life too high? But what choice did she have? If it had been the other way around, she hoped that her sister would have done the same for her. Besides, Hope wouldn't cope living on her own, physically or emotionally.

'What if no boyfriend can be honest? What if they all pretend it's fine about Hope but later tell me it's not?' Fighting back more tears, Faith added, 'How can I believe them? *Trust them?*'

'You're well rid of him,' Gavin said.

'We noticed he was changing,' Luke added.

'You didn't like him? You didn't say.' She blew her nose.

'It's not the done thing to say when it was "Andy this" and "Andy that".' Gavin renewed the hug.

Faith was grateful for the comforting gesture. 'But he was so kind... before...'

'Perhaps he was so nice to you at the start because there was no one else around—no offence—and then he got to understand what life would be like with Hope. If he can't accept her, he's not right for you.'

'How come I didn't see it and you did?'

'We're very astute when it comes to dating men,' Luke said.

'I hadn't thought of it like that.'

What an idiot she'd been! She should have noticed,

understood that there had been a problem long ago. Now she remembered how his smile would fade the moment he turned away from her, whereas hers would linger on. That had been a sign and she'd missed it—or had chosen to.

'How many boyfriends have you had?' Gavin asked.

'You mean apart from the odd boy asking me out at school and going to the cinema a few times before it fizzled out?'

'Yes. How many boyfriends have you had that involved an intimate relationship? How many notches on your bedpost?'

'One.'

'That's it? You're twenty-six and it's only the one? And Andy's that one?'

'Sorry, should I have gone on Tinder to get a bit more experience?'

'I think,' Luke said, 'that's rather sweet. Holding out for a man who... What is it you do want from a man?'

'Marriage. Children. I want what Perdita's got. A life full of colour and vibrancy; she's so happy compared to what she used to be. I don't want a drab, boring existence, like living in a black and white movie.'

'It's not much you're after then,' Gavin said. 'How are you going to go about getting this dream life?'

'I don't know. I don't think I'll ever meet the right man. I don't even go to places where I could meet men.' Since dating Andy, no man had registered on her guy-hunting radar.

'You're not supposed to go to places to meet men when you're going steady,' Luke said. 'What you need now is a girls' night out. Have some fun. Stop worrying about finding a man for a while.'

'Luke's right,' Gavin said. 'It's no good rushing into things or being involved on the rebound. You don't want to get involved with another loser. A girls' night out is just what you need.'

'Which is hard to set up when I'm the only one who's not married out of the very few school friends I managed to keep in touch with.'

She'd lost touch completely with all those who'd gone to uni. Their paths had diverged too much and, for a long time, Faith had been eaten up with jealousy, hearing about their lives away from home, the parties, the clubs, even the exams as they were also something she could not share in. Because she'd been needed at home…

She thought back to the thrilling day she'd got her A-Level results. And then the letter she'd written to the University of Chester a heart-breaking week later, regretfully declining her place on the Health and Social Care course. Hope had been in bed with post-glandular fever fatigue and their mother had just been diagnosed with bowel cancer. The treatments the oncologist had had in mind had included surgery, chemotherapy and radiotherapy. Their dad, Keith, had been devastated, and it was all he could do to turn up to work to financially support them all, including her brother Charlie, who'd only been twelve at the time. Faith had ended up being a carer to Marion and Hope and, at times, mum to Charlie, and her dreams of becoming a social worker had been firmly put aside. The day that letter had been sent to give up her place at uni had been the day her hopeful, excited life had ended.

'Go out with a married friend then,' Luke said, 'but not Perdita as she's not up to it.'

'I know. Her pregnancy is taking it out of her.' Faith mentally trawled through the possible women she could ask to go out with. Finally, she recalled a school friend she'd not completely lost touch with. 'I've got it! I'll call

Jade.'

'Before you go, let's have a stand-up group hug.' Luke rose to his feet.

The feel of the arms of two strong men around her made Faith feel loved and protected.

# 6

On Saturday morning, Tom was presiding over a lengthy Nuptial Mass in the Parish of St Michael in Marrow, Bleakset. The familiar smell of wood polish and incense that permeated the church was so poignant that he worried he might crumple to the floor in a heap of tears. This was going to be his final Mass and no one else knew it—yet.

Three congregants had already had to leave their pews in search of the disabled toilet installed at the rear of the church. He regretted having drunk so many coffees that morning. He couldn't leave the altar until Mass was over, and he had the jitters about the secret he'd not yet shared with a living soul.

Three more sentences to go. 'My dear friends, who are gathered here today, it is my pleasure to introduce you to Mr and Mrs Nolan. Mass has ended. Go in peace to love and serve the Lord, and each other.' How many congregants actually did that?

When the response, 'Thanks be to God', came, and the final hymn was in full swing, he led the newlyweds into the sacristy to sign the marriage certificate. The official photographer followed them to capture the moment.

Tom's own photographic side-line had begun when he'd stood in for an absent photographer after a last-minute hitch. He'd never enjoyed a wedding so much. Word soon spread and he became much in demand. Baptisms and then funerals were added to his list of events. His Excellency, The Right Reverend Brendon

Costello decreed that half of the "donation" should go to the parish and half of the proceeds could be kept for expenses such as camera equipment and photographic courses.

The paperwork in the sacristy was now complete and the photographer agreed they could leave. As they re-emerged into the nave, Tom signalled to the organist to strike up Felix Mendelssohn's *Wedding March.* The newlyweds walked down the aisle together and, as the best man and bridesmaids joined them, Tom snuck out by the side door and went to stand at the edge of the growing group outside.

If he left before the photographs started, he might be accused of unseemly haste. But the moment the bride and groom posed for their first picture as a married couple, Tom melted into the background and then charged back to the sacristy, as though the devil were nipping at his heels, to rip off his vestments—and go to the toilet.

After, Tom raced to his car wearing the mandatory black clothing for parish priests appearing anywhere in public. He turned the key in the ignition and pressed on the accelerator. The car sputtered, coughed and died.

Dread seeped into Tom's veins. If he missed the Bishop he'd have to continue working as a parish priest until The Right Reverend Brendon Costello returned from Rome. Tom thought he might be sick.

# 7

Faith had been halfway to the supermarket to do her usual Saturday shop when she'd recalled that the sore reminders of her failed relationship from Andy's place were still in the car boot—where Luke had always told her to stow groceries to avoid a back injury. She turned off the main road and headed for home again. As Hope hadn't been up by the time Faith had left, she decided to sneak back in quietly so as not to wake her.

She left one bag by the drawers in the hallway and was about to take another carefully to her room, tiptoeing all the way. But she didn't manage to get past Hope's bedroom.

'Ugh. That hurt,' she heard Hope say.

'Is this any better?' a deep male voice asked.

'Mm. Now that's good. Yes, do it like that... oh, yes.'

Rooted to the spot, Faith couldn't understand how, in the time since she'd left, Hope had invited a man into her bedroom—and it sounded like they were up to something very intimate.

Should Faith slip out and feign ignorance or bang on the door and demand an explanation? Gavin had said that Luke wanted a baby of his own. Is this how he was going about it? For as sure as Faith was single again, that had been Luke's voice she'd heard.

'How does this feel?' Luke asked Hope behind the door.

'Lovely.' Hope's voice was dreamy.

Faith didn't know whether to bang on the door and yell at them or leave as quietly as she'd come in. There were times her sister was selfish and didn't think enough about other people, but surely she wouldn't get Luke to cheat on Gavin? How could Luke behave like this? Yes, Hope was gorgeous and could have been a model if she'd not been unwell, and her long, wavy, blonde hair gave her a chocolate box sweetness appeal, but all the same... Should Faith cause a scene now or later? Would it be more productive to speak to Hope or Luke alone? Could there be an innocent explanation? She couldn't think of a single one; her brain was so frazzled by what she'd heard, her frontal lobe was in a stupor.

With an enormous effort, Faith instructed her brain to instruct her leg muscles to retreat to the front door. Just as she was struggling through the main door to the building with both of her bags—she couldn't leave evidence that she'd been back home—Gavin emerged from his flat.

'Would you like a hand with those? I saw you bring them in earlier, but I'd just come out of the shower and wasn't properly dressed for the occasion.'

Faith kept her head bowed as she didn't want Gavin to see her appalled expression until she'd tutored it into blandness; looking cheerful was way beyond her present capability. 'Oh, thanks.'

'Are they the same bags?'

Feeling cornered, Faith said, 'Um... no. No, they're different bags.'

'They look the same to me.'

'Well, the actual bags are the same. But the contents aren't.'

'When I saw you earlier, I thought you were bringing in the things you'd had at Andy's.'

'I was. I... er... realised that I wouldn't have anywhere to put them so when I left your place last night, I had a bit of a clear out.'

Gavin laughed as he followed her to the street. 'It's more than a bit. What are you going to do with it?'

'Oh, I'll take it to a charity shop.'

'Which one?'

'No particular one.'

'Well, look, I can save you the trip. We've been having a clear-out too, and I can take your bags along with our stuff.' Gavin reached into his pocket and produced some keys.

'That's very thoughtful of you, but I couldn't possibly impose.'

'It's no trouble.' Gavin aimed the key fob at the green VW Golf and its lights winked. He strode towards it with things she still needed and whatever else that was in the bags that she'd not already recalled.

'No! You mustn't.'

'Why not?'

As he turned his head, Faith took in his bemused expression.

'I don't want them taken today. I'm going to take them another day.' She was tugging the bags out of his hands. 'Please. I need them in my car.'

Gavin held fast. 'I want to help. Let me.'

'No. Now hand them back.'

Gavin's focus sharpened into a question as he let go.

'I have a problem,' she improvised, her frontal lobe thankfully reviving. 'It's very hard for me to chuck stuff out. So, when I do, it has to live in my car for a few days to make sure I can really part with it. If I can't, I can bring it back in. If I do get rid of it, I have to take responsibility so that I don't vent my frustration on anyone else.'

There was no way she wanted her things to be taken to a charity shop and this was the only excuse she could think of to keep Gavin's hands off them. She'd bring them in later, when he wasn't around. Better still, when no one was around so that curious questions couldn't be asked by anyone.

'Did Andy know you're like this?'

'Nooo. It's something I feel very embarrassed about so perhaps we could keep it just between the two of us?' She waggled a finger in the gap between them.

'What about Luke? Can he know?'

'No!'

If Gavin told Luke, Luke would know she'd been in the flat while he'd been in Hope's bedroom. Faith needed time to think things through before she did anything—caused upset where there might not be any need.

'Fine. Don't worry.' Gavin locked his car again. 'Let me pop them in your boot for you. I must say, I think you're very brave trying to get rid of this much at once under the circumstances.'

'Thanks. Oh, and please don't mention it to Hope either.'

Gavin cocked his head to one side. 'Hope doesn't know?'

'No.'

'How can she live with you and not know?'

'Oh, well, she did know but she thinks I got better,' Faith said, winging it. 'It would upset her to know that I still need to do it.'

'Have you been to your GP about this?'

Faith flapped both of her hands down in the gap between them. 'It's not that bad to warrant a trip to my doctor. Honestly.'

When the items were safely stowed away again, she said, 'Where's Luke this morning?' Did Gavin know about Luke's arrangement with Hope, whatever that was?

'Oh, he's with a client.'

'He works Saturdays?'

'Sometimes, if a client has a problem with other times.'

'I see.' She did indeed. 'You don't mind?'

Gavin shrugged. 'I work Saturdays too, sometimes.'

So, Gavin was definitely out of the loop with whatever was going on between Luke and Hope—or all three were in on it and didn't want her to know. But that didn't make sense either—if Gavin knew what Luke was doing with Hope, he'd know that Faith had just been in the flat and would have discovered Luke there.

'Well, I'd better get off and do the shop or we'll have nothing to eat.'

By the time Faith drove away, there were patches of cool in her armpits. She'd need another shower by the time she got home from all the stress—and what was she to do about Hope and Luke?

# 8

Normally, Tom would have invoked the power of prayer, but he'd suspected that God was displeased with him and that's why his Halora refused to work. God knew what he was about to do and was trying to stop him. That was it. Tom had tried hard to get the car going, thinking he might have flooded the engine, and then waited a while and tried again—and again.

Well, now he would show God a thing or two. Although public transport wouldn't get him to Snaresbury in time, bearing in mind the scheduled engineering works and the change he'd have to make, he was a member of the Automobile Recovery Service. Switching his phone back on—he'd had to ensure his favourite Gregorian chant couldn't blast out during the nuptials—connection to the ARS was almost instant.

It wasn't long before the blue and purple van appeared and a portly man in blue and purple overalls stepped out. Tom explained the difficulty. After the repairman had fiddled under the bonnet, he said, 'I'm afraid it's your fuel pump. Your car needs to go to a garage. Although, with the Haloras, repair is always a temporary measure. Terrible cars.'

Tom's muscles were so tense, he feared he was turning into a statue to complement the ones displayed in St Michael's Church. He'd never buy a parishioner's car again. But then he remembered that, after today, he wouldn't have any parishioners.

'Oh. Could you take me to Snaresbury? I've got silver membership. I'd be very grateful.' Without realising he'd managed to move, Tom found the palms of his hands had come together in a supplicant gesture.

The ARS man scratched his nose with a calloused, oily finger. 'Are you under some religious obligation to go to Snaresbury? Is it a matter of life or death?'

'I don't have long to get there...' That wasn't a lie...

'The Last Rites? I'm one of the flock myself—not from your parish, mind.'

'Er... yes... the Last Rites.' Tom's ethics seemed to be melting in proportion to the urgency of reaching his goal.

'Don't you need a special oil?'

Tom had nothing in his pockets apart from his wallet, keys, rosary, Fruit Pastilles and phone. 'Oil of the Sick? He's the one who blesses it. He'll have a stock of his own. The Bishop always does.'

'As you're my last job, I'll tow your car to a garage; we'll post the keys through their door. After, I'll drive you to Snaresbury myself, even though I'm not supposed to take a customer without their car.'

'That's very kind of you. Thank you.' Tom's fingers travelled along the olive wood beads of the rosary as he began to pray by way of penance for misleading the ARS man for his own benefit.

When they were on their way, the mechanic said, 'Would you pray for my dad? He's got cancer.'

Although unsure whether his prayers held any currency with the Lord anymore, Tom said, 'Of course. What's his name?'

An hour later, the ARS man pulled up outside the Bishop's residence.

'Thank you so much,' Tom said.

The door to the presbytery opened and the stocky figure of His Excellency emerged, his hair looking slightly greyer every time Tom saw him. Fudge.

'Has another priest got here before you, then? Hang on,' the ARS man said. 'He's the Bishop. He's wearing a big cross!'

'You're absolutely right.' Tom feigned surprise and squinted at the clear-as-day solid-gold pectoral cross that hung from the Bishop's neck. 'Shouldn't have left my specs in the car. It certainly is *a* bishop but as to whether it's *the* Bishop...'

The Right Reverend Brendon Costello came level with the nearside window, next to where Tom was sitting. 'Well now, won't you be coming in? I can see you in there.' His Excellency's Irish accent was still strong.

The ARS driver lowered the nearside window and leaned across Tom. 'Is Father here in time for giving Extreme Unction?'

Tom unbuckled his seat belt.

'What in God's name is he talking about?' The Right Reverend Brendon Costello demanded.

Tom grappled with the passenger door handle and the Bishop stepped out of the way. The fresh air, free of the odour of oil and mechanics' grease, was very welcome. He climbed out. 'Bye now! Careful how you go.' He slammed the door shut and waved.

But the driver's eyes were blazing, his mouth pressed into a grim line. 'The Bishop. He said the Bishop was dying. That's why I drove him here.'

'Do I look like I'm dying?' the Bishop said.

The ARS driver fixed Tom with an acute stare. 'Is this *another* bishop or *the* Bishop? Sounds to me like he's *the* Bishop.'

'Now that he's close up, I can indeed confirm that he's *the* Bishop. Remarkable recovery... a miracle. Praise be to God!'

The ARS driver's eyes narrowed and the sides of his

mouth turned down menacingly. 'I don't like being taken for a ride.' He released his seat belt and opened the driver's door.

With a commanding voice, The Right Reverend Brendon Costello said, 'Wait! Could it be that we have our wires crossed, don't you think?' He glowered at Tom. 'It wasn't me who was dying, you eejit. It was Father McKenna.'

*Father McKenna?*

The Bishop addressed Tom. 'Didn't my housekeeper tell you she was going to call me, too? Because you took your time, I got here before you.'

The ARS man scratched his head. 'But I thought you live here.'

'Of course I live here. But wasn't I away, meeting with the Archbishop? Didn't I come as soon as I heard Father McKenna had taken a turn for the worse?'

Tom found his voice. 'I'm so sorry for the misunderstanding, Your Excellency. I quite thought it was you who was ill. Imagine my surprise when I saw you walking towards me.'

'You didn't.' The ARS man frowned. 'You said you couldn't see who it was without your glasses.'

The Bishop's eyebrows lifted, registering his surprise at the notion that Tom's eyesight was not perfect.

'When His Excellency got close enough,' Tom said, 'I recognised him.' Mortified at how one little lie had multiplied, he looked away.

'If Father Sheridan hurries, he'll be able to say goodbye because, when I came out just now, Father McKenna was still with us. So, if you'll excuse us...'

'Certainly, Fathers.' The ARS man shut his door and tugged his seatbelt back into place.

'Thanks again,' Tom called as the passenger window

was raised, shame making it near impossible to meet the man's eyes.

'Stop your blasted waving,' the Bishop said. 'And you can confess your untruths to a priest in your own parish. I don't have time.'

Tom wondered to whom The Right Reverend Brendon Costello would confess his falsehoods.

They entered the plush study of the Snaresbury presbytery.

'I think you have some explaining to do,' The Right Reverend Brendon Costello said.

So Tom explained.

The Bishop tutted. 'Don't Haloras spend more time in the garage than on the road? As a parish priest, it's your duty to have a reliable car. And you can't be lying to laypeople. To anyone for that matter.'

'I apologise, Your Excellency.'

The Bishop flicked an impatient hand. 'Call me Brendon.' He crossed his arms. 'Now, Thomas, are you going to tell me what is so urgent that you broke the Eighth Commandment and took advantage of a kind soul to get you here?'

'I've thought long and hard about it...' He'd not just thought about it, he'd agonised over it, torn between his commitment to God and the love of his parishioners and the need for family life. 'I want to leave the ministry, and I want a dispensation from the obligation of celibacy.' Yes, he wanted to live like most blokes his age could, without the stifling rules.

The Bishop was about to scratch his head but his hand stilled in mid-air.

'I want to get married. I can't bear the loneliness anymore. I want a woman's company, someone special to confide in, someone to hold—and I want children.'

The Bishop's face darkened. 'Would I be right in

thinking you've been having an affair? Is the woman pregnant?'

'No... and no.'

The Bishop leaned back in his chair. 'Let's wait then until I return from Rome, and we can talk about it fully.'

'No. I want out. Immediately. I don't want to say another Mass, hear another Confession.' Tom's tendons were so taut, he bet the parishioner harpist would be able to play a tune on them. Would Brendon agree to let him go or would Tom have to abscond and cause undue upset all around?

'How long have you been feeling like this?'

He cleared his throat. 'It's been growing over the past few years.'

'You didn't feel it was incumbent on you to say something before now? If you're in crisis, Thomas, you are meant to talk to your bishop about it.'

'I am now.'

'Before now. This is a serious business.'

'I know. The reason I didn't tell you is that I don't want my mind changed. I want to find a woman to share my life with.' He didn't just want it, he yearned for a partner to share his life and bed with so much that the fantasy he craved would break into his prayers, interrupting his concentration.

He even daydreamed during Mass, only mentally coming back to the altar when a parishioner finished reading the selected piece from the bible or their bidding prayers—prayers of the faithful.

He wished he could put in bidding prayers for what he wanted, but a priest was not allowed to ask God for a family, a life of love and passion. He wondered what the prayer would be if he could: *Let those clergy who feel isolated and alone, longing to have a family, find their soul mate. Lord in your mercy. Hear our prayer.* What would his parishioners have made of that? What would the Bishop have said then?

The Bishop's eyes were half-closed as he regarded Tom speculatively. 'Don't you have a housekeeper?'

'Not that kind of a woman. A woman to love. To become intimate with.'

'Have you never harboured impure thoughts about your housekeeper?'

'No.' Clearly, the Bishop had never met her.

'Have you never become intimate with a parishioner?'

'No!'

The Bishop appeared pained. 'Well, this is a... shock, Thomas.'

For not having had impure thoughts about his housekeeper and not having had an affair with a parishioner? 'Plenty of popes were married in the past. We should go back to our roots.'

The Bishop created an arch with his hands. 'Priests might have been married but they were still celibate.'

'Only after Pope Siricius. He's not exactly a good role model, abandoning his wife and children.'

The Bishop's face turned an unhealthy shade of plum, and his mouth was working in silence. 'The Church goes forwards, not backwards,' he finally said in a rush.

'In many ways, the Church has gone backwards in going "forwards". The clergy was told to only have one wife in the First Letter of St Paul to Timothy, Chapter Three. Now they are allowed no wife. Even very early on among the orders, celibacy used to be optional...' Tom had come prepared, to make the Bishop aware of how unfair it all was. 'It's ridiculous, I counsel spouses in crises and prepare couples for marriage when I haven't got a clue about living the stresses and strains of a modern-day marriage.'

'Hasn't your training prepared you for that?'

'It can never replace first-hand experiences.' Judging by the way the Bishop's eyes were glowing like the ends of the cigars he sometimes liked to smoke, Tom knew that Brendon might soon lose his temper. But Tom was not going to be deterred by fear of the Bishop's wrath. 'It's also not fair that had I been an Anglican priest with a family, who wished to convert to Catholicism, I'd have been accepted. So why can't we all have families if we want?'

The Bishop's nose created an unpleasant sound as air whooshed through the narrow nostrils. 'Rabbis marry, don't they? Isn't it compulsory? Do you want to become a Rabbi?'

Tom visualised his sour and disapproving mother, Judith. 'Not at all. I'm Catholic through and through.' Why had he been born to a Catholic father and a Jewish mother to complicate his life?

'Despite your mother?'

'Yes, despite my mother. Now I just want to be free to marry and have children.'

'Are you sure that this isn't related to entertaining doubts about your faith? That might be the root of your troubles and, if so, I believe I can help.'

Tom wanted to keep his faith issues to himself. The main problem, the way he saw it, was that he wanted a wife.

'What are your plans, then? You can't stay at St Michael's.'

'Go back to my home town. Find something to do.' He wanted to be a professional photographer and hoped to God he could make a success of it. Perhaps he could find a cheap room to rent. How long would he be able to afford even that?

'You know that you can't be given an indult of laicisation from His Holiness immediately? It takes time. Even after you've applied officially. But applying doesn't mean you'll get it.'

'Yes. I know.' Tom wished it didn't take so long or that there were so many hoops to jump through to become an ordinary, non-priest, layperson again—if the Pope allowed it.

'I'll give you a year so that you can think about it. From the date you send in the form that I'll post to you—after you've had some time to think about it some more.'

Tom bowed his head. He'd have to accept the protracted wait.

The Bishop's voice became stern. 'You'll be needing to find a new career for yourself. You know that the Church forbids—'

'Laicised priests to teach religion or theology.'

'And you can't live anywhere you've been a parish priest.'

'I'm aware of all the rules.'

'When the indult comes from His Holiness, if it comes, I'll hang on to it until you come to me again. You won't be receiving your dispensation without visiting me in person.'

Tom nodded.

'And Thomas, you are to remain celibate until your dispensation, if it comes.'

Although initially despondent, Tom cheered up when he remembered that if he married, he would become laicised by default and then celibacy would be irrelevant to both his personal values and the values of the Church. Marriage would be a rather neat solution. But how likely was that within the year, and where was he to find himself a wife?

'You're to leave St Michael's without saying goodbye to your parishioners or telling them why you're leaving.'

Now, this was going a tad far; it wasn't on any list of rules that he remembered reading. 'If I just disappear,' Tom protested, 'they might think I've left because I've done something wrong.'

The Bishop's back straightened. 'You are doing something wrong. Very wrong.'

At that moment, the door to the living room opened. A smart-looking woman in her early forties popped her head around and said, 'Brendon, I've just finished your packing.' Then she blushed. 'Oh. You've still got company.'

The Bishop said smoothly, 'Father Thomas Sheridan of St Michael's.' Addressing Tom, the Bishop said, 'You remember Mrs McGuire, my housekeeper?'

'Yes, of course.' Although Tom recalled the woman, he didn't remember her as smart and made-up as she was now—and had she lost weight?

'How do you do, Father?' She opened the door wider.

He replied, 'Fine, fine. A pleasure to meet you again.'

Mrs Caraleen McGuire quickly made a retreat. She hadn't wished to disturb Brendon and, judging by his expression, it was clear that he was quite perturbed about something. She closed the door but her ear had somehow become glued to the outside panel.

She heard him speak. 'As I was saying, you are doing something wrong. Very wrong.'

'Leaving my parishioners without saying goodbye or explaining to them is what's wrong,' Father Thomas Sheridan of St Michael's said.

Caraleen gasped and quickly moved away in case she was discovered. Father Thomas must have done something deeply wrong for the Bishop to banish him like this. She wondered how Brendon had found out. But what misdemeanour could it be? Perhaps Brendon would tell her later. She was going to miss him while he was away.

# 9

It was evening and Faith was sitting in semi-darkness in the living room of her flat, waiting for the coast to be clear so that she could finish what she'd started that morning without risk of discovery. While waiting, she reflected on her second trip out with the car, after she'd left Gavin.

Needing some time to herself, she'd gone to a café before braving Sainsbury's, stirring her cappuccino listlessly and gazing unseeing through the window, her mind numb with indecision.

But by the time she'd slowly gone up and down Sainsbury's grocery aisles, she'd settled on being bright and cheerful when she got home so that Hope wouldn't suspect there was anything troubling her. Faith would play wise and let the mystery unfold before crashing in to possibly ruin Luke and Gavin's lives.

When she'd carried the first bags of groceries into the kitchen, she'd left them on the floor to find Hope. She'd been in the living room.

'Hi.' Faith had taken in the reclining figure, resentful that so much of the housework was, like most things, her responsibility. 'Could you help unpack the groceries? I've got to go back to the car to get the rest in.'

As Hope had sat up, she'd cast aside a thick tartan blanket to reveal yellow pyjamas covered in brown bunnies. 'Of course I'll help.' She'd tied back her long blonde tresses to keep them from getting in the way. Hope usually had a scrunchie to hand.

She'd moved about the place as though she'd been well-rested from a long night's sleep and a relaxing day. Faith had bought some cleaning materials too and had considered introducing them to Hope. After all, if she'd got sufficient energy to do things in her bedroom with Luke, perhaps she could do more to keep the kitchen and bathroom sparkling? Or perhaps Luke had done all the moving about and that was why Hope hadn't been the worse for wear? Or had Faith missed something?

All she could hear now from inside the block was the TV from the flat above. She got to her feet and put on her coat ready to retrieve the stuff she'd left at Andy's from her car boot. Furtively, she opened the front door and began to make her way to the Jazz. Just when she was back inside the communal entrance with bags in hand, Gavin appeared.

'Hello,' he said.

'Hi,' she replied weakly.

'You couldn't manage it then?' Gavin pointed to the bags.

'Um, no.' She forced a smile. 'Too much of a wrench.'

Luke joined them. 'I thought I heard voices. Hello, Faith.'

Doing her best to appear nonchalant, she said, 'Hi, Luke,' while digging her nails into the palms of her hands to stop her from demanding an explanation.

'What's all that you've got there?'

'More stuff from Andy's,' Gavin said. 'Faith didn't manage to bring it all in this morning.'

She tried to stop him from saying more with her eyes, but he didn't notice.

'How do you know she hadn't managed to bring it all in?' Luke asked.

'I saw her just after my shower. I offered to help her

with the rest of it, but she was in a hurry to get to the shops and said it could wait.' Apparently pleased with his invention of the events, Gavin shot Faith a smile. She could only offer a feeble one in return.

Luke shifted his weight onto his other foot. 'Are you sure Faith brought the first lot in just after your shower and not before?'

'Of course. What difference does it make?'

Faith stared at Luke defiantly. Accusingly. Then she saw understanding in his grey eyes. He knew she'd been in the flat while he'd been in Hope's bedroom. *Ha, caught you out.* 'Must get on. It'll take me ages to sort this lot out.'

'So, you're keeping it all?' Gavin asked.

Faith aimed icy eyes at Gavin. She wished he'd kept quiet about the whole bag thing.

'Well, er, if you need any help with anything, just let me know,' he said. 'Need to look for my phone. I think it dropped out of my pocket when I was driving.'

As soon as Gavin's figure retreated down the path, Luke whispered, 'We need to talk.'

'The sooner the better,' she hissed and went inside with the bags.

# 10

Back at the presbytery in St Michael's, courtesy of South Eastern Trains, Tom found the Fathers in the living room. He steeled himself for a difficult time as they were not likely to take it well, especially as he'd kept his leaving a secret.

He joined Father Patrick Maher on the sofa and addressed them all. 'I've asked His Excellency to be laicised.'

Gasps and exclamations came from the Fathers. When Patrick recovered, he asked, 'Would that be why you were in such a fraught state this morning? Don't think I hadn't noticed. You should have talked to us—or me—about it first, Tom.'

'I didn't want to be persuaded to delay my decision. I want a wife and family. I can't bear it any longer.'

Father Matthew Blessing cleared his throat. 'It's an enormous step for you to be taking. We could pray with you.'

Tom was done with praying over this issue.

'Sure, there was a time,' Patrick said, 'when I was tempted to leave. But had I done, I do believe I would have regretted it.'

'I might regret it,' Tom said, 'but if I stay, I believe I would regret it more.' There. How could they argue with that? 'I'm sorry I kept it from you, but I wanted to work it out on my own. I hope you'll respect my decision and not make it any harder for me than it already is.'

'I'll be taking your Mass in the morning then,' Father Peter Quade said after a long silence. 'And I'll redo the rotas.'

'I take it you'll be leaving soon?' Patrick asked.

'As soon as the Halora's fixed.'

Matthew wandered over to a bookshelf to retrieve something. 'A letter came for you.'

As Tom grasped it, he knew the Fathers would know who it was from as the envelope was addressed to Malakai Gold-Sheridan. His mother, Judith Gold, was the only person who called him by his first given name. He held the letter up in the air by way of farewell and left for his room.

Letters from Judith generally unsettled him as she resorted to print whenever she had something particularly unpleasant to say. With a heavy heart, he extracted the page and began to read.

*Malakai,*

*I have lived a long and lonely life. It seems I am to have a long and lonely death. The day you were ordained killed the last of my hope that you would lead a normal life. What's wrong with living close by, marrying and having children?*

*This is your final chance to see sense before I write my Will. I do not want you to inherit by default as you would only give it to the Church. Knowing your stupidity, you would not keep it for yourself.*

*Should you have any remnant of sense left after all that brainwashing to re-think and remain my only heir, I will even provide you with an escape route. An office suite on the top floor of Siskin House has become available. You could make use of it with that photographic hobby of yours. I will give you one month to consider my proposal before I instruct the manager to advertise it again and make that appointment with my solicitor.*

*Mum*

Tom sank onto a chair. He didn't want to return to the family home, to the House of Dread. To Judith. She was the most unmotherly mother he'd come across in his formative years, and she was no better now. But, being short of funds... would he be obliged to accept? It would mean he wouldn't have to find rent money for a home or an office...

Earlier, he'd suspected God of trying to prevent him from taking the path he'd chosen. But it seemed He was in cahoots with Judith. Tom's mother might crow at his return to the fold, but at least there was an open door there for him. At least he had a refuge and a means to start making a living outside of the Church.

But, later that night, misgivings about what his future life might be like took hold of his mind and heart. He'd hoped to feel free and relieved of a great burden. Instead, he was feeling like he'd cut off one of his limbs—a vital part of himself that he'd become so accustomed to having. Would it be freedom or Hell being separated from his flock?

# 11

Monday lunchtime, Faith met up with Luke at one of the many cafés on Whiteladies Road, a busy thoroughfare with all kinds of businesses selling goods and services as well as more places to eat and drink. Outrage had built up over the weekend and it had been an effort to contain the fierce emotions bubbling inside her.

Although she'd been tempted to pound on Luke's door and haul him out to make him explain himself—mentally picturing a firing squad at the ready—she'd been mindful of Gavin. It wouldn't have been fair to challenge Luke in front of his partner without the certainty of what was going on. Also, Luke was better able to handle confrontation than Hope, and Faith didn't have to live with him after potentially upsetting him.

Before confirming with Luke that her fears had not been a misunderstanding, it wasn't safe to risk a great bust-up with Hope. Faith had decided to keep secret Andy's reason for the break-up from Hope, but Faith might let it slip in a confrontational situation and that would add to the friction that would develop between them. She'd avoided her sister over the weekend as much as possible by feigning a sore throat and headache after the grocery shop and had stayed in her room bingeing on Netflix. Hope caught infections very easily and was more unwell and for longer than other people generally were. So she'd been grateful that Faith had been out of the way.

'So, Luke,' Faith said, stirring her cappuccino with an outward calmness she did not feel, 'are you going to explain what you were doing in my sister's bedroom before I throw the table aside and try to strangle you?'

'I understand you're angry. But let's talk about this quietly.'

'You'd better have a good explanation. Although, I believe I've already guessed, and I think the two of you have behaved incredibly badly.' She took a savage bite of her bacon and egg bun while glaring at him.

'You have?' Luke fished a radish from his salad and popped it into his mouth. Although he looked serious, he didn't seem to appreciate the true gravity of the situation.

'Mm.' Tomato ketchup was threatening to leak from behind Faith's lips.

'And you don't mind?'

She shielded her mouth with her hand as she spoke. '*Mind?* Of course I mind. I'm furious. I'm struggling not to shout and throw my lunch at you. I'll be affected by this, you know.'

'Hope said you'd be upset.'

'Damn right, I'm upset—and what about Gavin? It was obvious that he didn't have a clue either. How long has this been going on?'

'It started about six months ago. I'll tell Gavin tonight.'

'*Six months?* Shouldn't you have talked it over with Gavin and me first, before you and Hope got "started"? And how could you do that to him when he trusts you, loves you?'

Luke downed some mineral water. 'I think you're overreacting here. It's not as though it affects him much. I work on Hope when Gavin's not around.'

Faith's previously elevated opinion of Luke plummeted even further. 'Not affect him much? When you and Hope…? Surely, Gavin's not going to stand for it, having Hope come between you like that?'

'She doesn't come between us. I told you, Gavin's not around when I'm seeing to Hope.'

Faith's lips turned down in disgust. 'I think your attitude is despicable; you're as bad as Andy. Hope will certainly come between you once she's pregnant.'

Luke's head slowly tilted, his eyebrows closing in. 'Pregnant? Why would Hope get pregnant? What's Andy got to do with anything?' Then understanding showed on his face. 'You think Hope and I...?' Luke bellowed with laughter.

'Aren't you?'

Luke chuckled. 'Wait till I tell Hope.'

'Well, are you going to enlighten me?' Faith stripped off a piece of her bun with teeth bared.

'Hey, steady on. There's no need to give me a hungry wolf look as though you want to tear me apart. I can't help it if you add up wrong.'

'How else am I supposed to add up when a man and a woman are alone together in a bedroom when they think no one knows they are there, and I hear things that sound like you are being too pally with each other?'

Luke rested his elbow on the table, tittering behind his hand. 'It's hilarious. You know I'm gay.'

'I only know that you are attracted to men. For all I know, you can be attracted to women as well. Bisexual.'

Luke shook his head, smiling. 'I'm not bisexual.' Then his expression took on a more serious note. 'Actually, I'm surprised you thought it of either of us, cheating on Gavin. And I'm disappointed you thought we were.'

Under Luke's censorious gaze, Faith squirmed. Wouldn't any other sane person have jumped to the same conclusion with the pointers she'd had?

Luke was halfway through his salad when he gave

her a searching look. 'Why did you think Hope might be pregnant? If I was having an affair with her, wouldn't I be using protection?'

Under his keen gaze, Faith's stomach knotted. How could she protect Gavin's confidence about Luke wanting a baby? 'I see how you are with Petal. It made me think you'd like a child of your own.'

'And you thought I'd persuaded Hope to be a surrogate?'

Faith wished she could start the conversation over.

'You're right. I do want a child. But I hadn't thought of Hope helping out.' He spoke as though Faith had bestowed spiritual enlightenment.

'You can't. It wouldn't be fair to her.' *Or to me.* 'What does Gavin want?'

Luke rounded on her. 'Leave Gavin out of this.' There was a fire in his eyes she'd not seen before.

Trying to keep her annoyance in check, she asked, 'What were you doing in Hope's room?'

'I was giving her a massage. A sports massage.'

Faith weighed this new information with the sounds she remembered hearing from outside Hope's bedroom door. It actually made sense. 'I didn't know you could give sports massages; I don't think you said it was part of your job.'

Luke shrugged. 'Do you tell me everything you do at work?'

He had a point. 'Why give them to Hope?'

'I've been helping to increase her strength and stamina—and to ease her increased pain now that she's doing more. She's less reliant on painkillers than she used to be.'

Faith took a slurp of coffee as her mouth had become dry. Hope's request for repeat pain prescriptions had become more spread out but even so...

'Apart from a couple of glitches where she went backwards for a while, she has come on great. She's able to sustain a small amount of physical exercise every day.'

'That's why she's so tired in the evenings when I get home? Because she's been doing more than she lets on?'

'Yes.'

Why couldn't some of that exercise include cleaning the bath, kitchen sink—or loo?

'Why did you keep it a secret?' She couldn't keep the harshness from her tone.

'Because of Hope's big relapse a couple of years ago affecting you so badly when she tried to up her activity. She felt bad about it and thought you wouldn't support her in this programme I set up for her.'

It was true. Any downturn in Hope's health affected Faith.

'We've been doing things in a very careful way. Any bad effects on her energy levels or other symptoms and we step down for a while. But, if you compare how she is now to how she was six months ago, you'll see it's working.'

Faith stared through the window at a pub on the other side of the road as she compared memories of Hope six months ago with how she was now. Luke was right, Hope was stronger, able to do more things for herself, as well as often cooking for two. Her improvement had crept up so slowly that Faith hadn't fully appreciated the progress her sister had made. Faith shifted her eyes slightly to focus on Luke.

'Don't get me wrong. She's still far from well, and I don't know if she'll ever fully recover. You know what ME's like. You've helped her enormously in so many ways; you've been amazing. I want to do my bit, help Hope make the most of what she does have. Because she wants more from her life.'

Faith cleared her throat as it had become tight. 'What does she want?' Her voice caught as she spoke.

Luke leaned back in his chair. 'That's a conversation you definitely need to have with her. Now, I need to rush. I have a client at two.' Having finished the last of his salad, Luke stood up to go.

Faith stared miserably at the empty chair until she, too, was ready to go.

# 12

That evening, Faith broached the subject of Luke's rehabilitation programme with Hope. 'On Saturday, when you thought I'd gone to the shops,' Faith said, her feet on the pouffe as she relaxed in the armchair, 'I came back—'

'I know, Luke texted me.' Hope's expression, as she lay on the sofa, didn't change. 'I know he told you why he keeps coming round. But he didn't tell you I want to get a job.'

A jolt of panic shot through Faith. Would she have to pick up the pieces again if Hope had a relapse?

'But you're sick. You can't work.'

Faith couldn't have her job taken from her too… It had been awful during the last relapse trying to juggle everything and Edison was a stickler for punctuality… First, her dreams of uni gone, then Andy… she couldn't lose her job too because Hope needed more support.

'It would have to be a very little job, where I don't have to do much.'

'You can't do much.'

Hope held Faith's gaze squarely. 'I'm scared of having a relapse just as much as you. A few hours a week—that's what I've been working towards.'

Faith picked at her fingers, trying to keep her reservations in check, torn between doing what was safest and what Hope wanted. 'Look, I'll help you all the way—but if you feel it's too much, you must stop working before you get terribly ill again.'

Hope's eyes sparkled. 'Deal. I need this, sis, more

than you can imagine.'

Faith had been hurting so much that she hadn't fully taken on board how Hope had been feeling. She'd do her best to help Hope get more out of life. 'Okay... Where do we start? I haven't a clue how you'd find a job to suit your needs.'

Hope grinned and said, 'I do.' She plucked a scrunched page from her pocket and chucked it across to Faith.

She caught it as the paper dived downwards and spread it out thinking that this must have been the piece of scrunched-up paper Hope had hidden in the sofa the other day. It was a page torn from the *Bristol Post* and there was a red circle around a job advert.

Faith's gaze locked onto Hope. 'You want to work at my place? At Siskin House?'

'Yes.'

Faith re-read the advert: *Receptionist required: 8.00–10.00 and 12.00–14.00.*

'Well, you'd get there all right as I could leave earlier than usual. But what would you do between ten and twelve, and between two and five?'

'That's the thing. I don't know. Do they have an empty room I could lie down in, set up an airbed?'

Faith shook her head. 'There's a vacant office on my level, but someone is bound to take it on soon.'

'It's a shame we don't have a camper van. Then I could lie in that.'

'Let me do a search on eBay.' Faith went to get her tablet and then joined Hope on the sofa.

'What do you think my chances of getting the job are?'

'I don't know. But I bet it's going to be hard for them to find someone to do those hours.'

'Why do they need someone for those times?'

'For sorting the post when it arrives and taking calls—Cassie, the full-time receptionist, doesn't usually get in until nine. And, at lunchtime, she needs a break— the people working in the offices divert calls to Reception if they go out and urgent messages might need to be relayed using private contact details.'

'It sounds like I could do it.' Hope's eyes sparkled.

Faith was picking at her fingers again. How would Hope feel if she didn't get the job?

'Look, I'll do my best to make it work for you. Here we are.' They peered at the screen as the page loaded. 'Oh. Too expensive.'

Hope's shoulders sagged. 'I know.'

'How about an ordinary van?' Faith typed letters into the search box.

'Anything's fine if I can make a bed inside it. I've still got the money Grandpa left me.'

Faith clicked on five different vans and let out a long breath. 'Any that are in a reasonable price range have done a huge mileage. You might buy one and then find that it spends more time in the garage than driving us to work.' Hope would be reliant on Faith to be a chauffeur as she had never learned to drive.

'Why don't we ask the boys for advice?' Hope said.

It was Luke who answered the ring at the door wearing a maroon bathrobe. When he saw it was Faith and Hope, he leaned against the door jamb as though to block their entry. 'If you've come to cause trouble, I've already told Gavin.'

'Hope's told me everything and I understand. We're here for advice,' Faith said.

Luke's serious expression broke into a friendly grin. 'Then come in, and we can have a pow-wow.'

The hallway smelt of something cheesy, like pizza.

By the dirty plates on the coffee table, Faith guessed that Luke and Gavin had only just finished eating. Gavin was on the sofa and he, too, was wearing a bathrobe. Had she and Hope barged in on their cosy evening together?

Faith took a seat next to Gavin and Hope sat at the end of the sofa.

'We need some advice,' Faith repeated. 'Hope needs a van to lie down in, between her shifts and up to me finishing work—if she gets the job. Vans that Hope can afford have a tremendous number of miles on them.'

Gavin clapped his hands together, startling Faith. 'I've got a better idea.'

Hope craned her neck as she looked past Faith. 'Tell me, and how much would it cost?'

'The big boss woman is about to advertise the oldest in the fleet. It's company policy to upgrade every so often.' Gavin mentioned the sum. 'It has low mileage for its age.'

'A *hearse*?' Faith turned her head to see what her sister made of it. 'I don't—'

But Hope was laughing. 'I think that would be fun.'

'*Fun?* Wouldn't you worry about what people say?' Faith asked. 'You'd be ridiculed.'

'People who don't know me are often nasty anyway. What difference would that make?'

It was true that some people had been judgemental of Hope, calling her lazy and a malingerer, and telling her she should get a job, not understanding how unwell she was.

'But there's no need to encourage more negativity.' Faith was concerned that Hope might regret the purchase.

'I want a more normal life, and if this job and the hearse is the way to get it, then I'm in.'

'But it's a bit too much money—you'll have to pay

road tax and insurance as well.'

Gavin looked between Hope and Faith.

'Ask your boss if she can give a discount,' Hope said to Gavin.

Part of Faith hoped that Gavin's boss had a hard business head and the rest of her felt guilty for feeling like that.

'Even if I don't get the job,' Hope said, 'it could be useful if Faith and I go on a day trip—we've never been able to do that because I have to come home to rest as I need to lie flat.'

Faith caught the longing in Hope's glance. 'Of course we could go on day trips. But, if you get the job, you'll need the weekends to rest up.'

'If I get the job, I will do everything I can to keep it—and to keep myself well.'

'I'll make that call.' Gavin took to his feet and then froze for a moment, making Faith wonder if he'd been taken ill with sudden pain. But he began to move again and turned to Hope. 'You said you want to lie down in the back? Would you like a proper bed to lie in?'

'As it's an *undertaker* who just suggested that,' Faith said, 'I hope you're not thinking of a coffin.'

Gavin placed his hands on his hips in a theatrical manner that Faith had not witnessed in him before. 'We are *funeral directors*. We are highly skilled with a diverse job description. Not many people can cut it, dealing with the departed.'

'No, I'm sure they can't,' Faith said. 'But Hope isn't Dracula!'

'I can be,' Hope said. 'It's like I'm coming back from the dead, don't you think? And no one needs to know what's in the back of the hearse, do they?'

'Which would you prefer? A coffin or a casket?'

'What's the difference?' Hope and Faith said

together.

'Coffins have more sides—they fit the shape of the body. Caskets are four-sided, rectangular and they can have two hinged lids.'

'A casket,' Hope said decisively. 'More room. The hinged lids would make it more private as well as cosy in cold weather. I'd have to have breathing holes at the head end, of course.'

'You're in luck. We have a mis-measure in our store from a trainee who didn't realise how snug the fit is meant to be. It was for a large client but he'd have been sliding around in there. The big boss woman would be glad to get shot of it.'

'Really? Can you ask about the casket when you ask about the hearse?' Hope asked.

'Are you sure about this?' Faith was filled with misgiving. No one had asked her how she would feel driving a hearse around. Hope might be okay with the idea, but Faith had not yet bought into it.

'Yes, I'm sure,' Hope said. 'You have no idea how much I want a life outside of the flat.'

Faith pressed her lips together, wondering whether Hope's words were a reprimand in the belief that Faith could have done more or a show of jealousy over having been denied the life Faith was enjoying. Either way, it made Faith feel bad. She truly had done everything that was reasonably in her power to do.

Gavin made to leave the room. 'I'll call the big boss woman.'

'Now, Faith, have you arranged that girls' night out?' Luke said after Gavin had left.

'Yes.'

'Who's going?'

'Well, me, obviously, and Jade.'

'You're a bit short on friends,' Luke said.

Faith bristled. 'Hey, it's hard keeping up with people when I'm such a busy person.'

How could she have kept up with all her school friends when she'd been taking care of Hope as well as doing all the laundry, cleaning, shopping and cooking—and going to work full-time? She'd only met Andy because he'd attended her parents' house following a buildings insurance claim for a collapsed drain. Keith and Marion had seemed delighted that their daughter had met a man at last, and perhaps it had made them feel less guilty that her life had been interrupted.

Gavin returned. 'Brace yourself.'

Hope leaned forward. 'Yes?'

He gave a reduced price, and Hope whooped with glee.

'She won't have to pay commission now for selling the car so that's why she agreed to lower the price. The hearse is yours, and she'll throw in the casket for nothing.'

Hope flung herself at Gavin and gave him a noisy kiss on his cheek.

'I'll give you the number of a friend of mine. He can make sure you can get in and out of the casket in situ and fix it to the base of the car.'

Faith wasn't confident she could manoeuvre such a long vehicle. 'Do you think I could have a test drive, before any money exchanges hands?'

# 13

It had taken a week for the garage to get Tom's Halora fixed. On Monday, the repair guys had been too busy to lift even the bonnet. On Tuesday, they confirmed the fuel pump was at fault. Then they had difficulty sourcing the part. When it came, it wasn't the right one. When the correct part was eventually fitted, a second fault was discovered. By the time that had been fixed, it was another Monday morning, and February had turned into March.

The atmosphere at the presbytery had been far from comfortable, so it was with relief that Tom was finally able to load the car with his belongings and head for the motorway. By the time he'd travelled from the south east to the south west of England and the sign for the Leigh Delamere services' exit on the M4, between Swindon and Bristol, came up, Tom's stomach and bladder were protesting. He indicated left and not long after, headed towards the massive car park to access the services. There were no spaces close to the entrance, but he didn't mind that; it would be good to stretch his legs.

Once inside the building, Tom fancied getting some sweets to help while away the time during the rest of his drive; sucking on a Fruit Pastille helped his concentration. He usually had a packet in his pocket with his rosary. Standing by the confectionery display, he studied what was on offer.

A young, spindly boy came to stand next to Tom. He smiled, but the boy looked uncertain.

'Hello,' Tom said. 'Going somewhere nice?'

A thickset man appeared. 'Leave my boy alone.' He put a protective arm around his son.

'It's okay. I'm a priest. A Catholic priest.'

'Get away,' the man ordered the boy. 'That lot are the worst.' They retreated, looking over their shoulders at Tom.

As he glanced around, Tom saw other customers glaring accusingly at him. Not at all how his parishioners used to regard him. Did the customers suspect him of trying to groom the boy? Mortified, he slunk towards the back of the shop to avoid any question of him following the child by mischance. Tom would abandon the notion of buying Fruit Pastilles, wait a couple of minutes to allow the man and boy to be clear away, and then visit the loos.

But that idea was quashed when Tom spied the child and his dad ahead of him, aiming for the same opportunity. So he joined the queue at the food self-service counter.

Later, eating an all-day breakfast at a table along the perimeter of the dining area, Tom took in his surroundings. Actually, that was a lie. He was trying to spot women who might be single.

A dark-haired woman addressed him.

'Pardon?' He gawped stupidly at her. My goodness, she was attractive. Those curves, the pale tops of her breasts visible in the V of her blouse as she bent low to speak to him—and her dazzling smile.

'I asked if this seat was taken?' Her voice was rich and silky-smooth.

'Oh, no. No, it isn't. Please sit down.' Too late, he realised he ought to have gestured to the empty place diagonally opposite him as he recalled how she'd placed a hand on the chair next to his when she'd asked her question.

'Thanks.' The word was breathed as though she was overcome with gratitude. 'I don't like to watch other people eat,' she added as she lowered herself beside him, displaying a generous cleavage.

Conscious of the indelicacy of his gaze, he averted his eyes. The proximity of unfamiliar female flesh disturbed him, and being penned in between the food court barrier and this incredibly sexy woman made it worse.

She transferred a plate of salad and a pot of raspberry yoghurt from her tray to the table. Twisting around, she dumped the tray on the table behind, which had a pile of other things waiting to be cleared.

How did one chat up an attractive woman like her? 'Lovely day for driving.'

'Is it? And, despite the sun, you're wearing a scarf?'

Tom squirmed. Finishing his mouthful of bacon and baked beans, he decided to come clean. 'It's to disguise the clerical insert collar—because I've removed my dog collar. I've just left my parish.'

The woman laughed. 'That's the funniest joke I've heard all week.' She forked a cherry tomato into her mouth.

'It's not a joke.' A wave of vulnerability washed over him.

'Isn't it?' She ate some lettuce.

He opened his scarf to reveal the truth.

'Oh my God.' She almost choked. 'It's true. Why?'

'Catholic priests aren't allowed to marry. I want to find a wife.'

'When did you become a priest?' Her tone changed to a more serious note.

'I was ordained in my twenties. But I knew I wanted to be a priest when I was in my teens.' It was great to have someone who was not another priest to talk to, to share his burden.

The woman regarded him keenly. 'Does that mean you've never...?'

'No.' He was unable to hold her gaze. But then looked up, apprehensive about her reaction.

But an idea seemed to form in her mind. 'I've never slept with a—'

'Please.' He scanned the area. It was not something he would want the whole world to know. He choked back a gasp. What if she were a journalist? 'What's your line of work?'

He tucked into his egg and stacked up some sliced mushrooms with the tines of his fork. It was the next best thing to having a rosary to keep him busy at this difficult time.

'I'm in sales. I have my own business.'

Well, he was safe from journalists then. 'What do you sell?' Feeling jittery, he began to wolf down the rest of his lunch.

'How shall I put it? Personal pleasure equipment.'

Tom frowned. 'What's personal leisure equipment? You mean, like an exercise bike? Steppers, gym ball, that kind of thing?' She didn't strike him as a fitness enthusiast. She was all make-up and heels.

The woman smiled. 'Personal... *pleasure...* equipment. I could show you if you like.'

Her words left him speechless, but when he felt a lingering, hand-shaped pressure on his thigh, he found he couldn't move any muscle in his body.

'There's a motel here. We could book in, and I could show you my samples. It would be interesting to know what you think about them. Market research.'

His heart beat to the steps of a platoon of Christian soldiers on the go, his cutlery almost slipping from his fingers. 'Oh, I've got to get on.'

'Enlightenment can come in many guises. I could help show you what to do...' Her fingers walked up his inner thigh. '... for when the opportunity strikes again.'

To his chagrin, his body responded with an almost painful throb, He worried he might split his seams.

Her fingers trailed even higher.

'I've got to go.' He dabbed at the corners of his mouth with the napkin.

Her lips gave a slight downturn. 'It would be a new experience... for both of us. Having a go with a Catholic priest is a fantasy of mine—unleashing the innocence and finding the beast within.'

Beast? He was no beast. Tom stood up cautiously, angling away from her so that he could adjust his trousers and ease his discomfort while concentrating on an image of Christ's suffering on the cross. That usually helped.

'Please excuse me.' He twisted around to face her, his hands hiding his pelvis. 'I've got a long journey ahead.' He expected her to get up as well, to make way for him to leave as the chairs were fixed to the floor, but she didn't.

'You're afraid.' Her laugh tinkled around the tables, and he could see people looking their way. 'I'm offering myself up to you, oh Holy One, and you're not accepting the gift I have to offer. That makes Roxy a very sad girl.' She got up and pressed her body against his.

He'd never pushed a woman before, and he wasn't going to start now. God had provided him with long legs and he was going to use them. He leapt over the barrier as best as he could, hampered by his still stiff middle wicket, and took to his heels. It was only when he got to his car that he remembered he'd forgotten to use the loo. But he daren't go back in. He had to remove himself from the danger zone.

# 14

On the M4, all Tom could think of, in between bouts of mortification, was the discomfort down below. Now that his sudden rush of lust had receded, it was paramount for him to pee. He hung on as far as the M32 but knew there was no way he could hang on until he reached Bristol.

Tom pulled over to the hard shoulder and switched on the hazards. Then he clambered out of the Halora and made towards the grass verge. There was no coverage of foliage, but he was a bloke. With his back to the traffic, it would be quite discreet.

Halfway through the ritual of relieving himself, he was aware that a car had pulled up after his, and there was a blue flashing light. He turned to see the familiar blue and yellow squares of a police vehicle reversing towards him. He gave himself a shake and tucked himself away. Two officers emerged from the patrol car and strolled towards him.

'Good afternoon.' Tom wasn't sure whether it would be polite to proffer his hand, but considering the two officers had just witnessed his recent activity, neither one was likely to accept his gracious gesture. So, Tom kept his hand by his side.

'Did you know it's a criminal offence to stop your vehicle on the hard shoulder for non-emergency situations, sir? Public indecency is also a criminal offence.' The officer who spoke in a strong West Country accent was a bald, portly, middle-aged man who sported a thick, brown moustache.

'I'm very sorry, officer. It was an emergency. I couldn't hang on any longer.'

'Whether you came westbound or eastbound on the M4, you would've passed service stations. Should've stopped there to take care of your bodily needs,' the younger officer said in a similar burr. He was shorter and slimmer than his counterpart and had a full head of curly, brown hair.

'I did. I was going to. But then this woman made improper advances towards me, and I had to get away.'

Officer Large smirked at his younger sidekick. 'Made improper advances, sir? And what might they be?'

Tom's tongue struggled to form the sounds as he began to explain. 'She... she put her hand on my thigh, moved her fingers even higher.' Heat spread to his scalp. 'And suggested we booked into the motel so that she could show me her... samples.'

'Most men, sir, would consider this was their lucky day,' Officer Large said.

'I'm a Catholic priest! I do not fornicate as I'm a man of the cloth.' He made to tug at his scarf, which was closely wound around his neck, and then he remembered that there was no clerical collar to show.

'I'd like to see your driving licence, sir.' Officer Large held out his hand.

Tom plucked the plastic card from his wallet. Officer Large glanced at it, raised his eyebrows and handed it to Officer Small, who handed it back when he'd read the necessary title.

'It's still an offence to stop on the hard shoulder in a non-emergency situation,' Officer Large informed.

'I'm sorry. I didn't know.'

'And to expose your private parts in a public place. You were in view of oncoming drivers,' Officer Small added officiously.

Tom squeezed his eyes shut while pinching the bridge of his nose. What would His Excellency make of him being questioned by the police over indecent exposure?

'Where are you heading?' Officer Large asked.

Although tempted to make something up, Tom considered it would be worse if he were caught out. 'Bristol.'

'Whereabouts in Bristol?' Officer Small asked.

'Clifton.'

'That's our patch. And my mother-in-law lives there.' Officer Large's tone suggested he was not overly fond of his mother-in-law. He stared at the car. 'Is that a Halora?'

'Yes.' Tom braced himself, expecting some terse comment to follow.

'I've never heard of a priest driving one of these,' Officer Large said.

'I only needed it to fulfil my duties of visiting the sick and so on.'

'Really.' Officer Large made an unpleasant sound through his nose that indicated derision.

'You aren't wearing your dog collar,' Officer Small said.

Tom's scarf had come loose from the half-hearted tug he'd given earlier before he'd remembered his dog collar wasn't inserted into the tabs.

'I can explain. I've left the clergy. I don't want to be bound by the rules anymore.'

'What rules might they be?' Officer Large rocked on his heels, appearing amused.

'Marriage... and celibacy.'

Officer Large turned to his partner. 'There's something here that doesn't add up. First, he says that he's been sexually harassed and can't be intimate with a woman because he's a priest. Now he tells us he doesn't want to be a priest anymore because he wants to have sex.'

Tom cringed under their scrutiny.

'Would you mind opening the boot of your car, sir?' Officer Large asked.

Obligingly, Tom raised the lid of the boot.

'Well, well, well. What do we have here?'

'It's my camera equipment.'

Officer Large rubbed his hands and eyed Tom sternly. 'So I see. Take a lot of photos, do you?'

'A fair amount.'

'Who do you photograph? Children?'

'Yes, if they're part of the family. I think of myself as a Sacramental Photographer.'

'A Sacramental Photographer. Now, what's that? Some ritualistic photography?' Officer Large spoke disparagingly.

It was hard to keep his cool, but Tom knew that authority like this was not to be trifled with if he hoped to escape a trip to the police station. 'I take photos to mark events related to the sacraments of Baptism, Confirmation, Holy Orders and Matrimony. I do funerals too, as it happens. Anything that takes place in a church, I'm your man.'

'Do you have proof that this is what you do?' Officer Large sounded sceptical.

'Of course.' Tom rummaged to find a box of large photo albums. He'd made up a portfolio of his work.

As they leafed through the pages, Officer Large said to Officer Small, 'These are good. He knows his stuff.'

'Yeah. He's good.'

The men exchanged a meaningful glance, the thrust of which eluded Tom entirely.

A car pulled onto the hard shoulder, ahead of the

police vehicle, and reversed towards them. When the driver stepped out, Tom groaned and the police officers looked up.

In desperation, Tom hissed, 'That's the woman who... touched me. She said she sells personal leisure equipment—or was it pleasure equipment?'

Interest was clearly sparked. The officers grinned at each other. Then they faced the woman with serious expressions as she drew closer.

'Did you know it's a criminal offence to stop your vehicle on the hard shoulder for non-emergency situations, madam?'

'I'm sorry, officers,' she gushed. 'I'm just a woman who stopped to help out a friend. Father here had lunch with me, and I saw that he was in trouble. I thought I'd offer my help.'

'Is it true,' Officer Large said, 'that you placed your hand on his thigh?'

The woman faltered. 'Er...'

'Is it true that you suggested to this man that you book into a motel and that you wanted to show him your... samples?'

'Er...' Roxy began, but failed to finish.

'Would you mind opening the boot of your car please, madam?'

'Officers, I was just trying to help.'

'Open the boot of your car please, madam. We suspect you might be carrying suspicious merchandise.'

Then, as though suddenly filled with confidence, Roxy grinned, spun around and sashayed towards her car. Tom was intrigued. What did the woman sell? He followed the police officers—and Roxy's swinging hips.

Inside her car boot was a multitude of plain boxes and two unzipped sports bags filled with... samples. Tom's jaw was slack and his eyes were stretched wide.

He glanced up and caught Roxy's attention. She winked at him, licking her lips salaciously. Tom swivelled on his heel and headed back to the safety of the Halora. The officers would protect him. Imagine if he'd broken down in a lonely area and she'd come along...

Had the devil sent her to test him? Well, he wasn't interested. That kind of woman wouldn't make him the kind of wife he was looking for. That kind of woman needed someone more like herself. Another predator.

The police officers were approaching their car now, smirking and holding a couple of boxes each. They stashed them away before coming towards Tom, who lowered his window. Roxy was signalling to go back on the motorway and was already picking up speed in readiness to cross to the inside lane.

Officer Large reached Tom's open window first. 'As you know, you have committed a couple of offences, Father... Do we still call you Father?'

'Just call me Tom. And yes, you've made it very clear I was in the wrong.' He considered the boxes the coppers had appropriated and wondered if he could try something along the same lines. 'If there's anything I could do...'

Officer Large's face loomed closer. 'Well, Tom, as it happens, my friend here is getting married soon and needs a photographer...'

'I...' Tom's tongue was unable to complete the sentence.

'Well, that's mighty kind of you, volunteering like that. I was going to ask if there was someone you could recommend, but seeing how you're offering to take the pictures out of the kindness of your heart, I think we'll be able to overlook the offences on this occasion. My friend would, of course, cover basic expenses... on the production of all receipts.'

Officer Small's nodding head popped into view.

It seemed, thought Tom, that a deal had been struck and that he only needed to pass on his mobile number for the coppers to allow him to continue his journey to the House of Dread.

# 15

The cloud of Tom's journey still hung over him when he arrived at the House of Dread, the family home where he'd spent an uncomfortable childhood and had escaped for good at the first opportunity. It was a sprawling Georgian building with fat pillars, rectangular windows in angular bays and a sizeable rear annexe that, as far as he knew, was unoccupied. The green area of the front garden was as manicured as ever and its boundary hedges trimmed with professional neatness. He parked the Halora next to the white BMW that Miranda, his mother's personal assistant, drove, since Judith could no longer cope with the pedals and had been stubborn about getting an adapted vehicle.

There were three shallow steps. At the top, Tom knocked using the rapper and only glanced at the mezuzah fixed to the right of the door. Before long, the door opened, and Miranda's sturdy form appeared. Her straight, dark hair was always cut short. Tom supposed it was very practical. Like a nun's haircut.

'Miranda. It's good to see you.'

She smiled. 'And you. Judith's in the study. Shall I get you something to drink?'

What he could really do with was a shot of whisky. But he knew that was not what Miranda had in mind. Tom smiled back. 'Tea would be very welcome. Thank you.'

'Biscuits?'

His smile broadened. 'Not your homemade kind?'

'The very same.' Miranda's back straightened and

pride shone in her eyes.

'You've twisted my arm.'

Beaming, Miranda turned towards the kitchen. Tom strode to the study, breathing in the familiar scents of furniture polish and baking. On knocking, Judith's voice boomed, 'I heard you come in. There's no need to dither outside.'

Taking a deep breath, Tom pushed the door open. Judith was sitting at a gargantuan desk in a winged chair. Had she had a fluffy, white cat on her lap, Tom would have suspected James Bond's Blofeld of having undergone gender reassignment. Judith's demeanour was so forbidding, so menacing...

She indicated the chair opposite.

Pens and papers, Tom had expected to see on the table. But a pair of binoculars appeared out of place amongst the stationery. Ignoring the chair, Tom went around the side of the desk.

'How are you, Mum? It's good to see you.' As he placed a hand on her shoulder, he planted a kiss on her lightly rouged cheek, catching the scent of sandalwood.

She patted her bleach-blonde hair in what seemed like annoyance. 'You know very well how I am. Crippled with arthritis.'

Of course, she was. The Zimmer frame by the window was proof enough. He noticed that the view took in the side elevation of Siskin House. Was that why she had the binoculars? To spy on the place? He determined to avoid using that entrance; he didn't want Judith watching his every move.

He took his chair as Miranda walked in bearing a large tray with a pot, a jug, some sugar and cups and saucers—it was far too inelegant of Judith to drink out of something as crude as a mug.

Miranda beamed at him again. 'I'll be right back

with the biscuits.'

When she left the study, Judith said, 'I see she's buttering you up with home baking. I wouldn't let her get any ideas.'

'Ideas?'

'About you. She is a spinster, you know.'

'Oh.' Tom shivered.

When Miranda returned and offered him a biscuit, his smile was tight. It wouldn't do if she got the wrong impression. When the door shut behind Miranda again, Judith poured and handed Tom a cuppa.

'So,' Judith said, 'you finally saw the light, did you? Or was it the lure of family money?'

'Neither. I've been troubled for a while. I don't want to live a celibate life—I want to get married, have children.'

'You've not got your housekeeper pregnant, have you?'

Tom frowned. 'No, of course not.'

'My God! You've never cashed in your V-card, have you?'

Tom fidgeted under her eagle-eyed gaze. He'd only been back five minutes and the familiar spite was already in force—and what was she doing using lingo like that?

'I'm right, aren't I?'

Tom stared back at her. How was he going to handle living with her again? The sooner he became financially independent, the better.

'Well, do you have any fair maiden in mind? I take it you're on the lookout for another V-card holder? You wouldn't want to sully your priestly disposition with someone who's "experienced".'

How had Judith's tongue become so acidic? Embittered, he supposed, by Dad leaving her. She'd changed after he'd gone and had never forgiven him, even when he'd lain dying in Ireland. Perhaps it had been a struggle to bring Tom up alone while managing her property business—before she paid people to do that for her. But it seemed she'd taken the firing of barbs to a more elevated level of destruction than previously; he already wanted to escape to lick his wounds. The years had not mellowed her.

'I have no particular person in mind. I'll wait and see who comes along.'

Judith harrumphed. 'I don't have much faith in you finding someone. It's taken you so long to work out that you want to have sex that it will take you another lifetime to fix on the right person—or a wrong-un that you mistake for the right person. I bet you know nothing about the world of relationships.'

'I've had tons of experience in couples counselling.'

'But nothing hands-on—in both senses of the expression?'

Should his mother be talking to him like this? At the biggest stretch of his imagination, he might think it more the job of a father to concern himself about the private life of his son. But his *mother?*

'Mum, please show me some respect and allow me some privacy. I don't dictate to you how to spend your life and point out your flaws—although, at times, I'd very much like to.'

'If I didn't tell it to you straight when I get the chance, I wouldn't know whether I'd have the opportunity again. You've not exactly been a frequent visitor.'

'You talk to me unkindly and wonder why I've stayed away?'

'But now,' Judith said, 'you're taking me up on the offer of office space?'

He wished he had the means to turn the proposal down. 'Yes. Thanks.'

'You could sound a bit more grateful. Or do you feel it's like you're here with a begging bowl?'

He flinched. She was spot on.

'I would have thought that you would be used to begging bowls. Isn't that what you hand round every Mass?'

Well, Judith was certainly on form today. Tom's stomach was already feeling like it had been reinforced with steel, and his jaw was beginning to ache. She drove everyone around her away—except, surprisingly, Miranda.

'Unless,' Judith said, 'you consider that begging from total strangers is more palatable than from family?'

Actually, it was. He wasn't the only one begging in a church, and there was well-established precedence that the offertory bag got passed around. Congregants expected to give. It was a collective gift and it didn't go to him in person but to the running of the parish.

'I'm tremendously grateful that you have given me an easier way out,' Tom said stiffly. 'Your... offer was timely.'

'Couldn't bear to see the family wealth go to charity?'

'I didn't know about your letter until I'd already seen the Bishop.'

Her beady eyes studied him hard. 'Well, what a coincidence.'

'Yes.'

'Do you have plans for the office space?'

'As you suggested, it would allow me to take up photography.'

'If you need money—with equipment and so forth—

just ask. There's plenty of it as you know, and it will all be yours one day anyway. You need to get a thriving business up and running in triple quick time since you're starting from scratch. I don't believe a lady would want to hitch herself to a penniless ex-priest with a crumbling business.' She tapped her chin. 'Can it be called crumbling if it's never got going?'

Tom could detect the signs of a looming headache—a tight scalp and the warning sensation behind his eyes. *Turn the other cheek*. He often used it as a mantra when dealing with Judith.

'Miranda's got your room ready for you.'

He wished Siskin House had a shower, then he could live there.

'You know,' Judith said, 'I have a mind to find you a wife myself. I bet I'd do a better job of it.'

Tom made his escape by saying that he needed to unload the car. He only appeared in Judith's presence again when it was time to eat—by that time, having popped two paracetamol capsules. He excused himself as soon as he'd cleared his plate.

He wanted to look around Siskin House. The intruder alarm was something he was familiar with, and Judith had given him the code to disarm it. Taking the stairs, he charged upwards, finding the sudden burst of physical activity a release.

On the third floor, he poked around the oblong kitchenette, looking into the cupboards and the fridge, wondering about the people who worked here. There wasn't much to go on. The usual tea and coffee stuff. Biscuits—bourbons and custard creams. A pot of yoghurt in the fridge. A bag of apples. Not much of interest.

As he stood outside the door to what was now to be his office suite, he braced himself. By unlocking the door, he unlocked the next step to his future life—and where he would begin to find his future self.

There was a desk with a phone and, surprisingly, a chaise longue. He tried it out. Mm. It was something to bear in mind should his relationship with Judith deteriorate beyond endurance.

Going through the main room, Tom found two smaller rooms and a box room. He was impressed. The box room could be a dressing room. One of the smaller rooms could be a props room—and where he could store some of his equipment, and the other smaller room— which wasn't at all small—could be his studio. There he could set up lights, put up a backdrop and so on.

After he'd locked up, he noticed a door that had a ventilation grille close to floor level, next to another door with an electricity warning sign on it. He tried the handle of the door with the grille. Going through his bunch of keys, he found one that fitted the lock.

As Tom flicked on the light switch outside, the small room lit up. There were shelves on either side of a walkway stacked with cleaning materials, towels, cloths and, finally, toilet tissue.

The room turned to the left, presumably making use of the space behind the electricity cupboard. Here, he discovered a vacuum cleaner, a rectangular bucket and three self-wringing twist mops of different colours, similar to what the presbytery housekeeper used. There was a slight earthy smell as though the mops had taken too long to dry. But somehow it wasn't particularly unpleasant.

Tom contemplated the space that was hidden from the view of the door. It was a bit like a confessional, although this room lacked the scent of polish and incense. Even so, he felt harboured, secure, as though the walls were protecting him.

He upturned the bucket and sat down. When he reached for the rosary in his pocket, he fingered the olive wood beads as he pondered how to reconcile his faith—or perhaps lack of it—with his rejection of ministerial life.

# 16

It was Monday evening when Faith read a text from her friend, Jade; someone from their school had contacted her on Facebook, asking to join them tomorrow night. Faith agreed to the proposed plan, thinking it would do her good to broaden her depleted social network.

But when they all met outside the nightclub, Jade and the newcomer arriving together, Faith had no recollection of Roxy at all. Armed with drinks, they weaved their way into the dance area and found somewhere to leave their things. Faith had thought the place would be reasonably quiet as it was a Tuesday. But she'd forgotten how loud thumping dance music got. She wished she'd brought ear defenders; the kind road workers wore when using a jackhammer.

After a few dances, Jade suggested taking a breather with a fresh round of drinks. As they entered a quieter room, a group of women, wearing pink headbands with wobbly antennae sporting the words "Hen Party" at the tips, left their table. Faith sped up to claim it.

'Phew. That was lucky.' She placed her cola on the sticky surface as she sat down; she didn't think it wise to have more alcohol, bearing in mind she needed to be at work in the morning. Jade sat next to her. Roxy sauntered off towards the bar again after saying she needed another re-fill as she'd gulped the last one down on the way to the table.

'Who's the woman you brought with you?' Faith asked.

'You don't remember her?'

The name Roxy still didn't ring any bells. 'No.'

'Roxanne. Roxanne Miller.'

Faith goggled at the back of the brunette who had hair like the woman on the Galaxy advert, all chocolatey and shiny. That was Roxanne Miller? No, surely she was an imposter?

'Incredible, isn't it?' Jade said. 'I didn't recognise her myself.'

Faith dimly remembered a podgy, shapeless girl with pigtails. How had she turned into the excellently proportioned, voluptuous woman she'd been dancing with a moment ago?

'I'd have passed her in the street, easy.'

'Me too,' Jade said. 'In the taxi on the way here, she said something that I think meant she has a liking for married men as it leaves her free; you know, no commitment needed. Anyway, what happened with you and Andy?'

'Out of the blue, he dumped me. He said it's because of Hope, and he found our time together boring.'

'Oh, I'm so sorry. Sure there's no one else? Could be just an excuse.'

Faith shook her head. 'I wondered that too. But he insisted there was no one else.' Then she spotted Roxy approaching, a Cosmopolitan in hand. Without a bra, her generous breasts bobbed with every move of her swinging hips, and Faith wondered how they managed to stay inside the flimsy creation of her dress. The way men were ogling Roxy suggested they were hoping for a wardrobe malfunction. 'What was Roxy's Facebook page like?'

'Didn't pay much attention to it. When she requested to be a friend, I just accepted, remembering who she was and feeling sorry for her. Thought she was too embarrassed to have her own pic up as she'd posted a photo of some scenery. When she asked to meet up with us, I took pity on her. But I think she's quite happy with her life and whatever it is she gets up to. However, I don't like the way she talks; it wouldn't be funny if it was my husband she seduced.'

Roxy was almost back, sashaying between the tables, smiling at the men as she squeezed past, brushing her front elevation against their chests. 'So, what have I missed?' She slid onto a seat.

There was a tense silence, so Faith fibbed. 'We were wondering what you do. For a job.'

'Oh.' Roxy grinned. 'I sell personal pleasure equipment.'

Excited they had something in common at last, Faith said, 'I sell leisure equipment too. Among other things. Adaptations for the disabled.'

'Not *leisure*—although it could certainly come under the category of leisure. I said pleasure.'

'What is it that you sell?' Jade asked, appearing to be as befuddled as Faith felt.

'Personal... *pleasure...* equipment.' Then Roxy winked.

'I've got it now,' Jade said. 'I understand.'

Faith did too.

'I had a really funny experience yesterday,' Roxy said. 'I was at a service station when I met a Catholic priest.'

'What's funny about that?' Faith asked.

'Wait till you hear the end.'

Jade exchanged a glance with Faith. *Humour her*, it said.

'Well, when I heard he was a priest, and hadn't ever been with a woman, and had just left the priesthood to find a wife, I thought hey, this is a fantasy of mine. A *virgin priest*.'

'I don't think I want to know,' Faith said.

'Anyway, I put my hand on his thigh and suggested we booked into the motel. Do you know how he responded?'

'He went for it?' Jade suggested dryly.

Faith would have guessed the same—what sex-starved man would have turned down a freely available woman looking like Roxy?

'No. He *ran* away.'

Faith laughed; good on the priest, the one that got away. Faith wondered where he was now. She imagined him a hero who held out for the right woman and, once he'd found her, would never be unfaithful, never lie and never cheat. Never do anything underhand at all. She wished she could meet him.

'I was gutted I missed the chance to—'

Faith found the line of conversation distasteful. 'We were also discussing trips away.'

Jade asked Roxy, 'How was your holiday? You've not long come back, have you?'

'Fabulous,' Roxy said.

'Where did you go?' Faith asked.

'Vienna. It was lovely.'

'I bet.' Faith was filled with envy.

'Who did you go with?' Jade asked.

'A man.' The way Roxy said "man" was filled with meaning.

'Oh?' Jade queried.

'Told his wife he was going to Helsinki on business and she believed him because he's some liaison guy for a client out there—until she found the guidebook to Vienna in the pocket of his luggage. And now, unfortunately, she's told him to find somewhere else to live.'

'Has he moved in with you, then?' Faith asked.

Roxy looked horrified. 'He can't do that. I've got a boyfriend!'

Faith exchanged a disbelieving glance with Jade and then puckered her brow. 'Doesn't your boyfriend know?'

Roxy took a slurp of her Cosmo, catching a cranberry that was floating on top of the red liquid. 'No, he doesn't know. He works away from home a lot and, until recently, he was spending a lot of time with his girlfriend. But they've split up now. He wants more time with me. So, it will get a bit more awkward.'

Faith needed to check she'd heard right. 'You were both cheating? So, what would he care if he knew you messed around with other men?'

'If he'd known about Danny, he wouldn't have left that girlfriend of his. She didn't know anything about me—she was often busy doing stuff with her sister.'

'Her... sister?' Faith's skin became cold, which was odd considering the heat in the place. Tingles of chill sensations found their way into her fingers and down her legs, and her stomach tensed with foreboding.

'Yeah. Her sister's sick or something, and they often just hung out at their place. He dumped her a while ago.'

Faith's heart was picking up speed. 'How long ago did he dump this woman?'

'I don't know. A week and a half? Why?'

Faith flung a shocked glance at Jade that Roxy didn't notice as she'd picked up her glass for another slurp. In a strangled tone, Faith said, 'Curious, that's all. What's his name?'

Roxy laughed. 'Oh, I'm discreet about things like that.'

Feeling reckless, Faith said, 'Did Jade tell you I'm psychic? I could probably tell you his name.'

'Never?' Roxy looked intrigued.

'Yes.'

'This isn't a good idea,' Jade said.

'Don't worry.' A bolt of blistering anger threatened to overspill Faith's self-control. 'I know what I'm doing. It's quite safe. I'm used to communing with the spirit world.'

'Wow, you can do that?' Roxy asked. 'Commune...?'

'Yes. But I have to hold your hands extremely tightly while you think of the man so that I can get a good picture.'

'She's not really psychic,' Jade said. 'Take no notice. We should go, Faith.'

'Jade's just scared of spirits,' Faith said. 'It always makes her afraid when she sees the power I have. Are you afraid?'

'No. I don't get scared easily,' Roxy said. 'I guess that's why it's so easy for me not to worry about getting caught by wives and girlfriends. Anyway, it's not my relationship, is it?'

'How true,' Faith murmured.

'What do I have to do?' Roxy asked.

'This really isn't a good idea,' Jade said. 'Let's leave now. Before it goes too far.'

'I never believe in psychics, but if Faith can do what she claims, I will never doubt ghosts and so on again. Come on, don't spoil the fun.'

'Give me your hands,' Faith said.

'Hey, that hurts,' Roxy protested.

'I have to grip you tightly. It has to be a good connection.'

'It's late,' Jade said. 'We should go. Come on, let's break this up.'

'No, I want her to do it. I want to see whether she really is psychic.'

'No talking,' Faith said. 'Now, shut your eyes tight and think of the man. Concentrate hard.'

Roxy squeezed her eyes shut.

'A spirit is with me, come to help me. I can see an image forming. It's very misty. Are you thinking hard of him?'

'Yes.'

'Oh, that's better. He's blond?'

'Yes.'

'Blue eyes.'

'Yes.'

'There's a letter coming through now... It's an A.'

'Yes!'

'His name's Andy... Andy... Sutton.'

'How did you do that?'

'I told you, I'm psychic. I can tell you his job too.'

'Gosh, can you?'

'I'll have to squeeze a bit harder.'

'Agh. Can you be quick about it? Ooh, you're hurting me.'

'He's a loss adjuster,' Faith said.

'That's brilliant.' Roxy tried to pull her hands away, but Faith clung on. 'I'm convinced. Can I have my hands back?'

'It hurts, doesn't it?'

'Yes, too bloody right it hurts.'

'That's to show you what physical pain is like, since you can't experience emotional pain. It's good to understand that things in life hurt.'

'What are you on about?'

Faith let go and sloshed the rest of her cola into Roxy's face.

Spluttering, Roxy exclaimed, 'What the heck did you do that for?'

'Andy was my boyfriend. I hope you bring each other plenty of misery.'

'Hah!' Roxy recoiled. 'Really? He never told me you

were psychic... He said you were plain and boring. Plain boring.'

Jade was pulling Faith along to the exit but she broke off, running to the loos. As she vomited her food and drink, one hand clutching her long hair behind her, she bet she was the only sober, non-pregnant person who'd been sick in the club that night. How could Andy have cheated on her and then lied to her face when he'd said that there was no one else? There clearly had been someone else for some time. A long time, she thought, thinking back to when cuts in the office had affected his travel times. Had there ever been any office downsizing? Had that been a lie to cover up his relationship with Roxy? Had Andy enjoyed having two women in his life?

As she gripped the edge of the toilet bowl, another spasm heaved her stomach. What had she done wrong? What was wrong with her? Would other men see whatever flaw she must have and behave like Andy? If she'd not realised Andy was cheating on her, how could she trust herself to detect betrayal in another man? Would she ever find love and, if so, what kind of man would she feel safe with after this? Faith's eyes pinched shut with pain. He'd lied. He'd cheated. He'd conned her, and she'd fallen for it.

'Are you okay?' Jade asked from the other side of the cubicle door.

'No. How could he do that to me?'

'He's an idiot. He wasn't worthy of you. You're well shot of him, and you'll find someone far better.'

Faith opened the door and made straight for the sink so that she could rinse her sour mouth. She caught her betrayed expression in the mirror, her blue eyes large and dark with dismay.

'Here.' Jade held out a mint sweet.

'Thanks.' Faith forced a smile as she popped the

sweet into her mouth. She sucked on it gratefully. 'Roxy was very gullible, wasn't she?' But then, that's just what Faith had been, believing Andy's excuses, buying into his claim that he loved her.

'Roxy must be plastered, given the amount she's drunk—even though she didn't look it,' Jade said. 'Come on, let's go.'

They ordered a taxi each; Faith's arrived first. She gave Jade a brief hug and then climbed into the back of the saloon car. As it travelled down lamp-lit roads, anger seeped into every vein. The liar. The cheat. Andy had blamed it all on Hope, but Roxy had said that Andy wouldn't have finished the relationship had Roxy not declared herself to be serious about him. Was that because he'd been biding his time with Faith until a better prospect had come along? Had his mates gatecrashed her dates with Andy for the sake of time efficiency, to free up extra hours and nights with Roxy? Had they known? Faith bet they had and she felt as though he'd shamed her, that they'd all had a laugh at her expense. Hatred bubbled up inside her.

Just how much of Andy's straying was due to Faith being plain and boring and needing to meet Hope's needs, and how much was to do with Roxy's loose knicker elastic and Andy's unzipped trousers? Faith determined that if she got involved with another man, she would make sure he was caring and empathetic enough to understand her love and responsibilities towards Hope. And, if he told even one lie, he'd be out!

She wondered how Andy and Roxy had met. Then guessed. Hadn't she said she'd met that priest at a service station? If Roxy travelled a lot, she'd have probably met Andy travelling a lot too. Service stations were clearly great venues for following up an instant shot of lust with instant opportunity—like with the motel by the service station Roxy had wanted to lure the priest to. Where was he now?

Faith barely took in the route across the Plimsoll Swing Bridge. She'd lived in Bristol all her life and took the presence of water and the multitude of bridges for granted. Then they were driving past the entrance at the bottom of Clifton Rocks Railway, the imposing cliff face rising above them, the uneven surface of dark rock interspersed with green vegetation. It reminded her of her evening at The Horse and Groom with Andy—and his words replayed in her head; there was no one else, he liked to be straight about these things. She felt so deeply betrayed.

She began quietly at first, but soon the gulping sobs alerted the driver.

'Are you all right, love?'

'Fine, I just... need... to get home.' Faith fumbled in her bag for a tissue and then buried her face in it, trying to stifle more anguished sounds that just wouldn't stop coming.

'Do you need help? Have you got someone at home to look after you?' he asked as she caught him staring at her in the rear-view mirror.

'My... sister.'

By the time the taxi pulled up outside the flats, her throat was hurting, and she'd got through a whole packet of tissues. She assured the driver she'd be fine and that her sister would look after her just to get rid of him. Faith wanted to be alone and knew that Hope would be fast asleep.

In bed, she texted Andy.

*You are a liar and a cheat and you deserve a liar and a cheat. And that's what you got.*

Faith wiped her tears, switched out the light and cuddled her childhood teddy to her chest. When her phone buzzed, she picked it up, blinking her eyes into focus.

*What the hell are you talking about?*

*Roxanne Miller. Do you cheat on her like she cheats on you?*

Her phone buzzed again. *How the hell do you know her?*

Faith blew her nose before replying. *Went to school together.* After sending, Faith blew her nose again and switched her phone off. It was time she got some sleep.

# 17

The next morning, Faith felt drained and fragile; it hadn't been a good night and she wasn't sure when she'd finally fallen asleep. When her radio alarm had woken her, she'd just wanted to stay under the covers and not have to remember. She'd considered pulling a sickie but hadn't wanted to blemish her work record at Siskin House. So eventually, she dragged herself out of bed and went through the motions of preparing for work.

She thought she'd get away with being a tad late since her boss, Edison Ekwense, was usually out doing his round of appointments first thing. But he was in the third-floor office taking a call. As he tapped his watch, he passed her a look of rebuke. She mouthed *sorry* and quickly got stuck in behind her own desk, delving into the emails that had come through overnight.

Edison ended the phone conversation with panache. There was something about his gentle public school accent that reassured and invited trust in clients. But then he skewered Faith with his gaze as he said, in a much firmer tone, 'How come you're late?'

'Sorry. Bad night.'

'You said you were going to a club with a friend. But that doesn't give you the right to roll in half an hour over time.'

'No, it doesn't. I'm sorry.'

Faith knew he suspected her of being hungover but he wouldn't believe her if she denied it. He'd ask for an explanation but she didn't want him to know about Andy and Roxy. She shouldn't feel less worthy because she hadn't been good enough for him to stay faithful to her, but she did. The solution, she'd decided in her sleepless hours, was to find a man who did consider her worthy. But she'd have her trust radar set to full sensitivity; she didn't want to be duped a second time.

'My first appointment cancelled so I came here first,' Edison said. 'You are meant to be answering the calls.'

'I know. I'm sorry.'

'Okay. Let's say no more about it.' He gathered some papers into his briefcase and left.

Needing to calm herself, Faith decided she'd better think of something other than Andy and Roxy. She thought of Hope and the phone call that she'd made to Faith the day after her interview.

'I got the job!' Hope shrieked. 'They just rang to let me know. Isn't it wonderful?'

'Congratulations!'

'Thanks. I'm going to call Gavin to hurry things along. He's supposed to be contacting a workshop to get them to make a foam base for the casket, and he said he'd put up nets for me so that people won't be able to see in.'

'Wow. You're moving fast.'

'I need to. I didn't tell the manager I was ill.'

'*What?*'

'There was this sporty-looking woman in the foyer and, at first, I thought she was there because she had an appointment with someone. But when Bill Carruthers called me in, he told her that she wouldn't have long to wait. So, I had to act.'

'Act what? Being sporty and fit and up for a marathon every morning?'

'When he asked me what my interests were, I told him I like to go running.'

'You *what?*'

'Well, I used to. Miss Sporty Pants would've been handed the job on a plate if I'd played fair.'

'But I work here too. You're my sister. It'll reflect badly on me.'

'The manager didn't mention you at all, so neither did I.'

'What happens when Bill sees you climbing in and out of a casket?'

'That's the tricky bit, I grant you. There's a side door to Siskin House that leads onto a small road. We can park the hearse there. I walked my Google Maps man very carefully down that side street and there are no yellow lines. To cap it all, it's a cul-de-sac. So, no one from Siskin House would be driving down there on their way to, or from, work. There seems to be plenty of space for staff to park in front of the building.'

Faith shut her eyes as she imagined being spotted getting in or out of the vehicle and being unable to explain to cover up for her sister's lies. 'Hope, a hearse is not an inconspicuous car. Someone will notice.'

'Not if we're at the office first, and I have to be there early because of my shift. Then, at the end of the day, when you're done, you can sneak out of the side door. No one will be any the wiser. No one will know I use that casket.'

'People will see me driving the hearse. Questions will be asked. It's loopy, and it's not going to work.'

'It's a tough world, and Miss Sporty Pants can't win every time.'

Faith was brought back to the present, to the office cluttered with disability equipment catalogues and samples, as her mobile began to send shivers down her spine. It was playing the *Jaws* theme tune. She'd switched the notification sound from the happy, innocuous trill to the menacing tune in the middle of the night when she couldn't sleep. Faith rejected Andy's call and her fears of being about to be eaten by a shark subsided. Then she saw a message from Andy appear in her Inbox: *I've made a terrible mistake. I see that now. Let's meet up. We can work this out. Andy x*

She ignored it.

At lunchtime, Andy appeared at the door with an apologetic smile and bearing red roses wrapped in red paper. 'These are for you. To make up for being such an ass.'

'You're calling yourself a donkey?'

'You know what I mean.'

'I have no idea what you mean.'

'There's no need to play dense. You know what I'm trying to say. I'm sorry, and I want you to give me another chance.'

'Another chance to dupe me?' Faith noticed a look of pain fleetingly fall across his face. 'Why don't you give the flowers to Roxy?'

'I had no idea she was like that. I thought she was really into me.'

'Like you were *into* her? Go away and make it up to her.'

'I'm not going out with a tart.'

'How many seconds had you known her before you sealed the deal to head for a bedroom—or wherever you ended up? I think you were well-matched whatever label you choose to put on her. Andy, go home, grow up and work out what you want for the next time you meet someone. Now, it's my lunch break, and I want to have time to myself.'

'We could spend it together.'

Faith sent a burning look of hatred his way. 'Leave and take the wretched flowers with you. I'm not interested.'

'I'm not giving up,' he said as he retreated.

'I'd much rather you did. Cardinal rule: do not cheat on your girlfriend.'

# 18

Four days after his return to Clifton—very early that blustery Friday—Tom ran up to the third floor of Siskin House to avoid curious questions from people he didn't yet know. Once in the main room of his office, he got stuck into work at the heavy dark-oak desk that had been left by the previous occupant. He spent hours researching prices he could charge, familiarising himself with the new professional photographic editing software he'd bought, writing to-do lists and planning how to furnish and decorate the office. The flaking taupe walls required a few licks of fresh paint to brighten the room and hopefully eliminate the musty smell that cold, fresh air through open windows had not. The carpet could do with a wash too, in case that was the source of the fusty odour.

Although he was lucky that Judith could provide a place to stay and a spacious rent-free office suite in Siskin House, it hit him hard that, as a grown man, he had to rely on her charity.

It was approaching lunchtime now and in that unfamiliar room, far from the people he knew so well, Tom felt incredibly, intensely alone. God seemed further away than He'd ever been before, and Tom couldn't tell whether He understood Tom's leaving St Michael's to live a new life. Could having abandoned his parish make God abandon him? Was this why Tom felt so utterly friendless?

The dark, tired walls seemed to expand while Tom shrank, feeling more and more insignificant and out of his depth in this new, previously unlived life. He lifted his hands to cup his tense face, his trembling fingers lightly drumming his skin. How would he fare outside of the protective cocoon of the Church, depending on a home and hand-outs from Judith? He brushed his palms over his short, almost buzz-cut brown hair, massaging his scalp to smooth out the tightness in his head.

There were so many administrative tasks awaiting him; the list kept growing. To break the panic that was squeezing his chest, constricting his breath, flooding him with adrenaline, he craved something familiar and comforting such as a mug of coffee, despite its caffeine content.

The shrill ring of a telephone cut through the stuffy air in the carpeted corridor. As Tom passed the lift, the ringing stopped. The voice of a young woman drifted out from the other office, pleasant and lively. Should he wait until the call was over and introduce himself? He hesitated by the loos and then decided to carry on. Not yet. Another day, perhaps, when he was ready to tell others in the building about his business and be ready to answer their questions, sidestepping any that were too close to the truth.

Memories of his journey to Clifton, and the people he'd encountered, still haunted him and, because of this, he was determined to keep the fact that he was a Catholic priest a secret. For as long as he could. Sharing information about his past did not feel safe, especially while he was vulnerable, struggling to adjust to his new life.

In the kitchenette, he helped himself to what he needed. When he began to walk back to his office, mug in hand, the sight of the door to the cleaning cupboard reminded him how sitting inside had helped him feel safe like when he used to sit in the confessional waiting for the penitent to enter. It didn't take long to select the right key from the bunch in his pocket that Judith had given him.

Soon, he was sitting on the upturned bucket in the dark, tucked away around the corner from the door. Aided by his focused breathing, he began to feel calmer. Tears that had started to form failed to flow. But Tom still needed to blow his nose. With the light from his phone, he found some toilet tissue nearby. He wrinkled his nose in disapproval when he discovered it wasn't quite the standard he was used to: far too abrasive. The presbytery housekeeper had always bought luxury paper; she'd taken care of the Fathers' bottoms. A row of pale, pampered buttocks provided a disturbing mental image.

Images! He must add memory cards to his list of things to buy. Tom had learned the hard way about needing to put a shoot onto several cards before they were full. A few years ago, he'd given a full card to a parishioner volunteer to take care of—who'd then gone to prop up the bar. At the end of the evening, the memory card—like the assistant's memory—had vanished.

This line of thought only served to remind Tom that he wouldn't be able to afford an assistant. Squeezing his eyes shut, he clutched the rosary he kept in his pocket. It took a while to find the words and then he began to pray for help in his new life, especially in finding a woman to love and who would love him back. *Where would he find her and what would she be like?*

Faith had been working alone fielding calls, online chat requests and emails since nine that morning. Being so busy had helped take her mind off lying, cheating Andy.

The phone trilled. Faith said, 'Good morning,

Enablement Solutions. How may I help you?... We provide equipment and software to help people with all kinds of disabilities. If you explain the problem, I can let you know what's available to help...'

When she hung up, Faith noticed that the clock on her monitor showed it was approaching one. Feeding time. Edison was making community calls undertaking assessments and advisory work. He should be back soon but, until then, she'd transfer all calls through to the switchboard. Leaving her handbag in her desk drawer, she snatched the office keys from her desk and locked up.

In the kitchenette, Faith retrieved her sandwiches and juice from the fridge. When she lifted the kettle, she discovered it was hot. Had Edison slipped back in for a cuppa and then slipped back out again? Clutching her hair to the nape of her neck, she leaned over the sink to peek out of the window in search of Edison's car. Although there was no sign of him, the familiar figure and blond hair of Andy striding towards the main entrance came into view, invoking the mental image of two naked figures in bed and neither of them was hers.

As her heart filled with heavy hopelessness, her stomach knotted. If he hadn't got the message by now, there wasn't much point in hanging around for a replay. She never wanted to see him again, let alone have him invade her personal space, touch her. Just knowing he lived in the same city was too close for comfort; she could run into him at any time. She pictured fixing an electronic tracking bracelet to his ankle, set up to send an alert to her phone the moment he was within a mile of her.

She changed her mind about having a hot drink. It would be a complete giveaway if the kettle hissed, bubbled and clicked by the time Andy reached the third floor. She fled the kitchenette, grabbing her sandwiches and juice on the way.

In the corridor, she froze, uncertain of where to go. It was no good locking herself in the office. If Edison returned while Andy was still here, Edison would unlock the door to get in, and Andy would barge in after him. The empty office suite was locked. She'd tried the door out of curiosity a week ago and, as far as she knew, no one had opened it since.

Hearing the ominous movement of the lift, and seeing from the display above the doors that it was descending, Faith knew that it could be for Andy. But there was no guarantee he would be using the lift and that the stairs, should she use them, would be free of him...

Where could she hide? The loos? Too obvious. Being the only woman working on that level, there would be nothing to deter Andy from crossing the threshold of a female preserve. The men's loos? But what if Edison were to stroll in and make use of a urinal? What if, believing the room to be empty, she chose that exact moment to creep out of the cubicle? She shuddered.

The lift display showed the cage was on its way up.

The lift was at Level One.

In desperation, she charged to the end of the corridor, past the lift and tugged at the handle of the door close to the empty office suite. The door opened. How this miracle had happened, she wasn't sure. Perhaps the cleaner had forgotten to lock up before she'd left?

By the time the lift pinged its arrival on the third floor, Faith was safely inside the cupboard in pitch-black darkness. Then she sniffed the air. *Was that coffee she could smell?*

Just as Tom's muscles were starting to relax, the door to the cupboard opened and closed again. There was the sound of someone else's breathing. He ought to reveal his presence, but with luck, the person would leave without knowing he was here. He could pretend that what was happening now had never happened and introduce himself properly, outside of the cupboard, when he'd troubled to shave and bought shirts without clerical collar tabs.

But the person didn't leave, and Tom felt obliged to say something. As long as there was no light, he'd be able to get away with not being recognised later.

'I don't want to frighten you,' he whispered in his rusty West Country accent that he'd not used since school when he'd wanted to fit in with a cool crowd, 'but you're not in here alone.'

# 19

When the man's voice reached her ears, Faith nearly screeched her way out of the cupboard. Goosebumps tugged at her skin and her stomach dived to the floor. But, with her hand cupped to her mouth, only a minimal squawk escaped while she considered her options. Was she safer inside or outside of the cupboard?

'I didn't mean to frighten you. I just wanted to let you know that you have company.' He was still whispering, in a deep local accent much stronger than her own. 'I'm here, around the corner.'

If she screamed, Andy would find her, and his presence—albeit unwelcome—would save her from any danger this other man might pose. But a rescue from this unknown man might not be necessary. What she wanted now was to be safe from Andy. She plucked up the courage to progress deeper into the cupboard, guiding her way with the outside of her wrists on the shelving either side of her as her fingers were gripping her sandwiches and drink. She steadied her breath and told herself that all was well.

'Turn to your left when you get to the end,' the voice whispered. 'Then I'll be in front of you.'

As she had free access to the door, she began to relax. Her skin smoothed, the chill sensations dissipated and her stomach was firmly back in place. The man's tone was pleasant—deep and rounded—suggesting confidence and dependability. Gut instincts told her she'd made the right choice. She was safe in here.

Whispering seemed like a good idea. Otherwise,

Andy would find her here, with this man. But was that a bad thing? He might leave her alone if he thought she'd moved on. She'd have to think about it. It all depended on what the man here looked like—assuming a damp mop was responsible for the slightly mouldy smell—and his age.

'How old are you?'

'Is there an age limit as to who you can share a cupboard with?' he whispered back.

Faith shook her head and then realised that the man wouldn't see it. 'No. Curious, that's all.'

'Thirty-four. You?'

Promising. Andy would surely be convinced she'd found someone else. 'Twenty-six. I'm Faith, by the way. Faith Goddard.'

There was a sound as though something had fallen to the floor and the man muttered something that hadn't sounded polite. The scent of coffee strengthened.

'Are you all right?'

'Dropped my mug. Coffee's probably gone everywhere. Here, take my seat if you're staying. I'll just mop where I think the puddle might be. There isn't another bucket to upturn, and I apologise for not being gallant enough to suggest it sooner. I suppose I expected you to leave.'

'Oh. Do you mind my staying?'

'No. Just thought you'd rather be somewhere else.'

'I... er... thought I'd spend my lunch break in here.'

'Fair enough... Do you do that often?'

'First time.'

'Me too.'

She tensed. 'Would you prefer I left?' Had she intruded?

'No. Not at all. I could do with some company.'

Relief flooded through her. She liked it here. With

him. It seemed she could do with some company too, as long as it wasn't Andy's.

As their bodies swapped places, Faith sensed that he was tall and broad, and she detected a subtle scent of soap and freshly-washed clothes. Andy had a bit of work to do if he were to meet this man's stature. Too much time sitting in his car and not enough at the gym. But what did she care about that now?

'Shall I guide you to the bucket so you don't try sitting in the wrong place?' the man offered.

'Thanks.' The hand that found hers was warm and strong. For some reason, Faith was reluctant to let go and, without thinking, outstretched her fingers so that they could slide along his, prolonging contact, as he pulled away. Had he noticed what she'd done?

'Do you believe in Divine Providence? Fate?' he asked.

That was an odd question. 'That's a bit deep for a lunch break.'

'Sorry, it's just that meeting you now when there's so much change in my life, and I came in here to escape—and it looks like you're escaping something too—makes me feel it's significant.'

Faith was stunned into silence.

'It's like it was meant to be,' he continued. 'That we were destined to meet. And your name...'

'Yes?' Her lungs stiffened as she fought for breath, feeling surreal.

'It's lovely.'

Faith was glad they'd swapped places because if they hadn't, she'd have been sitting on the man's lap. Her knees were insubstantial; her whole body was like jelly. Perhaps she required some sustenance? Her blood sugar was probably low. 'Care for a cheese and tomato sandwich?'

'Oh. Thanks. If you can spare it.'

Of course she could spare it. Their hands brushed again, and a thrill from the touch of his skin spread up her arm, branching off to tingle in other parts of her body. Faith rubbed her hand at the point of contact and the tingles subsided. Something strange was happening that she didn't understand. Was she so desperate for a man that she was responding to the slightest stimulus? Or did her body recognise that he was right for her?

Outside, Andy called her name. Why didn't he just give up?

'Why are you hiding from him?'

'He keeps bothering me.'

'Any particular reason?'

'He wants me back.'

'What do you want?'

Now that was a good question. She was warming more and more to this man. 'I want to get married. But not to him. Someone a lot nicer than him. Someone who doesn't lie and cheat.'

'He did that to you?' The man sounded genuinely sorrowful on her behalf. 'I wouldn't ever do that to you... if you and I were... sorry, I'm a bit ahead of myself here. But I know I would never do that to a woman.'

'Huh. Men always say that though.' She finished her sandwich and wiped her mouth clean of crumbs.

'I mean it.'

He certainly sounded as though he did. But still, Faith wasn't convinced. 'I've heard it said that when a woman offers herself to a man on a plate, he never says no. Just can't resist.' She opened her juice bottle and swigged.

'I have done. It happened on Monday. I legged it.'

'Are you gay?'

'No.'

Wondering what he was doing sitting in the cupboard, she was suddenly struck by a thought. 'Are you an albino?'

'What?'

'You know, someone who can't go in the sun. No pigment in the skin.' Or hair or eyes for that matter. Was that why he liked to sit in the dark?

'I'm not in here to hide from the sun. I'm just used to spending a lot of time on my own.'

Faith was drawn to the mellow sound of his whispers and wondered how he would sound at normal volume. Andy was calling out her name again and banging on what was presumably the office door. So, Edison hadn't come back yet. An idea occurred to her.

'If this door opens, would you pretend that you're kissing me? It would have to be in the view of the door though... Hello? Did you hear?'

'Yes, but I wasn't sure that I heard right.'

'If you don't like the idea—'

'I do. I just don't think I'd be very convincing.'

Did he suspect there was something wrong with her? 'Why wouldn't you be very convincing?' It sounded accusing, she knew. But why else would he have trouble playing the part of an ardent lover? Lover? Hey, hang on, she admonished herself. That's a bit quick.

'Because I've never kissed a woman before. So, I wouldn't know how to pretend.'

*What?* 'Could you repeat what you just said as I don't think I could have heard right?'

'I said, I've never kissed a woman before.' His whisper deepened.

Well, that was unexpected. In fact, she was floored by it. Then she understood. It was a wind-up. She smiled.

'Hello, can you hear me?' he asked.

She giggled. 'How old did you say you were?'

'Thirty-four. And don't laugh. It's not funny. Not for me anyway.'

Faith muffled another giggle with her hand. 'You're being serious?'

'Yes.' He sounded hurt. 'I'm not someone who lies about these things.'

Blimey. He was telling the truth. 'How come you've never kissed...?' If he'd never kissed a woman, did that mean...? Surely not? *A virgin?* She'd seen programmes on TV about virgin adult men who'd not been in a relationship and how they'd needed professional help to overcome their shyness with women. She thought it must be very difficult for this man too; he must feel like a reject, like she did.

'We were all single men where I lived. None of us had access to... relationships. I went straight there from uni. Even at uni, I was leading a sheltered kind of life.'

'Where were you living? After uni?'

'Erm... away... with my... flock.'

Well, no one could have guessed that one coming. She heard the rustle of material and guessed he'd shifted his position. 'All this time? With your flock?'

'Yes. I kind of got used to that way of life.'

Faith was pleased they were in the dark so that he couldn't have seen the face she'd just pulled. 'So, do you own lots of sheep?'

'They're not my... sheep.' He said the words slowly and carefully as though concentrating on what he wanted to say. 'It was a community that needed help. Part of a charitable organisation. We got paid for the work we did. I'm still all right financially. They give you time to get settled when you go back home. Coming back to Clifton is quite a culture shock for me, having been away so long, and that's why I wanted to sit in here a while on my own.'

'So, it wasn't just you?'

'There were a few of us. They're still there.'

Liberated by the darkness, Faith was freely shaking her head in disbelief. *Who would want to spend their lives looking at sheep?* Perhaps he'd been on some massive sheep-rearing station in the middle of nowhere? Maybe they were short of local men. She'd read about Merino sheep and how they had to be sheared more often than other sheep.

'It must have been very hard work.' She wanted to come across as empathetic because she was.

'It... was different. I did enjoy it. But I hadn't wanted a normal life back then. I chose to be away from family—and friends. Now I've changed my mind, and I want to settle down.'

'I want to settle down too but—' She was just about to tell him about having responsibilities towards Hope and then realised she should keep it secret. He might mention her sister's ill health to someone else in the building and Hope would be livid with her.

'But?'

'It's not working out so far.' She heard more banging outside. 'He's still out there.'

Why was Andy so persistent? Then she guessed he'd spotted her car outside on his way in, had called her mobile and had heard it ringing from inside her desk. It would have been enough to convince him that she was in the office. Perhaps she should broach the subject with the man again.

'Shall I...?' She trailed off, unable to finish. *How could she even think such a thing?*

'Shall you...?'

'No. I can't. It's too forward of me.'

'Go on. Don't be shy. I won't think ill of you. Who

could?'

'I was thinking... I could show you how to kiss...'

It was strange how quickly she'd become drawn to him, how it made her realise how much she missed having a man in her life. Perhaps it would comfort her, being in this man's arms? And she could help him like the women on the TV had helped men.

There was silence in the cupboard. Perhaps Andy had gone, given up.

'You want to show me how to kiss,' the man murmured, 'so I can give a convincing performance should this other man find us in here?'

The knot in Faith's stomach relaxed a bit; he understood. 'Yes. Unless you'd r...rather not.' Would this man like kissing her? She didn't think Andy had ever given feedback. How was she to know if she was a good kisser?

'I can't think of anything I'd like better.' His voice sounded husky now. Sexy husky. 'But I'm afraid I've not shaved the last couple of days... or so.'

He still had lips, hadn't he? What did the guy look like? As she rose to her feet, a tremor of anticipation sped through her. She reached out her hand and found the man—and his chest. He was wearing something warm to the touch but with a rough weave. Was it a jumper, she wondered, made from the fleece of the sheep he used to look after? If so, they hadn't been Merino sheep; their wool was much softer. Gosh, he was tall. As she raised her head, his coffee breath tickled her skin. As her hands walked upwards, they met his neck, and she could detect taut muscles. Was he anxious, like she was? Then her fingers reached cheeks that scratched like one of those coir doormats. She wouldn't be needing a facial scrub for a while after this then, but, at this moment, what did she care?

'Just the lips, okay?' Faith whispered.

'Okay.'

'I do something, you copy it exactly.'

'Okay.'

With a hand behind his head, resting on very short hair, which made Faith wonder whether he'd had a light buzz cut, she applied slight pressure. Soft lips pressed against hers and warmth began to seep into her body. His lips were pleasant, but the prickle of the stubble wasn't. Gently, she kissed his top lip. She could taste coffee and wondered what she tasted of—orange juice? He kissed her top lip. So far so good, her heart rate rising and warmth spreading to the further reaches of her body. She tried kissing his bottom lip. He kissed her bottom lip, same pressure, same length of time. She repeated the process but lingered on each lip and then so did he.

Faith was enjoying being in control. Andy had always been the one to take charge. Even when she'd initiated a kiss, he'd take over. This guy was pliant and did everything she asked, making it a heady experience. Becoming lost in the kisses, Faith pressed closer and his arms tightened around her, pulling her into him—and his arousal. Whoa, this was steamy stuff. She broke off for some air. He sounded in want of air too.

Should she go back for round two or should she call it quits? She knew what she wanted and she knew what she ought to do, but they weren't the same thing.

'How was I?' he asked.

'Fine.' It had been more than fine but she wasn't prepared to admit it.

His fingers pulled gently through her locks as though feeling the texture. 'You've got very long hair. How far does it reach and what colour is it?'

With tight lungs and a melting body, she whispered

faintly, 'It lies between my shoulder blades and waist, and it's black. What colour is yours?'

'Dark brown.'

When his hands released her, she experienced a sense of loss. That wasn't what she wanted. 'Another practice?'

He pulled her tighter and she enjoyed the feel of him, the strength in his arms that left her weak and trembling. It was only when common sense finally managed to break through the rush of desire that she broke away. 'I... I'm sorry. I don't know what came over me.'

'It is I who must apologise...'

'I started it.'

'And I agreed.'

Overcome with awkwardness, Faith said, 'I... I should go... I think Andy's gone.' She waited for the man to say something but when he didn't, she added, 'It was...' Nice to meet him? A pleasure? No, that was too forward, too close to the truth as it had indeed been an immense pleasure. '... interesting.' *Interesting?* How dumb did that sound? 'I mean, I'm glad that I met you.'

'Me too.'

'I... I'd better go.'

'Yes... I'll... I'll wait a while.'

# 20

Faith was in a dither about her experience that lunchtime. As she needed to gain some perspective, she phoned Perdita to ask if she could visit her home in Westbridge, after work.

As soon as Perdita's front door opened, Faith, having braved the Friday evening traffic out of Bristol, blurted, 'I'm so glad you said I could come.'

The smell of cooked meat and cheese wafted out to greet her as Perdita adjusted the high ponytail of her mousey-brown hair. She was wearing navy trousers and a jumper—her pregnancy bump didn't yet show.

'It's no trouble.' Her smile put Faith's mind at rest. 'Saul won't be back for hours. He's run into an old school friend. I think, from the sound of it, he's in a spot of bother.'

'I am too. I think,' Faith said, dazed and unsure of exactly what had happened to her today.

'Come in. The food's ready.' Perdita indicated the reception room on the right that doubled as a playroom.

A sizeable-portioned pepperoni pizza, two plates, napkins and a carton of apple juice with glasses were already on the coffee table. Petal's toys had been tidied away as the floor was clear of the usual display of jigsaws, cars and farm animals.

'So, what's the problem?' Perdita poured out the juice and then handed one of the filled glasses to Faith as she sat down. As Perdita settled in the other armchair, she shifted the cushion into the small of her back.

Faith took a deep breath. 'I met a man in a cupboard,

and I think I've fallen for him. I couldn't tell the boys... they'd think me barmy.'

Perdita's eyes widened. 'Is this cupboard thing a new speed-dating craze?'

'No. It's just a cupboard that has all the cleaning supplies and equipment. I hid in it when I saw Andy coming.'

Perdita's trim eyebrows lifted in surprise. 'I've never noticed a cleaning cupboard when visiting Saul.'

Faith worked in the same building as Perdita's husband, Saul. His legal practice was located on the floor below Faith's office. 'There's one on every floor, on the same side as the loos; the layouts are identical. Luckily, Andy hasn't ever noticed the cupboard either. He's harassing me.'

'Oh, dear. Have some pizza.'

As soon as Perdita indicated the pizza plate, Faith grabbed a segment and a plate to eat it over. The combination of bread, cheese and pepperoni aromas had been making her mouth water ever since she'd entered Perdita's home, and Faith had had to stop an impulse to dive in the moment she'd spotted the offering. Despite the sharp pangs in her stomach, she still didn't begrudge giving away half her lunch.

'This is great,' Faith enthused. 'I gave the man in the cupboard half my lunch, and my stomach's been protesting ever since.'

'Ah,' Perdita said as she reached for some food. 'Love at first sight?'

Faith shielded her mouth with her hand as she'd just taken an ambitious bite of the pizza. 'I don't think you can call it that,' she mumbled.

'Why not?'

Faith shrugged. 'I didn't actually see him.' She described the events that had led her to sneak into the dark cupboard and how, on hearing a man's voice whisper in a local, albeit strange, accent that she wasn't in there alone, she'd guided herself deeper inside until she'd found him.

'What's his name?'

What difference did that make? You couldn't tell a man's eligibility by his name. 'I don't know.' Faith flinched as her gaze took in Perdita's boggled eyes and parted lips.

'You don't know what he looks like, and you don't know his name?'

'He knows mine,' Faith said, as though that made everything all right.

'How long were you in the cupboard?'

Faith lowered her gaze, feeling chastised. 'It was my lunch break.'

'You spent a whole hour in a cupboard with a strange man?'

'He wasn't at all strange. He was very nice. That's why I think I've fallen for him.'

'What did you talk about?'

Faith pursed her lips while she considered. 'You know. The usual stuff.'

'No, I don't know. I've never met a man in a cupboard.'

Faith supposed she needed to tell all. 'Okay. I'll try to remember what we talked about. But you must promise not to tell anyone about this. Including Saul.'

'He's my husband.'

'And he works in the same building as me. I don't want it getting around or indeed back to the new cleaner.'

'Who's the new cleaner?'

'The man I met in the cupboard.'

Perdita was about to take a bite of food but lowered

her hand. 'Oh?'

'I think it's a stopgap job. While he adjusts to the culture.'

Although the man hadn't actually said he was the cleaner he must be. Otherwise, what would he be doing in there and how come he'd got a key? Faith hadn't got a key, and she wasn't sure whether Edison had either. If he was a new employee at the managerial level, he might be given a key but he would have a cupboard on his own floor to sit in. Why would he choose to come all the way to the third floor? That really wouldn't make sense. So the man she'd met must have been a cleaner.

'What culture does he have to adjust to? You said he had a local accent.'

'Although he was born here, he's been away a long time. He was a shepherd in a faraway place. To help the local community. That probably accounts for the odd twang to his whispers.' She wished she'd asked what country he'd been in. He hadn't said he could speak another language so he'd probably worked in an English-speaking country.

'Don't locals look after their own sheep? Wouldn't it be cheaper?'

'I suppose. Maybe they don't have enough strong men to work on the sheep station. How well-populated is Australia in the areas they rear sheep?' She'd sensed the man in the cupboard to be big and strong. Faith held out her hands in surrender. 'I know it sounds crazy...'

Perdita nodded in agreement.

'... but he was someone I could talk to. Someone who listened. It was like chatting with you—or with Luke and Gavin. But much more intimate. I didn't know a bloke could be like that.'

'Like what?'

'So understanding. So caring. He was really

interested in what I had to say. Not at all like Andy.' That was probably why she'd liked the man straight away. There was nothing about him that reminded her of her ex.

'From my experience, men flatter you to get you into bed.'

'He wasn't like that. Honest.'

'Why? Because there wasn't a bed in the cupboard?' Perdita compressed her lips and her gaze sharpened. 'Tell me there was no bed in that cupboard.'

'There was no bed in that cupboard.'

Perdita's mouth softened. 'Well, I can't understand why he was so nice then. Unless he's playing the long game. To get you into bed in the future.'

'If his kissing's anything to go by, I think I'd like to give it a go,' Faith admitted dreamily.

'You *kissed* him?'

By the sudden rise in temperature, Faith knew she'd had the grace to blush. Looking back, it did seem reckless to kiss a complete stranger she'd never even seen. Perhaps she was feeling her freedom from Andy? She could do as she pleased now. 'It's not what you think. We got to know each other first.'

'In the dark, during your lunch hour?'

She traced a finger around her plate. 'That's why I didn't go to the boys. I came to you. I thought you'd be more likely to understand as you fell for Saul in unconventional circumstances. I just had to tell someone.'

'So tell me while I eat more pizza.' Perdita reached for another slice.

'Okay. This is how things went...' Faith regaled all that had happened up to the offer of teaching the man in the cupboard how to kiss.

'You asked him, just like that?'

'Yes.' She reached towards the pizza plate and then realised she was about to grab the last piece and retreated.

'Don't worry about me,' Perdita said. 'Take it. Unlike you, I had all of my lunch today.'

'Ouch.' Faith was disappointed that Perdita wasn't taking her news well. Faith claimed the slice of pizza and took a slurp of apple juice before biting off a chunk. She supposed she'd have reacted like Perdita if Hope were to have told her the same story.

'So,' Perdita said, 'what did he say when you offered to show him how to kiss?'

'He agreed.'

'I can't believe I'm hearing this.'

'I know. But... in the cupboard, it was so peaceful, his company balmy. I felt so at one. Soothed. You know.'

'Mm.' Perdita had a distant look in her eyes as her hands nestled in her lap.

Was she recalling an experience with Saul? Had that got Perdita's heart beating faster like hers had been in the cupboard? Was this dreamy look an empathetic dreamy look? 'You understand?'

Like a switch being flicked, Perdita came back to the present and said, 'No. And I'm suspicious.'

'Suspicious? Of what?'

'Can I call a friend?'

This wasn't a TV game show. 'What about?'

'To ask whether it's likely that a thirty-something-year-old man—'

'He said he's thirty-four.'

'To ask why a heterosexual thirty-four-year-old man has never kissed a woman.'

'What friend?'

'Luke. He's sensible. He knows men.'

'I don't want the boys to know. It's supposed to be

just between the two of us. You promised.'

'I'll keep your identity secret.'

Perdita thumbed the screen on the mobile she'd picked up from the table, and, before long, Faith heard her purring down the phone. 'Luke? Hi. Quick question for you. Do you think it's possible for a straight thirty-four-year-old man never to have kissed a woman?... No, nothing wrong with him as far as we know... Well, he convinced a friend of mine he didn't know how to kiss, so she thought she'd give him a couple of lessons, and he, of course, accepted... She said he'd been living in a community where they were all single men... She didn't say he'd been a monk...'

When Perdita shot Faith a questioning look, Faith shook her head. The idea might have fitted but monks didn't look after sheep, did they? Even parishioner sheep. And he had been away, travelling, looking after flocks and shearing and so on.

'She mentioned minding sheep.' Perdita continued. 'Abroad, I think, on a sheep station, perhaps Australia. He mentioned culture shock coming back here... Thanks. I thought that might be the case.' Perdita tapped the screen, put the phone down and said, very softly, 'Luke thinks you've been conned. There's probably no truth in anything that man in the cupboard said.'

Suddenly, the bottom fell out of Faith's world. Then, she stuck it straight back on. 'I don't believe it. He was genuine.'

'I thought Petal's father was too. But it was all a game to him.'

Faith shook her head. 'This guy's different. Nothing flash, unassuming, gentle, not at all pushy...'

'He didn't have to be, did he? He got what he wanted without it.'

'It wasn't like that. Honest.'

'Supposing he's genuine then, what's next? You've not even arranged to meet up with him... Or have you?'

Faith hadn't. She wished now that they'd made plans. 'There's no need,' she said airily. 'We work in the same place. We're bound to bump into each other again.'

'I hope you don't take offence. I'm only going to say this as I'm worried about you. Do you think you could be experiencing rebound behaviour, jumping into a new relationship before you've properly dealt with the last? Latching on to a new man like he's the answer to all your problems? I read about it in a magazine, and I don't want you to get hurt.'

Sudden nausea rose in the back of Faith's throat. Was that what it was? A rebound thing? Since she'd never had a major break-up before, she hadn't got personal experience of it. Could that be the explanation for her uncharacteristic behaviour?

'I'll think about what you said.' So it hadn't been real? But it had felt so real—and it had seemed to be real for him. The way he'd responded to her...

# 21

After Faith had gone home, Perdita stacked the plates and glasses in the dishwasher as quietly as she could so as not to disturb Violet, Saul's aunt, who lived with them. Then Perdita made her way upstairs and into Petal's pink bedroom. Well, it had started off being pink, but Luke had used stencils to superimpose multi-coloured footballs, transforming the walls into a dynamic scene.

Petal was sleeping on her back, her short, dark-blonde hair haloed around her head on the pillow, her mouth barely closed. Her cheek, when Perdita stroked it, felt as soft as a rose petal and as chubby as the belly of Petal's teddy.

As Perdita came downstairs, the familiar sound of tyres crunching on the gravelled driveway told her that Saul was home. She opened the front door and waited for him to approach, her heart filling with pleasure as his athletic form strode towards her. The novelty of having a husband had not yet worn off; she still missed him when he was gone. They hadn't even been married a year yet; would she still yearn for his return after five, ten or twenty years? She hoped so, and she hoped he missed her just as much.

'How was your evening?'

Saul took the steps two at a time, his briefcase swinging in his hand. 'Let me kiss my beautiful wife, and I'll tell you.'

When he reached her, Perdita flung her arms around him, savouring the mixture of the scent of the car and

Saul's lemony aftershave she so loved. After she came out of the embrace, she led him inside and to the sofa in the reception room opposite the one she'd been in with Faith. When he sat down, she lowered herself onto his knee.

'Well? How did it go with this friend of yours?'

'O...kay.' He sounded doubtful.

'You don't seem very sure.'

'Well, as you know, I bumped into him today, on the stairs. He's taken the empty office suite on the top floor. He recognised me from our school days, but I didn't recognise him. That could have been down to his stubble though as well as not expecting to see him.'

'The top floor, as in the third floor, where Faith works?'

'Yes.'

Faith hadn't mentioned anyone new working on her level. Other than the cleaner, but he didn't count as he wouldn't be renting the office. But then she recalled Saul mentioning stubble. Didn't Faith say that the man in the cupboard had stubble? Well, it was common enough. Perhaps Faith could transfer her interest to the man renting the office suite—it was more normal than meeting a man who liked to sit in a cupboard.

'Do you know, it's the most bizarre tale I've ever heard.' Saul shook his head in a disbelieving kind of way.

'Really?'

'However,' he warned, 'I promised not to say a word.'

'You can't make a comment like that and then expect me to leave it! What was bizarre? His life story?'

'Not exactly. Although he filled me in on what had happened since uni and the last few days... it was more to do with today.'

She straightened and fixed him with an eager gaze,

feeling the stirring of connections. Stubble, Siskin House, top floor, bizarre tale... Could the man who was renting the office have been the man in the cupboard, pretending to be a cleaner because he was too embarrassed to admit the truth, whatever that might be?

Fondling Saul's ear lobe, she said sweetly, 'Give me a clue as to what you talked about. That bizarre tale...' She suspected that Saul had indeed just spent the evening with the same person with whom Faith had spent her lunchtime.

Saul gave a gesture of helplessness. 'I can't, I promised. But, I must say, he had a very... interesting time today.' Saul chuckled.

'Really? Give me a clue. Please?'

'Oh no. You'd want more. You wouldn't stop at that.'

'One word. A keyword that sums up the thing about today.'

'Uh-uh. No way.'

'Well, I had a very interesting chat today, too. How about if I give you a keyword and you give me a keyword and neither of us need say anything more?'

Jumping up, Perdita opened a narrow drawer that held stationery. Taking out a small pad, she tore off a sheet and then ripped it into two. She proffered a pen to Saul and walked to the chair normally used by Violet. After scribbling on her sheet, Perdita stared challengingly at Saul who'd sat unmoving. Even his hand holding the pen remained still.

'Oh, all right,' Saul conceded. 'One word and one word only and then we're through?'

'Promise.' She watched him as he began to write.

They swapped folded pieces of paper.

She unfolded her scrap. It read: CUPBOARD. When Saul looked up sharply, having read her word, she giggled. 'Snap.'

# 22

It was Saturday evening, the day after Faith had met the man in the cupboard, and she had nowhere to go. She was in her favourite armchair with her feet up, comfort-eating a bag of Dolly Mixtures as compensation for having to visit the sexual health clinic that morning. Faith didn't seem to have caught anything; the clinic would let her know the last of her results only if there was a problem.

Hope was lounging on the sofa. 'The hearse looks good, doesn't it?'

Gavin had delivered the vehicle that afternoon, and they'd gone out for a spin. Faith decided that she would drive it again tomorrow to get some extra practice in before Monday.

'The net curtains make it look cosy, like a bedroom,' Hope said. 'No one will see when I'm in bed with a duvet and pillow. I filled a plastic shoebox with some essentials too. My spare alarm clock, moisturiser, lip balm, tissues and eye mask.'

It was unlikely that the eye mask would be necessary since it had been pretty dark when Faith had tried lying in the casket with both lids down. Only minimal light had sneaked in through the breathing holes and she'd felt as snug as a bug...

'I like the handles on the inside of the lids. It's easy to close myself in. If it's cold, I could stick a heat pad in the microwave before going out for my sleep.'

'Yes, you've thought of everything... But not an indoor toilet should you be caught short.'

Hope grinned. 'All in hand. Bucket with lid. For emergencies.'

'Wow. All mod-cons.'

'Absolutely.' Hope twiddled with the belt on her dressing gown. 'When Luke came round this morning, he didn't just give me a massage. He made a proposition. He said it was your idea actually.'

'My idea?' Then Faith recalled having lunch in the café with Luke to discuss what he'd been up to with Hope in her bedroom. 'Oh, no. That wasn't an idea—'

'Well, Luke thought it a good one. He asked me to think about it.'

'What's there to think about? You can't have a baby with him! And you've no business coming between him and Gavin. Does Gavin even know?'

Hope held up her hands. 'I told Luke I'd think about it, that's all. He plans to talk to Gavin about it if I decide to go ahead.'

'I can't believe that Luke is doing this behind Gavin's back.' She couldn't believe it of Hope either.

'Luke said there's no point in upsetting Gavin if it doesn't come to anything. It's because he cares about Gavin that he's not involving him at this stage.'

'At this stage? How can you even contemplate it? It's saying it's okay to betray his partner; it's like saying what Andy did to me was okay. What about your health? What about Gavin? How could it possibly work?'

'There's no need to lay on the guilt. I haven't decided to do anything yet. Do you think Luke suggested having a baby with me because he likes me?'

'You're not developing feelings for him, are you?'

Hope gave the tiniest of shrugs. 'We have cosy chats and so on. He's so there for me—and he is gorgeous.'

'Luke's a great friend. Anyway, you're wasting your time. He won't be interested in you, he's gay. You can get pregnant without sex being involved, and I'm sure that's what Luke has in mind. If you continue thinking along the lines you've just said, I'll think even less of you. You have no business interfering in someone else's relationship!'

'I know that really. When he first mentioned having a baby with him, I was stunned. Then I was quite taken by the idea—I'd love to have a baby.'

'When you're better, and you're out in the world more, you'll meet someone. Then you can have babies as a natural progression of your relationship. Not as an unnatural progression of someone else's relationship.'

Hope hmphed. 'What do you mean, unnatural relationship?'

'Unnatural *progression*. You getting between Luke and Gavin is not a natural progression of *their* relationship. And you should put an end to it right now.'

Hope opened her mouth, but whatever it was she wanted to say was forgotten when the intercom sounded. They exchanged looks that confirmed neither of them was expecting anyone.

Faith pressed the talk button. 'Yes?'

'Faith, it's me. Please let me in.'

There was a plummeting feeling in the pit of her stomach. She wished he'd give up. Clenching her teeth, she said, remembering a children's tale, 'Not by the hair on my chinny-chin-chin.' Faith glanced at Hope and mouthed, 'Andy' and then switched the talk function off.

The intercom buzzed again. Faith sat down.

Then knuckles rapped on the glazing, and she could see Andy outside, through the nets. With the evenings becoming lighter, they hadn't yet drawn the curtains.

'For heaven's sake,' Faith said to Hope, 'how many times do I have to say no?'

'Is he a bit slow?'

'He's as wily as anything. He's a loss adjuster.'

'I suppose.'

'But he's not adjusting to this loss very well.'

Faith stomped over to the window, lifted the net and motioned to Andy to go away.

He mimed her opening the window.

She opened it a fraction. 'What?'

Andy held up a box of chocolates he'd been holding behind his back. 'Peace offering.'

'Not interested.' She was about to close the opening but then had second thoughts. It was a delightfully wrapped parcel of Belgian chocolates, going by the writing on the packaging. As Andy turned to go, she increased the gap. 'Hey!'

His eyes adopted a hopeful puppy expression as his gaze took her in. 'Yes?'

She beckoned, put out her hand, and he passed her the box.

'Thanks. This is the last box you can buy me, Andy. Think of it as compensation for disturbing us.' She shut the window and then pulled the curtains across. As she made her way back to the chair, she said to Hope, 'Fancy a chocolate?'

# 23

It was almost a quarter to eight the following Monday morning when Faith, disguised in a baseball cap and clear-lens glasses, parked the hearse by the side entrance to Siskin House. Hope had donned a headscarf to help keep the secret as they drove along roads bound to be shared by other employees of the building. Although the long car had a fuel-guzzling engine, the reverence of other drivers was a bonus. Accustomed to waiting to turn at junctions, Faith had been pleasantly surprised when other drivers had readily given way.

Faith wasn't sure which of them was the more nervous on Hope's first day of work. As they removed their surplus accessories, Hope gave Faith a *help, get me out of here* expression.

'It's bound to be hard,' Faith said. 'Cassie's ever so nice; you'll be fine working with her.'

'I don't want her and Bill Carruthers to find out I cheated at the interview.'

Faith worried about that too and patted Hope's arm. 'Come on. Let's go in.' Perhaps the secret wouldn't matter once Hope had had a chance to prove she was worthy of the job. But, until then, Faith would do her best to avoid her sister being rumbled.

The side door was operable with the same key card that was used for the main entrance. Hope headed to Reception for her training with Cassie while Faith sprinted up the stairs to the third floor. As she was so early, she wondered whether the cleaner would be still here.

After she'd opened up the office and stashed her bag in the desk drawer, she tried the handle to the cleaning cupboard, her heart fluttering wildly. But the door was locked. Her heartbeat steadied.

Believing she was alone, she barged into the kitchenette, keen to have some coffee—and collided with a hunk of a man she didn't recognise. He was carrying a mug of something on his way out and the drink splashed over them both. They screamed and pulled at their wet shirts to save their skin from being burned.

'Sorry,' they said together.

'My fault,' they said.

'No, it's my fault,' they said.

'How about we share the fault?' Faith suggested.

The man shrugged. 'That sounds reasonable. Which part of the blame shall I take? Carrying a mug of coffee?'

'I'll take responsibility for walking in at the wrong moment.' She could tell that the man's black shirt was wet, but she bet that as soon as it was dry, there would be little to show for the mishap.

He smiled, showing a row of even teeth. Then he extended his arm. 'I'm Tom Sheridan.' His physique was better developed than Andy's, and Tom was way more attractive, his mesmerising brown eyes drawing her in. Had rules of propriety been different and she had not met the man in the cupboard first...

She grasped his hand. 'Faith Goddard.' The brief grip of his hand had been strong and warm but he let go when she introduced herself.

'Faith! Oh, er... nice to meet you.' Tom's complexion developed into a rosy hue. No, make it red; the colour was deepening by the moment.

Faith regarded him sideways on wondering how he came to be so shy at his age. He must be at least thirty.

'I've, er, taken on the other office. I'm a photographer.' His voice had an appealing masculine timbre. His accent was closer to Edison's than local.

'Oh.'

'Oh?'

'Sorry, I just wouldn't have guessed you're a photographer.'

Tom raised a curious eyebrow. 'What would you have put me down as?'

Should she say? Why not? He'd ruined her cream shirt. 'A magician. A performer.' When she saw the gap between Tom's eyebrows narrow and the slight inclination of his head, she added, 'The black clothing... I don't think we've had a photographer in the place before. Are you moving studios then?'

The colour in his cheeks had begun to recede, but Faith saw it return with a vengeance. 'I decided to branch out on my own. So, it's my first studio.'

'What do you do? Portraits? Schools?'

'Sacramental photography.' He must have noticed her blank expression. 'Weddings, baptisms, funerals...'

'*Funerals?*' Was that why he was wearing black? He was going to a funeral? When her nan died, Faith wouldn't have wanted someone taking snaps of them all in tears. As Tom was still blocking the doorway, Faith pointed with the flat of her hand to the area past him.

'Oh. Sorry.' Tom stepped back. 'Here, let me get you a cloth. Your blouse...'

He dampened the dishcloth under the tap and squeezed out the excess water. Then he motioned as though to wipe the stain himself but passed her the material instead, looking flustered, as though realising how inappropriate dabbing at her shirt front would be.

Faith's efforts at removing the stain were ineffective. When she discovered that Tom had disappeared, she closed the kitchenette door and pulled her shirt over her head with most of the buttons still done up. A good scrub under the tap with the nail brush from under the sink and a dash of washing-up liquid worked far better. As she was wringing the shirt out, the door opened. She swung around in horror and caught Tom staring at her.

No, that was not true. He was gawking at her balconette bra. No, that wasn't true either. He was gawking at the generous display of breasts that the balconette bra was designed to expose to maximum effect. She grasped the sopping shirt in front of her.

He blinked. 'I'm sorry... I didn't realise... I just came to get a top-up.' His intent gaze was fixed on her eyes now but then it flicked downwards for a moment.

Pushing past him, Faith made to the loos and the hand dryer. She still hadn't had any coffee... that was in a mug.

# 24

Tom cringed as Faith brushed past him. By the set look on her face, he knew she regarded him as a lech. He wasn't. But he'd never seen an almost half-naked woman so close before. Faith was beautiful. Her body was... perfect. Her breasts—or what he'd seen of them—were amazing.

When they'd first met in the doorway of the kitchenette, Tom had been full of hope and now it was gone—Faith couldn't have been more eager to get away. Saddened, he decided to take some mailshots he'd prepared the previous evening to Reception for posting. Other human interaction might help to dispel his deep disappointment about how his first meeting with Faith had gone.

As he approached the desk, he observed a short-haired woman on the phone and a pretty blonde woman next to her.

'Hi, I'm Tom Sheridan from the third floor,' he said to the blonde woman. 'Is there anything for me?'

'Hi.' The woman checked the post and handed him a single letter in a white envelope. 'We're still waiting for today's delivery so there might be more later.'

'Thanks.' He wondered if the envelope contained a response to one of his earlier mailshots to local churches. 'I'm new here.'

The woman's smile was enchanting. 'Me too. I'm Hope.'

The mailshots Tom had been holding slipped from his fingers, scattering about his feet. Something uncanny was happening. On Friday, when he considered his faith was in crisis, he met Faith. Today, when his hopes about Faith were dashed, he met Hope. God was working in a very mysterious way. Fumbling to pick up the envelopes as he puzzled over the recent events, he decided he would visit Clifton Cathedral later that day in the hope that God would guide him in his new life.

He straightened up. 'Hope. That's a lovely name.'

'Thanks.'

He placed the envelopes he wanted posting on the desk and fiddled with the letter she'd just given him. 'Did you know there's a Faith working here?'

Hope glanced at the woman who was intent on her call and said quietly, 'She's my sister.'

Tom was disappointed, preferring a supernatural explanation. 'And is there a Charity lurking here, too?'

'Our brother's called Charlie. He's in Sydney for a gap year.'

After returning to his office to pick up a few things, Tom left Siskin House to call on some funeral directors. He bet that few, if any, had connections with photographers so it was likely to be the biggest untapped market around. Boxten Funeral Directors had caught his notice because of the positive reviews, and the business was the first on his list to merit a visit.

Fresh, appealing flowers in the windows made him wonder how often the displays were changed. Beyond, he glimpsed a smart, simple interior. As he pushed open the door, a bell sounded. He hadn't got as far as closing it behind him when a solemn male voice greeted him.

'Hello, sir. How can I be of assistance today?'

A handsome man in his twenties stood before him, kitted out in black apart from a white shirt.

'I'm a photographer, and I'm here to offer my

services.' Tom tapped the thick photo album he'd brought.

The man appeared doubtful. 'We don't do photography as part of our package.'

'If I might be permitted to show you...' Tom tapped his photo album again.

'The manager's not here right now, but you could talk to me. I'm Gavin.'

Tom held out his hand. 'Tom Sheridan. Sacramental photographer.'

Gavin led him to one of the sofas in the main area and motioned to him to sit down.

'I specialise in taking photos during the sacraments of Baptism, Confirmation, Matrimony and Holy Orders. My work from these areas brought in clients who asked me to take photographs during the Funeral Liturgy, Rite of Committal and at the reception after.'

Gavin shook his head. 'I don't think...'

'Please, let me show you.'

Tom opened his album. There were photographs of all the wreaths with messages on, gathering guests, the church, the casket by the altar and at the graveside, the reception, the food, guests laughing, children playing outside. It was a varied mix, and Tom considered it represented his funeral work well. He had to struggle to keep his voice steady. He'd devoted years of his life to the parish, to the congregation. He'd known all the families involved in the funerals he'd shot.

'You see,' Tom explained, 'funerals are not just about loss. They are about celebrating the loved one's life, remembering good times, gathering to share the suffering.' Apart from, Tom thought, when it came down to the reading of the Will. 'These photos remind mourners of the interconnectedness of people and how together, they are strong.'

'I have to say, I was very sceptical. But there might actually be a market for it. These are excellent pictures. I'll mention it to my manager when she comes in, and, if she's interested, she'll give you a call.'

'Thank you. That's very kind of you.'

'Do you have a card?'

Tom fished into his jacket pocket and produced one of a pile he'd had made up.

'"Tom Sheridan, Sacramental Photographer",' Gavin read as he took the card. 'Is that why you're wearing black today? To blend in with the mourners?'

Tom fidgeted. 'It's just how I happened to dress today. Coincidence.'

'I see.' Gavin pursed his lips. 'You know, we don't just have Christian burials.'

'I'm open to any kind of funeral. I'm very familiar with the Jewish traditions.'

'By the way, I didn't recognise the church from the photos—or the cemetery. I've been to most in a fairly large radius.'

'I've only just moved back into the area. I've been working by the east coast.'

'That explains it. Do you have a website?'

'Soon.'

'What about for your previous business? Is there a site for that?'

'I didn't need one. I had plenty of commissions through word-of-mouth. And it wasn't the only thing I did.' Tom wanted Gavin to think he'd been far too busy and successful to need a website.

Gavin inclined his head, inviting Tom to elaborate.

'Couples counselling. Assisting couples through their difficulties.'

'Do... you still... do that?'

'No.'

Gavin wore a thoughtful expression. 'If you were to do that kind of thing, how much would you charge?'

'I can't say... I just don't do it anymore.' Tom had never charged for counselling so had no idea of rates, and that part of his life was over now.

Gavin tapped the card against his thumb as though he wanted to say something but was too nervous to come out with it.

'What is it?' Tom asked gently.

'How about a deal?' Gavin said. 'I praise your photography to my boss so that she takes you on as part of the package we can offer clients, and you support my partner and me with our personal problems?'

'I'm sorry, I...' Tom's gut instincts were to leave well alone.

'We could help each other...'

'I've given up that line of work.'

'But you still have the expertise, the experience.' Gavin's eyes were wide in a silent plea. 'Look, the situation with us has reached a crisis.' He placed a hand on Tom's arm. 'I need your help to save our relationship.'

Tom decided his calling meant that he could not ignore a cry for help—and he needed to drum up business. 'It's a deal.'

# 25

When Tom had cleared his plate of roasted rosemary lamb chops served with garlic potatoes and green beans, he reflected how kind it was of Saul, and his wife, Perdita, to invite him to dinner and to meet Violet, Saul's aunt.

Pregnancy certainly agreed with Perdita. She had fresh skin and happy eyes. What, Tom wondered as he let his unfettered imagination run wild, would Faith look like pregnant? He'd barely glimpsed her since their coffee collision ten days ago and, when he had, she'd scurried back to her office, acknowledging his presence with only the quick flash of a smile that hadn't reached her blue eyes. Since meeting Faith in the cupboard, he knew she was the one for him and no one else. He'd been praying for a way to bring them together.

Petal, who was a delight, had been whisked off to bed soon after his arrival. What would the child look like if he and Faith...?

'Tom, Perdita asked you a question.' Saul was regarding him with faint annoyance.

God, how rude of him. 'I'm so sorry. I got caught up in the family atmosphere, wishing I could have a family of my own one day.'

Perdita gave an understanding smile. 'I asked if you'd met up with old friends—or made new ones.'

Tom eyed Saul. Had he told Perdita about the cupboard? 'I haven't yet caught up with any old friends—apart from Saul, of course.'

Perdita's smile was bland. 'And have you made any

new friends?'

Tom laughed uneasily. 'I haven't been back long.'

'Well, we're having a party in the summer,' she said, 'and we'd like to invite you. You'll be able to meet more people then.'

'That would be great. Thanks.'

'It's our last chance to have a bash before I get too big to want to be bothered. I hope you didn't mind having lamb.' She waved her hand over the virtually empty serving dishes.

'No, not at all. I like lamb.' Why wouldn't he? He hadn't said he was vegetarian.

'My wife,' Saul stated proudly, 'craves lamb when she's pollinated.' Tom's incomprehension must have shown because Saul explained further. 'When Perdita was pregnant the first time, she was in denial and, as a coping mechanism, used botanical terms for anything to do with her own pregnancy.'

'Apparently, I'm to blame,' Violet said. 'I was the one who told her that it was the brightly-coloured flowers that attracted the bees, and that gave her the idea to use plant references when she succeeded in attracting a bee.'

*Pollinated? Bee? What in heaven's name…?* Tom decided to ignore the revelation regarding Perdita's favoured terminology in case he said something that caused offence.

'Why did you think I might not like lamb?'

'I…' Perdita floundered. She exchanged a glance with Saul, but Saul looked blank and appeared to want to know the answer to that question himself. Violet, too, wore an enquiring expression. Then Perdita beamed apologetically. 'I had some idea you were fond of live sheep, but I can't remember where that came from, so just forget I mentioned it.'

*Sheep? Live sheep?* Since coming back to Clifton, there was only one person who'd mentioned sheep and that had been Faith, when they'd been in the cupboard and he'd talked about his flock... Was Faith linked to Perdita? They were about the same age. Saul worked at Siskin House and so did Faith. Was there a connection there? Suspicion solidified.

'Do you... er... know a Faith Goddard by any chance?' Saliva had collected at the back of his throat, making him sound as though he was talking through water.

Perdita's heightened colour told it all. So, she must know all about him being in the cupboard with Faith. But how could he blame Faith for telling when he'd done the same with Saul?

'We're friends,' she said. 'Very close friends.'

He thought he might be sick.

Violet must have sensed his discomfort because she asked cheerily, 'How about some pudding?' She clearly hadn't sensed his nausea.

Saul and Violet stood to clear the table. As Perdita rose too, Tom touched her wrist. 'Can I talk to you? In confidence?'

She fixed him with a steady gaze and sat down again.

'You've chatted to Faith?'

Perdita nodded.

'How did you know she was in the... er... with... me?'

'Faith came to see me while Saul was seeing you. It wasn't hard to make the connection. Saul knows Faith is the only woman who works on the third floor. We know but we honestly haven't shared our conversations.'

'Oh.' His stomach began to unclench, and his nausea receded.

'Can I tell Faith I met you?'

Horrified, Tom said, '*No.* Please don't say anything about me.'

'Why not?'

'It might mess things up. She's met me—as you see me now—but she doesn't like me.'

'Why on earth not?'

'She doesn't like what I wear, and she caught me staring at her breasts.'

'Through her top, you mean?'

'... No... she'd taken her shirt off.'

A disapproving glint appeared in Perdita's eyes.

He raised a hand to say, whoa, it's not what you think. 'Faith was in the kitchenette. I went to get more coffee and there she was, at the sink, scrubbing out the stain.'

'Stain?'

'From the coffee I spilt over her earlier—which was why I needed a top-up so soon. I couldn't help staring. I tried very hard, but I couldn't stop myself. So, you see, she doesn't like me.'

'But she likes the man in the cupboard?'

Tom nodded. 'Yes... and I'm sure she thinks I'm a lech.'

'That's too bad. After Andy and all that.'

'The man who cheated—?'

'Yes.' Perdita appeared to be mentally wrestling with something. 'You know I promised to keep your secret?'

'Ye...es.' Was Perdita about to renege on not telling Faith about him being the man she'd met in the cupboard? Or had Saul told Perdita about his being a priest after all and she was referring to that?

'Well, I'll keep it secret for now...'

*For now?*

'...unless you and Faith need some assistance.'

Tom bridled. The secret Perdita just mentioned had to be about his previous career. Tom must have told her about his being a priest. 'You said you hadn't shared the conversations. Saul promised not to tell you.'

'Not to tell me what?' Perdita was looking at him now with those big, brown eyes of hers, inquisitive and encouraging.

'About my past.'

Perdita bit her lip. 'What in particular about your past?'

It was possible she didn't know. That Saul hadn't told her. Tom needed to be careful. 'What secret are you talking about?'

Perdita's lips widened into a playful grin. 'What secret are *you* talking about?'

Saul and Violet came back into the dining room, and Tom was in a state of agitation: had Saul told? And what did Perdita mean by safe for now, and what kind of "help" did she have in mind?

'You two look cosy,' Saul said.

'We were talking about secrets,' Perdita said.

'Oh?'

'Have you told any secrets lately, Saul?' Tom asked, challenging Saul to tell the truth.

He seemed to cotton on at once. With every indication of veracity, he said, 'No, I haven't.'

Tension in Tom's arms began to ebb away.

He saw Perdita's lips compress, presumably because she wasn't in on the "secret" when she thought she had been. Well, there were two secrets. As far as Perdita was concerned, secret number one was out—he had been in the cupboard with Faith. But secret number two about him being a Catholic priest looked safe for now in Saul's hands.

'Who's for apple crumble?' Violet was holding a serving spoon over a steaming casserole dish that was crusted brown around the edges. The aroma of warm fruit and baked topping filled the room.

'I'd love some.' Tom rubbed his hands together in a hearty fashion, hoping to break the awkward atmosphere. The appearance and comforting smell of the pudding had dispelled the last of his nausea.

Violet began to dish up. 'Do you like custard with your crumble?'

'Yes, please.'

After they'd all been served, Tom addressed Perdita. 'Earlier, you mentioned getting brightly-coloured clothes. To attract the bees.'

'Yes?' Perdita stopped eating to eye him quizzically.

'Well, I think I need help there. I need to attract a bee.'

'Women need to attract bees, not men,' Perdita explained. 'Men can't be pollinated.'

'Then I'd like to be the one who does the pollinating...' Tom trailed off as Perdita's gaze burned into him as though she was trying to set him alight. 'I mean I need brighter clothes. I don't want to put women off. I was told that I look like a magician.' Why had he chosen black shirts to replace his clerical ones?

'Who said you look like a magician?'

'Woman at work.' Dinner was becoming more excruciating by the moment when Perdita's mouth opened and then closed, indicating she'd guessed who Tom was referring to. 'I only have black clothes, you see.'

'That's depressing,' Perdita said. 'Don't you get bored of wearing the same colour all the time?'

Tom flashed Saul a warning look. 'Yes. I do. It's time I was more adventurous. The thing is, I looked round some shops earlier today, and I hadn't a clue what to pick. What would make a flower want me to... pollinate her...' Perdita's penetrating stare of disapproval made him trail off. 'After marriage, of course.'

The taut muscles in Perdita's jaw relaxed. 'I'm glad to hear it. Look what happened to me—'

'We had a child before we were married,' Saul said.

'And I'd no man to call my own.'

'I wasn't the bee who pollinated Perdita,' Saul explained. 'The first time.'

'What you've got to do,' Perdita said, 'is go to a store with a personal shopper service. Book an appointment because they might not be able to help you if you turn up on spec. I was an instant bee trap after going to one. It's just that the first time around, I trapped the wrong bee.'

'Thanks,' Tom said. 'This is all very new territory for me. I'm so nervous when I'm around F—women.'

'You sound like Perdita used to be,' Saul said. 'Complete innocent. Brought up in a convent.'

Now that was interesting. 'Really? I've had a rather sheltered life too. Which is why I'm finding the idea of being a bee scary.'

'With some help,' Perdita said, 'I nabbed myself a great husband and a wonderful aunt to boot.'

When they finished their pudding, Saul got up to clear the things away and offered coffee. Tom began to make his excuses to leave but a sharp kick under the table from Perdita brought him to his senses, and he said that would be very welcome.

Violet's gaze caught Perdita's and Perdita said, 'Keep Saul busy in the kitchen for a few minutes so that I can chat to Tom about some help.'

Violet looked uncertain. Tom reached inside his pocket for his rosary, teasing it between his fingers, feeling the small, wooden beads.

'Are you really and truly naïve?' Perdita asked Tom while Violet dithered in the room.

Unsure of the consequences if he did admit to it, the

faint hope that Perdita might be able to help drove him to be reckless. 'Absolutely.'

Perdita straightened her back and squared her shoulders. 'Violet, do keep Saul occupied so I can tell Tom where to get help. It sounds as though he needs it—like I needed it.'

Violet's expression relaxed as she smiled. 'You Catholics do band together, don't you?'

Tom didn't recall introducing himself as Catholic, and Saul had promised he'd not spilt the beans. Tom eyed Violet sharply, and she winked at him. Then she pinched her sleeve and waggled it while nodding at his clothes. He looked across at Perdita to see if she'd witnessed Violet's antics regarding his black priestly clothing. But Perdita was too intent on writing something on a napkin. He supposed there was no paper to hand and they were short of time; Saul could interrupt them at any moment. Would Violet tell she'd guessed he was a priest?

As soon as Violet left with the near-empty jug of custard, Perdita handed him the napkin.

'You need to go to Bristol Central Library, around noon, on a weekday, to the downstairs lending area. Find the person on this piece of paper. No one else. She's middle-aged and dresses like Miss Marple. Explain what you need help with and tell her that I sent you. Be prepared to be humiliated. Don't give up. Insist that you need the same kind of help that...' She flushed a beetroot red and swallowed hard. '... well... the kind of help she gave me. It is through Barbara Roach's efforts that I learned what to do. With Saul. And this is between you and me. No one else. Do you understand? It's a secret. Pretend you're a priest in the confessional and you can't say a word about it to anyone.'

# 26

Faith was bored and lonely. It was seven o'clock and Hope had already gone to bed, exhausted by her job, and it was only Tuesday. It was over two weeks since Faith had met the man in the cupboard, and she'd not seen him since. As she fancied company, she decided to call on Luke and Gavin.

But when Luke's baby-blond hair appeared at the opened door, he was looking tense and did not seem at all pleased to see her. He was still in sports gear so probably hadn't changed after work.

'Oh. Is this a bad time?'

'Who is it?' Gavin came into view wearing jeans and a T-shirt.

'Yes, it's a bad time.' Luke was about to shut the door.

'No, it's not.' Gavin grabbed the edge of the door so that Luke couldn't shut it. 'Ideal person and ideal time.'

'It doesn't look like it. Hey, guys, I think I'll go—'

But as she made to leave, Gavin lunged forward and grabbed her arm. 'No, you won't.' He pulled her across the threshold. 'I expect you're just as shocked as I am and, if you hadn't come over, I'd have come to see you myself. We've got to thrash this out.'

Faith gave a bemused look.

Luke shrugged. 'Come in.'

'If you're sure.'

'Yes, we're sure,' Gavin said. 'Here, sit on the sofa with me. Luke can sit on his own over there. If he's not careful, he'll be staying on his own.'

'If this is a tiff you two are having, I don't think I should be here.'

'It involves you,' Gavin said, 'so of course you must be here. It involves all of us.'

'It does?'

Gavin flung his arm in the air. 'Luke has asked Hope to have a baby with him. He said it was your idea.'

'No, it wasn't!' *How could Luke put this on her?*

'Before Faith knew about the sports massages,' Luke said, 'Faith thought Hope and I were having sex to give me a baby.'

'But that doesn't mean I meant you and Hope to have a baby,' Faith said.

'But it's a good idea,' Luke said.

Faith flapped her hands downwards as she said, 'It's a crap idea.'

'That's what I told Luke, but he doesn't agree.' Gavin's voice broke. 'I said it's me or the baby. Guess which he chose?'

'No!' Faith couldn't believe it. Choose a baby over Gavin, the love of his life?

'Yes.' Gavin's eyes shone with moisture.

'Gay couples have children,' Luke said. 'It's normal these days.'

'But I don't want a child!'

'And I do.'

'Who would the baby live with?' Faith thought this would help to ground Luke. She wanted him to see the impracticalities of such an event, and how it just wouldn't work out.

'We could share her.'

Faith didn't want a screaming baby in the flat unless it was her own. 'Hope's ill. Pregnancy could make her relapse. She can barely look after herself so how would she manage to take care of a baby?'

'That's what I said!' Gavin's eyes were wide with what might have been a mixture of fear and indignation.

'I would help, and I hoped that Gavin would help too. And...' Luke appeared sheepish now, '... you.'

'*Me?*'

'You'd be the baby's aunt.'

'Yes, but that doesn't mean I'd want to be a mum to the baby if Hope's too ill to look after the child. Would you give up your job? Because I'm not prepared to give up mine.' Another vision of a monochrome existence came to mind.

'I want a baby,' Luke said with grit.

'Why not adopt?' Faith said, thinking that would leave her and Hope out of the picture.

'Both of us would have to agree. And I'd like my DNA to be involved. I want a baby that's part of me.' Luke got up. 'I'm getting some air.'

'Hope's in bed resting. Don't go there,' Faith said.

Luke disappeared from view. Moments later, she heard the front door open and slam shut.

Gavin puffed his breath out through his lips while shaking his head. 'I can't believe this is happening, that Luke's being like this.'

'It's a ridiculous idea, and I don't know how Hope could come between you and Luke like this. I'll try to talk her out of it again.'

'You do that...' They sat in silence for some time. Then Gavin said, 'I met someone recently; a photographer who works with funerals and is based where you work, actually—it turns out he's a couples counsellor. His pictures are good, so I expect his counselling skills are too.'

'Tom? *A couples counsellor?*' Tom hadn't struck her that he would be good with relationships of his own, let alone helping other people with theirs.

'Yes. I've asked him to help with Luke and me, and he's agreed.'

'That's... great.' Should she tell Gavin to check Tom's credentials?

'Yeah.' Gavin sounded despondent. 'Otherwise, it's going to be the end of the road for us. I don't want to be a dad.'

'When you met Luke, did the question of children come up?'

Gavin laughed. 'Not at all. It wasn't until Perdita got pregnant that Luke became obsessed with kids. Do you know, he read the same pregnancy magazines as Perdita when he was at work and hid them in his locker so that I wouldn't find out?'

'It just goes to show, you never really know someone, do you? You think you've got them sussed, and it's all a lie.'

'You're talking about Andy now?'

'Yes, and there is no Andy now. I'm lonely.'

'I bet you're missing sex.'

'Well, yes. I have met a man I like, but it's not going anywhere.'

'What you need is a rabbit.'

Faith considered this but couldn't see the link. 'Aren't they an awful lot of work?'

'Batteries take all the work out of it.'

'What can it do?'

Gavin's expression was hard to read. 'What you want it to do.'

'You mean, I can train it?'

'No, it's not programmable. It's a matter of switching it on, selecting the speed and whether you want rotation and it's ready to go.'

'So, it hops around the room? In circles? Is it realistic?' Faith wasn't warming to the notion of having an electronic pet. It sounded gimmicky and how did that help the fact that she was missing sex?

'I think we're on different planets, Faith.'

'We are?'

'It's an adult toy...' Gavin raised his eyebrows meaningfully. 'I'm not talking about a cutesy little rabbit. I'm talking about the kind of rabbit that gets you going. In bed.'

It all clicked into place. 'And you think it would help?'

'It would probably be better than with Andy,' Gavin suggested disdainfully.

'Really? Where do I buy this rabbit?'

# 27

Relieved to get out of the chill March wind that Thursday—it was giving him earache—Tom entered the grand building of Bristol Central Library on College Green, next to Bristol Cathedral. He walked through the vaulted entrance with marble and turquoise mosaic arches. The hush of the place made him feel conspicuous.

To give him the best chance of succeeding, Perdita had told him to get to the library around noon, but she hadn't explained why. Barbara Roach, Perdita had said, was middle-aged. At first, he thought that particular librarian couldn't be working today but then he spotted a likely-looking woman by a trolley that held a stack of books.

'Excuse me,' Tom said on his approach, 'are you Barbara Roach?'

The solid woman, dressed in a skirt and brogues, straightened. Her short, brown hair was flecked with grey. 'Yes?'

He bent towards her. 'This is a rather delicate matter. I was told that you're the only person who can help.'

'Help you how?'

'I don't know exactly.'

'How can I help you then?' Her tone was tinged with irritation.

'She said you would know when I mention her name: Perdita.'

Barbara gave a start. '*Is this a joke?*'

'N... no...'

'I can't assist you in this matter.' Barbara picked up another book from the trolley and examined the spine.

'Please. I'm desperate.'

'Surely you have friends to ask...?'

'I'm a thirty-four-year-old virgin Catholic priest. I've met a woman I like, but I wouldn't have a clue what to do if she liked me back.'

Barbara pulled herself up even straighter. 'How dare you come to me to ask for help? You're a Catholic priest. You took a vow of celibacy.' Although she'd started off talking softly, in her outrage, she'd forgotten to keep quiet.

Tom cast around the immediate area. Yep. Other people had heard, and they were all looking pretty much disgusted with him.

'I've left my parish. I told the Bishop I want a wife. But how am I to get a wife when I don't know what to do?' Corinthians, Chapter 7 came to mind: *...For it is better to marry than to burn with passion.* He couldn't remember what verse it was in. Somewhere close to the beginning. Well, Tom was burning with passion for Faith, the woman who'd taught him to kiss, and he wanted her as his wife.

'Shouldn't you be married before you consider doing anything like that?'

'Of course I should be. But there's plenty to... play around with before you get to the final bit. If I'm no good at that, she wouldn't risk marrying me, would she?' Tom knew he'd already bent the rules by kissing Faith, but he would not cross the final boundary of intimacy before they were wed. The Church had not lost its grip on him entirely.

'Have you formally left the Church?' Barbara asked.

This must be how a ribeye steak felt under the grill.

'There are formalities to be gone through, but I've already left my clerical duties.'

'It doesn't look like it. You're head to toe in black.'

'On my to-do list,' he said defensively.

'You know, I can't help you. Perdita shouldn't have sent you.'

Having got this far, Tom was not prepared to give up. 'Whatever you did for Perdita, it worked. She's very happily married.'

Barbara lowered the book she was holding. 'Really?' She sounded genuinely pleased. 'I did wonder from time to time what had become of her.'

'She's having her second child, you know. Lovely husband. Lovely home. Lovely aunt living with them.'

Barbara looked at him in wonder. 'So, it worked?'

'Seems so,' he said, still none the wiser as to what "it" was. 'And I want the same.'

'Mm.' Barbara had a pensive look.

'Does the library stock—?'

'No,' she said sharply.

Then what was he doing here? 'My future happiness seems to be hanging in the balance.' He looked around and saw that the people had gathered nearer and they were all holding open books—but not one of them was reading them. They were all glancing his way. Was this what Perdita had meant when she'd said he had to be prepared to be humiliated? He certainly felt humiliated. He met the librarian's gaze. 'Please?'

Sighing, she replaced the book on the trolley. 'Wait for me by the exit while I get my bag and coat.'

'Where are we going?' Tom asked when she joined him by the doors to the street.

'It's clear Perdita didn't tell you, and it's best you don't know in advance.'

Barbara marched forth, her green and yellow

headscarf flapping behind her from the strong wind.

Tom's unease increased. 'You're not taking me to a brothel, are you?'

'How dare you suggest I go to brothels?' she shouted against the blustery breeze. 'This is the very last time I am prepared to do this. Do not send any of your priestly friends to me. Do you understand?'

Tom was ready to agree to anything as long as he got the help she had the power to give. 'Yes, of course.'

After a few minutes of brisk walking, Barbara suddenly stopped, and he almost collided with her as she made her way towards a shop front.

Oh no... no, he couldn't. *Mother of God...*

'There's no need to worry. I'll look after you.' She sounded kinder now.

'I... I... don't think I can...'

'That's why you need me with you. It's not the place you would manage to go to alone, is it?'

He shook his head. So, Perdita had come here. With the librarian. He swallowed. Should he have trusted a woman he considered barmy?

'It's okay. I will take care of you.' Barbara's voice was even softer now, but he still hesitated. She grabbed his arm and said in a changed tone, 'Inside. Now.'

They were through the door. Tom blinked at the multi-coloured twinkling lights, took in the soft music, the lingerie, the scary leather—or was it PVC?—clothing and displays of... something he decided not to name. He had to get out.

'No, you don't.' She grabbed his arm again as he made to leave. 'We're seeing this through. I'm not having you turn up another day begging me to bring you.'

Pulled towards the rear of the shop, Tom saw... breasts. *Terrifying breasts.*

'Stop gawping at the DVDs.'

'Wouldn't they... help show...?'

'Do you want a wife or a sex worker?'

'A wife... of course, a wife.'

'Then if you did anything to her like you'll see in porn—unless she's used to being... treated like that during the act—you'll put her off you more surely than inefficient fumbling on your part.'

'Oh.'

'Listen,' she said sharply. 'That is no material for a priest.'

A couple of heads turned their way. A woman dressed in fluff sidled closer swishing a long tail. Then she gathered it into the crook of her arm. 'Can I help you?' the woman with a fox tail asked.

Tom whispered in Barbara's ear. 'Don't tell her I'm a priest.'

'This man needs a beginner's book on how to please a woman. He is not a Catholic priest, but he is a virgin.'

Tom hid his face behind his hands. This woman was...

'Hey, do I recognise you?' the shop assistant with the fox tail asked.

'Probably,' Barbara admitted.

'Aren't you a librarian?'

'Yes.'

'It's brilliant you support your customers like this.'

'I don't. Personal favour.'

'It's still brilliant helping people who are too shy to come in on their own.'

'Can we just get on with it?' Tom ground through clenched teeth, having unpleasant thoughts about Perdita, whose advice had put him in this situation.

'Yes, we don't have much time,' Barbara said. 'What would you recommend for my non-priest friend?'

His mortification was absolute. He couldn't possibly sink lower than this.

'Let's see...' The shop assistant perused the bookshelf.

Each time she picked up a volume to flick through, he saw that the explicit covers gave all the hints one could possibly need to identify what kind of book it was. How would he get his purchase home undetected? Damn. He'd have to ask for a bag, but then he'd be seen with a bag from this shop.

He was feeling ill. He had to leave. 'I'm sorry, I...'

Barbara clutched his arm tighter than before. 'Oh no, you don't. You begged me to bring you here. You're staying.'

'I didn't know we'd be *here.*'

'You can take it up with Perdita.'

The shop assistant said, 'Oh, are you two friends? I remember her. Convent girl, wasn't she?'

'Please, please let us finish this quickly,' Tom begged.

Barbara Roach checked her watch. 'He's right. Time's ticking on, and I still have my lunch to eat.'

# 28

At the start of her lunch hour, Faith had listened out for Tom as she'd not wanted to get into conversation with him if she'd run into him in the corridor. But she'd heard sounds of him locking up and then his rapid footsteps on the stairs. She'd given him a short head start before catching a bus into Bristol town centre as trying to park a hearse in the multi-storey wasn't a hot idea.

Gavin had told her exactly where to go and now that she was standing outside the unprepossessing storefront, she was feeling confused. There was a pet shop next door that looked far more appealing. When she leaned up to the window, shielding her hand from the light, she saw, deep inside... cutesy little bunnies.

But then she remembered why she'd come and pulled herself away from the glass. Once inside the shop Gavin had directed her to, she noticed the lights. Very pretty. Yes, she could cope with this. But where did they keep the rabbits? When she spotted a bunny girl, Faith went up to her and said, very softly, 'Excuse me, I'm looking for a rabbit.'

The young woman smiled. 'I'll show you.'

Faith watched the movement of the little bunny tail as she followed behind the woman and asked, 'Is there any particular one you'd recommend?'

Bunnytail plucked something from a display where items were hanging from racks. 'This is our most popular.' She passed it to Faith and she found herself grasping it before she'd had time to consider.

It was a huge, purple, missile-shaped contraption.

Faith pretended she was taking in the wording on the gaudy packaging.

'Would you like me to show you how it works? We have a demonstration model.'

'No, it's okay. I'll play around with it when I'm home.'

'Enjoy.' Bunnytail winked.

That hadn't been what Faith had meant. She was torn between running away and hot-footing it to the cash desk. 'Do the batteries come with it or—?'

'You can ask for them at the counter.'

Faith smiled her thanks and headed towards the cash desk. She didn't want to admit failure to Gavin.

*Damn.*

*Double damn.*

Tom Sheridan, photographer, had frozen mid-stride. His wide brown eyes and gaping mouth could have been those of a burglar caught in the act. A middle-aged woman stood next to him.

Faith quickly hid her package behind her back.

'Hi,' he said, clutching something to him as though scared that whatever was there might just leap out and show itself to her. By the dark corners, she thought it could be a book. Or a DVD.

It was rather an odd place to bring his mother. There was no way Faith was going to join the queue ahead of him so that he would see what she'd selected. Nor was she going to be one place behind since the girl serving would have her purchase in full view on the counter before he was out of the shop—and she'd have to ask for batteries.

'Just browsing.'

'Me too.' He aimed a look of appeal at his mother.

His mother raised her eyebrows as though to ask him a question, and he nodded. What did that signify? Was it to do with her?

Then she realised. Tom must have told his mother about seeing her breasts. His mother must have asked him just now whether Faith was the girl he'd talked about, and he'd nodded to say yes. *Hardly a gentleman.*

Feigning confidence, Faith held the package behind her back in her left hand and extended her right arm to Tom's mother. 'Hello, I'm Faith. I work on the same level as Tom.' How was she going to get the purple missile back on the shelf without either of them seeing what she'd chosen?

Tom appeared desperate to be liberated from the tangle too by the way he was aiming pleading eyes at his mother, who'd blatantly ignored Faith's proffered hand. She lowered her arm. Perhaps Tom got his gauche manner from his mother—she didn't appear to have acquired social niceties and so probably had failed to help her son navigate the social arena smoothly.

Without warning, his mother stepped between them, snatched the item Tom was holding and then went to queue.

Great. Tom's mother had relieved him of his embarrassment but what about her? Who would rescue her?

'Rather awkward, isn't it?' Tom said.

'Mm.'

'Would you like me to look away while you go to pay for... whatever it is?'

What chivalry. If he'd just clear off, the problem would be solved.

Bunnytail had gone but there was another woman dressed in fur with a long fox-tail approaching.

'Can I help you?' Foxtail asked. 'Is there something else you were after?'

'No,' Tom said. If he'd been much louder, he would

have been shouting.

Foxtail regarded them benevolently. 'Are you two friends?' she asked while looking Faith over.

'Please...' Tom began.

'Yes?' Foxtail asked.

'... just go,' he finished hoarsely.

'We work in the same building,' Faith explained. 'But I barely know him.' She didn't want to either. 'It's the first time I've met his mum.' She thought it worthwhile to use the opportunity to have a dig at Tom having to come with Mummy. To show him not to have any ideas about her as Faith wasn't the least bit interested in him as a man.

'Oh, that's not—'

Tom raised his hands. 'Don't say another word. Please, you're making it worse.'

Intrigued, Faith said, 'Let the lady finish. It is polite.'

Foxtail laughed. 'No worries. Client confidentiality. I won't say another word. Just one last thing before I go...'

'... Yes?' Tom asked.

'Could you say a prayer for my nan? She's been very poorly of late—'

'Yes. No problem. Now, if you'll excuse us...'

'Have a good day.' She smiled and gave a little wave to Tom as she walked towards the rear of the shop.

'Looks like you made a hit there. What's with the prayer?' Faith asked.

'No idea.' Tom adopted a befuddled expression.

Then his mum came back and handed him a bright yellow carrier bag. 'Right. I'm off,' she announced.

'Thanks,' Tom said.

'Say hi to Perdita,' his mother said and headed towards the door.

Faith's ears pricked up. '*Perdita?* You know Perdita?'

'Um... yes,' Tom said.

'How come?' Faith asked sharply.

'I went to school with her husband. Why, do you know her too?' The tone in which he asked the question suggested he already knew that Perdita and she were friends. That meant they'd discussed her.

Faith gasped. Had Perdita told him about the man in the cupboard? 'I've got to go.' But she was still holding the purple missile. She couldn't risk being arrested for shoplifting. What would the *Bristol Post* make of that? She waited for Tom to follow his mother out of the shop before she made her purchases.

# 29

There wasn't time for Faith to stash the purple missile in the hearse before going back to the office. As it was, Edison frowned at her for being five minutes late when she arrived at her desk, and it was clear that his annoyance at her punctuality failures was increasing. When he left to make afternoon calls, she sat with her head in her hands recalling the excruciating humiliation of having Tom find her in that shop.

It was unusually quiet. The phone hadn't rung since Edison had left. Emails could wait. Her fingers crept to the bright-yellow carrier bag she'd hidden wrapped in her jacket. She retrieved a pair of scissors from the top drawer of her desk and snipped at the brittle casing. There, it was out. It had a certain amount of give. She wiggled the ears. Mm, promising. Now, where were the batteries? She might as well have a go since she'd missed out on the demonstration model.

It was when she'd inserted the batteries and switched the thing on that there was a knock at the door and then it opened. She chucked the purple missile in the bottom drawer and slammed it shut as Tom approached.

'Hi. Um, sorry to bother you, but I wondered if I might ask a favour?'

She smiled with forced brightness in the hope that it would encourage him to say what he wanted and leave.

He cocked his head to one side. 'What's the noise?'

'My phone... Set to vibrate.'

Tom put his hands in his trouser pockets. 'Aren't you

going to answer it? I don't mind waiting.'

Faith shook her head. 'No. If it's important they'll call back.'

'Well, they're hanging on a long time.' He stepped closer.

She wouldn't be able to open the drawer without risking Tom seeing its contents. 'What is it you want?'

'I'm looking for someone to help me at a wedding in a couple of weeks. On a Saturday. Someone to look after my camera gear and help switch lenses.'

Surely, he wasn't expecting her to do it? 'I can't think of anyone. Sorry.'

He reddened and rubbed his chin with his hand. 'I wondered if you might come with me?'

Was this some crass chat-up line? She almost laughed. 'How much would I get?'

His feet shifted. 'There's supposed to be a splendid buffet.'

She raised her eyebrows. 'I'm to work for my supper?'

'Sorry, I'm finding your phone extremely distracting... Would you mind?'

She wondered if the reverberating vibrations could be heard from Saul's offices below. The drawer seemed to be amplifying the sound instead of muffling it. 'You're right, I should answer it. Could I pop into your office afterwards?'

He backed away as though aware he was intruding. In fact, he looked as though he regretted coming in. 'See you in a little while then.'

Faith smiled politely. When the door was safely shut, she removed the batteries from the overactive device. Honestly, Gavin must be mad suggesting she bought a rabbit. With the racket it made, the entire building would know what she was up to. Products like this ought to have decibel values. One purple missile sorted. Now one photographer to be sorted.

Two hours later, Faith packed up to go home. As an afterthought, instead of heading straight for the lift, she made for the cleaning cupboard. She'd not met the man in the cupboard since that first time, despite her trying the door most days. She grabbed the handle. The door opened, and her heart missed a beat and then quickened.

With the door open a crack, Faith's fingers wandered towards the light switch.

'Please, can we keep it dark in here?' the man in the cupboard whispered, apparently guessing what she had in mind. 'I... I'm quite shy, and I feel safer in the dark. It helps with my... anxiety about leaving my old place.'

Faith's hand dropped, her heart somersaulting when she realised that he was suffering from his change in lifestyle. She wished she could help by doing more than just letting the cupboard stay dark. Perhaps getting to know him, becoming his friend, would make the adjustment easier. She checked the corridor for the photographer before sneaking inside and shutting the door.

'Here. Have my pew,' the man whispered when she reached him. He guided her towards the upturned bucket.

'I didn't expect you to be here at this time of day.'

'I don't keep regular hours.'

'You'll never guess what kind of day I had,' she said, and then wished she hadn't. If she took out her visit to the rabbit shop, there wasn't much to tell. She didn't wish to share a rabbit story with this man.

'What happened?' he asked in a barely audible tone.

She decided to have a good grumble about Tom. 'Well, there's this new photographer working here. He's asked me to work, on a Saturday. For nothing. What kind of a mug does he think I am?'

'That's... um...'

'I bet he makes a mint from weddings—and the spin-offs from all the prints people order. He expects me to be his slave for the day for nothing other than a few bits of food provided at the reception.'

'Are you sure he's being paid for this wedding job?'

Faith laughed. 'Why on earth wouldn't he be? He would be a right numpty if he did it for nothing.'

'It may be that this particular job—'

'He didn't say he was doing it for nothing, and he expects me to give up my Saturday.'

The man was silent for so long that she wondered if he'd been listening. Just as she was about to ask him if he was mentally still in the cupboard with her, he asked, 'Do you think he might like you but be too shy to ask you out for a drink so he asked you to help him in his work instead?'

*What the...?* 'If that's the way he shows he likes a woman, it makes him even odder. Do you know, his eyes were glued to my breasts when he caught me with my shirt off?'

'Um... that's... terrible.'

'Isn't it?'

'Do you think he perhaps might not be used to seeing women's breasts and so stared because it was such a new experience?'

This idea didn't wash with her. 'No. He's probably used to taking photos of nude women.'

'Not all photography is the same. Did he say he did nudes?'

'No. But I bet he'd like to, judging by the way his eyes kept homing in on my chest.'

'I like to keep an open mind—until I know all the

facts.'

Faith almost blurted out about seeing Tom with his mum in that shop. But then she'd have to explain what she'd been doing there and she didn't want this virgin of a man to know. A man like him would never have been in such a place.

Faith was the first to leave the cupboard again. It was only when she was on her way to the hearse that she realised she'd forgotten to ask him his name. It was also strange that he hadn't asked how come the photographer had managed to see her with her shirt off.

Leaving by the main entrance, Faith passed the bus stop—and a litter bin, where she disposed of the bright yellow carrier bag and her recent purchases. When Faith reached the hearse, she opened the tailgate. 'Time to go home, Hope.'

The lid of the casket opened, and Hope stretched her arms in the air and yawned. 'This is such a great arrangement, isn't it?' Her smile was wreathed in slumber.

'It is.' Faith helped Hope climb out of the back of the car.

# 30

Judith was standing at the window, behind the nets, with her binoculars aimed squarely at the two young women by the hearse.

'What's going on out there?' she shouted when she heard Miranda come back into the house. Judith had sent her to get some stamps for the correspondence she'd started to tackle.

Miranda came in and put the stamps on the desk. 'I don't know.'

'I mean to find out. Those two girls keep coming and going through Siskin House side door. That means they both work there.'

'Probably.'

'Not probably. There's no other explanation. Has Malakai mentioned these girls to you?'

'No.' Miranda's sad tone told Judith that she must be harbouring hopes regarding Malakai.

Well, she wouldn't have a chance with girls looking like that. But did they have the personalities to match their pretty faces? She didn't want Malakai drawn in by females who were not worthy of him. Of her bloodline. Of her fortune.

'Why didn't that black-haired girl come out of the side door like she usually does?'

'I don't know. I saw her come out of the main entrance as I was driving in.'

'Why would she do that?' Judith didn't like mysteries. 'Surely it's much closer to that bloody hearse to come out of the side door?' She turned to Miranda.

'Well? Do you know why she changed her routine?'

'I saw her put something in the litter bin at the bus stop.'

'What was it?'

Miranda shrugged.

'Get it. Unless it's foul rubbish. Anything else, I want it.' Judith was determined to get into the heads of these girls to assess their suitability as a daughter-in-law.

She watched as Miranda walked down the path and headed in the direction of the bus stop. Returning the binoculars to her eyes, she saw the hearse drive away. A bit later, it passed Judith's house again, having turned around at the end of the cul-de-sac.

As Faith headed right, out of the cul-de-sac, she passed a stocky woman in a puffy, pink anorak by the bus stop. Faith stared disbelievingly into her rear-view mirror as the woman retrieved Faith's bright yellow carrier bag. She slammed on the brakes.

'What is it? Did you hit a cat?' Frantically, Hope scanned the road.

*What to do?* Nothing, Faith's internal voice advised. That woman couldn't know who'd put the purple missile in the bin and hadn't even turned around at the squeal of the brakes. Anyway, what could Faith do about it? Snatch it from the woman? Then Faith would have to explain her behaviour to Hope and the whole tale would come out.

Faith put the car into first gear and depressed the accelerator. The woman could only be fishing in there by chance.

'I can't see a cat.' Hope was looking behind them. 'It must have got away.'

'I was mistaken. I thought I'd seen something, but I hadn't,' Faith said.

When the vehicle accelerated away, Miranda knew she was safe. She realised she should have waited until the hearse was clear of the area, and she'd nearly been caught.

It was hard to make out what was in the bag. There was something purple underneath the plastic casing, and she stuck her hand in to take it out. Hastily, she shoved the gadget back. Well, Judith might not be so keen on the black-haired woman being the future Mrs Malakai now. That left the blonde woman as Miranda's only opponent. With luck, there would be something unsuitable about her too.

As soon as she closed the front door behind her, Judith shouted, 'Well? What is it? I saw you carrying something.'

Miranda walked up to Judith and silently held out the bright yellow bag, then pulled it back again. 'I think it might be better if you sit down first.'

'Why?'

'You'll understand.' Miranda wanted to enjoy this moment. Trying to predict the look on Judith's face when she took that purple thing in her hand was proving difficult. For once, words might fail her. Miranda suppressed a giggle.

Judith's sharp eyes focused on her as she lowered herself into the chair. 'What is it?'

Miranda just handed her the bag.

It was a picture she would never forget; Judith holding aloft a purple male member-shaped object in utter bewilderment. But then she fished in the bag and found two batteries. After inserting them, she pressed a button. The noise the thing made was terrific. Then she pressed another button, and Miranda's eyes stretched open as wide as they'd ever been. The male purple member started to rotate.

Judith rummaged again and found the till receipt. 'Bought today. It's brand new.'

'She must have changed her mind.' When the front door banged shut and Malakai's footsteps approached, Miranda screamed.

Judith threw the purple member into the drawer of her desk and rolled the bag up on her lap.

Malakai rushed into the room. 'Is something wrong?'

'No. It's all fine,' Judith said.

'I thought I heard a scream.'

'Miranda. She thought she'd seen a spider, didn't you, Miranda?'

'Yes. But it was just a bit of fluff.' She bent down to pick up an imaginary piece of fluff and pretended to throw it into the waste paper basket next to Judith and out of Malakai's line of vision.

'What's that noise?'

'Noise? Oh, that. Probably my mobile,' Judith said.

'Set to vibrate,' Miranda added to back up Judith's story. The last thing she wanted was for Malakai to know that she'd personally fished that thing out of the bin in the street.

Malakai scrunched his eyes as though recalling something. 'It sounds just like someone else's phone.'

'Does it?' Judith asked.

'Yes. A woman I work with. Well, not with. Just on the same level.'

Miranda and Judith exchanged glances. Miranda felt that Judith had come to the same conclusion; Malakai had caught the woman trying out her purchase, just as he had with Judith now, and the woman had chucked it into her desk drawer as Judith had done. And then, Miranda guessed, the woman had lost her nerve and had decided to deprive herself of the pleasures it might offer.

It made sense now.

'Aren't you going to answer it?' Malakai asked.

Judith pursed her lips. 'It's not convenient now.'

'Well, I'll be on my way then.'

As soon as he was out of the room, Judith gathered the trove and handed the lot to Miranda. 'I don't care what you do with it. Just get it out of here.'

Frantically, Miranda twiddled with the buttons. The male member started whirring, twirling and vibrating worse than before, and she was worried that Malakai would return.

'On second thoughts,' Judith said, 'you'd better hang on to it. It will be the closest you get to getting it.'

# 31

After work on Friday, Faith and Hope swapped the hearse for Faith's Honda Jazz so that they could park easily at Sainsbury's. Perdita had persuaded Faith to switch her grocery shopping plans from Saturday to Friday. This was to take advantage of a new range of clothing, as well as a good bargain rail at a department store in Bristol. Although Faith didn't need anything new, Hope had begged to go.

'Ugh,' Hope said when they were inside Sainsbury's and she saw the number of other shoppers. 'I'll get the electric scooter.' There was only one left from the usual line-up.

'You sit on it while I get the key.' Faith didn't want her sister to pass out on her. When Faith returned, she unplugged the scooter from the mains and dealt with the trailing cable. 'It should be ready to go now.' She hoped it didn't conk out partway through shopping as it was the end of the day. Sometimes the battery was too low to last, and Hope would get stranded at the far end of the store. The scooter might have only been plugged in for two minutes before they'd arrived, having a depleted battery already.

Hope grimaced. 'I don't like having to be in one of these when you're walking.'

'I know. One day you won't need one. You'll have enough energy.'

'Well, I suppose I'll have to settle for just being employed for the time being. Fruit and veg, here we come.' Hope squeezed the trigger and the cart began to move.

They'd only got as far as putting the week's vegetables in the front basket and were approaching the fruit aisle when Hope clutched her stomach. 'Sorry, Faith. I'm going to have to dash to the loos. It's been building up a while, and now it's urgent.'

'Okay.' She didn't think Hope would be able to dash anywhere. The place was teeming with people.

'I'll leave this with you.' Hope got off the scooter platform. 'It's quicker to walk. See you back around here.'

Faith thought she may as well have a rest while she waited for Hope to return. When she noticed a tall rolling cage packed with banana trays being pushed into the centre of the fruit aisle, she edged closer. Parking next to the tower, she selected a bunch of Fairtrade bananas.

Then she noticed the apples further down the aisle. As she pulled the trigger to move forwards, she realised that the banana cage was following her. She released the trigger and the scooter came to a halt. So did the bananas.

'Faith!'

Spinning around, she saw the photographer. *Damn.* 'Tom. Hi.'

He drew his trolley up beside her. 'I didn't know you had a disability.'

'Oh, this isn't for me.' When Faith saw his eyebrows lift, she added, 'No. Really. It's not for me. I'm just looking after it for someone.'

Tom inclined his head as though he disbelieved her.

Since Hope was bound to return soon, there was no point in trying to keep her secret from him any longer. 'It's for my sister. She'll be back in a moment.'

'I couldn't help noticing that you've got caught up in this tower thing.'

So, he'd observed her moving off, hitched to the bananas. But, as she wasn't the least bit interested in him, what did she care? She stood up. 'Perhaps I can shift it off.'

'I wouldn't dream of letting you. Allow me.'

'I can manage.'

'Please. Let me help.' His voice was so deep, so... manly... that she let him.

He parked his trolley to one side and made for the end of the banana tower. With his overcoat open, Faith glimpsed his broad chest encased in a black jumper. It fitted him well. Photographer he might be, but she bet he'd done some work to develop a chest like that.

He shifted the cage, arms spanning the outer sides. 'I think that's done it.'

She tested the scooter by slightly edging away. It was free. 'Thanks.'

'No problem.'

'Well... I... er... best get on.' *Where was Hope?*

'Have a good weekend.' He shot her a heart-melting smile before turning his attention to the vegetables.

'You too,' she called as the scooter crawled away.

He caught up with her. 'If you have trouble reaching for something, let me know.' He overtook her and went out of sight.

It was patently clear that Tom hadn't believed a single word she'd said. Well, he would know she'd been telling the truth when Hope swapped places with her. With a bag of Cox apples in the basket, Faith steered towards the bakery section. Tom was already there.

When he saw her, he said, 'Why don't we go around together? I could help you.'

Just then, Hope sidled up from nowhere. 'Hi, Tom.' She spoke in a sugary tone that Faith hadn't heard before.

Initially, she was at a loss as to how Hope knew Tom but then realised that, of course, they would have met through her job as a receptionist.

Tom's smile lit up his face, his attraction hitting Faith in the stomach. But it was a shame about his clothes. Less of the black and he'd—actually, he looked pretty good in black too.

'So, how are you settling into Siskin House?' Hope gushed.

'Fine. Great.' Tom's gaze shifted to Faith as though expecting her to join in the conversation.

'That's brilliant. I'm so glad it's working out for you.' Hope was all but simpering over him.

Did Hope really like Tom? Perhaps she was behaving like a desperate woman because he was the first available male she'd come across having been cooped up at home for the past few years. Well, she was welcome to him.

Faith stood up to allow Hope to take her place. 'There you go.'

Her sister's eyes blazed with an angry passion before she turned to smile at Tom again. Was that because she didn't want anyone from work to know she had a health problem or was it because she didn't want Tom specifically to know she'd got difficulties?

Light dawned. That was why Hope had been gone so long. She hadn't wanted Tom to see that the mobility scooter was for her. She'd held off for as long as she'd thought practicable. Then she'd sallied forward in the hope that Tom would notice her, single her out. And... take the attention away from Faith.

When they were back in the car, Hope breathed ecstatically. 'Isn't Tom gorgeous?'

'He's okay.'

'Okay? *Okay?* That's all you've got to say about him? I take it that means the field is open for me?'

Hope deserved some happiness if it worked out with Tom. 'Have him.' Faith liked the man in the cupboard.

'Seriously? You're not interested in him?'

'I don't warm to men who gawp at women's breasts and ask them to be their slave.'

'You mean seeing your bra when you were trying to get that stain out of your shirt and asking you to help at the wedding without paying you?'

'Exactly. Now, why wouldn't you get in the scooter after you'd been to the loo?'

'Oh. I had a surge of energy.'

'It looked like I was the one who had a problem.'

'Now you know what it feels like. Having everyone look at you differently, treat you differently, like you're a lower species.'

'Tom didn't. He was kind to me.' It surprised Faith that he hadn't been at all put off. It seemed to have given him the confidence to step up. He'd not been at all nervous.

'Really? That's so sweet. I told you he was nice.'

By the time they were home and the shopping unpacked, Hope said she was shattered and nauseous.

Faith regarded her sister sternly. 'You should have used that scooter.'

'I just need a rest.'

'I'll get you a hot drink. Tea?'

'Mm.'

When Faith was back with two steaming mugs, she put one of them on the coffee table by the sofa where a white-faced Hope was spread-eagled with her eyes closed and then went to sit in the armchair. Faith thought it was high time to pin Hope down about the baby business.

'Have you come to any decision about having Luke's baby?' Faith asked in a tone that indicated there would be trouble if she did not get the desired answer.

Hope shrugged.

'It's mad; it would risk your health and do you know, Gavin has told Luke that if he goes ahead with the plan, he's leaving? It's him or the baby.'

'And?' Hope's voice was cool and detached and her eyes remained closed. She'd clearly overdone it.

'It looks like Luke's opting for the baby. They're meant to be getting some kind of couples counselling though. From Tom.'

'*Tom?*' Hope's eyes opened and a searching gaze was directed Faith's way.

'Yes, Tom. He's supposed to be experienced in couples counselling as well as photography. He visited Gavin's premises to offer to take pictures at funerals—and they got talking.'

'Oh…' Hope shut her eyes again. 'Do you think Gavin would really leave Luke if there was a baby on the way?' Her vowels were flattened and the words slurred with exhaustion.

'Definitely.'

'Not even Luke's child?'

'Not even Luke's. So, if you were to have a baby, it would be with a single, gay man—who might be on the pull for a new man. You might end up being left with a baby you're too ill to look after, and you wouldn't have the strength to work as well, even if you could afford childcare in the daytime.'

'Mm. I can see you're right. But there's one angle you've not thought of.'

'Oh?' Faith tensed. Which way would this unforeseen element swing the dial? Neither she nor Gavin wanted Hope to have a baby with Luke.

'How would Tom react if I got pregnant with Luke's child? I think that would make things between him and me more unlikely, don't you?'

The dial, it seemed, was swinging Faith and Gavin's way.

# 32

The next morning, Faith drove to Bristol's Cabot Circus shopping centre and claimed a disabled parking space using Hope's Blue Badge before Hope took charge of a scooter she'd booked at the Shopmobility centre. Then they made their way to the large department store Perdita had suggested. She'd been quite insistent that they should get there before the store was too crowded.

When the scooter's basket was full of garments Hope had selected to try on for wearing in her new job, they headed to the changing rooms. After a short wait, Hope was passed a plastic card stating the number of items she'd chosen and then she was through.

From the armful of clothes Hope had taken in with her, Faith judged it safe to spend time browsing for herself while looking after the scooter, and she began to navigate around the aisles. To clear out of the way of the crowd, Faith aimed for the men's section, planning to double back further down the store to women's apparel.

'Faith!' It was a man's voice.

'Tom.' It was difficult to look pleased to see him because she wasn't. The misunderstanding about who needed the mobility aid would become more entrenched now.

Tom's awkward body language mirrored her own feelings as his gaze shifted from side to side, a deep flush pervading his face. There was a man wearing a store badge carrying a couple of coloured shirts. Was he helping Tom depart from wearing black? And was it just a coincidence they were in the same store at the same time or had Perdita known that Tom would be here? Was that why she'd persuaded Faith to come at a particular time? But then Faith dismissed the idea. Why would Perdita do that when she knew that Faith didn't like Tom and was keen on the man in the cupboard?

She tapped the handlebar of the scooter. 'I'm looking after this until Hope's done in the changing room.'

'You know, it doesn't make any difference to me that you have a disability. There's no need to hide it.' His voice had the same mesmerising kindness he'd shown when they'd run into each other at Sainsbury's, but he was so wrong.

Faith's clutch on the handles tightened. 'I'm not disabled.'

'It's nothing to be ashamed of.'

'I'm not ashamed.' She wished she could blurt out the whole truth, but Hope would be mad at her.

Tom smiled sheepishly. 'I'm just getting some new clothes.'

Faith's eyes slid to take in the badge the store assistant wore. It gave the man's name and job title: Personal Shopper. When she glanced up, she saw that Tom hadn't missed what had caught her interest. Any redder and he'd combust. She wondered what it would feel like, to touch his burning face, and whether it would make a good hand warmer. But did she want to feel his skin against hers, to feel his heat? The fact that she wasn't sure gave her something to think about.

The personal shopper said, 'This tie, sir, would go very well with this shirt.'

Having lost the desire to browse, Faith slowly edged back to the changing rooms. Hope hadn't come out yet. But, deep in the women's section, Faith was safe from Tom—and the stirring of some unsettling thoughts. Did liking two men at the same time make her fickle? What about Hope's interest in Tom? Faith determined not to interfere, to leave a clear run for Hope as she deserved some love.

When, finally, her sister did show her face with only half an armful of clothes, Faith jumped up, and Hope slumped on the mobility scooter. Repeatedly changing clothes was a tiring activity for her.

'By the way,' Faith ventured, now that Hope was safely seated, 'I met Tom in here.'

'*Tom?*' Hope looked around, half-standing.

'Tom,' Faith confirmed, wondering why Hope's enthusiasm disturbed her. She ought to be glad for her sister—if Tom liked her back. It was high time Hope had a life of her own.

'Do you know, I think it would do me good to walk a bit.' Hope stood to full height.

Faith shook her head. 'No way.' Hope's expression was drawn and if she continued to push herself physically, she'd be in bed the rest of the day to make up for the over-exertion.

'Sis, take my place. Do this for me.'

'He'll have to know sometime. Anyway, I told him I was keeping it warm for you.'

Hope's eyes narrowed. 'Did he believe you?'

Faith shrugged.

'He didn't, did he?'

Although Faith was sorely tempted to lie, she admitted, 'No.'

'Then take my place. Please?'

'He will know eventually, whatever you do. The hearse is a dead giveaway.'

'But it will buy me time. Give him a chance to get to know me first.'

'You really like him?'

'Yes, I really like him. Now whereabouts did you see

him?'

'He's probably gone by now.' Faith caught Hope's stern look. 'In the men's section.'

'We'll go via the men's to the cash desk then.'

Defeated, Faith sat on the scooter and led the way.

It wasn't long before Hope was waving her hand in the air behind Faith, shouting, 'Hi! Tom!'

She'd spotted Tom before Faith had. But that was hardly surprising considering Faith was travelling below the display line.

'This way,' Hope directed, branching off behind Faith and almost dancing, her feet tripping daintily along the floor in the heels she'd worn so that she could look the part when trying on clothes.

Miserably self-conscious in jeans, hoodie and trainers, Faith executed a rapid three-point turn, increasing the speed to catch up with Hope who was already out of view. The scooter whined its way between aisles of clothes. The going was tougher, as though there was a steep incline. But she wouldn't worry about that now. She must be close as she heard voices: Hope's high-pitched trill that she'd used with Tom in Sainsbury's and Tom's deep timbre.

A man stepped into sight, walking backwards. Faith braked but it was too late. The side of the scooter knocked him off balance. Then he was on her lap, one hand gripping the handlebar and the other... her breast. She gasped at the shock of having a substantial volume of tissue cupped by Tom's large hand. Although she wanted to brush his hand away, her arms were pinned down by the heavy body sprawled across her. The longer his fingers clutched her breast, the stranger things became. Through some pain of having his hand grab her, other sensations emerged, shy at first but gaining strength as awareness of Tom as a man grew, ripples of desire springing from her tingling breast.

'Faith!' Tom and Hope exclaimed.

Then Hope said, 'You should have been more careful.'

Tom pulled himself up, snatching his fingers away from Faith's breast, staring at his hand as though it didn't belong to him. 'I... I'm terribly sorry.' His face was very close to hers and she caught the scent of something sweet. Had he recently eaten a fruity sweet? 'I... didn't mean to...'

'Grab my breast?' Faith finished for him, but then she recalled the garlic she'd eaten in her meal last night and worried that her breath could not match his for pleasantness. Had he flinched when she'd spoken? She didn't know as she'd been unable to tear her gaze away from his errant hand, wondering what it would feel like if he'd touched her tenderly instead of grabbing her.

Tom moved to stand up and Hope was there, gripping his arm. 'Let me help.'

As he got to his feet, he said to Faith, 'I'm very sorry. I didn't see you coming.' He glanced at his hand again and then at Faith's right breast.

'Faith, how could you?' Hope said.

'It must be the lack of practice with this thing.' Faith rubbed her breast to erase the remaining pain and the unwelcome tingles, giving Hope a baleful stare. 'You should give me lessons.'

Hope glowered at her, but Faith didn't care and glowered back.

'You're a danger to shoppers,' Hope said.

'Well, it was your idea.' Faith still had the memory of Tom's weight on her.

'I'm so sorry, Faith.' He was frowning as though he couldn't believe what had just happened. She couldn't either.

'It wasn't your fault,' Hope told him. 'Faith was speeding. Weren't you, Faith?'

'No, it's been sluggish. There's something wrong with it.' Her gaze met Tom's and there was an intensity in his focus that recalled the stirrings of desire.

'Don't make excuses. It was dangerous driving,' Hope declared. 'Are you okay, Tom?'

'*What about me?*' Faith asked.

Showing concern, Tom asked, 'Did I hurt you?'

Tom appeared so worried and so downcast that Faith said, 'I'll live.'

His gaze kept sliding downwards to watch the soothing massage she was giving her sore breast. Out of guilt? Or had he been recalling the feel, the density and the volume? And what conclusions had he drawn? She lowered her hand.

Then his expression changed as he looked beyond her. 'Faith…'

Twisting around in the chair, noting the rearrangement of the store's clothing, her heart dived.

'Oh, my goodness,' Hope said.

Faith realised Hope must have tracked Tom's gaze too.

'How could you?' Hope said.

The personal shopper stepped into view. 'Let me help.'

Two other shop assistants appeared. Faith was surprised they'd not noticed sooner.

Hope opened her mouth wide as she took a deep breath. 'How many clothes rails have you brought with you? Didn't you feel that you were dragging something along? Didn't you look where you were going?'

'Don't worry, Faith,' Tom said. 'We'll soon get you free.' To her astonishment, he addressed Hope harshly. 'I think a bit more sensitivity would be in order. Life must be very hard for Faith as it is. I don't think giving her a good telling off when she is disabled is particularly helpful or kind.'

Faith saw the colour rise in her sister's cheeks, the fire burn in her eyes and the lips of her mouth part indignantly. 'I'll have you know, *I'm* the disabled one!'

Tom flicked his gaze between Hope and Faith and then it rested on Hope. 'Faith is on the scooter, not you, which means she must need it. She deserves to be treated with sympathy and respect and she was treated with neither.' Then he met Faith's eyes, and she saw a determination in his expression—and a desire to protect.

She regretted telling her sister she could have Tom. At that moment, Faith wanted him all to herself. Feeling like a traitor, she crossed her fingers in the hope that this unwelcome attraction wouldn't last.

## 33

When they got home, Faith put Hope's shopping bags next to the sofa. Hope followed her in and sat down but Faith remained standing, too agitated to sit still.

'I think I deserve an apology for your behaviour in the shop. You as good as made me use that scooter when you wanted to see Tom and then, instead of being sympathetic, you had a go at me for dragging the clothes rails along. And you got angry that I knocked Tom over, but he stepped back into *my* path.'

Hope's eyes watered. 'Faith, I'm sorry.' When she broke eye contact, she stared at her hands, her shoulders hunched forwards. 'I don't know what came over me. As soon as we were back in the car, I realised how mean I'd been and Tom... Tom thought I was nasty too.'

'Yes, he did and you were, weren't you? Instead of criticism, some gratitude would be more appropriate after all I've done for you.'

'You're right.' Hope's voice cracked as she looked up. 'Of course I'm grateful. I don't know why I was so horrible in the shop. Maybe because of Tom but that's no excuse.'

'No, it isn't. I'm not going to cover for you again.'

Hope's hands cupped her cheeks, tears spilling out of her eyes. 'I'm sorry, really. I won't do it again, I promise. Even if Tom is around. And you're right. I should have used the scooter. I don't feel so good now.'

A gentle tap in her temples warned Faith that a full-blown headache could be looming; she needed to relax. 'Okay. Let's leave it now.'

After lunch, her headache was still there but had not developed further, so when Hope went to bed, Faith left the flat for Bristol city centre. They needed something to appreciate together, to help heal their wounds and loneliness.

Nearly two hours later, she returned, feeling better for her time away, and her head had cleared. As she was hauling the last of her purchases into the communal hallway of the flats, Gavin appeared. 'I thought you needed to get rid of stuff, not buy tons more.'

'I took your advice.' Faith slightly opened one of the boxes. 'Take a look.'

Gavin peered in. 'Now that's not the kind of rabbit I advised you to get when we had that particular conversation, and you know it isn't.'

'But it's the kind of rabbit I've ended up with. It didn't work out when I went to the shop you meant me to go to.'

'How come there are two?'

'Hope's not got a man either.'

The door to Luke and Gavin's flat opened, and Luke stepped out. 'What's going on?'

'Come in and help, then you'll see.'

With the racket Gavin and Luke were making with the erection of the hutch in the living room, Hope surfaced in light-blue pyjamas with pink spots underneath her pink dressing gown, yawning. 'What's... going on?'

Faith grabbed her hand and got Hope to stand over the box the rabbits were in before she opened the flaps completely.

'Oh, they're so cute.'

'Remember how you always wanted a rabbit but couldn't? I think it's time we put that right.' A wave of uncertainty washed over Faith. 'You still want a rabbit, don't you?'

'I don't know how old you think I am. I'm not a child anymore.' Then Hope laughed, lowering herself to the floor. 'Silly. Why would I ever grow out of wanting an itsy, bitsy, bunny wunny?' Hope's hands were already delving into the box. She picked up a tiny brown rabbit with small white patches.

The rabbit's sister was mostly white with small brown splodges. 'One each,' Faith said. 'They get lonesome on their own.'

'Just like me. Oh, that's so kind of you. Whatever made you buy them now?'

'It was Gavin's idea.'

Gavin cleared his throat. 'That's not the kind of rabbit I meant.'

Hope glanced at Faith and burst out laughing. 'Did you misunderstand him?'

'No.'

Gavin coughed.

'Well, at first,' she admitted. 'Gavin explained where to buy it. But there was a pet shop next door...'

'I didn't know you've been giving Faith sex advice.' Luke stared at the rabbits as though something was bothering him.

'You needn't worry,' Faith said, assuming Luke was concerned about the physical health of the rabbits. 'I've got this collapsible run so that they can exercise safely while we're at work.'

'Don't rabbits normally live outside?' Luke was looking very troubled now.

'The run can go outside in the warmer weather,' Faith said, but his expression didn't clear. 'Is something wrong?'

In a tremulous voice, Luke said, 'If Hope's considering having a human baby, how come you've just got rabbit babies? Is there something you haven't told me?'

With her heart free-falling to her toes, Faith aimed a glance at Hope. It was her call after all to give Luke her decision.

'I'm very sorry...' Hope began gently and tears began to trickle down Luke's cheeks. 'I've thought about it very carefully, really I have.'

'But?' As Luke sniffed, his hurt palpable, Faith's heart squeezed in sympathy.

Hope stood up and hugged him. 'It's not right for me at the moment. And, when I do have a baby, I'd like a partner to go with it.'

'I could be... your... partner.'

'Not that kind of partner. A madly in love kind of partner. A man who's crazy about me and wants me—not just my baby.'

Luke nodded, unable to look at any of them. Gavin's face sagged in what appeared to be relief.

Faith touched Luke's arm. 'I'm sorry, Luke.' She glanced at Gavin for help, but he just lifted his shoulders. 'Maybe you'll have a baby someday. Just not yet.'

# 34

The first Saturday in April—a week after Tom had run into Hope and Faith in the city centre—he loaded the Halora with his camera gear and was all set to go. Except, when he turned the ignition key, the Halora was not set to go.

After repeated attempts, he gave up. If the warning light on the dashboard had diagnosed the only problem, he guessed that he needed to fork out for a new battery to resurrect the engine. His body tensed at the thought of being late. Officers Large and Small were expecting him. Well, Officer Small's fiancée was. Tom was soon due at Cerys's house to take shots of her getting ready with the bridesmaids and then with her all dolled up and ready to wed.

The idea of calling out the Automobile Recovery Service appealed to him for about two seconds. Thinking of alternatives, he could only fix on one: Faith. But she'd refused. After fishing out his mobile, he selected Saul's number.

'Hello? Tom?'

'Hi. I need to ask a favour. My car won't start. Could Perdita plead with Faith on my behalf to help me out? I wouldn't ask if I weren't desperate...'

Faith was getting ready to leave for the supermarket when her mobile rang. 'Hi, Perdita, what's up?'

'Tom called.'

*Tom? Photographer Tom?* 'Oh?'

'His Halora's broken down. He's desperate for help

with that wedding he mentioned to you. He called me to put in a good word for him and to beg you to pick him up right away from Siskin House's car park.'

'No can do. I've got plans.'

Perdita sniffed. 'Sainsbury's?'

'Yep.'

'That can wait, can't it? Listen, he's a very nice guy. Please help him out. Be a Good Samaritan?'

'He's not dying by the roadside.'

'No, but his business will if he messes up—no one will want anything to do with him.'

'Why should I work on a Saturday for free? He'll be raking it in.'

'He's not being paid. Cost price for the prints. He's practically skint.'

'And that's my problem?'

'I think you'll like him when you get to know him. He's got a good heart.'

'No.'

'Faith, do you trust me?' There was an edge to Perdita's tone.

Faith wondered where this was leading. 'Ye-s.'

'Then trust that this is the right thing to do. That's all I can say.'

'What's going on?'

'Faith, I've been bound not to tell secrets. Like I keep yours, I must keep his. Now, please say yes as Petal needs me.'

Faith sighed. 'Okay, I'll do it.' Part of her had wanted to anyway. Pride had held her back. Tom was odd, but there was something about him that interested her, despite Hope having first dibs on him, and despite Faith having wished that her unwelcome feelings for him would go away.

She'd tried to make them vanish, but had failed. The

way he'd stood up for her, thinking she was disabled, had made something change deep inside her. She'd been wrestling with that sudden attraction ever since. But what of her feelings for the man in the cupboard? She'd need to get to know both of them better to be able to answer that.

As she pulled up outside Siskin House in her Jazz, wearing makeup and a pretty dress and heels to be suitably attired for the event, Faith saw a Halora alone in the frontage used as a car park. Assuming the figure inside the car was Tom, she flashed her lights.

But was it Tom? The man who got out was... gorgeous. He had on a shiny grey suit, white shirt, plum tie and something plum sticking out of his top pocket. He stashed his photographic gear in the back of the Jazz and soon the front passenger door opened, and the new Tom slipped into the seat beside her, the smooth scent of his aftershave accompanying him. She couldn't help inhaling deeply in an attempt to identify, remember... savour it.

'It's so good of you to do this. I do appreciate it. Wow.' Tom's gaze appeared to take in every detail of her appearance.

The way he was appraising her was not the leery, lusty way that Andy used to ogle her. Tom's look was more... reverent. As though he was in awe of her beauty, and she liked that. She liked that a lot. She smiled. 'Tell me what you want me to do.'

Faith drove Tom to the bride's home. There, he was so at ease with everyone, paid so many compliments to the bride and her mother, that his charm made Faith feel like she was breathing thin air at a mountaintop.

'That was a fabulous shot of you, Cerys. One to remember. Now, how about another of you in the garden?'

Cerys's brown hair was piled high with loose ringlets that cascaded down, framing her face. She was wearing a sumptuous off-the-shoulder white dress with a tight, lacy bodice. Faith wondered whether she could ever look as good on her wedding day. Assuming she eventually had one.

'Well,' Tom said as he packed his camera away, 'that's all for the time being. We'll see you at Christ Church and your next shot will be of you getting out of the car.'

When Faith was driving towards Clifton Down, an expanse of green near the beautiful, old limestone church with its arched windows and steeple, she said, 'Perdita mentioned that you're not getting paid for this job. Is that true?... Hello?'

Tom gave a sigh that seemed to originate from deep within him. 'Yes, it's true.'

'How come?'

'Oh, you know how it is when you get your arm twisted.'

'Like my arm got twisted?'

He met her gaze. 'I don't know what Perdita said to you to get you to change your mind since you'd turned me down so firmly when I'd asked you myself. But I doubt whatever lever she used would have had any similarity to the lever used on me. It would be like comparing the smallest Allen key to the biggest crowbar.'

'Who used it on you? Cerys? Is she an ex-girlfriend of yours?' Faith's tone was a little too sharp. Why did she care?

Tom began to laugh.

Faith bridled. 'Are you going to share the joke or just keep it to yourself?'

Tom sobered. 'Sorry, that was very rude of me. Cerys isn't an ex-girlfriend. As you saw, I was introduced to her for the first time today.'

'I wasn't sure if pretending you were strangers was a scene for my benefit.'

'Faith, I don't know what bad experiences you've had with men—but I assure you I am not like a bad experience.'

'What about staring at my chest?'

The air in the car froze. She shouldn't have brought it up.

'I couldn't help it. I'm sorry. I've never seen such... magnificence.'

'Are you calling my boobs humongous?' A 34C cup was hardly out of the ordinary.

'Not at all,' he said quickly, as though realising he was on wobbly ground. 'They are the nicest breasts I've ever seen and... so soft.'

'*Soft?*' Faith's grip tightened on the steering wheel. 'You can't tell that from looking at them.' In her peripheral vision, she could see Tom turning over his right hand and guessed he was staring at his palm.

'That day... in the store...'

'When you grabbed me?'

'I didn't know breasts could feel like that.' There was a hint of wonderment in his voice.

Faith's lips curled downwards. 'Are you lusting after them?'

'N...no.' Tom's voice wavered. 'They're so... feminine. The embodiment of femininity.'

When she briefly flicked her gaze from the road to his face, she thought he wanted to say more along the same lines, but then he said, 'I'll try very hard not to look at your breasts again... as long as you promise—'

'Not to take my shirt off in a communal area?' Faith

risked another glance.

Tom's smile brought creases to the corners of his eyes. 'Yes, something like that.'

'Deal.'

# 35

At the church, Faith stood next to Tom, minding his camera cases in case he needed to change lenses. He kept asking her if she was all right. She supposed he still didn't believe that the scooters she'd driven had been borrowed for Hope. After the words had been out of Hope's mouth about her being the disabled one, following the clothes rail debacle, she'd reverted to being schtum about it and no more had been revealed. Faith didn't say anything now because it wasn't her secret.

The wedding ceremony was beautiful. Her throat swelled and pressure grew behind her eyes as she fought tears, perhaps because her own dreams of marriage had been destroyed. She knew she'd had a very lucky escape from Andy. But how was she to find her ideal man if not in a cupboard?

Tom repeatedly arranged groups of guests, snapping them when they finally stood as he'd requested and organising others as soon as he was satisfied with his shots. Faith ticked off his list of groupings and finally, with relief, told him he'd finished. They could go now, following the bride and groom in the chauffeur-driven car.

It was not long before they arrived at the Clifton Pavilion. At the sight of the 1920's-style building with numerous arched, art deco windows, her mood lightened. It was a splendid place for a happy gathering. The flamboyance of flamingos wading in shallow water as they enjoyed the sunshine made her want to slip off her tight high heels and cool her hot, swollen feet. But she was here to help Tom, and he only had time for a few shots of the guests before a uniformed man called everyone inside for the wedding breakfast.

If she were ever to marry, she'd like something similar to the white-clothed circular tables, chairs covered in white, the backs tied with oversized pink bows. She considered the multi-coloured centrepieces of arranged flowers to be works of art.

Tom said, 'I'll get plenty of candid shots of guests as they come to get their food.'

The groom, a slim man with curly, brown hair, strolled up to Tom and slapped him on the back. 'Well, how's it going?'

'Fine.'

'How long will I have to wait until I get the prints?'

'A couple of weeks and you'll get the proofs.'

The man shook his head. 'Uh-uh. Make it one week.'

'If I have two weeks, I'll be able to do a better job.'

'Make it a week—and a good job.' The groom eyed Faith but addressed Tom. 'I see you've got over your scruples about being with women.' Then he walked off.

Faith bit her lip. 'What was that about?'

'He's one of the men who twisted my arm. His sidekick should be here somewhere too.' He began to scan the room.

Faith was recalling the cars she'd seen. 'Do they work for the police?'

His glance briefly rested on her before he searched the room again. 'Yes.'

If it was a cop wedding, then... what had Tom done? Then it hit her. *Tom. Tomcat. Peeping Tom.* Was that why he'd looked away? He was ashamed? 'Have the police got something on you?'

Tom's gaze shot back to her face. 'No. No, nothing

like that.'

Was he telling the truth?

A big, bald man with a thick, brown moustache tapped Tom on the back. 'How's it going then?'

'Fine.'

'When can we see the prints?'

'Two weeks.'

The large man sucked air in through his teeth. 'Make it one week.' Then he turned to her and said, 'Amazing what the threat of indecent exposure can do.' Then he winked and sauntered off.

'*Indecent exposure?*'

'It's not what you think. I stopped on the hard shoulder for a pee. Then Officers Large and Small stopped too and could have charged me—for the exposure and stopping on the hard shoulder for a non-emergency reason. But they said they'd let me off if I took the pics. So that's what I'm doing.'

Injustice burned in her chest. 'That's it? They made you do all this just because you needed to pee?'

'Yes.'

'The bullies.'

'That's something I like about you, Faith.'

When she heard the catch in his voice, her mouth became dry. 'What do you mean?' Heat rushed to the surface of her skin.

'You stand up for what you believe in. You're feisty, and I believe you're fiercely loyal.'

Her heart bounced and would have danced if she hadn't recalled that the first man had mentioned Tom's scruples about being with women. What had that been about?

She didn't have a chance to ask as he was very busy, and then they had to take the opportunity to grab some food before the guests gobbled everything in sight.

Apparently, Tom had insisted the arrangement he'd made included their access to refreshments.

When the dancing began in another room, with a live band, Tom took a few shots of the bride and groom enjoying their first moves together as a married couple, and then of the guests.

He lowered his camera. 'Would you like to dance?' Without waiting for an answer, he indicated he needed to ditch his gear and strode off to find someone to mind it.

She followed him. Snatching his sleeve when he was free of the photographic equipment, she asked, 'What did the first policeman mean when he mentioned you getting over your scruples about being with women?'

Tom's eyes squeezed shut. 'Do you think I could have a free pass on that one?'

She was about to say certainly not and then thought better of it. Tom's expression was mournful, as though revealing the truth would hurt him. She didn't want to cause him pain. He hadn't pressed her about the scooter so perhaps she shouldn't press him about this? Perdita had said to trust him... 'Okay, I'll trust you.' *For now.*

When they joined other people on the dance floor, Faith put her hands on Tom's shoulders, and he put his hands on her waist. His physique was similar to that of the man in the cupboard. Without thinking, she stepped forward so that their bodies were almost touching. She found, as Tom tightened his hold, that having warm, fuzzy feelings was not in the sole preserve of being physically close to the man she'd met in the cupboard.

'Are you all right?' Tom murmured in her ear. 'Do you need a tissue?'

'What do you mean?'

'You keep sniffing. I wondered whether you had a cold. Or hay fever. Or were... crying.'

Tom's aftershave was intoxicating. Short of running her nose along his cheek, there had been little she could do other than inhale deeply. 'Perhaps some dust was tickling my nose. I'm good now. There's no need to worry.' She kept her head at the optimum angle for catching scented air wafting her way and resisted the urge to sniff. She'd not noticed the scent before and wondered if Tom only used the aftershave for special occasions. Either that or it was new.

By the time the melody ended, Faith wasn't sure whether a drunk man wearing builder's safety boots would have made a better job of leading her about the floor. Tom's galumphing around had made her long for her torture to be over.

'I... need the loo,' she said when they dropped their arms as the music stilled.

She limped all the way, her squashed feet protesting with every step.

'I'm so sorry I hurt you,' Tom said later when he found her rubbing her toes in a corner of the room.

'I didn't know accepting your invitation to dance would be so dangerous.'

'I wish I were a better dancer.'

'I don't think your movements came into the category of dancing at all.'

'I'm sorry... Here, let me rub your feet.' He crouched down and started to work on her left foot.

She recalled the dampness inside her shoes when she'd taken them off and wondered if her feet smelt unpleasant. She pulled away. 'It's okay, it's much better now.'

But he stayed kneeling in front of her, one knee on the ground and one in the air as though he were about to propose. 'Thank you for rescuing me today. I'm very pleased you came.'

She swallowed. 'Me too.'

He sat beside her. 'It's been very hard starting a new business from scratch.'

Briefly, Faith covered his hand with hers and then put it back on her lap when she realised he might misinterpret the sympathetic gesture as a green light.

There was an awkward silence before Tom asked, 'Do you like your job?'

'I love it.'

'What is it that you do?'

Faith explained, giving recent examples of how she'd helped customers: the mother who needed eye-tracking software for her son who was unable to use a computer mouse; the wife who needed cushioning to preserve her husband's skin integrity in his armchair; the woman who need kitchen aids that were easy to grip and a cardholder so that she could play with her grandchildren. Faith decided to leave out the phone call she'd had that morning about the rocker bench that allowed the paraplegic man to gain the right action for achieving intimacy with his sexual partner. She thought it would make the awareness of Tom—and perhaps his of her—all the more awkward.

'How come you chose the job?'

Faith took her time in answering. 'I missed out on going to university—I'd wanted to be a social worker but my mum had cancer, and I stayed back to care for her.' She left Hope out of the picture as it would give away her sister's secret—Tom hadn't believed the scooter had been for Hope.

'When I was able to, I attended carer support groups and it was through one of the other carers that I found out about this job. Edison trained me, and I stayed.' It suited her as there was no overtime required and it was very rewarding, but sometimes she wished she didn't have to go home to another person in need. 'Then I found a place of my own.' Hope, who just hadn't a shred of hope at that time, had needed Faith and had left home with her. Would Hope always need her? 'Dad was coping better after Mum started to get her strength back and now she's in remission so it's only her osteoporosis troubling her.'

'Why don't you go to uni now? There's still time to get a new career.'

'Uh-uh. I don't want that anymore. I can't face going back to studying. I like working and earning my own money.' Besides, there was still Hope to consider. Faith didn't want to have to study evenings and weekends, writing essays and completing assignments—not anymore.

'You're a very kind person,' he said, 'to have given all that up to help your mum.'

'I haven't been kind to you.'

Tom chuckled. 'I'm not sure that counts. Weren't you like that for self-protection, because you've been badly hurt in the past? Inside, you're as soft as a marshmallow. What you just told me proves it.'

She let the compliment hang in the air, savouring it. But then she worried he was putting her on a pedestal without good cause. He didn't know the bitter resentment she swallowed down most days over her caring role never having quite ended and without any guarantee that it ever would.

'I think we all behave differently with different people and depending on the circumstances.'

'That's true. I'm guilty of that with my mother.' Tom glanced away, rubbing his chin. 'She's not someone you'd wish to meet.'

'Haven't I already met her?' Faith pictured the woman who'd been in the shop with Tom and how she'd rudely ignored Faith's offer of a handshake.

'Oh. Er... that wasn't my mother...' Tom stared at the floor. 'Can I have a free pass on that as well?'

Intrigued, Faith was about to protest but then realised he'd been polite enough not to ask what she'd been doing in the same shop. 'Tell me about your actual mother then.'

'Well, she's extremely intimidating and has a knack of finding the cruellest things to say.'

'She doesn't sound at all kind.'

'No. You really are the antithesis of her and that's why I like you.'

Faith wasn't sure if this was some kind of declaration or a casual, off-the-cuff comment that she should not read much into. She decided to accept it as the latter—*but what if it were the former...?* This was something she needed to think about, away from Tom. She asked when they could leave. Tom said they could go now; his job was done.

She was grateful to be able to concentrate on driving as it gave her an excuse not to talk. He didn't seem to have anything to say either or perhaps he, too, was deep in thought about having let on that he liked her.

When she stopped outside Siskin House so that he could store his camera equipment in his office, she said, 'Let me take you home.' Where did he live? She almost asked but there was a sudden tension in the air as though mentioning going home was a problem for him—some awkwardness in his manner that she couldn't account for.

'There's no need... But thank you. I'm going to start work on the shots tonight.'

It was clear she wasn't welcome to pry and, anyway, he might see her curiosity as an indicator for her liking him in return.

# 36

When Faith got back to the flats, she rang Luke and Gavin's bell as the light showing from their living room suggested they were still awake. Luke opened the door.

'Can I come in?'

'Sure. What's up?'

She marched inside and plonked herself down on the sofa. Gavin was reading the Daily Mirror. Well, checking out the TV programmes.

'I'm in a quandary,' Faith said.

Luke sat down in his usual armchair.

'Tell Uncle Gavin all about it.'

'And Uncle Luke.'

'I intend to. But neither of you must laugh. Promise?'

'We'll do our best, won't we?' Luke said, and Gavin nodded.

'There are two men I like, and I'm not sure which to go for.'

'Why not both?' Gavin suggested. 'Then you'll have two puppets to your string.'

'Don't you mean two strings to your bow?' Luke asked.

'That too,' Gavin said.

'I'd get rumbled as they both work on my floor. So, it would be impossible to see them both, even if I could bring myself to do it.'

'Who are these men?' Luke quizzed.

'One's a cleaner and the other's a photographer.'

'*Photographer?* Tom Sheridan?' Gavin asked. 'The

guy who's helping us out, starting this week?'

'Yes.'

'How come you're into the cleaner?' Luke asked.

'He's nice. Kind. I feel a connection with him. It's the first job he's got since settling back in the area again.'

'Again? He's been away?'

'Minding sheep. Voluntary work. That's his thing, apparently. Sheep.'

'This,' Luke said, 'is starting to sound familiar. Is this the virgin thirty-something who got you to believe all manner of things? The one Perdita called me about? You're that friend, aren't you?' Luke almost crowed in delight at having pieced it together.

'Yes, yes, yes,' Faith said huffily. 'But the "all manner of things" is true. It has to be.'

'As I said to Perdita, unless he's a monk, it's all tosh. You're a complete muppet, do you know that?' Luke said. 'You'll believe anything a man tells you.'

'How come you got chatting to the cleaner?' Gavin asked. 'Don't they go in really early or late or something? They don't work office hours.'

'Is it relevant?'

'How can we tell if you don't explain?'

Faith took a deep breath. 'I don't know his working hours. I just met him in the cleaning cupboard. In the dark.'

Gavin sniggered.

'I came here for advice, not to be ridiculed.'

'We'll be serious now, won't we, Gavin?' Luke fixed him with a steely gaze.

'Baa-aa.'

'That's it, I'm going.' Faith made to rise.

'No, stay. Let us help.' Luke threw Gavin a look of reprimand.

Faith relaxed into her seat again. 'Well, the problem is, both the man in the cupboard and Tom are nice guys. I've enjoyed the time I've spent with them. The man in the cupboard kisses exceptionally nicely—he had a good teacher—i.e. me—but Tom hasn't kissed me, so I don't know how I would feel if he were to kiss me.'

'Ask Tom to kiss you and then you'll know,' Gavin suggested.

'I can't do that!' Glowering at Gavin, Faith added, 'This isn't helping me decide.'

'How about choosing on looks if you can't compare the kissing?' Luke said.

Faith picked at her fingers. 'I don't know what the man in the cupboard looks like. It was dark, remember? I don't even know his name.'

'I've got your answer,' Gavin said, sounding chuffed.

'Yes?'

'Go for the least weird. Cupboard in the dark is definitely weird. Baa-aa.'

# 37

When Faith got to work on Monday morning, she tried, as she often did, the door to the cleaning cupboard. It was locked. Disappointment crushed her. How could she determine which man to choose if only one of them was available for her to get to know?

Hearing a sound from within Tom's office, and curious about the changes he was making, Faith knocked and walked in. Although she couldn't see Tom, she could smell emulsion and see the freshly painted ivory walls. Her attention was caught by several large photographs: a beautiful bouquet; a groom whisking his bride towards a white-ribboned vintage car; a tiered cake banded in cornflower blue with cascading flowers; the inside of a marquee with lanterns; tables decorated with flowers and folded napkins; and, finally, the one that appealed to her the most. This was of a bride lying on the grass with her head on the groom's lap as he bent to kiss her.

A distinct creak of something metallic reminded her that she had not yet made her presence known.

'Hi. It's Faith!'

'In here!'

She made her way into the next room. The sight of Tom, standing on a step ladder with a paint roller in his hand, wearing a tight, white T-shirt and blue jeans that hugged his rear, made it hard to breathe. The arm that was moving the roller back and forth on the ceiling had clearly defined muscles. Then she stared at the outline of his pecs and then his flat stomach. She swallowed.

'What can I do for you?' He rested the roller on the

tray.

*Ooh.* There was plenty he could do for her. But then she remembered the man in the cupboard. Where was her allegiance to him? Well, at this moment, things were swinging in Tom's favour. However, there was Hope to think of...

'I just wanted to see how things were progressing in here.'

His smile crinkled his eyes, and Faith experienced a falling sensation akin to travelling into a dip on a rollercoaster.

He came down a few rungs and rested his arms on the arch of the ladder. 'What do you think?'

'Fantastic,' she whispered, eyeing his physique.

Tom's eyebrows drew closer together. 'This room's not halfway done yet.'

What had been the question? 'Oh. I meant your office.' Faith raised an arm in the general direction. 'The pictures... They're... fantastic.'

'Which did you like the best?'

'The bride and groom together, on the grass.'

Tom grinned. 'Me too.'

'Did you get them to pose for that?'

He shook his head. 'Uh-uh. That was for real.'

'I thought it might be.' She smiled as she sauntered to the window to discover the view—which included the hearse—and then snapped her head away. Tom might ask about the vehicle, and then she'd have to start lying.

'I plan to start portrait photography,' he said, seemingly not noticing her sudden aversion to the sight from his window. 'This will be the studio. I'll paint it mid-grey. That wall, where my subjects will be...' Tom pointed, '... will be dark-grey to prevent light bouncing off the walls. With a blackout blind, I can control exactly where the light is coming from.'

'You seem to have it all worked out.'

'I hope so. When the website I'm having built is finished, customers will be able to order their prints through that. Until that's done—'

There was a commotion outside in the corridor. Tom came down the ladder and motioned her to stay where she was while he investigated the space outside, but then he abruptly flung his back hard against the door to close it. 'You don't want to go out there,' he whispered, his expression earnest.

There was something familiar about the whisper that tugged at her memory, but Faith couldn't identify what it was. The noise from outside was louder, and she recognised at least one of the voices. Indicating she wanted Tom to move, she brushed past him and stepped into the corridor. Instantly, she regretted it. They were outside the office she shared with Edison.

'Leave her alone.' Andy had his back to Faith and he was clinging on to a woman's arms as she struggled to be free.

Faith recognised the woman Andy was with as she writhed in his grasp.

'This is nothing to do with Faith,' Andy panted as he fought to retain his grip.

'It's everything to do with her!' Roxy yelled. She was dressed in impossibly high stilettos and a short dress that allowed her breasts to bob up and down. Her makeup was tear-smudged.

'You're the one who messed around!' Andy was dressed unusually for a work day in cords and a T-shirt. Mm. Not as well developed as Mr Photographer.

'You bitch!' Roxy screamed when she spotted Faith.

Andy gripped Roxy's wrists from behind.

As Roxy struggled to free herself, Faith addressed Andy. 'What's going on? How does she know where I work?'

'She's always known. I told her everything about you when we first got together. You know, as people do.'

Faith pulled a disgusted face. 'So how come you didn't tell me all about *her*?' When Andy didn't answer, Faith folded her arms. 'Well, what's with the drama?'

'I'm pregnant,' Roxy said. 'And because of you, he doesn't want to know.'

Was Roxy referring to the texts she'd sent Andy the night after the outing with Jade?

'Do you even know whose it is?' Faith brimmed with loathing for the woman who'd interfered in her life, taken her boyfriend.

'It's Andy's.'

'Really?'

'He was the only one I didn't use a condom with.' Roxy was still trying to break free.

'Congratulations, Andy,' Faith said. 'You struck lucky there. I hope you'll be very happy together.'

Andy's eyes were blazing. 'We're not together, and we won't be together.'

'Then I hope you'll pay Child Maintenance.'

Roxy flicked a hand free and managed a step towards Faith. 'He doesn't believe it's his.'

'How can I? When you've been picking up men all over?'

'I'll get a DNA test done as soon as it's born.'

'You're *keeping it?*' Andy asked.

'Yes. I'm keeping it.'

'I think I'm done here,' Faith said. 'Can you let me pass so that I can get into my office?' Or should she go back to the protection of Tom? Where was Tom?

'Andy, I think you've exaggerated in your mind how many men I've been with,' Roxy said. You've got it so wrong thanks to this *bitch*.'

Tom stepped into view. 'Actually, I think whatever Faith said might be right so there's no need to call her names.'

'And who are you?' Roxy demanded.

'Just some guy at a service station.'

Faith watched as Roxy appraised him.

Roxy glared at him. 'Never seen you before in my life.'

'Then how come I know you sell... what was it now? Personal... *pleasure...* equipment.'

'Bloody hell,' Andy exclaimed. 'How many men have you had?'

'Not this one. I'd remember.' Roxy was taking in Tom's body with a regretful expression.

If Tom had been with Roxy, it would put him out of the running. Faith studied him carefully—and she imagined Andy and Roxy doing the same.

'You're right,' Tom said slowly. 'You didn't have me.'

'I knew it!' Roxy exclaimed. 'I'd have remembered a body like yours.'

'But you tried, didn't you?' Andy said without any hint of triumph before walking to the stairs, looking grim.

It seemed as though Roxy's aggression had evaporated as she just ambled after him. Tom stared at Faith for a moment before retreating into his office, and Faith decided she'd better get some work done too.

It was then that the first faint throbbing in Faith's temple began. The endless calls and the stack of emails that followed involved intensive use of her monitor, which hadn't helped her headache. She'd tried turning the screen's brightness down in the hope that she could avert a full-blown migraine attack. But the closer it got to lunchtime, the more intense the pain across her left eye and down the left side of her face became.

'Do you mind if I go for lunch now?' Faith asked Edison, who'd been working opposite her for the past hour.

He consulted his watch. 'I don't see why not.'

'Thanks.' From past experience, she knew that having an empty stomach made her migraines worse, so she headed for the lift via the fridge and popped a couple of painkillers while she was at it.

After leaving through the side door, Faith made for the hearse. Already, she'd eaten the first sandwich, and she started on the second. She kept her knees bent as she walked in her heels to minimise the pounding on the ground that was maximising the pounding in her head.

She opened the tailgate of the car. There was no one around as she climbed in, tucking her empty sandwich wrapper in her bag. Then she lowered the tailgate, removed her shoes, hitched up her skirt to get into the casket and then tugged it back down to prevent it from creasing. After setting her phone alarm, she pulled the duvet partially over her as it was only slightly cool outside and shut the casket lids.

# 38

Judith was aiming her binoculars out of the study window that faced the side elevation of Siskin House. 'Miranda! *Miranda!*'

'Yes?' Miranda appeared at the study door.

'Did you see that woman get in the hearse?'

'Which one? Sooty or Blondie?'

'The black-haired one. Only two minutes after the blonde one had gone. What's going on?'

Miranda shrugged, but Judith could see that her interest was piqued.

'Go out and take a look.'

Judith watched as Miranda approached the black vehicle cautiously and then tried sticking her face against the glass while shielding her eyes.

When Miranda returned, Judith demanded, 'Well? What could you see?'

'Nothing. Apart from a coffin.'

'A coffin?'

'Yes. Sooty's not there.'

'She is. I saw her get in, and I've been standing here ever since. There's no way she got out.'

'Then she must be in the coffin.'

'And what would she be doing in there?'

'Maybe practising for when her time comes.'

'There's no need to be facetious. It's time we found out what those two are up to. Suspicious isn't the word.'

'I thought it was rather apt myself.'

Judith gave her a cutting glance. 'Inform the police there's a hearse parked outside my house every office day and that your employer is of a delicate disposition...'

Miranda's eyebrows shot up.

'... and that she is disturbed by the image of that monstrous vehicle. Tell them she is afraid that it's here waiting for her... Death, the Grim Reaper, whatever. I'm sure you can dress it up well. What you can't do in life with your clothes, you can do in words.'

Miranda winced. 'Wouldn't Death fear you more?'

'Probably.'

Judith watched Miranda dial 101 and listened as she gave a sob story, drawing on the basics that Judith had outlined.

'Oh, thank you, officer. That would be so kind.' Miranda replaced the receiver.

'Well?' If the black-haired woman left before the police arrived, Judith might not find out what the woman was up to.

'They're sending a patrol car. It shouldn't be long.'

It was twenty minutes later and the police still hadn't arrived. Judith was standing with Miranda at the window, shielded by the nets.

'What's taking them so long?' Judith griped.

'Perhaps they have some criminals to catch.'

Judith produced a sound not dissimilar to that of a snorting horse. 'For all they know, this hearse is linked to criminal activity.'

'My call didn't indicate it was.'

'Perhaps you ought to have embellished the story. Imagination isn't one of your fortes, is it?'

'What is?' Miranda mumbled.

'Looking after my interests. You're better than most.' It was probably the first compliment Judith had ever paid Miranda. But it would be best not to do it again for another year or so; she wouldn't want the commendation to go to Miranda's head.

'Here they are!' Miranda exclaimed.

Judith detected excitement. So, Miranda wasn't as cut off from playing games as she made out. Judith adjusted the focus to get a better look at the two officers getting out of their car. One was large, the other was smaller all around. The large officer walked the entire perimeter of the hearse, looking in. Then he rapped on the window.

The smaller man was using his radio. He was looking at the number plate so Judith assumed they were tracing the owner. Now the large man had his mobile out and the smaller man seemed to be telling him what numbers to dial.

Faith was snoozing when she thought she heard a knocking at the window. When it stopped, she assumed she'd imagined or dreamt it. Then there was the melody of the can-can.

She didn't rush to stop the sound as she didn't feel like moving. But then she heard voices. Men's voices. One of them said, 'Did you hear that? The phone was ringing inside the hearse.'

'Try again,' another voice said.

Faith's mobile began the can-can again. Who did she know who'd be calling her from outside the car? Gavin? Luke? But it didn't sound like them. She opened up the lids and pulled the net curtain aside. She screamed. A man—dressed in a police uniform—was peering in at her.

'It's a woman,' she heard the man say. 'Lying in a coffin.' The man rapped the window. 'Could you come out of the vehicle please, madam?'

What had she done? After scrambling out of the casket, Faith found her shoes and made her way to the front so that she could get out of the passenger door. She didn't want to have to ask strangers to open the tailgate for her. Outside she saw not one but two police officers. Had she gone through a red light? Been speeding? Why would they track her down here? Was it against the law to lie in a casket in a hearse on a public road?

'Hello, don't I know you?' the large one said.

'Yeah. I think I've come across you before,' the small one said.

Faith eyed them. Surely, they didn't think she was one of the criminals they'd had to deal with?

'We never forget the face of someone we've nicked,' the large one said smugly.

'Well, you've never nicked me. I was at the wedding on Saturday.' Faith recalled Tom's monikers for the officers: Large and Small.

'Well,' Officer Large said. 'Small world.'

'You were with the priest,' Officer Small said.

*Priest?* She'd not been with any priest. 'No. I was with the photographer.'

The officers smirked at each other. 'Why is the vehicle parked here?' Officer Large asked.

So, it was about the hearse. When had that become a police matter?

'That's where I work.' Faith pointed to the side entrance of Siskin House.

'Can you explain what you were doing in that coffin?' Officer Small asked.

'Having a lie-down. I get migraines. And it's a casket.' Faith's phone started to trill again. 'My alarm,' she explained, switching the sound off. 'It's time for me to go back to work.'

'When we've finished here. And we haven't done that yet.' Officer Large looked menacingly at her.

'I mustn't be late,' Faith protested. 'I'll get into trouble.'

'I'm sure you'll be able to explain that you were helping police officers with their enquiries.'

Edison might hit the roof. The last assistant had got sacked because of punctuality issues.

'What else do you want to know?'

'Well, it seems that this vehicle being parked here is scaring a fragile, old lady. She thinks the hearse is waiting for her to pop her clogs. Would it be possible to park it further up the street? Then the old lady won't be able to see it.'

Faith looked across the road at the only house—or was it a mansion?—opposite. There was a shadow at the window. Faith guessed that the old lady was watching them anxiously.

'No. This is the least walking distance from the hearse to the building where my sister works. The hearse and casket were bought for her use. She's not well and needs to rest between her shifts.'

'What's wrong with her?' Officer Large's tone lacked sympathy.

Did he think she was lying? 'She had a terrible dose of glandular fever and never quite recovered. It became ME.'

The officers frowned at each other, suggesting that they did not know what ME was.

'And she comes out to lie down in the... casket?' Officer Large asked.

'Yes.'

'So, are you refusing to park somewhere else?'

Too right she was. After the efforts she'd gone to over helping Hope, she was not going to jeopardise her sister's job now.

'It's not an offence to park here, is it?'

'No, but it will cause an old lady distress.'

'It would cause my sister considerable distress to

have to walk further. Repeatedly.'

The officers did not look at her kindly. Officer Large rocked on his heels a couple of times. 'How about if we verify this information with your sister?'

'No! You mustn't go in; they don't know she's ill. She might lose her job.'

The officers exchanged glances. 'I take it she didn't disclose facts that were material to her employment?' Officer Large asked.

Faith put a hand on the hearse, her heart hammering. 'Please. It's a very part-time job—her first. Can't I explain the situation to this lady? I'm sure she'd understand.'

The officers' gazes met and then Officer Large said, 'We'll accompany you. We can't allow strangers to call on the weak and vulnerable.'


'They're coming here. The lot of them. Get the door open, Miranda.'

With the aid of her Zimmer frame, Judith eased herself into the armchair and prepared to display a timid, nervous disposition.

Soon, two police officers and the black-haired woman were in front of her desk.

'As we've just explained to this lady...' The large officer indicated Miranda. '...we have responded to your call about the hearse, madam. And this here is Miss Faith Goddard. She'd like to apologise for scaring you and give you an explanation as to her activities with the vehicle.'

Judith turned what she hoped were feeble eyes towards Faith, doing her best to hide the zing of interest in the woman's name. Judith wondered what Tom had made of it since he must have heard it by now. 'Hello, dear. It's nice of you to come to talk to me.'

'Hello... er... Mrs...?'

'Mrs Gold. But call me Judith. Would you like some tea?'

Officer Large rocked on his heels again. 'We need to be going. If Miss Goddard would proceed with the explanation...'

'Oh, there's no reason for you to stay, officers. I'm sure that I will be fine with Miss Goddard—'

'Faith, please.'

'Well, if you're sure...'

When the officers had been shown out, Judith said, 'Miranda will make some tea.' Behind Faith, Judith saw Miranda glare. Judith bet Miranda wanted to stay to hear what Faith had to say.

'Please, no,' Faith said. 'I'm late for work as it is. I'm going to get into trouble even now.'

'Who is it you work for?'

'A man called Edison Ekwense. He's a stickler for punctuality.'

'Tell him you were visiting your grandmother. She had a fall.' As she tapped the handle of her Zimmer frame, she gave what she hoped was a friendly wink.

Tom had almost toppled from his ladder when he'd spotted police outside in the street below with Faith, trooping down the driveway to Judith's place. He'd recognised the coppers: Officers Large and Small. Not long after they'd all gone in, Officers Large and Small had emerged and driven away.

Faith was still there. Why? What was Judith doing to her? Should he rescue Faith? But then she would discover that Judith was his mother, that he'd got the office rent-free and had had to return—as a grown man—to living with "Mummy". Faith might even find out that he was a priest. So, he continued his vigil.

A few minutes later, Faith emerged from The House

of Dread. Suppressing an impulse to charge down the stairs to question her, he listened at the door to his office instead, planning to pretend that he needed to go to the kitchenette if he could detect her presence outside.

The stairs had been too much for Faith's throbbing head, which hadn't much improved, despite her rest. Edison caught her as she stepped out of the lift. He was holding a mug of a hot drink judging by the steam coming from it.

'You're late.'

'I know. I'm so sorry.'

Dimly, she was aware of a door opening behind her. It was humiliating being brought to book in front of Tom.

'This has happened too often,' Edison said stiffly. 'And as you asked to take your break early, the least I'd expect is for you to be back on time.'

'I know. I couldn't help it.' She'd hoped not to have to lie. But there was nothing else for it if she was to keep the hearse and Hope's ill health a secret. 'It's because of my grandmother. She's had a fall. I popped round to see her. She phoned when I was out at lunch.'

'And you didn't think to call me to explain?'

'I was so anxious about her that I didn't think of anything else.'

'You've not mentioned a grandmother before.'

Oh no. More lying. 'There was a bit of a rift. But it's healed now.'

Edison appeared only slightly appeased. 'I'll let it go this time. But in the next three months, I don't want you to be even a minute late. There has to be someone to answer calls during published office hours or we will lose customers...'

When Edison finished giving her a piece of his mind,

Faith risked a look at Tom. He was watching her with a strange, bewildered expression that was a mixture of pain and betrayal, as though she'd done something to wound him. Then he turned and went back into his office.

What had that been about?

Tom sat on the floor of the inner room that he'd been painting, running his fingers over his hair, confused. *Was Faith really his niece?* Or was it some kind of scam where she was hoping to get something out of Judith? But he was convinced that Faith was a good person... wasn't she?

Yes, she was. So that meant she was his niece, wasn't she? His fantasies of having a home and children with Faith were crushed, destroyed by that single piece of information. How could Judith have failed to tell him that he had a sister or a brother somewhere who'd given half their genes to Faith? How could Judith have let him find out that he had a niece like this? Why did he have to find out now, when he'd far from avuncular feelings towards Faith? And he'd *kissed* her! How had Judith even managed to keep such a secret from him when he'd been living with her? Had she gone away for a while, to give birth secretly to a sibling, and he hadn't remembered?

Feeling like his universe was falling apart, Tom groaned. Life was testing him. God was testing him. This was his punishment for leaving the fold. Although he couldn't really believe it of his mother, he had to know. He couldn't be left ignorant for a minute longer. He rang Judith from his mobile. 'Mum?'

'Yes?'

'I...'

'Yes, Malakai?'

'I suddenly have a memory that I can't explain. Of

another child. Did I have a brother or a sister?'

'What are you talking about?'

'Do I have a brother or a sister?'

'Don't be ridiculous. You know you're an only child.'

Tom was tempted to ask if Judith was sure she'd not given birth to another child, but of course she'd know. She was either telling the truth or lying. If she was telling the truth, what was the explanation of Faith coming out of her house? And the police being there? If Judith was lying, to what purpose? He recalled Faith mentioning Judith having had a fall.

'Are you all right? You're not hurt or anything?'

'Why should I be hurt?'

'No reason... I'll see you tonight then.'

With his head on his bent knees and his hands feeling the coarse fibres of the carpet, his mind numbed. He didn't know what to do—and then he did.

With trembling fingers, he searched the Internet for birth records. He had to create an account on an ancestry website and the first two weeks were free. But what he found was that Judith had given birth to one son named Malakai and he knew that was him; he had his birth certificate to prove it. Could his mother have given birth on another occasion secretly? Unlikely. *Or had Faith lied?* Perhaps Faith was *spying* on him and reporting back to Judith? But he couldn't truly believe that of Faith either, despite being well able to believe it of Judith.

# 39

Two days later, the reception area of Tom's office was just about complete. He still needed to buy a couple of big plants to soften the room, but he'd managed to find a suitable glass coffee table, which he'd placed between two nearly-new red sofas. It was quite an ideal setup, he thought, for that morning's business.

On the dot, there was a knock at the door. Gavin entered.

'Hi, how are…?' Tom trailed off, confused at the sight of who followed Gavin into the room.

'This is Luke,' Gavin said.

Tom should have said nice to meet you and then shaken hands. But he was too shaken up to do either.

'Is something wrong?' Gavin asked.

'You did tell him we're a gay couple?' Luke asked.

'Why would I do that? We're a couple, and he's a couples counsellor.'

Luke coughed. 'The statue look suggests he's not had a gay couple before.'

Tom cleared his throat. 'When you said you were having problems in your relationship, I took it to mean you were referring to your wife… or girlfriend.'

'You've never counselled gays?' Gavin asked. 'That's discrimination.'

Yes, it was. But that's how it was in the Church. 'I've not been trained in gay relationships.'

'How, in this modern day and age, can a couples counsellor not be trained to help same-sex couples?' Luke demanded.

Tom shrugged helplessly.

'We're not leaving,' Gavin said. 'We struck a deal, remember? I've already plugged your business to the big boss woman, and you've already had work from that come your way, so I've kept my side of the bargain. It's time to honour yours.'

'Please, sit down.' Tom's brain was whirring furiously, trying to work out what to do.

'You'll find that we're just like any other couple with problems,' Luke said as he lowered himself onto the sofa. Gavin joined him.

Tom stared blankly. Strictly speaking, he should leave well alone. Some therapists had not had formal training and could still legally practice, but it was a grey area.

'It would be wrong of me to undertake counselling without formal training,' Tom hedged.

'How come you haven't been trained?' Luke asked. 'We don't intend to leave without an explanation.'

In synchrony, the men crossed their arms.

Tom sank onto the sofa opposite. 'It's a secret.'

'We're good with secrets,' Luke said.

Tom had to come clean with these guys. It wasn't as though they were formally there as his clients; he was helping out as a favour. 'I was only trained to help heterosexuals as the Catholic Church does not allow same-sex marriages.' Tom waited for their understanding. 'All my clients were Catholic.'

'You worked for a Catholic organisation?' Luke asked.

Tom nodded gravely.

'Catholic counselling?' Gavin sniffed.

'Yes.'

Gavin appeared more disgruntled by the second. 'Why is this such a big secret?'

'You've only ever taken photos at church events, haven't you?' Luke asked.

'... Yes.'

'You've only covered Catholic weddings,' Luke said.

'... Yes. Until recently.'

'You were a priest, weren't you? A Catholic priest?'

'Actually, I still am. But I've stopped doing the clerical work. I want my freedom.'

Gavin made a sound that indicated disgust. 'In that case, why don't you leave your gay scruples behind and help us?'

Glumly, Tom shook his head. He didn't think he should tamper with things he didn't fully understand. Things he'd not been exposed to and things he'd been... brainwashed about. It wouldn't be fair on them.

'Come on,' Luke said. 'Let's go.'

Tom watched miserably as the men made for the door. When the door was open, Luke exclaimed to someone in the corridor, 'Hi Faith! How are you doing?'

Tom tensed. Then he heard her reply, 'Oh, okay.' Then, in surprise, she added, 'What are you doing here?'

'Counselling. Except...'

Tom was behind the door, out of Faith's sight, so quickly he could have magicked himself there. 'Please,' he whispered to Luke, 'can we have a chat? About confidentiality?' If he'd known they were connected to Faith, he would never have let on about his being a priest. He wanted Faith to think of him as a regular guy, just as he was trying to be.

'No,' Luke said to Tom, and then addressed Faith. 'As I was saying...'

'Yes?'

'I'll do it,' Tom hissed. 'I'll do it. Just don't say anything. Please.'

Tom watched as Luke raised a hand to Faith. 'It

seems we're not done here yet. Catch you later.'

'Okay.'

There was the sound of a door. Tom imagined Faith going back into her office.

Luke shut the door to Tom's office and raised his eyebrows questioningly.

Deflated, Tom said, 'I said I'll do it.' When they were seated again, he asked, 'How do you know Faith?'

Luke leaned back and stretched out his legs. 'We live in the same building.'

'I see.'

'I take it you're keen on her and that's why you don't want her to know you're a priest?' Luke asked.

Heat rose in Tom's face.

'I'd give up hope there if I were you. She's stuck on this man she met in a cupboard.' Luke's scrutiny made Tom feel very uncomfortable. Then Luke grinned. 'Do you, by any chance, sit in a cupboard on this level?'

Tom hid his face behind the palms of his hands.

'I take it that's a yes,' Luke said.

Tom nodded.

'You're the guy who was looking after sheep, aren't you?' Luke asked. 'I told her it was a load of codswallop unless the guy was a monk. But it's you, the priest—a *parish* priest. So, I wasn't far off then, was I?'

'You're brilliant for working that out,' Gavin said.

Tom lowered his hands and forced himself to make eye contact. 'Do we have a deal? You keep quiet about what you know, and I'll do my best to help you?'

'What do you think?' Luke asked Gavin.

Gavin shrugged. 'I don't know why he didn't just help us in the first place. It would have been a lot more straightforward.'

Tom learned that Luke was a personal trainer—healthy eating and keeping fit were absolute priorities.

He did most of the cooking and grocery shopping. Gavin was a funeral director and did most of the cleaning, washing and ironing. Luke paid bills, organised insurance and undertook other administrative tasks. Gavin sorted out everything to do with their cars.

'Okay,' Tom said, now that he'd broken the ice, 'tell me what's brought you here.' The guys looked at each other. 'How about you, Gavin? Tell me why you asked for counselling.'

Gavin gave a short cough. 'We've got a major difference of opinion. Luke wants a child, and I don't. I asked Luke to choose between me or having a child—and he's going with the child.'

Tom tried to keep his expression bland. He'd expected that one of them might have felt neglected or that they were gradually growing apart without knowing why. But it was a completely different kind of trouble they were in.

'I do want a child,' Luke said. 'Desperately. But I'd like to keep Gavin as well. I don't know if anything can be done to change Gavin's mind...'

'I'm not here to change anyone's mind or to tell either of you what to do,' Tom explained gently. 'My role is to allow safe exploration of your feelings, improve communication between the two of you and work at ways to enable both of you to feel more supported, more secure in the relationship—and to help you find an acceptable compromise over differences you might have.' Tom smiled at them to put them at ease. 'But before we talk about the main issue, I'd like to explore the relationship between the two of you. Gavin, would you tell Luke what he means to you?'

Gavin began to trace patterns on his thigh with his fingers and the tendons in Luke's hand stood proud as his grip tightened on the arm of the sofa.

'Gavin?' Tom prompted.

Gavin's chin trembled and tears overspilled his eyes. 'Luke means everything to me. He's the love of my life.'

Tom shifted a box of tissues close to Gavin. 'How are your feelings affected by Luke's desire to have a child?'

'I feel shut out. Like I'm not enough for him.' Gavin reached out for a tissue, dabbed at his eyes and blew his nose. 'But Luke's plenty for me. I've never wanted anyone else since I met him. But it's obvious when Petal's around that he can't think of anyone else but her.'

'*Petal?*'

Luke spoke. 'She's the daughter of a mutual friend of ours. Petal's over more often now that her mum's—'

'Pregnant.'

'Blimey,' Gavin said, wiping his eyes with a second tissue. 'How did you know?'

Should Tom have mentioned that he knew? But there was nothing there that was confidential. He'd just not tell Saul or Perdita that Luke and Gavin were his clients—of sorts.

'I've been to dinner at Saul and Perdita's place. I've met Petal briefly.'

Luke grinned. 'Then you know how adorable she is.'

Tom noticed a shadow fall across Gavin's expression. 'How is it when Petal's around?'

'Brilliant,' Luke said.

'I feel like a spare part no one wants,' Gavin said.

Luke's happy face became sombre. 'Really?'

Gavin sniffed. 'Yes. You're not interested in me when Petal's with you. So how much worse do you think I'd feel if you had a child around all the time?'

The atmosphere became tense. Tom asked, 'And what does Gavin mean to you, Luke?'

Luke seemed to be struggling for an answer.

Eventually, he said, 'I love Gavin. I want to share my life with him. But he's not enough. I yearn to have a child of my own so much, it's gobbling me up.'

Tom was surprised at how much the guys were revealing. Men in therapy often had trouble communing with their emotions let alone voicing them.

'Luke, how do you think you could help Gavin feel more valued when Petal is around?' '... I'm not sure.'

It didn't seem that Luke had ever considered how to help Gavin. 'Gavin, is there anything Luke could do to make you feel more valued?'

'When he reads Petal a goodnight story, he always does it on his own.' Gavin's voice wobbled and was higher pitched than before. 'I've never read Petal a goodnight story. He's never even asked me to—or tried to include me.'

Luke stared. 'I... I'm sorry. I didn't think you were interested; I thought you didn't like kids.'

Gavin dabbed at his eyes again and wiped his nose. 'I haven't been given a chance to like them. I don't know how I feel. I just know that they take you away from me.'

'Well,' Tom said after a long silence, 'I think we've covered enough ground for the time being. There are things you can talk about, and think about, over the next couple of weeks, before I see you again.'

The guys got up to leave, appearing diminished compared to their confident entry.

Despite knowing he shouldn't use his connection to Luke and Gavin to ask questions about Faith, Tom couldn't help himself. 'Can I ask... has Faith ever mentioned a grandmother to you? Someone who lives just across the road from here?'

Luke frowned. He checked with Gavin, but he shook his head. 'No. Why?'

'There's a minuscule possibility that Faith is my

niece. But as you don't know of a grandmother there's probably been a misunderstanding. Please don't mention it to her.'

*So was Faith Judith's spy?* But how were the police involved? It just didn't make any sense.

# 40

A week had gone by since Tom had seen Faith come out of the House of Dread and he needed some answers. Observing her hadn't provided them. He hadn't spotted her going to Judith's again.

Familiar with Faith's routine, he knew that she would soon arrive for work. He waited in the unlit cupboard in the hope that she'd try the door handle and allow the mystery to be cleared up. The deception was wrong but it was the only way he could safely fish for information. He hadn't risked it before because of the effect she had on his emotions. But now that the chance of her truly being his niece had slimmed considerably, he decided he must take the plunge and find out the truth. To his relief, he saw the influx of light from the door being opened.

'Are you in here?' Faith whispered.

'Yes,' he whispered back. He was pleased she hadn't switched the inside light on—he knew that one day she might and then he'd be rumbled.

When she groped her way to him, he guided her to the bucket seat and sat on the cold, hard floor in front of her.

'It's been a long time.' There was an accusation in her tone.

'Yes. I've been busy.'

'How are you adapting to life back in Clifton?'

'Oh, so-so. Getting established again in a community takes time. I'm still finding it hard to adjust to things; everything's so different now.'

'Do you miss your sheep?'

Tom felt guilty for having misled her but now that he had, talking of sheep served a purpose. 'I do. Terribly—and everyone else I left behind.'

'I'm sorry—it must be so hard for you. Have you made any friends here?'

'I've met lots of people. Perhaps some will become friends. I'd like to think of you as a friend.'

There was a pause before she answered. 'Thank you. But I look for you and you're not here most of the time...'

He'd held off being in the cupboard in the hope she'd get to know and like him as Tom the photographer. Then the man she'd met here could disappear, and he could try to forget his shameful deception. But he had that burning, unanswered question. 'Do you have family in the area?'

'Just my sister. My brother's in Sydney for a gap year—he's got hotel work through a family friend—and my parents are staying with him at the moment. They deserve the break. They'll be back before Christmas. Mum's been very ill and has recently got the all-clear.'

'I'm sorry to hear about your mum. I hope they all have a great time. What about grandparents?'

'They died a while ago.'

He wanted to keep his connection to Judith a secret, but he couldn't let the subject pass yet. 'Really?'

'Why sound so surprised? Do you have grandparents then?'

'No.'

'Well, why do you expect me to?'

He couldn't think of a suitable reply.

'Actually,' she said with a giggle, 'it's funny you should mention grandparents because I acquired a fictitious granny last week.'

'What do you mean?'

'Someone said to pretend she was my grandmother to stop me from getting into trouble at work because she delayed me. So, I did. I told my boss she had a fall to excuse my lateness.'

Tom almost collapsed with relief; Faith was not related to him, he'd done nothing wrong and she wasn't a spy for Judith.

'Are you okay?' Faith sounded panicked.

'Yes. Why?'

'I heard a whoosh sound. Like you're ill.'

*Drat.* He'd been holding his breath from the tension and had then let it out all at once. 'I'm fine,' he said, and then, to divert attention away from his breathing, he asked, 'What was she like? The old woman?'

'Oh, very friendly. She wanted me to stay for a cup of tea and some homemade biscuits, but I couldn't. I was already running late. So she's invited my sister, Hope, and me after work next week as that's better for Hope.'

'Better for Hope?'

'She's been very ill and is still adjusting to being employed. After another week here, I hope she'll have enough stamina to cope with a short visit. But her health problems are a secret, so please don't tell anyone.'

He'd been a fool. 'No, of course not.' He should have believed Faith when she'd said that the scooter hadn't been for her—then she might have confided in his photographer self. 'What's wrong with your sister?'

'She had a terrible dose of glandular fever and never quite recovered. It became ME.'

'I'm sorry to hear that. What a shame. I know how awful that can be.' Several parishioners had developed the illness and a couple of them had been given Holy Communion at home after Mass as they'd been too ill to attend in person. 'Well, I hope you and Hope enjoy taking tea with the old lady.'

Judith wasn't yet seventy and her brain was as agile and sharp as it had ever been but it was her arthritis that aged her. He wondered why she would have invited Faith and Hope and then the answer came to him. Judith had threatened to find him a wife. She was probably vetting the women as possible matches.

'I feel sad that you're missing your sheep. There are plenty of farms outside Bristol. There's a big one on the way to my friend Perdita's place...'

'It's... okay. I think I need to do something other than looking after a... flock. It had been such a heart-wrenching decision to leave but now that I have... although it's hard... I'm glad as it's meant I met you.'

Apart from a brief letter from the presbytery, he'd had no news from his parish and he guessed that the Bishop had forbidden the Fathers to keep in touch. He did miss their evening chats and the sociability of mealtimes...

'I still don't know your name.'

'Fa—' Tom had just been about to introduce himself as Father Thomas Sheridan. To cover his blunder, he fixed on the first name that came to him. 'Farquhar.'

'That's... different.'

'Don't you like it?' He should have planned ahead. He had an idea. 'My middle name is Thomas. If you'd prefer to call me that...'

'There's a Tom working up here. Have you met him?'

Had she just changed the subject to hide the fact that she hated the name, Farquhar?

'I know who you're talking about.'

'He's a bit weird, you know.'

'Is he?' Had he been? How weird?

'Not long ago, I helped him out at a wedding. He was so confident, so charming, so in control of the job and guests and not at all shy with me. I... quite like him.' She said the last sentence apologetically as though aware of the fact that Farquhar's feelings might be hurt.

Tom would have liked to have commended her for flagging up the possibility of his having a rival, playing fair with him. 'Yes?' Perhaps he could encourage Faith to prefer the office Tom rather than the cupboard Farquhar?

'Well, lately, he seems to have been avoiding me. He's got some very odd mood changes.'

'Perhaps he likes you but is clumsy in the way that he shows it?'

'Are you suggesting he's shy? He doesn't strike me as that shy. At the wedding, he couldn't have been more extroverted.'

Tricky, Tom thought. 'Maybe it's because he wasn't so concerned about what the guests thought of him. But he worries what you think of him?'

'I doubt that. He was strange when I first met him. As for his terrible dancing…'

'Perhaps he's never danced with a woman before?' Tom was hoping to nudge her onto the right track.

'Impossible,' Faith said. 'A man looking like him and with his physique…'

'Looking like what?' What did he look like to Faith?

'You must know if you've seen him.'

'Men's perspectives are different to women's.'

'Well, he's probably one of the most attractive men I've met—handsome, broad-chested and has very strong-looking arms. He's bound to have had loads of women after him.' She was silent for a while and then added, 'Sorry. That's probably not what you'd like to hear.'

She was wrong, of course. He was very pleased to hear how attractive she thought him. 'No need to apologise. Anyway, I've been told that I'm rather like that, and I haven't had loads of women after me.'

Faith laughed. 'You explained your situation, being away from civilisation, looking after sheep. He's a photographer, for heaven's sake.'

'My experience in life tells me that one should always look below the surface and never be too quick to judge.'

'Are you some kind of guru? Spouting wise stuff? Why do you stick up for him?'

He'd gone too far. 'I'm sorry. It's just that...'

'Yes?'

'People have been too quick to judge me and misunderstandings happen that are hard to put right.'

'But,' Faith said, 'you're sticking up for a man you don't know. I thought you'd sympathise with me. But you've taken his side *again.*'

He sensed her stand up so he scrambled to his feet. Faith brushed past and soon left—and he still didn't know why Officers Large and Small had become involved with Faith and Judith.

# 41

'This is very nice of you,' Faith said after she and Hope were seated in Judith's plush living room: heavy brocade curtains, traditional furniture, plump cushions and a deep pile carpet. There was a strong smell of beeswax as though the furniture had been polished in her and Hope's honour.

Judith smiled kindly. 'It makes a change to have people around. It gets lonely here all day with just Miranda to talk to, and she's often busy.'

'Don't you have any family?' Hope asked.

'I have a son, but he's not around much. Malakai's a law unto himself. Tell me, Faith, did you get into trouble for being late the day you came here?' Judith sounded more interested than concerned.

'Yes. But I told Edison that my grandmother had fallen over, and I'd been called to see her.'

Judith gave a satisfied, smug smile. 'And he believed you?'

'Yes.'

Judith's smile broadened. 'Did you find it easy?'

'Find what easy?' Prickles of discomfort settled in her scalp, and Faith hoped she'd misunderstood the thrust of Judith's question.

'Lying? Does it come easily to you?'

Under the older woman's scrutiny, Faith could tell she'd reddened. She did not like the suggestion that she was a habitual liar. 'Actually, no. I didn't like it, and I said it as a last resort. Edison was very angry with me so I need to make sure I'm punctual in future.'

'Quite so,' Judith agreed, as though she hadn't had anything whatsoever to do with Faith's tardiness the last time.

Miranda entered with a tea tray. Judith urged Faith and Hope to help themselves from the biscuits laid out ready on the coffee table.

Hope was the first to reach out. 'These are yummy!' She coaxed stray crumbs into her mouth.

'Miranda's handiwork,' Judith said, without any hint of pride in her employee's skill.

'Try one, Faith,' Hope said. 'They're lovely. I'd buy these if they were in a supermarket.'

Miranda glowed from the praise.

Faith bit into a biscuit. 'Mm. They are good. Hey, the boys would love these.'

Judith's posture stiffened. 'Boys?'

'Friends of ours,' Faith said.

'Boyfriends?' Judith was so snappy, it was like taking tea with a crocodile.

Was this the same woman who'd smiled so benignly after their arrival?

Miranda gave a small cough.

Judith looked up at Miranda and then back at Faith and Hope. Her expression broke into a warm smile. 'You two look too young to be having boyfriends.'

'We're in our twenties,' Hope said. 'And Luke and Gavin aren't boyfriends. They're a couple.'

The shocked look on Judith's face stopped Hope dead.

Miranda gave another cough, and Judith said, 'How interesting. I've never had gay men as friends. A bit like having female company, is it?'

'No... not really,' Faith said.

'It's like having very safe male friends,' Hope said. 'You know, men you can have a laugh with yet know that they aren't going to want to pounce on you.'

'I'm not sure,' Faith said, in what she trusted Hope would recognise as a warning tone, 'that Judith appreciates—'

'Oh, don't mind me,' Judith purred. 'I'm an old fuddy-duddy. I do apologise for coming across as disapproving.'

Miranda asked how they would like their tea and busied herself pouring it out.

'Tell me about these two lads.' Judith was watching them with an expectant beam.

'Well,' Hope began, 'Gavin's a funeral director. It was through him that we managed to get hold of the hearse and the casket for me to lie in.'

Judith nodded understandingly. 'Which company does he work for? I've been considering getting one of those funeral plans.'

'Boxten—'

'Boxed In?' Judith pulled a sour expression. 'That's not a very tactful name.'

'Box-ten,' Faith enunciated.

'Gavin's terribly conscientious. I can recommend him,' Hope said.

'And Luke's a fitness instructor,' Faith said quickly before Hope could give Gavin's work address. Judith was a tad too nosey for her liking. 'He's into healthy eating and exercise.'

'And he wants a baby,' Hope said.

This was far too much information.

'Really?' Judith's keen gaze bore into Hope.

'He wanted me to give him a baby, but I've decided against it. So, he'll just have to find another woman who wants a child and is happy to share with him.'

The clatter of crockery as Miranda missed the coffee table with Faith's cup of tea interrupted the conversation.

'I'm sorry.' Miranda bent to pick the cup and saucer up and ran out. Before long, she was back with a cloth and a towel.

As soon as Miranda had stopped fussing with the stain, Judith asked, 'How do you like working over there?' She waved a hand in the direction of Siskin House.

'I love it,' Hope said.

'I like my job too.' Faith took her new cup of tea direct from Miranda. The sooner she'd drunk it, the sooner they could leave. There was something creepy about Judith, as though there was more to her questions than a lonely, old woman passing time pleasantly with her guests. Miranda was odd too.

When Hope was given her cup of tea, Judith asked, 'What about the people who work there? Are they nice?'

Faith nodded.

'All very nice,' Hope said.

'As you two don't have boyfriends, I expect you're on the lookout for one?' Judith suggested.

Wasn't she being overly intrusive?

'There's a really handsome man on the top floor,' Hope said. 'I wouldn't mind having him as my boyfriend.'

'Oh? What's his name?'

Before Faith had any chance of kicking Hope, she blurted, 'Tom.'

There was some agenda Judith had that Faith did not understand. These weren't ordinary, casual questions. They were far too focused for that.

'Do you agree with your sister?' Judith asked Faith. 'Do you think he's handsome too?'

'Oh, Faith's not interested in him,' Hope said. 'She's left the field open for me.'

Judith appeared peeved.

Why would Judith care whether or not Faith was attracted to Tom? What had Judith got to do with the goings-on in their private lives and Siskin House?

'Did you ever work there?' Faith asked innocently to hide the fact that she was suspicious.

'No,' Judith said. 'But it's hard not to be curious when I live close by. So, tell me more about the hearse and casket.'

As soon as Faith deemed they'd stayed long enough to be polite, she suggested that they leave.

'Oh, so soon?' Judith's lips were downturned in what appeared to be disappointment.

'Yes. We must go,' Faith said. 'We've got rabbits to feed.'

# 42

'So,' Tom said to Luke and Gavin, 'How's it been?' They were all in his office again in the same places they'd taken just over two weeks ago.

'Difficult,' Luke said.

'In what way was it difficult?' Tom asked.

Luke rested an ankle across his other leg, making a large triangle. 'We had a lot to talk about.'

'It was painful,' Gavin said, 'talking about our feelings.'

Tom nodded understandingly. 'Revealing deep emotions can make you feel vulnerable.'

'That's it exactly,' Gavin said. 'Having to let your guard down, expose yourself.'

'It sounds like you managed it. That's good. Isn't it?'

Luke crossed his arms. 'It is if it moves you forward. But it feels like there's a big, gaping wound. It feels worse than it did before we came here.'

Tom nodded again. 'Without sharing your deeper feelings, there can be no moving forward. Being prepared to open yourselves up like this indicates your commitment to saving the relationship.'

'So, it's a good thing?' Gavin sounded doubtful.

'I believe so.' Tom spread an arm along the back of the sofa. Luke and Gavin appeared tense. By spreading out, Tom hoped that they would feel more relaxed and be encouraged to open out their postures too. 'Did you come to any conclusions or decisions through your talks?'

The men exchanged glances.

'I agreed to let Gavin help bath Petal,' Luke said, 'and read her a goodnight story before I read one. When we go to the park, Gavin can push Petal on the swing.'

'Yeah, but she's so used to Luke that she kept calling out she wanted him to bath her, push her on the swing and for him to read a goodnight story. I wasn't wanted. She rejected me time and again.'

Luke put his hand on Gavin's arm. 'I told her to listen to you and play nicely. It's different now.'

'You shouldn't have needed to speak to her! It's obvious she prefers you.'

'That's only natural since you've not been interested in her. How's she to understand that she's not the rejected one anymore? Because that's what you did, Gavin. You rejected her all this time!'

'I'm not now.'

'She understands that but you need to understand too that she's confused because, from her perspective, it's like you suddenly changed the agenda, there was no gradual lead-up. But it's got better, hasn't it? Instead of telling Tom all the bad stuff, why don't you say where we're at now?'

Tom intervened. 'Where are you at now, Gavin?'

Gavin glanced down at his hands. 'We... er... had Petal over on Saturday as usual. And it was better. She seemed to even like me.'

'How about you, Luke? How did it feel having Gavin more involved?'

'It was, er, hard to break the routine I'd got going with Petal. But the day went well, Petal was responding more to Gavin. When we'd both finished saying goodnight—Gavin stayed sitting on the bed while I read my story—it felt good leaving the room together. I felt...'

When Tom saw Luke's throat working emotionally, he said, 'Yes?'

'... I felt...' tears began to fall, '... like we were... a... family.' Luke broke into a sob.

Tom was gratified to see Gavin's hand cover Luke's. Tom nudged a box of tissues closer to Luke.

Gavin's chin was trembling. 'I felt it too. For the first time, I felt it too.' Tears coursed down Gavin's face, and he helped himself to tissues also.

'That's good, isn't it?' Tom said.

Luke and Gavin nodded their agreement while dabbing and blowing.

'And how has it been between you when Petal wasn't there?'

The men swapped glances again.

'Luke? How about you start.'

'Well, er...' Luke sniffed. 'It's been a bit more strained.'

'A lot more strained,' Gavin chipped in.

Luke shrugged. 'It was like we were being over-polite to each other all the time. That's not how we usually are.'

'It hasn't been usual for quite a time,' Gavin said.

'Tell me what usual means to you,' Tom said.

'Spending evenings together or with friends, going out for a meal, seeing a film. That's largely stopped since Petal's been coming round so much. And Luke's been keeping secrets. I don't understand why he didn't tell me he's been giving Hope all these massages.'

'Hope?' Tom asked. 'Hope from Reception?'

'Do you know everyone in our circle?' Luke asked.

'I wouldn't have thought so.'

'And then,' Gavin said, 'he asked Hope to have a baby with him.'

'Which she subsequently turned down,' Luke said. 'Got a rabbit instead.'

'It sounds as though there is resentment between

the two of you over these things,' Tom said.

'We're partners,' Gavin moaned. 'We're not meant to have secrets.'

'Helping Hope to build up stamina,' Luke defended, 'and help relieve her muscular pain was her secret, not mine. She didn't want Faith to know.'

'You could have trusted me to keep the secret,' Gavin said.

Tom was intrigued. 'Why didn't Hope want Faith to know?'

'Because,' Luke said, clearly irate, 'Faith might have flipped at Hope's plans to work. It's been genuinely hard on her taking care of Hope, especially when she relapsed a couple of years ago. Faith was the one who had to pick up the pieces. My input was to help prevent the possibility of deterioration while getting Hope to improve her tolerance for physical activity.'

Hearing about Faith caring for Hope just raised her another ten notches in Tom's estimation. First her mum and then her sister. Faith must have sacrificed so much...

'You weren't meant to say anything about Hope,' Gavin said. 'It's a secret that she's not well.'

'You brought her up as one of your grievances,' Luke said.

'Okay,' Tom said. 'So some awkward things are going on here. This would be an interesting time to explore how you each deal with differences of opinion—your arguing styles, if you like.'

After a ten-minute discussion on the subject, and a five-minute role play re-enacting the time Gavin had found out about Luke giving Hope massages, Tom said, 'The role play was a way to demonstrate the possibility of doing things differently. If you don't change what you do, you can't expect anything different to what you've been getting, can you? Whereas if you change something, that induces further change.'

'I get your point,' Luke said. 'But we're not going to transform overnight.'

'No way,' Gavin agreed.

'It's not meant to be a quick fix. It's showing you possible ways of moving forward. For next time, I'd like you both to consider what things have worked well for you in the past and why you think that was. Both of you have resources within you to get through difficulties in life. The solutions are in you right now. My job is to help you find them.'

Luke stood up. 'How much do we owe you? The deal you made with Gavin wasn't meant to last forever and it wasn't meant to include free help.'

'How about another deal?' Tom suggested. 'I never wanted to charge you in the first place—I don't do counselling professionally anymore. I just wanted the custom for my photographic business—and I did rather get my arm twisted.'

'Depends what it is you want us to do for you,' Gavin said.

Tom steeled himself. 'I want you to teach me how to dance with a woman so that I won't be treading on her toes if she risks a second try with me.' He was relieved they hadn't sniggered or smirked.

'We're talking about Faith here?' Luke asked. 'Didn't you think there was a slight chance you were related?'

'It turns out it was a complete misunderstanding.'

Luke grinned. 'Are you thinking of Perdita's garden party? You know there'll be a band.'

Tom nodded again.

Luke slapped Tom on the back of his shoulder. 'I'm your man.'

Gavin slapped Tom on the other shoulder. 'And I'm your chaperone.'

# 43

It had been another two weeks since Tom had last met Luke and Gavin in his office and the weather had become noticeably warmer.

'So, how's it been?' Tom asked once Luke and Gavin were settled opposite him, where they could all enjoy the slight breeze from the open window, with scents from someone's freshly mown grass wafting in.

Luke cleared his throat. 'We've been more considerate of each other's feelings.'

'And I've tried to understand how Luke feels about children,' Gavin said, 'rather than concentrate on how it affects me. You know, thinking that I was enough for Luke and then finding out after Petal was born that I wasn't.'

Luke placed his hand on Gavin's thigh. 'You are plenty enough for me in the partner line. It's just that there's another part of me that needs something else as well—something you can't give me. It's not a slight on you.'

'I understand now,' Gavin said.

'How has this understanding come about?' Tom asked.

Gavin gave Luke a shy smile. 'I was on my own with Petal on Saturday for an hour while Luke popped out. She was more responsive than she's ever been towards me. Probably because Luke wasn't there. I was scared I'd do something wrong, that she would cry, and I wouldn't be able to stop her. But she loved it. We've got this Fuzzy-Felt game where you can stick pieces onto a special board. She sat next to me while she was doing it and kept looking up at me to see what I thought of her picture. I felt a bit like I imagine a dad does.'

'Whose idea was it for Luke to go out so that you could have alone time with Petal?'

'Mine,' Luke said.

Surprised, Tom asked. 'How did you feel about pulling back?'

'It was hard. But I can see that I was selfish wanting Petal all to myself. As it turned out, I was excited about returning when the hour was up. It felt good coming home to Gavin and Petal... That family feeling again.'

'It seems,' Tom said, 'that you have both learned quite a lot since I saw you last. That's great.' The men nodded, and then Tom addressed Luke. 'If you remember, last time, I asked you to think about things that had worked well in the past. Gavin said that he's felt threatened by Petal's presence—what do you think would help Gavin feel more secure in your relationship?'

Luke's eyes rolled upwards and he bit his lower lip. 'I think,' he said slowly, 'I should pay Gavin more attention. As we don't go out on Saturdays anymore, we could have another night that's our night. We could also do stuff on Sundays, after Petal's back with Perdita.'

Tom caught Gavin's gaze. 'What do you think about Luke's ideas?'

Gavin nodded his agreement. 'They're good.'

'There's something else I would like you to think about,' Tom said. 'When you're a couple, you can lose sight of who you are as an individual—your personal identity. Is there anything you used to do—a hobby, for example—that's been pushed aside because of the relationship?'

Luke looked down, up, across, anywhere in fact but at Gavin.

'Go on, say it,' Gavin said. 'You gave it up to spend more time with me.'

Grudgingly, Luke admitted, 'Five-a-side football.'

'And what about you, Gavin? Is there anything you don't do anymore?'

'I used to go to flower-arranging classes, and I occasionally helped out at a local church, teaching the volunteer parishioners how to do the flowers.'

'Do you think you both might be happier if, as well as having special together time, you also have special time apart? Do you think that if you do one thing for yourselves each week, it could bring freshness back into the relationship? And with those special dates Luke mentioned earlier...' Tom left the sentence hanging and waited.

'Yeah,' Luke said, sounding surprised. 'I think it would.'

Gavin brightened. 'We'll try it.'

After ending the session, Tom clapped his hands to help dispel the serious atmosphere. 'So, did you get suitable tracks for teaching me to dance?'

Luke fished out his mobile. 'The playlist's on here. The sound's pretty good so I don't think we need additional speakers.'

'As I'm the official chaperone,' Gavin said, 'there's an adaptation I want to make.'

'Oh?' Luke said.

Gavin picked up a cushion from the sofa and undid his tie.

For a moment, Tom was worried that this was going to get weird. But when he saw Gavin strap the cushion to Luke's pelvis, he understood. Gavin was jealous at the thought that Luke might become aroused. He didn't want to chance Luke's and Tom's pelvises brushing against each other. Having a pelvis guard would make things less awkward. Luke was clearly up for the cushion idea so Tom grinned at Gavin when the job was done.

Lately, Faith had been spending lunch breaks chatting to Tom in the kitchenette. After all, the man in the cupboard was nowhere to be found. Not even in the cupboard.

Faith had discovered that Tom's parents had been divorced. His Irish Catholic dad had gone back to his roots after the split to run a pub and guesthouse in Kerry, in the west of Ireland, where Tom had spent his summer holidays.

'What did you do in Kerry?' she'd asked.

'I learned to ride a horse. We went pony trekking. Dad put me to work doing lots of washing up in the kitchens of the pub and guesthouse. And I cleaned and changed beds... And my aunt took me to church.'

Faith pulled a face. 'We had to go to church too.'

'You didn't like it?'

Faith shook her head. 'Boring.'

Tom rubbed his chin. 'I rather liked it. In fact, I got baptised there.'

'How come you'd not been baptised before? I was baptised as a baby.'

'It was one of the things that my parents argued over. So Dad said he'd put it to me when I was old enough to choose. I was ten. My mother was furious when she found out.'

'Isn't she baptised?'

'No.'

'Oh. Did she forgive you?' Faith asked this playfully, thinking it a small thing, nothing out of the ordinary for someone in the UK, with an Irish Catholic parent, to get baptised. But there was sadness in Tom's eyes when he replied.

'No, she didn't. I'm not sure she ever will. She's not the forgiving type; even when Dad was dying and asked to see her, she wouldn't go with me. I've seen her as little as possible ever since. Well, even before that. She's a hard woman and even harder to please.'

As Faith devoured a bacon roll, she asked, 'How come you didn't move to Ireland permanently as you liked it so much?'

Tom shrugged. 'I've got a life here as well. I still go back for my holidays. Always have done. I think you'd like Ireland.' His intense look made her heartbeat rise and that made her feel guilty as she couldn't help thinking she was betraying Hope.

Now, Faith was in the kitchenette again and was disappointed not to find Tom. Feeling bold, she grabbed her coffee, juice and sandwiches and made for his office. She could be friends with the guy, couldn't she? It was difficult not to be when they worked on the same level. So far, she'd never seen Tom show the slightest interest in Hope.

It was difficult to get a good rap on Tom's door as her hands were full. But, with her elbow, she managed to press down on the lever of the handle and shoulder the door open.

The Commodores, singing *Three Times a Lady*, hit her ears. But that was nothing compared to the visual jolt that bulldozed her. Tom was smooching with Luke, their arms around each other, and Gavin was watching. Very peculiarly, Luke had a cushion tied to his pelvis.

Had she just walked into a kinky threesome?

Faith tried to back out but, at that moment, Luke and Tom's dancing rotated them such that she was in Tom's line of sight. He let go of Luke and stepped away.

'Faith!' Tom flushed.

She tried to get out but couldn't with her hands so

full.

'Faith!' Luke and Gavin were gawping at her.

'It's not what it looks like. Let me explain,' Tom pleaded.

'I've seen enough. I don't need any explanation.'

Luke's commanding voice stopped her from struggling with the door handle. 'I was teaching Tom to dance. So he doesn't stand on your toes next time.'

*Next time?* What made any of them think there would be a next time?

'It's true,' Tom said. 'You're the first woman I've ever danced with. I need practice. I don't want to mess it up again.'

Faith stared. 'I don't believe you.' She wasn't going to fall for another man's lies. She liked Tom but perhaps he swung the other way? And what about Hope? She'd got her sights on him needlessly.

'We believe him, Faith,' Luke said.

Gavin nodded. 'Pure as the driven snow—whatever that means.'

'It means—' Luke began, but got interrupted by Faith.

'You must think I'm a numpty.' How could two thirty-something-year-old men on this floor be virgins?

'I've been saving myself.' Tom sounded desperate.

'Oh yeah?'

'For the right woman and you—'

How could that be true? She decided to sacrifice her coffee. She could always make another one. Placing it on the floor by the door freed her right hand so that she could escape.

Wait till she told Farquhar about all this.

# 44

It was uncanny how the man in the cupboard—Faith had used the title for too long to surrender it entirely—appeared in the cupboard at times when she needed someone to confide in. Someone she could trust. Although, remembering the last time, could she trust him? He had sided with Tom at every opportunity.

'Hi,' she whispered as she opened the door at the end of the day.

'Hi,' he whispered back. 'Have my seat. I'll sit on the floor.'

'Thanks.' Faith found the upturned bucket. 'I'm sorry that I got angry the last time I was here.'

'That's all right. I understand.'

'Do you?'

'Yes. Think no more about it. You wanted my support, and I didn't give it. I'm sorry.'

His gracious apology did much to restore him to her good books. 'You know, you're not here very much. I do look for you.'

'You're right, I'm not. That's... something I want to talk to you about.'

'Oh?'

She got the impression that it was difficult for him to reveal what was on his mind, since it seemed an age before he began to whisper again. 'When you start down a path, you think it's easy to find your way back. But I don't know how to go back and put things right without making everything so much worse.' His words were steeped in apology.

But why? What had he done? 'What things?' Faith deliberately filled her voice with sympathy, to help him feel safe opening up to her.

There was another long stretch of silence. Eventually, he said, 'I'm leaving. This will be my last time in here.'

The shock that hit her was similar to the one she'd experienced when her TV blew up. She didn't know what to say, what to admit to.

'Did you hear what I said?'

'Yes,' she whispered faintly, bereft, barely gathering the breath to make the sound. 'Why?'

'I've messed up, and by my leaving, I can undo some of the mess.'

'What do you mean? I don't understand.' What would she do without him? Without the hope of seeing him again?

'I promise you that one day, you will understand.'

'Have I done something?'

'It's not you, it's me.'

Ha! As if she believed that line. 'It is me, isn't it? You're going away because of me.'

'I'm going away as it's the right thing to do.' His words were spoken slowly as if he'd chosen them carefully to conceal the problem. It piqued her at the same time as filling her with sorrow.

'I don't have to come in here, to bother you.' Her fingers interlocked, pressing them tightly as she did her best to keep her voice even.

'You don't bother me. I like it in here with you.' The warmth in his tone touched her heart.

'Then why...?'

'I have to leave.' Now his tone was resolute.

'What about your job?'

'Taken care of.' Dismissive.

'This is goodbye?' She did her best to hide her panic.

'Yes.' Firm, unchangeable.

'Oh, and that's it, is it?' She couldn't help the miffed, peevish ring to her sharp whisper.

'Yes. I'm sorry.'

'... How about... a goodbye kiss?'

'Do you think that's a good idea in the light of my having to go away?'

Was he hoping she'd press for a kiss? 'Would you like to kiss me?'

'I'd love to kiss you. If that's what you want.'

Boldly, brazenly, Faith took to her feet and reached out her hands. He was standing exactly where she expected him to be. This time, he didn't need any help in finding her mouth, and there was the added bonus of there being no prickles. She detected the scent of soap that was provided for the Siskin House wash basins. Had he washed his face here? Was he so poor that he couldn't afford his own toiletries?

They repeated the gentle kisses of the first time in the cupboard together but now an intense surge of need made her sick with longing. His hands strayed from around her back to her sides and brushed the edge of her breasts—and her hands strayed and rested on the curve of his buttocks, pulling him into her.

Coming up for air, Faith said, 'You don't need any more practice. I think you're fully qualified as it is.'

'I take it you enjoyed it as much as I did?' His voice was husky and breathless.

'I think I need to jump into a pool of cool water.'

'I think I need to join you.' He caressed her face. Then he grazed his lips against her neck and it was too much. Faith had to pull away or she'd be at the buckle of his belt.

She sat down.

'Are you all right?'

'Yes. Just need to take stock. I don't think kissing's safe anymore.'

'I agree. Far too scrumptious.'

'Best to concentrate on something else.' Faith closed her eyes, trying to calm her ragged breathing and stop her hands from shaking. She'd found someone and was going to lose him before getting to know him properly.

He cleared his throat. 'I agree. Tell me what's been going on.' His tone was more neutral now.

'Today, an odd thing happened.'

'Yes?'

'Well, I went into Tom's office and Luke and Gavin—a gay couple I'm friends with—were there. Luke was dancing up close to Tom to *Three Times a Lady*.'

'You're worried that Tom's gay?'

'Well, he was dancing with a man. Up close.'

'Did he give a reason?'

'He said Luke was teaching him how to dance so that Tom didn't step on my toes again—like he did when we danced at the wedding I helped him out with.'

'So, what's the problem? You do like him, don't you?' There was a hopeful note to the question and it seemed out of place.

Faith's eyebrows puckered. 'It sounds as though you want me to like him.'

'Does it? I just like things to be fair. Give someone a fair hearing, a fair chance...'

'What is it with you and Tom? Do you know him?'

'I've met him. He seems like a decent bloke.'

'But he's a photographer. He must be used to women. How come he can't dance? And how can he not have had any experience with women? A man his age? I ask you!'

'I'm a virgin.' Farquhar sounded embarrassed.

Wanting to reassure him that she'd not got a problem with *him* not being experienced, she said, 'But you've explained that.'

'Have you asked Tom?'

'No. It was Luke who told me that Tom's a virgin. Luke and Gavin have clearly been taken in by him. But honestly, it can't be true.'

'Isn't Tom a... sacramental photographer?'

'Yes. He takes photos of ceremonies.'

'Well, you know... I've thought of a possible explanation of why he's not had much experience with women.'

'What's that?'

'Do you think, by any chance... he could be... or has been... a Catholic... priest?'

Faith burst out laughing.

# 45

That evening, just after Faith and Hope had finished their cheesy Bolognese, the doorbell rang.

'The boys are here,' Luke and Gavin said when she opened the door.

*As if she couldn't see that...*

Luke added, 'We need to sort this out.'

'I'm not sure I want to talk to either of you at the moment.'

'That's not an option.' Luke barged past and Gavin followed.

'Why are you being like this?'

'What's going on? Has something happened?' Hope edged around the dining table to join them.

'It's about Tom,' Luke said. 'There's been a misunderstanding, and we're here to clear it up.'

'Tom? Has Faith been unkind to him?' There was indignation in Hope's tone as she turned accusing eyes towards Faith.

'I caught him slow-dancing with Luke in his office while Gavin looked on—it looked like a cosy threesome.'

'Tom's gay?' Hope's shoulders fell inwards.

'Shall we sit down to discuss it?' Luke gestured to the sofa. 'Faith knows damn well that Tom is not gay.'

Faith folded her arms. 'I think you should leave. I don't want to hear any more ridiculous stories about Tom.' She'd been duped before but not again, and she was not going to take Luke's word when she'd not heard it from the man himself.

'What ridiculous stories?' Hope asked sharply.

Luke regarded Faith with a frosty expression. 'I want you to remember what you just said. Don't blame me when you find out it's all true as you don't want to listen.' He motioned to Gavin to follow him.

'Will someone tell me what's going on?' Hope demanded.

'Tom is mad about Faith, but she's too dumb to see it,' Gavin said.

'Faith? He likes *Faith*?'

'Does the sun rise in the west every morning?' Gavin said.

'I think you mean east,' Luke said.

Faith's lips thinned. 'No, I think Gavin got it right the first time around. What I saw doesn't tie in with your version of events. But I'm glad there's no black tie around your pelvis now, Luke, holding that cushion in place. It didn't suit you.'

'What the hell is going on? I want to know! And is it true that Tom likes Faith?'

The boys turned to stare at Hope. Then three pairs of eyes fixed on Faith.

'I think we'd better let your sister explain,' Luke said. 'I'm sorry, Hope.' The boys walked towards the hallway.

'No! I want to know now, and you can tell me since Faith has failed to do so.'

'Then stay calm and we'll all sit down,' Faith said.

When they were all seated, Hope said, 'Let's be hearing it then.'

Luke cleared his throat. 'Tom asked me to teach him how to dance so that he won't stand on Faith's toes again when they go to Perdita's party.'

Hope's head snapped towards Faith. '*Again?*'

She picked at her fingernails. 'I danced with Tom at the wedding I helped out at.'

'Why didn't you tell me? You knew I liked him.'

'Because I felt bad about it.'

'If you felt so bad about it, why dance with him at all?'

Faith dug her toes into the pile of the carpet. 'When you asked me, at the supermarket, whether I was interested, I wasn't. And I'm still not sure whether I am. Sometimes I like him and then I don't—and then I like him again. My feelings keep changing, and I'm confused.'

'What's so confusing about being honest with me?' Hope's blazing gaze made Faith feel even worse. 'You should have talked to me about it.'

'I didn't want to hurt your feelings—but I have, haven't I?'

'By not being straight with me. Why keep my hopes up for longer than necessary? Although, I suppose I knew Tom only had eyes for you ever since that day we went clothes shopping and he told me off for not being more considerate of you. He looked at you in a way he's never looked at me. And he never chats when he comes to pick up his post—he's polite but he just doesn't hang around more than he needs to. I suspect he doesn't like me because of you.'

'*Because of me?*'

'If you weren't in the picture...'

'Are you proposing to bump your sister off?' Gavin asked. 'I'm sorry and all that, but don't be a sore loser. He wants Faith. Always has.'

'What do you mean by *always*?' Hope asked.

'From their first meeting.'

'When he caught her with her top off?'

Gavin exchanged an uncertain glance with Luke and Luke replied for him, 'We're not sure of the exact day the moment struck him but take it from us, he's smitten.

Move on.'

Hope rounded on Faith. 'If you truly want him, you're welcome to him—he was clearly never mine. If you'd said you really liked him, we wouldn't have had all this upset, would we? And I... I... You should have confided in me.' Hope turned to leave and soon after, a door slammed shut.

'That was well-handled,' Luke said dryly. 'If you'd said Hope was after Tom, we'd never have pushed in.'

'You're right, I didn't handle it well. I'll apologise to Hope when she's had a chance to calm down.'

'Do you believe now that Tom only has eyes for you? Not us, not Hope, but you and only you?' Gavin said.

'*Only me,*' Faith whispered. 'I didn't know.'

'And do you,' Luke said, 'like Tom back?'

*Did she?* 'I'm not sure. The last time with the man in the cupboard... it was so nice. But the more time I spend with Tom, the more the memories of Farquhar...'

'Farquhar?' Gavin said, and he and Luke exchanged glances and burst into laughter.

'He's... called... Farquhar?' Luke tried but failed to smother his amusement. He and Gavin dissolved into another bout of laughter.

'It's rude to make fun of someone's name!'

'Sorry.' Luke tittered.

'Yes, sorry,' Gavin said and renewed his laughter.

Sobering, Luke said, 'I'm sorry we rudely interrupted you. Please carry on.'

At first, Faith was unsure whether she could remember the thread of the conversation but then managed to pick it up. 'My feelings for... the man in the cupboard blur and the feelings I had for him seem to get mixed up with my feelings for Tom. Even when I think of Farquhar—'

The boys bellowed with laughter, bending over their

laps.

'Are you going to let me finish what I want to say or are you going to act like silly children the rest of the evening?'

Luke cleared his throat. 'Please, carry on.'

'Well,' Faith said, 'I find that I'm putting Tom's face onto Farquhar's imagined body—' Faith broke off to give time for the boys to stop their sniggering, 'and although Tom is a bit weird at times, at other times, he's brilliant. I'm up and down like a yo-yo and don't know where I am.'

'Forget... Farquhar,' Luke advised, another chuckle escaping his lips.

'I'll have to. He said he's leaving. So I probably won't see him again.'

'As he's out of the picture,' Luke said, 'it's definite you won't do better than Tom if you want a decent husband. He'd never cheat on you.'

'Husband? That's a bit premature. And the man in the cupboard said he'd never cheat on me.'

'He's gone,' Gavin said. 'A man in the hand is worth more than a man in the cupboard.'

Luke smiled. 'Although you didn't get the saying quite right, I agree with the sentiment. And Faith, we both recommend Tom. We have good instincts for men, remember? And your taste in Andy was definitely flawed. Think of the guy in the cupboard as a bad rebound relationship thing and forget about him.'

The boys plumping for Tom was all very well, but they didn't have the dilemma of experiencing butterflies every time she thought of either Farquhar or Tom. How could she like two men at the same time?

If only she could eliminate Farquhar's unexplained absence and annoying support for Tom while retaining his empathy, tenderness and affection. And if only she could eliminate Tom's aptitude for hiding the charm and charisma she'd glimpsed at the wedding while hanging on to his handsome face, skill as a photographer and availability. And if what she'd valued of Farquhar and Tom were merged, well, then she might have the perfect partner.

# 46

Faith spent a disturbed night, wrestling with complicated feelings for both Tom and Farquhar. In the morning, without having reached any conclusion as to which man she preferred, she decided to clear the air with Tom about his dancing with Luke. There was an hour to spare before she had to be at her desk. So, before she even got herself a cup of coffee, she knocked on Tom's door.

His deep timbre gave her permission to enter. Through the widening gap, she saw that the casement window was flung wide open. When she'd been getting in and out of the hearse, she'd never thought to look up. Had Tom been watching?

When he caught sight of her, he sprang out of his chair like a jack in the box. 'Faith!' He was wearing camel chinos and a white shirt. Her heartbeat strengthened.

'Can we have a chat?'

'Of course, take a pew.'

She settled on the sofa, crossing her legs and allowing a high-heeled shoe to swing from her toes. It helped to dampen her nervous energy. Tom sat opposite.

'How nice to see you.' His tone lacked conviction and his face resembled a ripe Braeburn apple. His gaze dropped to her swinging shoe. Was he too embarrassed to look her in the eye?

'The boys confirmed last night that they were teaching you how to dance. I feel embarrassed about the conclusion I came to, and I apologise.'

'*Boys?* Luke and Gavin? Is that what everyone calls them?'

She detected hurt in his tone. Was he feeling he'd been left out of their friendship group? 'Yes.'

'That's... a relief. It troubled me to think that you believed...'

'Well, I don't anymore. At the time...'

'I understand. Thank you for telling me.' Tom cleared his throat and then cleared it some more. 'I... don't want to break your toes if you are brave enough to accept another turnabout on the dance floor with me. Would you...? Do you think...? If I were to ask you...?'

'I'll risk it,' Faith said. If she could tell Farquhar about having feelings for Tom, surely, she should tell Tom about having feelings for Farquhar? 'But I have met someone else—although he's gone away. I... thought you should know.' Faith expected Tom to look crestfallen if what the boys had told her about him being mad about her was true. But he took it in his stride with barely a flicker of acknowledgement in his eyes.

'You're so attractive, that doesn't surprise me.'

She was just about to inform him that the man she'd referred to had never actually seen her, but she managed to curb her tongue in time. 'My ex-boyfriend was not so taken with my appearance that it stopped him from straying.'

'How come he... strayed?'

She inhaled deeply a couple of times. 'He said he didn't like the amount of time I spent with Hope. I just tried to include her as I didn't want her to be on her own.'

'Because she's not well?'

Faith jerked her head up and stared at Tom and then at the window.

'The scooter had been for her, hadn't it? And in the

shop, Hope said that she was the disabled one.'

'It's a secret.'

'Don't worry, I'm used to keeping secrets. Does the hearse outside have something to do with it?'

Faith gulped. 'You noticed?'

'A bit difficult not to,' he said apologetically. 'It is somewhat conspicuous, and I've seen you drive it... But I didn't like to mention it as we all have things we want to keep private, and I'd hoped you'd tell me about it.'

She wished now that she'd trusted him like she'd trusted Farquhar—but Tom wouldn't know she'd told the man in the cupboard and now he wouldn't find out. 'Sorry—I wanted to explain the situation to you properly but it wasn't for me to say. Do you think anyone else has noticed the hearse? The offices below yours have the same aspect.'

Tom smiled. 'I don't think you need to worry there. The therapist on the ground floor has the blinds permanently shut for privacy, and Saul's rival legal firm has filing cabinets along that wall, including in front of the window. I know because I went in to introduce myself and hand out business cards.'

'Well, that's a relief. But it won't be long before word gets out. With luck, Hope would have proved her worth by that time and it shouldn't matter.'

'The hearse is for Hope, isn't it?'

'There's a casket in the back so that she can rest between shifts and while she is waiting for me at the end of the day. It's very comfortable. I tried it out one lunchtime as I had a migraine. But the old lady opposite got anxious and called the police. It was a close shave as I thought Hope's poor health was going to be exposed. But everybody was understanding in the end.'

'Ah.' Tom grinned and leaned back as though relieved, which was strange considering Faith had said that the woman opposite had called the police. *Shouldn't he have shown some concern?* 'What did you make of the old lady?' Tom's finger rubbed his upper lip.

'A bit weird,' Faith said. To her surprise, he nodded. 'Why did you just nod? Do you know her?'

'I... I've seen her and... I thought she looked weird too.'

As Faith was leaving, Tom said, 'You know, it's been nice meeting up before work. We could have coffee together before the daily grind if you like... When you're not busy.'

Why not? She'd enjoyed their time together too. 'Okay. Your place or mine?' She'd meant it as a joke but then realised he might interpret it incorrectly. But, with the speed of a ball bouncing back from the wall, his reply was ready.

'Mine.' He must have sensed her surprise as he added, 'I've got sofas.' Then he seemed to have trouble with his reply as though realising the implication of what he'd said and added, 'What I mean is, we'll be more comfortable here.' Tom's mouth worked silently and then he added, 'What I mean is, your office doesn't have any comfortable chairs.'

'And we're less likely to be disturbed here?' she teased.

'Er... that, too.' He stared at the floor. 'What I mean is...'

Faith chuckled. 'I know what you mean, it's okay.' He was like a flustered teenager, and she understood what the boys were trying to tell her. She believed he was, like Farquhar, totally inexperienced with women. She forgave Tom for staring at her breasts when she'd been scrubbing out the stain on her shirt.

She hadn't minded Farquhar's innocence, and she found now that she didn't mind it about Tom. In fact, it had become an endearing trait considering she'd been put off the likes of Andy, who'd had a bit too much experience. The boys were right, Tom was not likely to cheat on a woman and something inside her softened, close to the point of melting.

# 47

It was a balmy July evening, perfect for Perdita's garden party, and Tom had been commissioned to take photographs. After taking shots of Saul, Perdita and Petal in the garden, he went to stand at the front of the house to capture the guests as they arrived. One of the first was... no... how the hell?

'Mum. What are you doing here?' Tom's tongue had trouble forming the words as he took in the makeup and the heavy gold chain, earrings, rings and bracelet Judith always wore when she'd been invited to a social gathering. How had she managed to inveigle her way into his social arena? He glanced at Miranda for a clue, but she just smiled.

Judith was pushing her rollator towards him, struggling with the gravel and her medium-height brown shoes, before she said, in a superior tone, 'Do you think you have a monopoly on the area and the people in it? It's strange since you haven't seen fit to bother with either for years. Oh, I see,' she said, glancing at his photographic gear. 'You're here on a job. Well, I hope you're charging the going rate.'

Why had they invented foldable rollators for cars? 'They're friends. Of course I'm not charging the going rate.'

'Can you afford to have friends, if they squeeze you dry?'

'I hope I will always afford to have friends. You should try it.'

'I have friends, otherwise I wouldn't be here.'

*Really?* Then he recalled Judith informing him that she'd recently updated her Will. He bet Saul had been given that privilege. Because of Tom's connection with Saul, he'd probably thought it kind to extend his hospitality to include Judith and Miranda.

'Are you here because they are friends or because Saul is a business acquaintance?' Tom challenged. The pursed, twisted lips showed him he'd scored.

'Since we are on the subject of friends, you will certainly have to make new ones now that you're not allowed near your old ones anymore.'

Miranda gave him a sympathetic smile—which he returned tentatively while trying to avoid gawping at her unusually tasteful outfit. Was it for the benefit of single men on the invitation list? Whatever effort she'd put in, time and expense had been worth the elegant cream ensemble.

'Can you keep quiet about my past?' Tom glanced between the two of them.

'Do you think your previous career is something I would like to publicise?' Judith said.

His muscles relaxed. It was time he got Judith and Miranda to move on. 'If you go around to the left, you will get to the garden.'

Soon, he was involved with snapping other guests. Many he didn't know—including a nun and a priest he decided to take pains to avoid getting into a conversation with as there was a risk of him being rumbled. Those he did know included Edison, Luke, Gavin, Hope and Faith. Below the hem of her floral strappy dress, Tom could see Faith's beautifully shaped calves and slim ankles, and wished he could see more of her.

Tom's shiny, grey suit rekindled Faith's memories of when she'd helped at that wedding—and her sore toes.

Had it been a rash move to wear open-toed sandals this evening? Had the boys done a good job at teaching Tom to be more like a dainty flamingo than a clodhopping dinosaur?

At the wedding, she'd been unable to fully appreciate being held by Tom as she'd barely known him, and her thoughts had kept fluttering to the man in the cupboard—when they weren't distracted by the pain in her feet from Tom's clumsiness. But now that she did know Tom, and the man in the cupboard had truly disappeared, she couldn't wait to feel his embrace again. Perhaps it was because she'd mentioned his rival to him that he hadn't made any move at all towards her outside of friendliness. Tonight, she hoped that would change. Anticipation sizzled inside her.

'How are you doing?'

Faith turned to see Luke was standing next to her. 'Fine. You?'

'Great.' Luke nodded towards Tom. 'Where are you at with Tom?'

Faith stiffened. 'What do you mean?'

'Have you discovered his positive points yet and developed feelings for him rather than for the man in the cupboard?'

'Tom has grown on me,' she admitted, not wanting to divulge by how much. She dreamed of him often, and he was the first thing she thought of when she woke up. Then she would imagine how it would be, kissing him, having him hold her, make love even. 'Ask me again after tonight.'

Luke's jaw dropped. 'You're not going to pop his cherry, are you?'

Faith thumped Luke's arm. 'That's not what I meant. I was talking about Tom's intention to ask me to dance. He still plans to do that, doesn't he?' But if tonight led to more... she wouldn't complain. His reserve during their regular chats had made her want him perhaps more than if he'd been flirting with her the whole time. Maybe tonight, he would want her too...

'Oh, he plans to ask you to dance all right.' Luke's grin was wide.

Shivers went up and down Faith's legs and settled in her stomach. 'Do you think he'll kiss me as well?'

'Is the Pope Catholic?' Luke said.

'Is that what he told you?' Did Tom share everything with the boys?

'No. It's what I've intuited. Remember, I'm good at reading men. I don't think after waiting so long, Tom could possibly hold out any longer—especially after a couple of slow dances. I bet you won't be able to either.'

Faith wondered what Tom's place looked like. Would he take her there tonight? The boys could take Hope home... 'You and Gavin haven't been making bets, have you?' Faith asked, aghast.

'No point. We're on the same page here.'

'Mmph.' Faith surveyed the lawn and what she could see of the inside of the marquee. 'Perdita and Saul have splashed out a bit, haven't they?'

'They didn't have a big do after the wedding. Maybe they're making up for it now.'

'Mm.' Faith's gaze sharpened. 'Hey, what's that old woman doing here?'

'Who?'

'Judith. The old woman with a mobility aid sitting inside the marquee talking to Hope. There's another woman with Judith who's her helper. Miranda.'

'How do you know them?'

'Judith called the police when I was lying in the casket, trying to get rid of a migraine one lunch hour—she said having the hearse parked opposite her house scared her. I went in to explain but the whole thing made me late for work, and Edison had already had a go at me for another time I was late. I didn't want to lose my job. She suggested I told him I was with my grandmother who'd had a fall. I'd have preferred to have told him the truth but then he'd know about the hearse and Hope's poor health. Judith even invited Hope and me for tea once. But she's a bit strange—in a creepy way.'

'I think we'd better rescue Hope then.'

As Faith marched with Luke towards Judith, Edison and Tom joined them. Their paths converged in front of her. Edison was looking amazing in a white jacket.

'Lovely party,' Judith said politely.

'Yes. It is. How are you?' Faith asked flatly.

'Mustn't grumble,' Judith replied. 'Now, are you going to introduce me?'

'Oh, yes. This is Luke, a friend. Tom—who works on my floor—as you can see, he's a photographer. And Edison, my boss.' Faith pointed to each of the men in turn as Luke shook Judith's hand first. 'And this is...?' Faith floundered, unsure of how to introduce Judith. Her gaze met Judith's eyes and there was a hint of a smile. *How should she refer to Judith?*

'I'm her grandmother,' Judith said, deciding the matter for Faith. 'So pleased to meet you. I'm sorry I made Faith late for work. My health...'

Luke gave Faith a hard look, and she knew he disapproved of her lying to Edison and allowing that lie to get bigger. He was right, of course; the situation had become more difficult. And now Tom would think that Judith was related too, and he'd wonder why Faith had never mentioned her.

Edison took Judith's hand. 'It's a pleasure to meet you. I understand there had been a crisis.'

Tom, however, seemed to hesitate before proffering

his hand to Judith. For some reason, Judith laughed as she shook it, and Tom appeared discomfited. Had he detected strange vibes too?

Faith noticed Hope catch Edison's gaze. 'I'm Hope. Remember me from the desk?'

'How could I forget?'

Edison's gaze was appreciative—Hope was looking delectable in a knee-length red chiffon dress, lined for respectability's sake. Her hair, made extra curly for the occasion, tumbled down one side. Faith had made up Hope's eyes to give them smoky appearance.

'I'm Faith's sister.' Hope was simpering again like she had with Tom weeks previously.

Edison's smile crinkled his eyes in a way that Faith wasn't sure she'd seen before.

'I had no idea she had a sister as beautiful as you.' He turned to Faith. 'You've kept quiet about the connection.'

Faith cringed. *Her boss and Hope...*

'Why don't you all grab chairs and join me?' Judith suggested in her spiderweb tone.

Luke excused himself to find Gavin.

'I must mingle.' Tom indicated his camera.

'Would you like an assistant again?' Faith was desperate to escape and wanted to spend time with Tom anyway.

Hope remained seated, and Edison pulled up a chair next to her.

'I'd love to have you as my assistant again.'

Tom gave her a smile that was different to his usual pleased expressions. This smile was a private, intimate sunbeam of a smile that warmed her to her core, and he held her gaze as though he was conveying a message of... promise. It made her heart flutter.

When they were out of earshot, Faith said, 'I'd hoped

to rescue Hope, but it seems she likes Judith.'

Tom mumbled something that Faith didn't catch and then abruptly stopped and turned to face her. 'May I take your photo? Here, against this tree?'

'Why?'

Tom shrugged. 'I'm here to take photos of all the guests.'

His answer disappointed her.

'But with you, I confess it's more for me than for Saul and Perdita.'

That was more like it. 'Like this?' She stood like a statue with her hands clasped in front of her.

'Could you walk away and then turn your head towards me on the count of three? There's a slight breeze and it will create movement in your hair as you turn around—and you can give me one of your lovely smiles.'

Tom counted to three and then she turned. But she felt too self-conscious to adopt a happy face.

He was staring at her, his camera by his side. 'You're very beautiful, you know.'

A shiver of something strange went through her. 'You didn't take the picture.'

'I didn't want to lose the moment through a lens— it's far removed, not so personal. We can try it again if you like, and I'll take the shot.'

Faith walked back to the starting point and then walked away again to the count of three. When she turned, she didn't smile again either. Instead, she gave him a searching look, trying to understand the tidal wave of longing that stole her breath.

'That was even better.' Tom lowered the camera. 'What were you thinking?'

'I don't know,' she said in confusion.

'Were you thinking of me? I was certainly thinking

of you. You're about all I do think about.'

Faith gulped. *Tonight, something would happen between them.*

# 48

Miranda had followed Luke across the lawn like a greyhound after a rabbit, unable to believe her luck in having met him here so easily. But it had been hard to keep up in her dress and heels. As she'd needed to nab him before he'd got talking to someone else, she'd let out a cry before falling to the ground. He'd turned. She'd stayed on the ground. He'd come over. *Bingo.*

Luke had helped her to a patio chair, explaining that he was trained in sports injuries.

Once she was seated, a man came up and placed his hand on Luke's shoulder. 'Is everything all right?'

'Fine.' Luke looked up from studying her ankle. 'This is Gavin.'

'I'm Miranda. How do you do?' Miranda gave Gavin her hand.

'Does any of this hurt?' Luke pressed different parts of her ankle and foot.

'No. It's great. Honestly, I'm fine.'

'Good.' Luke rested her foot on the ground.

He had nice hands, she noted. The other people turned away and resumed their conversations; some wandered off. Only Gavin remained.

'Gavin,' Miranda pleaded, doing her best to look vulnerable, 'could you get me a glass of water, please? I... I'm feeling a bit dizzy.'

A flicker of concern showed. 'Sure.'

Off he went. But he'd be back soon as a trestle table providing soft drinks had been set up nearby. For the moment, it was just Luke and her; her and Luke...

'There's something I'd like to say.'

Luke appeared surprised. 'It was nothing. Anyone would have—'

'Not about my foot. That was just a ruse to get your attention. To try to have a private word with you.'

Wariness flickered across Luke's expression. 'I'm gay.'

'I know.'

Luke's brow puckered, and he regarded her speculatively.

'I hear you want a baby. I do too.'

Gavin was back with her water. 'There you go.'

'Thanks.' Miranda didn't take it from him. 'Oh. Could you put some ice in it, please?'

Obligingly, Gavin went away again.

Luke sat immobile. It was a moment before he spoke and his tone adopted a rigid reserve. 'How do you know I want a baby? I haven't advertised the fact.'

'Hope mentioned it in my hearing.'

There was more silence, and then Gavin returned with the iced water.

Luke stared, studying her face.

'Thanks.' She gulped half of the drink.

'What's up?' Gavin eyed them keenly. 'What's going on?'

'I don't keep secrets from Gavin,' Luke said.

Miranda shrugged. 'Just make sure you keep it between yourselves then. I don't want my employer getting wind of it.'

'Wind of what?' Gavin folded his arms and aimed his enquiring gaze at Luke.

'We need to go somewhere private.' Luke had a hand on Gavin's arm.

Gavin shrugged the hand away. 'Private? At a party?'

'My car,' Luke suggested.

About three minutes later, Luke and Gavin were in the front of Luke's red Ford Fiesta and Miranda was in the back.

'What's this all about?' Gavin asked tetchily, twisting around in his seat to get a good look at her.

'I'm interested in having a baby. With Luke,' Miranda said.

'*Oh, how long has this been going on?*'

'I never met the woman until five minutes ago.' Luke scowled at Miranda.

'It's true.' She explained how she'd come into the picture. 'Now, I'm a healthy thirty-six-year-old who will probably never have children—unless we come to an agreement. But I would need to know an awful lot about both of you to decide whether to go ahead with the idea.'

Although Luke's face was filled with wonder, Gavin's face was filled with dread. She fished in her bag and retrieved a till receipt. She scribbled her number on it and handed it to Luke. 'Think about it. If you want to open up discussions, get in touch.' It was best, she concluded, to withdraw and let things take their course. She just hoped that Luke wouldn't keep her waiting too long.

Faith bumped into Hope coming out of the cloakroom. 'Hi... What's the hurry?'

'Edison's waiting for me. I don't want him to start chatting to someone else.'

'You own him now, do you?'

'I like him.'

'How come you're so into Edison all of a sudden?'

'Are you kidding? Don't you use your eyes? And his voice. Surely, you can't have failed to notice that?'

'You mean because it's such a posh accent?'

'Dynamite. And the black skin against the white jacket makes him look James Bond-ish, don't you think? That's why I've got to get back now,' Hope called over her shoulder as she left.

The fairy lights relieved the murk in the centre of the garden. As she couldn't spot Tom outside, Faith sauntered into the marquee, being careful to avoid Judith. Lights circled the dance floor and lit up the band that was playing a hit from the eighties. Several couples were dancing and two older children were holding hands as they moved.

Tom was chatting to a group of people, his camera on a table nearby. He broke off when he spied Faith approaching.

'Sorry to interrupt. I wondered if you'd like me to bring you something else to eat? You didn't have much earlier.'

'I didn't know you'd noticed.' His tender look affected her ability to stand.

'Shall I get you some?'

'No. I'd like to dance with you.' He held out his hand.

'Aren't you supposed to be taking pictures rather than inviting guests to the dance floor?'

'Special dispensation.'

'*Dispensation?*'

'I mean, er... I deserve a break for working so hard up to now.'

He led Faith to the square of hard floor, beyond the swathed poles, and took her in his arms. It was apparent that he, thanks to Luke, was now an accomplished slow dancer. As they swayed to the music, Faith began to relax, her movements became less wooden and her body softened against him. Anticipating that it would not be long before she got her first kiss from Tom, Faith wondered how it would compare with the kisses she'd had from the man in the cupboard.

When the music stopped, Tom didn't let go so neither did she. When the next song stopped, he still hung on as though his hands had become superglued to her body, and it was at the end of that song that he kissed her.

It was a gentle, teasing kiss on her top lip and then her bottom lip. Then he kissed the top lip again but lingered longer. It was when he was giving the same treatment to her bottom lip that she pulled away. Tom's kisses compared very well to the ones the man in the cupboard had given. Too well. The lessons she'd given to Farquhar seemed also to have been learnt by Tom.

'What's wrong?' he shouted in her ear, the music too loud to talk normally. 'Didn't you like it? Didn't I do it right?'

'The trouble is, you did it perfectly,' Faith shouted into Tom's ear. 'You're the man in the cupboard, aren't you?'

'Can we go somewhere to talk?'

'No, and you may well look sheepish. I expect it comes from having spent so much time with the animals.' Faith's eyes were stinging, and she wanted time alone. So she strode towards the house before breaking into a run, fearing giving way to an emotional explosion in front of all the guests.

Taking refuge in the upstairs bathroom, she sat on the loo seat. Bawling. Tom had deceived her, played her—and she'd lost two virgin men in one go.

There was a tap at the door. 'Faith, are you in there? It's Luke.'

'No, I'm not. Go away!'

'I've come to see if you're all right.'

A thought struck her. Tom must have gone to Luke for help. Luke had taught Tom to dance. *Luke was in on it.* She unbolted the door, grabbed hold of Luke's shirt, hauled him in and then shot the bolt back again.

'Steady on.' Luke brushed at the creases she'd made. He sat on the edge of the bath and she sat back down on the loo seat.

'You knew, didn't you?' She unrolled toilet tissue. 'You knew that Tom was the man in the cupboard.' She blew her nose hard.

'Yes.'

'He told you?' She helped herself to some more loo paper and wiped her face. The tears had travelled as far as her chin.

'I guessed.'

'And you didn't tell me?'

'He persuaded me not to. He wanted you to fall for him, not for the man in the cupboard.'

'And that's why he said he was going away—so that the man in the cupboard would conveniently disappear, leaving a clear run for Tom?'

'Something like that. I didn't like doing it. But he is genuinely into you. Big time. He didn't want to spoil things.'

'Well, he has.' Faith frowned in suspicion. 'Who else knew?'

'Gavin...'

'Anyone else?'

Luke displayed his palms. 'I don't know; you'll have to ask. Have you let Tom explain?'

'There's nothing to explain. I expect you all had a good laugh. Especially over that ridiculous name he chose. What was that all about?'

'No, we didn't have a good laugh, and I have no idea why Tom settled on Farquhar—you'll have to ask him. And you need to let him explain the whole thing. Then you'll understand.' Luke slapped his hands on his thighs as though to emphasise his advice.

'Why don't you explain? You seem to have the complete lowdown.'

'I don't, and you need to get it from the horse's mouth. I promised to keep his secrets like I've promised to keep other people's—including yours. Go and ask him. Get it cleared up, make up and make out.'

'You think it's that easy?'

'It's up to you.' Luke rose. 'Now, I've got a party to get back to.'

Lonely after Luke had gone, she supposed she'd have to have a showdown with Tom—after she'd washed her face and waited for the unsightly streaks from her tears to fade.

Faith spotted Tom sitting on his own under a tree lit by garden lights. She picked up a chair from the patio area and took it with her. 'Luke said I should ask you for an explanation,' she said when she got near enough to sit down and hold a conversation with him. 'So here I am.'

'Thanks. I'm so glad you came back.' There was a catch in his voice.

'I'm waiting.'

'The day you met me, I'd only recently come back from being away. I was finding it hard to adjust. The offices were too empty and too strange. I needed to feel safe, enclosed.'

'So, you went into the cleaning cupboard?'

'Just as you did.'

'That was different.'

'Not really. We were both escaping some aspect of reality. Anyway, when you asked me about my previous job, I talked about my flock.'

'Was that a lie then? You weren't a shepherd?'

'Of sorts. It's a metaphor. I tried to tell you, the last

time we were in the cupboard.'

The last time... Her thoughts flew back to the cupboard, and she recalled her laughter. '*You're a priest!*'

'Shh. Keep it down. It's a secret.'

'It's not though, is it? How many people here already know?'

Tom gazed helplessly at her.

*He'd lied to her.* She'd come to love and trust him and he'd *lied to her.*

'You kissed me. Three times now. But you're a *priest*. A priest. How could you?'

Priests were not meant to behave like that, were they? Didn't that count as cheating? It felt like the whole Andy situation had repeated, and she'd fallen for it. Again.

'How could I not have kissed you? And I've left my parish. I'm going to be laicised. I told the Bishop—'

How could that make it all right? He was still a priest, wasn't he? 'You lied and misled me. You're not the person I thought you were.' Without looking at him—it was too hard to see those brown, mesmerising eyes she'd come to love—she left to have it out with Luke and Gavin.

She found them by the bar in the marquee, their expressions miserable. They'd probably had another tiff over Petal. The band was still playing so she'd have to shout. 'Did you two know that Tom's a priest?'

The band stopped playing the instant she was on the name, Tom. But her volume hadn't lowered. She looked around the marquee and saw everyone looking her way. Except Judith. She, for some reason, had her hands over her face. For a moment, Faith wished she could crawl under the nearest table and become invisible. But she wanted answers.

Although the place was silent, Faith was not going to be deterred; she needed to know the extent of her friends' betrayal. 'Did you—'

'We heard you the first time,' Gavin said. 'Everyone did.'

'We knew. But it was—' Luke began.

'A secret?' Faith suggested sourly.

'Yes.'

'Why couldn't I have been in on the secret too?'

'Tom's rules,' Gavin said. 'We wouldn't have got our counselling without keeping to them.'

Everybody she'd known, everybody who was important to her had known and they'd kept quiet about it. Had they had a good laugh? Didn't they think Tom had done anything wrong? Didn't they think they'd done anything wrong?

The band struck up another smoochy song and people turned their heads away and resumed their conversations.

'Rrr...' Faith squeezed her hands into fists.

*Now, where was Perdita?* She was over by the far table, with Violet.

'Did you know that Tom's a priest?' Faith demanded as she strode towards her.

Perdita gave her an apologetic expression. 'Not at first, but the penny dropped later.'

Violet was nodding also, but Faith decided to ignore her. Faith's gripe was with the woman she'd thought of as her best friend. 'And you didn't think to tell me?'

'It was Tom's secret. He didn't want anyone to know.'

'Anyone, or just me?'

'Anyone, but especially you. He likes you. It might have put you off.'

'Being lied to puts me off. I had enough of that with

Andy. Did Saul know?'

Perdita nodded. 'The night you came to tell me about the man in the cupboard, Saul was out with him at the pub hearing all about it from his side. But I kept what you told me secret from him and Tom. And Saul wouldn't tell me what Tom had said to him.'

'Well, I'm through with men who deceive and tell lies.'

Faith scanned the room. Judith was looking over intently. Somehow, she was involved. She was far too interested in Faith's life. Judith had been eyeing Faith's movements at the party with more than a casual interest, and she'd covered her face when Faith had shouted out about Tom being a priest.

She made a beeline for Judith. 'Did you know that Tom's a priest?'

Judith nodded. Miranda, who was sitting next to Judith, nodded too. With rage boiling over, Faith marched to Tom who was standing awkwardly in the entrance to the marquee. She thumped him and pointed behind her. '*Even that old bat knew you were a priest!*'

'That old bat,' a voice boomed, 'is his mother.'

Faith gasped in horror and spun around to see Judith approaching fast with the rollator, dragon eyes boring into her. Miranda was by Judith's side, carrying her handbag.

Focusing on Judith, who was now level with her and Tom, Faith said, 'I'm so sorry, I had no idea.' Tom's mother must have been in her late thirties when she'd had him. She appeared to be in her seventies. Perhaps the arthritis made her seem older but the lines on her face didn't suggest a younger woman. 'Please accept my apology... It was so rude of me... I... I thought you were Jewish... How could you have a Catholic priest for a son?'

'*Oy vey.*'

'What's that supposed to mean?' Faith demanded of Tom.

'Woe is me. The full expression is—'

'Why are you interested in this *shikse?*' Judith shouted above the band.

'Because I love her!' Tom shouted back.

Faith's mouth fell open. He'd said those words. Out loud. Shouted them. *At his mother.*

'*Oy-yoy-yoy!*'

'Will someone translate?' Faith asked.

Miranda stepped forward. 'She's not overjoyed.'

'I gathered that from the way she's talking. I would like to know what she's saying to me. She called the police on me.'

'I did that,' Miranda said. Then, when she took in Faith's expression, added, 'She told me to.'

'Spying on me? To get me to come in?'

'Now she's getting it,' Judith said. '*Schlemiel.*'

Miranda leaned in and said in Faith's ear, 'Fool.' Faith pulled away and flung a hateful glance at Miranda, who raised her hands. 'There's no need to blame me. You asked for an interpreter. I've learned a lot working for Judith—and getting called names myself.'

There was a commotion on the dance floor. People were gathering around. Luke was running towards her. 'Hope's fainted.'

Edison appeared, carrying Hope. Faith's heart lurched as she saw the limp form of her sister with her long, blonde hair hanging over his arm, swinging with each step.

'Is there a sofa I can put her on?'

She and Luke led Edison into the house. Tom followed.

Once Hope was settled on the sofa and Edison was fanning her with a magazine he'd found and Faith was sponging her with a wet cloth, he asked, 'Does she do this often? Faint?'

Faith bit her lip. It was meant to be a secret. But she was done with secrets. 'She's not well.'

'Is she dying?' he asked with deep concern in his voice.

'It's not that big a secret,' she said, and then wished she hadn't. 'She hasn't been well for years, ever since she had glandular fever. She kept it hidden at work because she was worried she wouldn't be given the job.'

'I thought you were your mum's carer when you came to work for me.'

Faith met his gaze. 'I was carer to both of them—and still am to Hope.'

'Did I forget?'

Faith nodded. 'I was bringing up Charlie too. I just didn't talk about them... I wanted to show I was focused on the job I suppose—and have a break from thinking about them so much, a life separate to the life at home.'

Edison patted her shoulder. 'I'd no idea you had so much responsibility. And now your grandmother too. Amazing.'

Faith cringed when he mentioned Judith. Hadn't he heard her say she was Tom's mother? But then, he and Hope had been sitting close to the band and perhaps had eyes and ears only for each other during the commotion by the marquee entrance.

'She's coming round,' Luke said.

Hope's eyes fluttered and then they opened. 'I was doing well, wasn't I? No one guessed.' Hope's eyes closed with the effort of talking.

'No. No one guessed.' Faith squeezed her sister's hand.

'Don't worry,' Luke said. 'She's much more resilient now. After a long rest, she'll bounce back.'

'Can I help get her home?' Edison asked.

'Come around tomorrow,' Faith said. 'Hope might be up to talking to you then.'

'Can I come as well?' Tom asked. 'We've got things to talk about too.'

Slowly, Faith said, 'I think not.'

# 49

Luke carried Hope into the flat. 'Where shall I put her?'

'On her bed, please.'

When Luke had lain Hope down, he offered to make Faith a hot drink while she helped Hope undress.

'I'm tired,' Faith said. 'I think I should go to bed too.'

'What's the hurry? It's not as though you'll get to sleep anytime soon. Not after the evening you've had.'

Luke had a point. It was doubtful she would sleep at all. She was still reeling from the shock of having kissed a Jewish Catholic priest in a cupboard as well as on the dance floor, thinking they were two separate men and then insulting—and being insulted by—his mother.

Gavin stood outside the doorway. 'If Luke's staying, I am too—and I'll have some tea.'

Luke compressed his lips and then snapped, 'You can put the kettle on then.'

'And you can help me,' Gavin snapped back.

'Will you boys play nicely?' Faith pushed Luke into the hallway to be with Gavin and shut the door on them; she had to help Hope into her PJs.

Later, when the three of them were in the living room, Hope left to rest, Faith said, 'Well? Haven't you got anything to say?'

'What about?' Luke asked.

'I'll give you some keywords.' Faith resisted the urge to hit the boys with one of her cushions. 'Deception. Subterfuge. Lies—' Saying the words seemed to fire her anger up even further.

'Now hold on,' Gavin said. 'We didn't tell any lies.'

Faith couldn't sit still and began to pace the room in the hope that the movement would help quell the raging emotional storm that brewed inside her. 'By omission.'

'We needed to have counselling,' Gavin said.

Her muscles tightened. 'Tom was the only counsellor in the area?' It had been spoken in a half-shout in consideration of Hope's need for sleep.

'He was the only one we knew personally,' Gavin said.

'What's a Catholic priest doing counselling a gay couple? Hasn't homosexuality been outlawed in the Catholic Church?'

'Yes, if you're having sex. That was why he needed a bit of persuading,' Gavin said. 'It was either that or nailing him to the floor until he begged for mercy.'

Faith gave them her darkest scowl. Then she couldn't hold back any longer. Grabbing the nearest cushion, she aimed it at Gavin's face, since he seemed to be so smug and righteous about their part in what had happened. But he fielded it before the connection was made.

Luke eyed Faith with a concerned expression. 'I don't think this is helping Tom's cause. You need to calm down and wait until the shock has lessened before you think about it again.'

Faith quit her pacing, sat down and willed her brain to think of something else. 'Okay. My turn now. What's up between you?'

Luke conferred with Gavin by eye contact. Gavin shrugged.

'You went to see Tom's mother...' Luke began.

'I went to see a woman that I didn't know was Tom's mother. What of it?'

'While you were there, Hope mentioned me, didn't she?' Luke's voice was soft.

Faith tensed.

'What did she say?' Luke asked.

Faith gulped. *Were they in trouble?*

'Did she,' Gavin cut in, 'tell Miranda that Luke had asked her to have a baby with him?'

Faith recalled it clearly; it was difficult not to with the mess Miranda had made with the spilt tea. 'Yes. Although not to Miranda specifically. Why?'

'She wants to meet up with us. To discuss having a baby,' Luke said.

Now Faith understood the tension between the boys. She tried to get to grips with the news and wondered why she'd not understood the significance of Miranda's clattering crockery after Hope had said that Luke wanted to find a woman to share a baby with.

'How do you both feel about it?' Faith wasn't sure how she felt about it. Another woman in their circle would affect them all.

'I don't know what to think,' Luke said. 'I don't know who she is, what her health's like or what kind of mother she'd make.'

'You'll actually consider a complete stranger to be the mother of your child?' Gavin asked.

'I could consult Tom,' Luke said. 'He must know her. He's living in the same house.'

Tom had said that he'd been finding it difficult living at home again. But why hadn't he ever mentioned Judith to her when Faith had told him about her visits there? What other salient facts about Tom were yet to be unearthed?

'So,' Faith said, 'you guys knew all along that Judith was his mother? Yet you kept schtum?'

'Well,' Luke said, 'we didn't know. Tom told us he was living with his mother until he gets his business up and running. It was tonight that Judith declared herself to be his mother—after they'd pretended to be strangers. So don't blame us.'

'I've blown it, haven't I? With Judith. I called her an old bat. In public. In front of all those people.'

'It's not the best way to introduce yourself to your future mother-in-law,' Luke said.

It was hard to swallow. That's exactly what she'd been thinking. 'Hey, what's this with the marriage? I told you, I'm not interested in Tom. Not anymore.' She'd made her rule of one strike and he's out and it was safest to stick to it. She did not know him anymore.

Gavin rubbed his chin. 'That's why you're stressing about Judith? Because you don't want to get hitched to Tom? Well, I wonder what you'd be like if you did.'

She glared at him, annoyed that he saw through her. But she'd prove it to him—and to herself—that she was no longer interested in Tom.

'Come on,' Luke said, 'you can't fool us. We know you're into him.'

'And we know he's not been into you,' Gavin said, 'as it's against his religion. Before the wedding, that is.'

'Boys, boys, puh-lease.'

'Do you think you'll have to teach him what to do?' Gavin asked.

She'd play along—then it wouldn't give them the satisfaction of her rising to their taunts. 'I expect so. After all, I had to teach him how to kiss. And, I must say, he's a fast learner.'

'Sure he wasn't getting some practice in elsewhere?' Luke asked.

'He's not like that!'

'See,' Gavin said, pointing at her, 'you do like him.'

'I do like him. But I don't want a relationship with him. I like you guys but it doesn't mean I'd want to take it further.'

'But you haven't kissed us—and you have him,' Luke said. 'Even in public.'

'In front of all those people,' Gavin mimicked.

Unable to think of a sharp rejoinder, and deciding to lick her wounds later, in private, she changed the subject. 'So, what are you going to do about Miranda?'

'Meet up,' Luke said decisively. 'Hear what she's got to say for herself.'

'And I'm coming too,' Gavin said. 'I want to know exactly which way the wind's blowing.' Then Gavin burst into sobs with gulping, hiccupping noises.

Luke took hold of Gavin's hand. He leaned into Luke and Luke put his arm around him. 'He's feeling threatened about the Miranda issue.' Luke stroked Gavin's arm. 'We'll talk it over with Tom next week.'

*Tom?* Not long ago she'd been their confidante. *But then, how could she possibly outdo the skills of a Catholic priest?*

# 50

By the time Edison breezed into the office that Monday, Faith was already firing off emails, despite not having had to fall in with Hope's super-early schedule. Hope, and the hearse, were taking a break.

He dumped his briefcase on the floor. 'You should have told me what a brave sister you have. I haven't been able to stop thinking about her.' He leaned against the edge of his desk. 'And the hearse. The casket. You really do embrace the ethos of the company. Disability is no reason to stop living. You helped Hope live—not just exist.'

Faith took stock. How come he was so keen on Hope, despite hearing yesterday how ill she'd been and how she managed her condition to enable her to work just a few hours a week? There was a memory tugging at Faith's mind, urging her to think. It must have been about three years ago when his sister got the diagnosis and her fiancé hadn't stuck around long after that. When she'd needed the support the most, he hadn't been there for her. And the tumour had grown and multiplied, and Edison's sister had died.

'Edison, when you were with Hope at the party, after she fainted, were you thinking of Dinah?'

He crossed his arms. 'Maybe.'

'Were you thinking that you could be there for Hope as Dinah's fiancé could not be for her?' Had she been too blunt?

'I was interested in Hope long before I knew she was unwell. Finding out hasn't put me off. Hope charms me.

She's delightful. Being sick does not take that away.'

'She's a lot younger than you.' From what Faith could recollect, Edison was a good ten years older than Hope. 'She was still a teenager when she got ill. She's never had a relationship.'

'She has now. And what's the age gap between you and Tom? I saw you with him on the dance floor.'

'At the moment, there is no me and Tom... And he's the inexperienced one—he went straight into the priesthood before having any romantic relationship. Hope's not seen much of life—she's been stuck at home for years.'

'She's not stuck at home anymore. She's in her twenties and she wants the freedom to live her own life, doesn't she?' He put his arms behind him and leaned back on his desk. 'Tell me, would you prefer to have Hope meet a man none of us might know, be taken advantage of and messed around? I think you know what that's like.'

Did he know about Andy? 'What do you mean?'

'I heard about your ex causing trouble here a couple of times. Surely, you wouldn't want to risk Hope being involved with that kind of man?'

Faith shuddered.

'I don't mess women around. In fact, they've messed me around. There hasn't been anyone serious for a while. Trust me. I'm at that stage in life where I'm not looking for fun. You know what I'm referring to.'

Faith blinked. *Edison and Hope?* 'She's never had a boyfriend. She needs to have a life of her own before she thinks of settling down.'

'Why can't we share some enjoyable times together first—and after, if it gets that far?'

'I hear what you're saying. And it might be true for now. But what happens six months or a year down the line, when her heart's fixed on you and you realise the impact her poor health has on you and how limited your life has become?'

'What happens if six months or a year down the line, Hope decides I'm not the guy for her and she leaves me heartbroken? Isn't there risk on both sides? Love is always a gamble, isn't it? Do you think you're being judgemental without reason?'

Shame rose up into her throat. 'Perhaps I'm being overprotective. Sorry.'

'I would take good care of her. Make sure she doesn't get too tired. I understand these things.'

Dumbly, Faith nodded. It was true. With clients, he couldn't be faulted. She supposed it would be okay, and she ought to be happy for Hope. He was a good man: trustworthy, dependable, always polite. If it were between Edison and Andy types...? Of course, she'd choose Edison. Hope was lucky to have him.

'Now,' Edison said, 'I've been thinking about what you said yesterday.'

When he'd come round to see Hope, Faith had confessed about lying to him about Judith. She braced herself for a severe reprimand.

'I didn't want to give a knee-jerk reaction, and I had to bear in mind that you are Hope's sister and that you'd got into trouble because of keeping her secrets.'

Did that mean her job was safe? Because of Hope?

'So, I understand why you lied. But I always prefer the truth—and don't be late anymore.' His tone was crisp. 'I will understand if Hope needs your help and it's an emergency. But I do want the truth in future.'

Faith nodded. 'Absolutely.' She'd got off lightly and her breathing eased.

'If you'd not been Hope's sister and you'd not been doing what you thought best...'

'I understand.' She'd have been replaced.

'I need to trust my staff.'

'I know. It will never happen again.' She held his gaze for a moment and then he nodded as though to say the issue was over as long as she kept to her word.

'I'm seeing Hope after work. Perhaps I'll see you there?'

So they'd have to be sociable with each other.

'I will be seeing her regularly,' he said gently.

'Of course. I'll... see you there.' Could he get to know Hope at his place too? Then she remembered that Hope had had to put up with Andy's presence—had she minded when he'd stayed over? Would Edison stay over? Well, if he did, she'd be glad for Hope. She would. Hope was grown up now. Another thought struck her. If Hope settled down with Edison, she'd be free too. But alone...

At the end of the day, after Edison had left, Faith was puzzled about Tom as she'd not seen him around. But she'd seen two smartly dressed women enter his office after lunch. She wondered if they'd come to discuss an event. Now that Tom had left the church, he wouldn't stay single for long, especially with beauties like those to tempt him. Having a successor or two lay uncomfortably with her. But he'd lied to her, made a fool of her.

Yet, she missed him. With a mug of coffee in her hand, she tried the cupboard on impulse. It opened, and he was standing by the opening, making way for her.

'I hoped you'd come.' Tom dropped the accent he'd used in the cupboard as Farquhar.'I don't know why I did... it's probably a mistake. I think I'll...'

'Put your mug down,' he said.

'What?'

'Give it to me. I'll do it.' Warm hands found hers,

and she allowed Tom to take her drink and place it on a shelf next to some cleaning bottles. He shut the door behind her so that they were in darkness. Then he kissed her.

'Hey,' she protested, pushing him away. 'I'm not your girlfriend, you blew it.'

'I know. That's why I thought it best to settle our differences in a nonverbal way.'

'I don't—'

Tom nuzzled her face, his lips grazing hers. 'Oh, but I think you do.' His breath was pleasant as he kissed her again. He was bolder than before—and she liked it.

After what might have been an age, he broke off with a sound Faith could not interpret. 'Now tell me you don't feel something for me.'

'I do feel something for you.' *I'm heartbroken*. 'But I wish I didn't.'

'You prefer Andy types? The ones who cheat on you? As I said when we first met, I would never do that to you. And I proved it with that Roxy business.'

'I met Roxy on a night out, and she said she'd met a priest who'd run away from her. That was you, wasn't it?'

'It was. And because of her, I left the service station before having a pee, was desperate enough to stop on the hard shoulder and Tweedledum and Tweedledee—aka Officers Large and Small—pulled over to charge me. Hence the blackmail with the wedding shoot.'

'What about calling yourself Farquhar?'

'I lost track of who I was meant to be and almost introduced myself as Father Thomas Sheridan. The "far" sound was incorporated into Farquhar—the first name I thought of that would pass my mistake.'

'It all makes sense now. But I hate that you misled me about your past and tricked me in the cupboard.' *And*

*I can't stand your mother...*

'I hadn't planned to. But when I met you in the flesh... and...'

'Stared at my breasts?'

'Exactly. How could I tell you we were the same person when you thought me a lech? I was so taken with you that I didn't want to risk losing you altogether.'

'By my finding out that a Roman Catholic priest liked my breasts and had kissed me?'

'Yes. And I must say,' he murmured, 'your breasts are superb. Even now, as I'm holding you close, I can feel your softness.'

'I can feel your hardness.'

'Are you bothered by it?'

She wished she'd not brought it up. 'No.' But it was inappropriate behaviour for a priest. 'What would your superior say if he knew about what had gone on between us?'

'You mean raising my hopes?'

Was it just his emotions he was referring to? '... Yes.'

'The Right Reverend Brendon Costello is not in a position to cast a stone at me.'

Faith gave a derisive sound. 'Are all Catholic priests like that?'

'I doubt it. I certainly wasn't. Look, you were so judgemental towards me after I gawked at your breasts, giving you a totally wrong impression of my true character, was it surprising I didn't dare risk trusting you with my secret?'

'I would have understood.' Maybe. Maybe not.

'The stakes were too high for me to jeopardise our possible future together—you'd taken such a dislike to me. Can you forgive me for not being completely upfront with you?'

'No, I don't think I can. It's a deal-breaker.'

'You know,' he said gently, 'if you can't appreciate me, I will have to consider the boys' advice.'

Faith tensed. 'What advice?'

'They recommend I move on if you reject me for your future husband. So, don't worry, I shan't kiss you again.' Tom released his hold, and the coffee mug was placed back in her hands. He eased past, opened the door and then he was gone.

The boys... how dare they interfere? How dare they give Tom advice when they should have been consoling her? Then she recalled Tom's words. *Husband?* She clung to the shelf. She'd been going steady with Andy for two years and the subject of marriage had never been broached. Come to think of it, he'd never given her the impression he was madly in love with her. Whereas Tom... Tom... well, he'd certainly made it crystal clear. She clutched her chest and concentrated on steadying her breathing.

When she recalled the thoughts she'd had about the combined positive characteristics of the man in the cupboard and Tom making her ideal partner, she thought she might be sick. *The greatest man she'd ever met...* and she'd had to turn him down because, like Andy, he'd deceived her.

# 51

A week after Perdita's party, Miranda met up with Luke and Gavin in a pub; they were sitting at a table in a bay window.

'Why do you want a baby?' Luke asked over the top of his beer.

As Miranda watched the bubbles rise in her white wine spritzer, her thoughts filled with sadness at the lack of opportunities that had come her way. Then she looked up at the boys. 'Biological clock. I've no man. You guys aren't partner material so don't count. How much longer should I wait, when I haven't been lucky—in that or generally?'

'Aren't you?' asked Gavin. 'You met us even if we won't be sharing your bed.'

'Definitely not. I work for Judith.'

'She's right,' Luke said. 'That can't be lucky. I pity Tom.'

'Malakai. That's what Judith calls him; a Jewish first name, a Christian second name. And meeting you wasn't luck—it was desperation. I'd say I was lucky if it worked out.'

'So, what kind of arrangement do you have in mind?'

'Well, I'll have to see if I can persuade Judith to let me have a baby while still working for her.'

'The last time I saw her,' Gavin said, 'she was breathing fire. How is this angry woman going to be persuaded to take kindly to living with a baby?'

'I have some ideas. I can test the water with Judith when we've come to an arrangement. Before it's too late.'

'Too late?'

'Before I'm fertilised.'

'You sound,' Gavin said, 'pretty sure that you will be. Have you been... *fertilised* before?'

'No. But I don't see why I wouldn't be.'

'Optimist, are you?'

'I have to be—I keep hoping working for Judith will get better. That she'll learn to be kind.'

'Why don't you leave if she's so awful?' Luke asked.

Miranda didn't want to admit that she had nowhere else to call home—she was the product of the chaotic care system, having gone from one children's home to another and from one foster parent to the next—so she just shrugged.

'Now, you guys: what kind of dads are you going to make?'

Gavin gulped.

'Is there a problem here?' She picked up a beer mat and played with it in her lap, turning it over and over.

Luke answered. 'I want a baby. Gavin... well, we're having counselling to help us sort out... our differences.'

Miranda frowned. 'As you both came, I supposed that you were both on the same page now.'

'Tom's helping us sort things out,' Luke said.

'Malakai?'

Luke shifted in his seat. 'Yes. What's the problem?'

'I'm just surprised. His lack of experience with same-sex relationships—and with having babies.'

'He's very good at it,' Luke defended. 'We like him.'

'Oh, we all like Malakai,' Miranda said. 'What's there to dislike?'

'Have you got a crush on him?' Luke's tone oozed suspicion.

'Has there ever been anything between the two of

you?' Gavin asked.

Miranda pulled a rueful expression. 'I wish. But he's so into Faith, isn't he?'

'Hasn't got that far yet,' Gavin said. 'He's still a virgin.'

'What's wrong with being selective?' Miranda asked.

'To be selective,' Gavin said, 'you have to make a selection. He's not made any selection so far.'

'He tried to,' Luke said. 'But she didn't select him back.'

'I'll tell Faith about all the gorgeous bridesmaids Tom is meeting,' Gavin said. 'It'll drive her mad with jealousy.'

'Sounds good,' Miranda said without enthusiasm, recalling what she'd said about the dearth of luck in her life. There wasn't much hope of Tom turning to her for consolation then. Who was she kidding? He'd not turn to her even if Faith weren't around. He'd never shown the slightest interest in his mother's dogsbody.

'By making Faith insanely jealous, we'd be helping two friends at once,' Luke said. 'If we can get Tom and Faith back together.'

Miranda was beginning to feel that she was getting to know them. 'You stick by your friends, don't you?'

Gavin smiled at her. 'Yes.'

'Does this mean you think you could put up with us?' Luke asked. 'We are nice guys. We do care about people. Our friends. Family.'

'Maybe. But what happens if I get pregnant and then you two split up?'

'I will do everything I can to not let that happen.' Luke touched Gavin's hand. 'But if it does, then I will still be a father to that child. I think I've proved my commitment through Petal.'

Miranda glanced at Gavin. 'How do you take to Petal?

How does she take to you?'

Gavin flicked a glance at Luke. 'Quite well. I get alone time with her so we have a relationship of our own.'

'What would happen to her if I have that baby?'

'Nothing,' Luke said. 'She would be welcome as usual. She'd be like a big sister, part of the family.'

'Perhaps she wouldn't come quite as much,' Gavin said, 'if our spare time is taken up with the baby. Remember that Tom said we must have time together on our own and time apart to follow our interests? It needs to be balanced.'

'You're looking a bit overwhelmed.' Miranda squeezed the beer mat between her fingers and thumbs. Had she got her hopes up for nothing?

Gavin's Adam's apple bobbed up and down. 'I... I'm not quite with Luke on this one, but I'm getting there.'

Although this didn't bode well, they could have lied. Did it matter as long as Luke was on board?

'How much input do you envisage having with the baby?' Miranda asked.

'As much as I can,' Luke said. 'I want to be a hands-on daddy, sharing the ups and downs throughout his, her or their life. And I will guarantee, for as long as I have a job, that I will contribute towards the child's keep.'

It sounded positive. The enthusiasm and sincerity in Luke's reply was reassuring but she needed surety over his financial input too. Miranda narrowed her eyes to show that she was not going to be taken advantage of. 'An agreement would have to be drawn up. By a solicitor.'

'Fine,' Luke said without hesitation. 'I want to be acknowledged as the father.'

Gavin was looking out of the window and then at the door, as though wanting to escape.

Miranda laid a hand on his. 'It's too much for you, at the moment, isn't it? Are you feeling left out, perhaps?'

A tear trickled down Gavin's cheek, and he bit his lip—presumably in an attempt to tame his chin, which was working spasmodically.

'If it goes ahead,' Miranda said, 'and I have a baby, I consider that two fathers are better than one. A child can never have enough support. But you two are a couple. I could be the one to get left out.'

Gavin wiped away his tear.

Miranda squeezed his hand. 'It might be possible, don't you think, that we could all become a family? Let's take a while to think about it, okay?'

# 52

Tom was sitting with Luke and Gavin in his office. It was sweltering, even with the windows open, and sun blinds down so Tom had placed a selection of chilled Sprite and Fanta cans on the table. The boys had opened two cans the moment they'd sat down.

Tom had had several sessions with them now, but, since Perdita's party, he'd been very busy with wedding commissions, updating his new website and meeting prospective clients.

'I'm sorry that it's been a while since we last met. How have you been getting on?'

The boys exchanged glances, and Gavin nodded at Luke.

'Things have moved forward,' Luke said. 'We've found a surrogate mother. I didn't tell you before now because it wasn't certain. Also, the lady in question asked us not to tell you until we'd made a firm decision, which we now have.'

'How did you manage to find a surrogate mother?'

'We didn't. She found us. She heard about us from Hope. When Hope visited your mother.'

Tom's eyebrows pulled together. 'Mum's too old...' Judith was seventy-two.

Gavin shook his head. 'Not Judith...'

Tom couldn't think for a moment who it might be, and then he couldn't believe who it *might* be. '*Miranda?*'

Gavin nodded. 'They've been tested at the clinic to check they're free of anything nasty.'

'Except, as it turns out,' Luke said, 'Miranda needn't have been. But people sometimes lie about these things so we had to go together...'

'Why needn't Miranda have been tested?' Tom asked.

'Let's just say that if she becomes pregnant, Mary's won't be the only virgin birth,' Luke said.

Tom took a moment to take in what Luke had said. 'How do you propose...?'

'Turkey baster,' Gavin said. 'I'm not having Luke deflower her.'

'I don't think little Luke would be up to the job.'

Tom knew he had to pull himself together. Recover from the image of a pregnant Miranda—that followed a graphic image involving a long tube with a rubber bulb at one end.

'So, Gavin, how do you feel about the possibility of Miranda and Luke having a baby together?'

'I'm not as keen on the idea of Miranda being involved as Luke is.'

'Why's that?' Tom asked.

'It will mean that Luke will have an intimate, lifelong connection with another person—a *woman*.'

'I've never shown the slightest interest in any woman,' Luke said, 'and you should know that by now.'

Slowly, as though emotion was fighting logic, Gavin nodded.

Tom knew that having Miranda involved lifelong as the mother wasn't the same as having a baby handed over by a stranger. Only time—and Luke's hard work—would reassure Gavin that he would not be left out.

It was time, Tom decided, to explore the fathering issue. 'Gavin, how good a father figure do you think Luke would be on his own, without you?'

Gavin looked down at the black rug on the floor. 'I

think he'd be great. I don't think my presence makes any difference one way or the other.'

'Do you think Luke's answer would be the same?' Tom asked.

Gavin shrugged. 'I don't see why not.'

'Luke, could you tell Gavin how you think your role as a father might be affected if Gavin weren't in your life?'

Luke looked stunned. 'I... I don't know.'

'Gavin, how would you describe Luke's expression just now?'

Tom waited while Gavin considered.

'I think... he looks scared.'

'Might Luke be a good father figure now, with Petal, because he has your support? Because he has you in his life?'

A stunned expression was stamped on Gavin's face.

'It's true,' Luke said in surprise. 'It wouldn't be the same without Gavin. He's an integral part of my life.'

Tom cocked his head to one side. 'That's a big statement for Luke to make.'

Gavin nodded.

Luke rested his hand on Gavin's. 'It's true. I don't think I could do it without you. Be such a good dad. If I didn't have you in my life, I'd be—'

'Miserable. Heartbroken. Wretched,' Gavin said.

The guys stared at each other. It was clear to Tom that these two were simply meant to be together. There was no other way for things to work out, and it looked like they were realising it too.

'Homework,' Tom said.

They groaned.

'And for some of it, you are not to confer.'

Luke picked up his can for a long slurp. 'So, what do we have to do?'

'Having a child is a very grave step. It brings responsibilities. You need to think not only of the baby stage but all the stages through childhood and teenage years—and beyond.'

The boys nodded with solemn expressions.

'I want you, Luke, to write a list of all the ways in which you can help make Gavin feel secure—in the lead-up to the pregnancy, during the pregnancy and following the birth. Gavin, I want you to think up ways Luke could help you to feel secure at these stages—as well as ways in which you could help support Luke. And another list that you do together—how both of you can support Miranda.'

Tom took in their startled expressions. 'Miranda needs to know that both of you will take care of her; the mother of your child.' How would Judith take the news? Surely, she'd send Miranda packing? 'The baby and the health of the mother need to be the number one priority for all of you; they go hand in hand. There will be four of you in the family from the moment Miranda becomes pregnant. Never forget that.'

'I know what I can do to help Gavin feel more secure,' Luke said. 'It's been on my mind for ages.' Luke looked at Gavin. 'I'd like us to be a family. Parents to the child we might have?'

Gavin's expression became earnest. 'There's no one else I'd rather be with. You're my best friend. I can't contemplate a life without you. I... I don't know how it'll turn out with a baby, but I know I have to give it a try. I'm staying with you.'

'Then I can't hold back any longer,' Luke said. 'I want us to make it official. Get spliced. Hitched.'

Gavin's eyes widened and glistened, which made Tom a bit teary too.

'Oh, yes!' Gavin exclaimed.

Luke flung his arms around Gavin and kissed him.

'You've… er… taken me by surprise,' Tom said. 'Congratulations.' He stood up and so did they, and he soon found himself in a triple hug. A warm feeling flowed through him. These were real people, real lives. And they were real friends. *His friends.*

'I wish you could give us a blessing,' Gavin said, 'but you can't do that, can you?'

Tom's heart went out to them. 'I give you my blessing. I'm sorry about the way the Church is. I'll tell the Bishop what I think about it when I see him.'

'Are you still a priest?' Gavin asked.

'I am. The Bishop wants me to sign a document to say I should never have become a priest in the first place. Wanting a wife is not a serious enough reason to be granted the indult of laicisation. But I'm not prepared to do what's required by the Church in order to get laicised.'

'So, you'll be a priest forever?' Gavin sounded concerned.

'It's an automatic suspension if I get married. Job done. Thanks to Canon Law 1394.'

'You're a bit of a rebel,' Luke said admiringly.

Tom shrugged. 'I just don't want to sign something that's not the truth. I cannot testify to a lie. And I fully intend to get married.'

'Talking of marriage,' Luke said, 'would it still be to Faith?'

Tom grinned. 'Who else?'

# 53

When Luke called Miranda to let her know that he and Gavin had broken the news to Tom, it was time to broach the subject with Judith.

It was always hard to challenge Judith. Miranda intended to have a baby even without Judith's support. But the thought of being cast out was incredibly daunting, which was why she'd practised the conversation beforehand, even in her sleep.

'I'm trying to have a baby,' Miranda said. They were sharing a pot of tea. 'And I would like to stay here, working for you, if I get pregnant.'

It seemed to take a moment for Miranda's words to percolate through Judith's brain, and then her teacup clattered back into its saucer. She clicked her tongue. 'How could you have a baby?'

'Luke will be the biological father of my child. Gavin, a second dad.'

'The queers?'

'The gay couple. Don't disrespect them like you disrespect Malakai. They are likely to be in my life forever.'

'But they don't have to be in mine. You can hand in your notice the moment you find out that you are pregnant. I won't tolerate having a bastard in the place.'

It was exactly the reaction Miranda had expected from her employer. 'All you do is drive people away. No wonder you're so bitter and twisted. Malakai is firm friends with Luke and Gavin, and he loves Faith. You have the chance of hearing the laughter of children in this house—Malakai's and mine. Laughter that hasn't been heard for—'

'How dare you talk to me like that? Get out!' Judith's gravelly voice could have rivalled that of a death metal singer's vocals Miranda had once heard when she'd tapped the wrong radio station icon on her phone. She'd thought she'd been mistakenly connected to a foreign power's torture chamber.

'When you have a chance of happiness, you screw it up and chuck it away,' Miranda said. 'Haven't you learnt by now that your ways aren't working? You must change or you'll lose him for good.' Miranda wasn't sure whether Judith would regret losing her for good—or, at least, she'd never admit to it.

'Shut up! You're fired. Get out!' Judith's bellow could be heard from the street despite the double glazing; two startled passers-by looked their way.

'I could help you make it all right. But only if you help me.'

Judith's eyes narrowed as though generating a laser beam to create maximum damage.

'I could help you get Malakai back. I could help him get married to Faith. They'd give you an heir.'

Judith's laser-beam stare appeared to soften to a less dangerous form of light.

'I have a plan. But it's at a price.'

'I want my boy to marry a Jewish woman, not a gentile.'

Miranda gave a belly laugh. 'Do you honestly think a Jewish mother would allow her daughter to marry a Catholic priest? And weren't you considering Hope and Faith as possible candidates? You didn't mention that they must be Jewish at the time—you're making the rules up as you go along.'

Miranda had overheard Malakai telling someone

about needing to see the Bishop but he was going to delay it until he was less busy. She could use that event to get Faith back with Malakai.

'If you don't agree to my staying on—with my baby—I can also arrange it so that Malakai never has anything to do with you again. Ditto Faith.'

'Huh. And how would you do that?' Judith seemed diminished, scared.

'If they were to find out that you instructed me to fish out Faith's purchase from that litter bin, and how you examined that purchase...'

'You wouldn't,' Judith hissed, her chest rising and falling with increased rapidity, but Miranda wasn't concerned as she knew that Judith had a strong heart. Her mind was clearly whirring furiously as her eyes darted from one direction to another. 'I... They wouldn't believe you.' Judith sounded less confident.

'I still have the original bag, packaging, receipt and *unused* product.'

'*You didn't use it?*'

Miranda shrugged. 'I'm quite capable of doing my own shopping, thank you.' Picking up her cup, Miranda drank. She didn't like cold tea.

After about ten minutes' contemplation, Judith said, in a small voice, 'And if I were to let you stay...?'

'I would do my damnedest to get Malakai and Faith together and to reunite you with your son. But you would have to play your part and lay off being a bitch— including to Luke and Gavin.'

'... It would make an interesting diversion to find out what you have up your sleeve.'

'It would make it all the more interesting if you played along—for real. Imagine that. Experiencing true human emotion and connecting with a whole load of strangers. Including Malakai.'

Judith's tone rallied. 'Malakai's not a stranger.'

'He is to you. What efforts have you made to understand life from his perspective? Do you know what's in his head? What drives him?'

'Why do you ask me questions you already know the answers to?' Judith sipped from her tea. Her hands were steady. A good sign, Miranda knew. The crisis had been averted.

'Imagine yourself being sociable, nice to people, people wanting to spend time with you? Malakai hugging you? His friends enjoying your company?'

Judith replaced her cup. 'Are you implying...' Her brief bluster turned to defeat as she mumbled, almost incoherently, 'You may be right about everything you've just said.'

'I *am* right.'

'I... I'm not proud of who I've become.' Judith's shoulders sagged and her posture became hunched as she stared regretfully into the distance. 'But I don't seem able to change my ways.'

'I'll help you if you let me stay—with my baby. I can—' Miranda was going to say, be the daughter you never had, but she checked herself in time. 'I can make your life better... if you'll let me. I truly do want you to be happy.' Life for them all could be so much better, so much more enjoyable, if the conflict just disappeared.

Judith's head bowed and she was quiet again, and Miranda knew it was best to let her cogitate uninterrupted. Perhaps Judith was truly remorseful over her actions towards her son and the nasty comments she had a habit of making; perhaps her mind was playing a mental reel of all the occasions her barbs had been deliberately fired to hurt.

'Let me help you,' Miranda whispered.

Focusing moist eyes on her, Judith asked softly,

'What do I have to do?'

'Can I stay—with my baby if I get pregnant?'

'There would have to be rules.'

'Of course.'

'I'd still want you to help me and do what you normally do.'

'Of course.'

'No slacking.'

'Of course not. I'll do my best for you. I always do. But I would hope you'll be kind enough to be flexible and allow some changes.'

'I suppose so.' Judith looked her straight in the eye. 'So, what is it you want me to do to keep Malakai happy?'

Getting Judith to attend Luke and Gavin's wedding next month was a task Miranda would start work on another day. 'The first thing is to invite Faith to tea.'

'Again? Look what a disaster that turned out to be.'

'This time,' Miranda instructed, 'you're going to be genuine. You are going to apologise to her and explain you're a lonely and embittered old woman who'd deserved to be called an old bat... And, in the future, you must always refer to Malakai as Tom.'

# 54

Faith had been in the kitchenette, intending to get her lunch and take it back to the office, when the call came. She was still in the kitchenette but when she'd taken the call, from a number she hadn't recognised, she'd been standing. Now she was slumped on the floor, her legs out and her back against a cupboard door.

'Are you all right?' Tom had come in without her hearing his steps.

'I don't know,' she whispered.

He helped himself to a mug from the cupboard, stepping over her outstretched feet, and flicked the switch on the kettle. She was aware that he wasn't taking much notice. He hadn't been showing much desire to chat for ages now—and it hurt. What's more, Faith didn't know whether his seeming lack of interest was a genuine lack of interest or down to Luke's advice Tom had mentioned when they'd last been in the cupboard.

Finally, Tom's curiosity seemed to get the better of him. 'What's happened?' he asked, but with his back to her. She saw his arm movement and imagined him spooning coffee into the mug.

'Judith. Your mother. She just called to invite me over for tea. After work.' Faith could detect the stupefaction in her voice and wondered whether Tom could too. She bet Luke had given her number to Miranda.

He spun around. '*What?*'

'Judith—'

'Yes. But what's she playing at?'

Faith bristled. 'Why shouldn't Judith invite me for tea?'

'Why should she?'

'To apologise for being unpleasant and to say that she deserves my calling her an old bat.'

Tom was down on the floor opposite her. She moved her legs to accommodate him.

'My mother has apologised to you?'

'Yes. And she intends to do it again. Over tea. She sounded so... nice.'

'Are you sure it wasn't someone impersonating my mother?'

'Quite sure. Miranda dialled and handed the phone to Judith once I'd answered. She's a witness.'

'Is my mother ill?'

'How would I know? Don't you want your mother to be friendly?'

Tom stared at her. 'I don't remember her ever being nice... or friendly. Since Dad left.'

'Perhaps she's lonely and has seen the error of her ways?'

'The only errors she sees are the errors of everyone else's ways.'

Faith made to stand. 'Well, I've accepted the invitation.' She gathered her ham roll, yoghurt and juice.

'Are you sure you want to have tea with her?' He remained on the floor; it was obvious he wasn't in a hurry to leave.

Apparently, Faith's legs didn't want to leave either as her knees bent, and she was soon sitting opposite him again. 'Yes, because every time Hope and I go to the hearse or get out of it, I feel her spying on us. She might not be, but I feel prickles on the back of my neck.'

'I understand.'

'If I make my peace with her, then I might not feel uncomfortable all the time I'm by her house.' Perhaps she and Tom could also get on a friendlier footing as a result. After all, he was talking to her now all right. Giving her his full, undivided attention. She bet he'd want to know how it went afterwards too.

Faith believed that if she found excuses to spend more and more time with Tom, the issue between them might gradually, magically dissolve—and it should lessen the risk of him transferring his affections to a wedding guest or bridesmaid. Considerately, Luke and Gavin warned her of this possibility on a regular basis. So she determined to go back up to the third level after visiting Judith, to tell Tom all about it. She was often free to do as she pleased, now that Edison was spending so much time with Hope.

Tentatively, Faith knocked on Tom's door and then pushed it open. His office was deserted. 'Hello?' She walked in and decided to check the other rooms. The smaller one had a chaise longue in it, covered with bedding. A wooden crucifix was fixed to the wall and, on the floor, holdalls were bursting with clothes. So, he was sleeping here?

Then she glanced away and gasped. On the wall opposite the chaise longue was a blown-up framed, black and white print of herself. It was the image he'd taken of her at Perdita's party, capturing a searching, wistful expression. Strands of hair had blown across her face, softening her cheekbones and making her look... beautiful.

'What do you think of it?' Tom stepped into view.

She jumped. 'Amazing. I didn't know I could look like that.'

'That's usually what I picture when I think of you,'

he murmured in her ear, making her feel giddy.

'Really?' This wasn't what she saw when she looked in the mirror. She nodded her head towards the luggage on the floor. 'You're sleeping here?'

'Most of the time. I go back to shower, do my laundry and, if it's late enough, I might sleep there as well.'

'Judith said you'd fallen out with her.'

'I can't remember a time when we truly got on. She should never have become a mother.'

'That's rather harsh, isn't it?'

'You've met her, you know what she's like.'

'I know what she *can* be like...'

'Don't tell me you're best buddies with her now?' His tone hardened.

'No. But I could tell she was sincere when she said how much she wants to be reconciled with you.'

'I wonder whether you'd be so keen to make up if you'd had the childhood I'd had, if you'd had mean and nasty insults hurled at you, had experienced a motherly affection that had the warmth of a deep freeze.'

Faith was suddenly very grateful for her own childhood and for having loving and supportive parents. Perhaps she'd taken their love and affection for granted at the time but when she'd heard of Marion's cancer diagnosis, she'd been so afraid that she would lose her mum that Faith did everything she could to help—while having Hope to care for too.

'Please don't meddle in things you don't understand,' Tom said. 'If you want a new best friend, go ahead. But don't pretend to know my mother better than I do myself.'

'I'm sorry.' She brushed past him, the tone of his voice making her feel she wasn't welcome to stay.

'Wait. Tell me about it.'

She turned to glimpse his unreadable expression and

went to sit on one of the office sofas. If he was going to reprimand her further for having tea with his mother, she'd leave. She'd thought he'd be pleased that she and Judith were starting to get along, but she'd clearly misread the situation.

Why she was feeling so bad about it, she wasn't sure. She'd been the one to break things off with Tom. Yet she was hurting so much. Was there a path that would eventually lead them back together? Could she ever forgive his deceit? His actions as a priest? If Judith could forgive all, and if Faith succeeded in forgiving Judith for the insults flung her way, should Faith not find it in her heart to forgive Tom? But she didn't know whether she could as the arrow had gone too deep; she'd given him her full trust and then she'd found out that he wasn't the man she'd thought he was.

'Tell me about your visit.' Tom parked himself opposite. 'Although I do think she's using you to get to me.'

'She was very pleasant and wants us to be friends. She kept referring to you as Tom and wants to be on good terms with you too.'

He gazed at her disbelievingly.

'It's true, I'm not making it up. Miranda—'

'Witnessed it?'

'Yes.'

'But have you got it in writing?'

'You think Judith is lying?'

'What you are describing is uncharted territory for her.'

'Then you are in good company,' Faith said dryly, 'considering you have also stepped into uncharted territory—for a priest.'

'Perhaps,' Tom said heatedly, 'you should take a leaf out of Judith's supposed new book and start being nicer to me. It was your personality that drew me to you, but, lately, I've found it wanting.'

Faith blinked, feeling the rebuke. 'I'm sorry,' she said, 'really.' But the line of Tom's mouth was grim. 'It was very unkind of me to say what I did. I'm just finding it very hard to forget that you're a priest. And that you lied to me, made a fool out of me.'

'Sometimes the lie isn't as important as the motivation behind it. I didn't do it to hurt you. And who doesn't tell lies? What relationships do you know where there isn't some secret kept back?'

Faith wasn't sure it was fair he was putting her on the naughty chair.

'Luke wasn't honest with Gavin, was he, about the help he was giving Hope?' Tom said. 'But Gavin forgave him when he understood why. You forgave Hope for scheming behind your back with Luke. And didn't Hope lie to get her job? Didn't you help cover up for her? The same with the scooter, you didn't explain straight away to me what you were doing with it. You lied to Edison about Judith being your grandmother. Have you told him the truth yet? Did he understand?'

'Yes,' Faith said in a tiny voice, also recalling the lies she'd told Gavin about hoarding to cover up the fact that she'd discovered Luke in Hope's bedroom.

'So, your lies have been forgiven by other people and you forgive everyone else, but not me? Hasn't your hypocrisy struck you yet?'

Faith flinched. All that Tom had just said was true—including treating Tom differently to everyone else. She'd just compared him to Andy and then had written him off. Well, she'd tried to, but her heart hadn't been able to let go and was in a constant battle with her mind. With shame lurking behind her eyes, she dragged her gaze up to meet his and saw hurt and disappointment blazing towards her. 'I'm sorry,' she whispered.

'I am too,' he said. 'I thought you had a more generous nature; you have when it comes to caring for your mum and sister. But you've been unable to appreciate that living in a cocoon all one's adult life and then being spewed out into the adult world with no support network, no one guiding me in what to do or how to do it, is of any consequence.

'I was in that cupboard because I was struggling to cope, and the person who should have been giving me the most support at that difficult time was my mother. Yet, the way she behaved towards me would make anyone question whether she actually is my mother.

'What do you think it was like, being brought up by her? It was no wonder I escaped to Ireland whenever I could, and it was no wonder that I escaped her entirely at the first opportunity. So forgive me if I don't rejoice about the bond you claim to be developing with her. Now, if you'll excuse me, I've got things to be getting on with.'

He got up to open the door wide. Keeping her head low, so that her hair would shield her face, Faith concentrated on getting out without tripping up or bumping into something as her vision was down to about ten per cent of its normal acuity. She staggered in the direction of the loos, knowing that she'd broken something that could not now be fixed.

# 55

It was the last Friday of August, the day that Luke and Gavin were getting married. Miranda—in a knee-length dress, the blue of which matched the grooms' ties—was ready to leave to join them, but her employer was not.

'What do you mean, you're not going?' Miranda demanded from the doorway to Judith's study.

'I'm sure you can work it out.'

'You will go and the taxi will be here in fifteen minutes.'

'Since it appears that you require a hearing aid,' Judith said, 'I shall repeat myself a little more loudly. *I am not going.*'

'How can you not want to come to a wedding where I am groomsmaid to Gavin, your only child is best man to Luke and, God willing, Luke and Gavin will be dads to my baby?' Actually, Miranda had already performed a pregnancy test. But she wasn't ready to share the result with Judith yet—not until the daddies knew. 'Everyone in Tom's circle will be there and not one of them will take kindly to an obvious snub.'

Judith turned her head to the window, her expression impassive.

'Not welcoming Luke and Gavin into your life makes me feel unwelcome too, and I will have no choice but to leave your employ if I become pregnant.' Miranda aimed uncompromising eyes at Judith, confident she would buckle under the threat of abandonment.

No one had worked for Judith as long as Miranda had and they understood each other very well. Miranda had guessed early on that Judith's brusque manner was due to her divorce and feeling she'd not been good enough and never would be. So she drove people away rather than lay herself open to further vulnerability. Miranda had sensed this because she'd built her own walls; she knew that if she didn't change, she'd end up like Judith—a sad, lonely and scared old lady who was afraid she'd be left to cope alone.

'How many minutes do I have left?' Judith growled in her death metal voice. Then it softened. 'I was coming anyway—it was too much fun to pass up an opportunity to wind you up.'

'If that's true, be careful. One day, I might not take it anymore and leave.'

Miranda had so far hoped in vain for Judith to look upon her as a daughter she'd never had—and Judith could be the mother Miranda had never had. Perhaps, Judith would learn to soften by opening her heart to a new life like Miranda had opened her heart to Luke and Gavin. Then she might achieve something that jumping from one foster home to another had not given: a family.

Luke was with a group of people outside the Mayoral Room of the Old Council House on Corn Street in the centre of Bristol. When Miranda glimpsed him, she did a double-take. He could have been a celebrity in his white suit and royal blue tie. When he glanced her way, she mouthed, 'Where's Gavin?' He mouthed back that Gavin was in the toilets. Believing it her duty as groomsmaid to check on him, Miranda found the gents' loos and, since no one was about, knocked and boldly walked in, calling Gavin's name.

He was by the wash basin, splashing his face in cold water, looking almost as good as Luke in an identical suit except for the stricken expression.

'Are you okay?' Miranda asked.

'I'm worried I'll let Luke down in some way. I'm scared it will all go wrong.'

Now was not the time for Gavin to falter. 'You two are perfect for each other—and the three of us will work through any difficulties together. You won't be alone in the marriage or as a father if it all works out. It'll be a triple relationship. I'll help you not let Luke down, and I'll do my best to ensure that Luke doesn't fail you. We'll be parents together and that will make us all the stronger for it. Now, come here and let me hug you.'

When she and Gavin emerged from the loos, Faith was standing outside. She raised her eyebrows. 'And here you are... coming out of the gents. Is there a problem?'

Gavin smiled reassuringly, and Miranda squeezed his arm. 'Just a bit of a wobble,' she said.

'Don't worry, Gavin,' Faith said. 'It'll be fine, you'll be fine.'

Gavin nodded.

Faith handed Miranda a bouquet of white flowers. 'They're ready to go.'

When Gavin's Adam's apple bobbed up and down, Miranda squeezed his arm again and stepped away so that Faith could take her place—and Gavin's arm. His parents had refused to attend on account of their disapproval of his "lifestyle choices". When Faith had heard, she'd offered to give him away.

Faith and Gavin went into the Mayoral Room first. Miranda followed through the open doors and down the aisle.

It was quite a few minutes into the ceremony when Miranda noticed unaccustomed feelings welling up inside of her. It was so unusual that, for a moment, she suspected she might be ill. Blinking hard and taking long, deep breaths, she tried to concentrate on the flowers, the wooden panelling below the dado rail, the massive fireplace and the paintings of former Bristol mayors. In fact, anywhere other than at the boys. She'd spent a lifetime building walls to protect herself from hurt and emotions and now some flood of unfamiliar feelings was breaking them down.

Gavin had read out sweet, loving vows from his smartphone. Things like, 'I will always love you, I will be there for you through the difficult times, I will make you proud of me, and I will do all that I can to be a good dad when the time comes.'

Luke pulled out his smartphone. 'I vow I will cherish you, listen to you and support you, share in the bad times as well as the good, include you in all aspects of my life and be the best husband I can possibly be. Gavin, I want you to know that you are my soul mate and that today, by agreeing to be my husband, you are making me happy beyond my wildest dreams. Despite loving you so much, I still find my love growing, and I'm so grateful that you will be a part of my life for always.'

Through Miranda's tears, she could see that Gavin was trying to hold back tears of his own. She tapped Faith on the arm and whispered in her ear for a tissue. Seeing these two men together, a true couple, showed her very clearly what she'd missed out on. But all was not lost.

Although she'd never had much of a family and had experienced the care system from pre-school to leaving school at sixteen, she hoped now that she'd found a stable substitute family in Luke Challoner and Gavin Jenkins—soon to be officially Luke and Gavin Challoner-Jenkins. In time, she might even find a substitute mother in Judith Gold... Miranda wished she knew of a Jewish equivalent of "pigs might fly". Her gaze drifted to the side and she saw, with surprise, that Judith's customary hard-nosed expression had melted. Perhaps the imaginary pigs might grow some wings after all.

When the registrar said that magic phrase, 'I now pronounce you husband and husband, and you may kiss your husband,' it was as though Miranda's heart was being squashed in a press. Like a fruit being de-juiced, emotion was bursting out of her—and she needed another tissue. Was it her hormones playing up? Was that why she was so nauseous too?

Guests clapped as Luke bent his head and his lips touched Gavin's, their hands clasped tightly. This was what Miranda wanted for herself. A man who truly loved her and a wedding that made people cry.

It was after the food, the speeches and the toasts in a hired room in a pub that Faith made her way to the ladies. In the area just outside the gents, she saw a small gathering of people and wondered if a guest had been taken ill. 'Is something wrong? Can I help?'

'I don't know what's up,' a man said. 'I found him on the floor, crying.'

Faith stepped forward as guests allowed her room to advance. 'Luke,' she said in surprise.

At the sound of his name, Luke glanced up, his face streaked with tears.

Faith edged in and crouched next to him. She put an arm across his shoulders. Then, to the gathering, she said, 'Can someone find Gavin for him?' When three onlookers sped away, she said, 'Now, Luke, what's up?'

Luke sniffed. 'Gavin knows.'

'Knows *what?*' Surely the boys hadn't had a tiff on their wedding day?

'We saw her... not looking too good,' Luke said, with

a distinct slur. 'Insiss...ted she tell us... what's wrong.'

'Who?' Faith had a pretty good idea to whom Luke was referring.

'Miranda.'

So, it was Miranda's fault. She must have changed her mind about having a baby with Luke. How could she have upset the boys on their wedding day? Couldn't she have waited?

'What's the problem?'

Faith's heart somersaulted at the sound of Tom's familiar timbre. She turned to take in his dashing appearance. He was wearing his grey suit again, reminding her of being held in his arms when they'd danced at Perdita's party. And his delectable kisses... until it all went wrong. She longed to have his arms around her again and her body ached to be closer. She'd gone to sleep at night clutching a spare pillow, pretending it was Tom, pretending that he loved her still and that everything was all right.

She sat fully down to make room for him as he squatted to join them, his thigh brushing her bare arm, increasing her yearning. 'I don't know what the problem is.'

Now that Tom was right beside her it was hard to talk normally; it was as though the words had been held hostage at the back of her throat until her efforts to speak had given them freedom. She'd not been this near to Tom since the day in his office when they'd had that row, and she'd left crying. She'd done a lot of that lately—and wishing she had a magic clock she could turn back. Had she really blown it with Tom?

He reached out to put a hand on Luke's shoulder. 'What's wrong? Have you had a row with Gavin?'

In between gulps of what sounded like misery, Luke shook his head.

Tom's gaze rested on Faith. During that brief connection, she tried to convey how sorry she was, for not forgiving him for pretending to be two separate people. But when Tom looked away, she didn't think she'd succeeded. Tears stung her eyes. How could she put it right? She'd wanted to but just hadn't known how to make the leap. Now she was no longer confident that Tom felt the same about her as he had back then. *She'd spoilt everything.*

'He's coming!' someone shouted. 'Gavin's on his way.'

Gavin weaved as he approached, clearly under the influence.

'Gavin's here,' Faith said.

He stumbled and threw himself down beside Luke, shoving Tom out of the way, which prompted Tom to stand up. It wasn't just the increased physical distance between them that made Faith feel rejected. Tom had stood without acknowledging her presence and appeared as though he was preparing to walk away once he was sure the boys were okay.

'Is one of you going to tell me what this is all about?' Faith's voice was thick with emotion as she fought to stem the tears that threatened to overspill her lashes.

Gavin grinned. 'We're going to be daddies.'

Luke nodded.

'Hail to the turkey baster!' Gavin shouted, his hands high in the air.

'Congratulations.' She found a tissue to wipe her eyes. With luck, everyone would think they were tears of happiness and not connect them to Tom. When she felt brave enough to check for him, she found he'd already gone.

She must find Miranda to congratulate her and ask after her health. She'd sat next to Faith during the ceremony yet Faith hadn't known; she wished that Miranda had confided in her. She'd blamed Miranda just now for upsetting the boys but, in fact, Miranda had done something incredibly special for them. It was time Faith stopped being so judgemental.

Were the boys' lives moving away from hers? First, them going to Tom with their troubles and now sharing a life with Miranda? The ugly face of jealousy dangled before her, swiftly followed by loneliness and rejection. The others were moving on in their lives—as Hope was too with Edison—and Faith was fast becoming an outsider.

# 56

Shortly after arriving at the office the following Tuesday, Faith's mobile phone rang. She frowned. Miranda didn't usually call her. 'Miranda?'

'Hi Faith,' a breathless voice said, 'I'm calling to warn you. About Tom.' She sounded urgent.

'What about Tom?' A cold hand of foreboding clutched Faith's heart. What new disaster was this? How could her sleep patterns get back to normal with another setback?

'He hasn't signed the form.'

'What form?' Her stomach dived.

'To relieve Tom of his clerical duties. To become laicised. He's been sitting on it all this time.'

Faith didn't know anything about any form. But the mention of it filled her with dread. Why hadn't he signed it? Had he doubts over leaving his parish?

'I don't understand.'

'Luke said there's a formal procedure to go through. The first is a chat with the Bishop. Tom never got beyond that. He never filled in the form. So, step two hasn't been done.'

Faith gripped the worktop.

'Luke said Tom wants to see the Bishop again. I saw him getting into a taxi as I was driving out with Judith—dressed head to toe in black. When I wound down the window, Tom said his car had broken down and that he needed to get to the station fast to catch the nine o'clock train to Paddington.'

'To get to the airport?' Hadn't Tom served abroad?

Faith wasn't sure what the term was in the context of priests working overseas, but didn't the army use that word when personnel had a posting? Or, had she imagined him being abroad just like she'd imagined him sheep-minding?

'No. To get to Snaresbury.'

Faith thought of all the sleepless nights she'd had since that day in Tom's office when he'd asked her to leave, her mind spinning like a hamster on a wheel. She'd been filled with such regret. Why hadn't she let Tom explain his whole story before they'd fallen out?

'Where did you say?'

She heard Miranda sigh impatiently. 'Snaresbury. It's in Bleakset. Where his bishop lives.'

How could Faith not have known that? Why had she concentrated so hard on her grievances when she'd failed to show any interest in Tom's clerical past—even something so basic as to where his parish had been?

From the silence, Miranda must have sensed that Faith was quite ignorant of where Tom had been living before he'd come back to Clifton, as Miranda added, 'Tom's parish is in Marrow... And that's in Bleakset too.'

Faith was feeling lightheaded and slightly sick. 'Why are you telling me all this?'

'Luke thinks he's going to ask the Bishop to take him back.'

Faith's heart lurched. Tom? Leaving? 'But what about his photography business?' Her voice came out thin and reedy as she wondered whether she really would be sick.

'I don't know. But he is back in his priest clothing. I want to help you—and Judith. She doesn't want to lose him again.'

Faith thought that Judith had already done a good job of that herself.

'Are you going?' Miranda asked. 'You're the only one who can stop him.'

Would she go? Damn right she would. She'd lost out on being a social worker, given so much to her mother and Hope, and had lost so many friends, she was *not* going to lose Tom as well. She'd get him to change his mind, tell him how much she loved him and how sorry she was. She'd square it with Edison later.

'I'll call a cab.'

'I've already done it. It should be with you shortly.'

Faith grabbed her bag, coat and scarf. Her stilettos clipped rapidly on the stairs as she made her way down while donning her outdoor wear, too impatient to hang around for the lift. While she waited for her ride, Faith tried Tom's mobile to ask him to delay boarding the train until she reached him, but a voice told her the number was unavailable.

The taxi ride to Bristol Temple Meads railway station took ages because of the lights and traffic. When she arrived, Faith charged towards the departure board. The 09.00 London-bound train was due in only four minutes. She ran to the ticket gates.

'Please,' she begged the gateline assistant, 'could you let me through? I've got to see someone getting on the Paddington train.'

The assistant shook her head. 'Not without a ticket, you don't.'

'I might miss it.'

'You need a ticket.'

The queue to buy tickets from a person was far too long. Faith had no hope of catching the same train as Tom if she stood in line there. Luckily, the queue she joined at the automatic teller machines instantly shortened. A man had just gathered his tickets from the dispenser and left. The woman in front of Faith stepped forward to take his place.

Repeatedly, Faith checked the station clock. While she wasn't checking the clock or the progress of the woman in front, Faith cast about her for a sign of Tom. But with the train's arrival so close, he was unlikely to be her side of the ticket gates.

Anxiously, Faith jigged on the spot. Two minutes to go. Then she heard the announcement for the next train to London, Paddington. She knew she was going to miss it. Miss it. Miss it.

Or was she? The woman ahead of her bent to retrieve her printed tickets. Faith edged forwards, willing her to go. Just go; don't stop to examine your tickets. Make way for the girl with a mission.

It was Faith's turn. To recall the previously unheard-of town that was apparently Tom's final destination was way too much of a cerebral task when her mind was on the verge of panic. She'd been so dazed by what Miranda had been telling her that she'd not properly taken it in. Besides, she hoped she would be able to dissuade Tom from his undertaking while en route to Paddington. Then they could get the next train back to Bristol.

Jabbing frantically at the touch screen, making mistakes because her hand was shaking, Faith finally managed to get to the stage where she punched in her PIN. Payment authorised. Printing ticket. Faith put her plastic back in her bag.

After grabbing the ticket and receipt as soon as they dropped into the dispenser, Faith charged towards the ticket gates, weaving around passengers who weren't in quite as much of a hurry. She waved her ticket at the woman she'd spoken to earlier and yelled, 'I've got it!'

Obligingly, the woman beckoned her through the open disabled gate, and Faith was able to turn right and then head down the stairs towards the underpass.

It was a good job she was so fit—although Faith was used to running in trainers, not heels. But she wasn't going to let that deter her. When she heard the announcement saying that the train was approaching, she put on a spurt. She still had stairs to climb and wasn't quite there yet. Off came her shoes and she clutched them as she continued running, damning the dirt and the pain as her soles slapped on the concrete. It was a shame the entrance to the platform was so far along the underpass.

The rumble of a train—it had to be the Paddington train—drawing into a station made Faith think again that she wasn't going to make it. She puffed up the stairs towards the platform. Then she heard the sound of a guard's whistle. She was going to miss it. She was...

The train was still there.

'Wait!' she croaked as she crested the stairwell. The whistle must have just been a warning of imminent departure rather than one of immediate departure.

The guard saw her.

Faith staggered ungainly towards the open door. 'Thank you so much,' she panted and lumbered aboard. The door closed. She smiled her thanks to the guard through the window as he blew the whistle differently while raising the dispatch baton. The train began to move. But she'd no idea whether Tom was on it. What if Miranda had made a mistake? While she stood in the space between the carriage doors catching her breath, she thought of where she was supposed to be and was not.

What would Edison say? She put her shoes back on her now filthy feet and thumbed out a text message, claiming an emergency unrelated to Hope. Faith didn't want him stressing over his girlfriend. Then she called

Luke.

However, Luke didn't pick up. She tried Gavin, but Gavin's phone was switched off. So she couldn't verify what Miranda had said. Why hadn't the boys been the ones to tell her? Why hadn't they told her about the form and the Bishop? They'd always been there for her in the past and perhaps there was a good explanation as to why it had been Miranda who'd called... Perhaps Tom had asked Luke and Gavin to keep information about the form confidential from her?

Faith scanned faces as she swayed along aisles. She didn't see Tom. But he was probably further up the train. Would he have travelled first-class? No. He was a priest and owned a Halora. First-class travel would be an unnecessary extravagance.

Passing through all the carriages bar first-class, including the buffet car and the ones she'd double-backed on to cover the entire train, Faith ended up several cars from the front. She couldn't spend the entire journey walking up and down the aisles of the carriages, scanning faces, in the hope of seeing someone who wasn't there. Had Tom spotted her, he would have made himself known to her.

Unless...

Unless he *had* spotted her and didn't want her to see him. He could have deliberately evaded her...

'Are you all right, love?'

Faith came out of her reverie to see a burly man looking at her expectantly.

It was the second time she'd passed him at his table seat, and she would have continued past again if he hadn't just spoken to her. Faith opened her mouth to answer, but instead of finding words, she burst into tears.

'Here,' he said. 'Take my seat and tell me what the

problem is.'

'I'm looking for a priest.' Faith sobbed through the words as she sank onto his seat. 'I can't find him. I was told there would be a priest on the train, and he's not here.'

'What was that, love?' The man cupped his ear and leaned towards her.

The train was noisy with wheels clattering on the tracks, kids screaming and general hubbub. Why hadn't she broken down in the quiet carriage?

Faith shouted, 'I'm looking for a priest! I need to find a priest!' and then continued sobbing into a tissue she'd found in her coat pocket.

The burly man yelled, 'Is there a priest on board?'

'He'll... be... wearing black clothes,' Faith shouted helpfully through the sobs.

An old lady sitting opposite reached across and patted her hand, 'I think they all do, dear. Black's their colour.'

When the burly man shrugged his shoulders because no one had come forward, Faith wailed, 'I want my priest.'

The burly man shouted, 'Will anyone help me find a priest for the lady?'

Another two men stood up and offered to help.

'I'll go back that way, to double-check.' The burly man pointed in the direction Faith had come from, towards the front of the train. 'You two can check the rest of the train that way. Tell him it's urgent.'

The old lady patted Faith's hand again. 'There, there, dear. I'll look after you until they find you a priest. If there is a priest.'

# 57

Tom sat on the Paddington train in a reverie, recalling good times with Faith, before it had all gone sour. It would have been nice if they could have made this journey together. Then he could have introduced her to the Bishop. Tom could picture him now, turning that particular shade of plum and spouting stuff Tom was no longer interested in. He was making his own rules now and took what comfort from the Church that he could without dishing out the massive guilt trip he used to punish himself with.

Not long after the train had cleared Bristol Temple Meads station, he'd headed for the toilet. Although he'd dressed in his clerical clothes, he hadn't put on his clerical collar, not wanting the few remaining people in Clifton, who didn't yet know he was a priest, to know that he was indeed a priest.

Guided by the mirror provided in the cubicle, Tom had fitted the plastic collar into his shirt so that only a tab of white showed in the cut-out by his throat. It had felt strange seeing himself again like this. But now, he shouldn't be bothered by Roxy types, and he would be in the mindset to deal with The Right Reverend Brendon Costello. Feeling for his rosary in his pocket, Tom had decided to say a few prayers for good measure.

Later, he'd chosen the first non-reserved seat he could find. He listened to the clackety-clack of wheels on the track. Then Tom's attention was caught by the sound of someone coming down the aisle shouting. Was there a what on board? He wondered what had happened. A heart attack? Stroke? Seizure?

The man was approaching and this time, Tom heard what was called out: 'Is there a priest on board?'

Christ, it must be worse than he'd imagined. Someone was either dying or had just died. It was his duty as a priest to help with any sacrament if needed. The man was level with him now. Tom stood up. 'I'm a priest.'

'I can see that,' the man said. 'She's towards the front of the train.'

'Who's towards the front?' Tom asked the man's back as he hurried after him.

'It's all right,' the man called to another man who was further ahead. 'I've found a priest.'

The further ahead man shouted, 'Make way for the priest! Priest coming through!'

'What's the problem?' Tom asked as they marched through the two sets of glass doors and into the next carriage.

'Don't know,' the man immediately in front said. 'Got this hysterical woman who says she needs a priest. Not for me to enquire... Could be confidential.'

What could be so urgent?

'Priest coming through!' the man further ahead shouted.

They'd reached the connecting area with the next carriage and were going between the two sets of glass doors again.

'Nearly there,' the man immediately in front said. 'Just further up this carriage.'

Tom could hear the sounds of a woman bawling.

'We've found a priest!' the man yelled.

The passengers in the carriage began to clap. What was he walking into?

The ticket collector was trying to squeeze past. When

he saw Tom, he said, 'Hurry. She's really upset. They've tried to console her, but all she keeps saying is that she wants her priest.'

*Her priest?* The way was now clear for Tom to follow the backs of the two men ahead. The crowd was diminished by people returning to their seats and stepping away from the lady in distress.

'Here's the priest,' the man further ahead said.

Tom's view was barred by the high back to the chair. 'But is he *my* priest?' he heard her cry. It was a strangled, intense sound that grated. But he prepared his kindest, softest, most reassuring tone that he used with the bereaved as he crouched by her seat.

'How can I help?'

The blotched and mottled face that turned towards him was... the most beautiful face in distress he'd ever seen. 'Faith.'

'She's got plenty of that, mate. That's why she asked for you.' A burly man joined them. 'Glad they found you. I searched the other end of the train. I think you must be the only priest on board.'

Faith's eyes widened in wonderment when she saw Tom. A moment later, she flung her arms around him and held him tight. So tight, he was having trouble breathing. When she loosened her grip, he stood up and she did too, briefly placing a hand on his chest. It felt good.

'Oh, I'm so glad I found you!'

Tom found an extra-large tissue to pass to her, and she put it to use immediately.

The two men who'd preceded Tom into the carriage said, 'Actually, we found him.'

Tom gazed adoringly into Faith's eyes, and she gazed adoringly back. He kissed her face. It was still damp.

'Is he a priest-o-gram?' the old lady sitting at Faith's table asked.

Tom ignored her. But when he glanced up, he noticed the men who'd found him were regarding him expectantly. 'I'm not a stripper,' he said. 'I am a priest.'

'He's *my* priest,' Faith said in a voice that carried. 'Except I didn't know he was a priest when I met him.'

'How could you not guess he's a priest? His clothes tell you that,' the burly man said.

Tom took hold of Faith's hand. 'What are you doing here?'

'I came to stop you going to the Bishop.'

'Looks like he's been a naughty boy,' the burly man said to no one in particular. 'Not discreet about it either.'

Tom tried to block everyone else out. 'Why don't you want me to see the Bishop?'

'I don't want you to go back to being a priest. Back to your sheep.'

Tom smiled apologetically at the people nearest to him. 'My flock.'

'His human sheep,' Faith clarified to the audience, and then whispered to Tom, 'Please come back. Don't see the Bishop.'

'Priests like you give the priesthood a bad name,' the burly man said.

Faith turned. 'He's not been a naughty boy. I can vouch for that. And he left his parish before he met me.'

'Looks like it. Why's he wearing the garb then? Why does he look like he's just come from saying Mass?'

Tom raised his hands. 'It was to make a gesture to the Bishop when I see him. To take off my collar and chuck it on his desk.'

'You tell him, mate,' the man who found him said.

'But I thought you already told the Bishop?' Faith said.

'I have. He gave me time to reconsider and there are formal procedures for this.'

'The form you didn't sign?' Faith asked.

'How do you know about that?'

'Miranda told me.'

'Who told...? Oh, I get it. Luke.'

'So, you're definitely leaving your parish and all your other duties?' Faith asked. 'You're going to stay in Clifton?'

'Definitely.' Tom stroked her cheek. 'And I would like you to come with me to see the Bishop.'

'Why?'

It seemed that the rest of the occupants of the carriage wanted to know why, too, as no one interrupted or called out. There was complete silence apart from the rumble and clickety-clack of the train.

'Because I love you.' Tom dropped to one knee in the way that he would genuflect, but stayed down instead of making it a quick bob. Looking up at her, he said, 'Faith, would you do me the very great honour of becoming my wife?'

She looked bemused, stunned. He rose to his feet. She still didn't answer. But he wouldn't give up.

'So, you really want to marry her?' the old lady said. 'She doesn't seem keen on the idea herself. Although I do like a romance myself.'

'You bet I do,' Tom said with feeling. To Faith, he said, 'I intend to marry you, Faith Goddard, and The Right Reverend Brendon Costello can put that in his pipe and smoke it!'

Encouraged by her silence and look of awe, Tom bent his head and kissed her full on the lips. When Faith's arms wound around his neck, he ended the kiss. 'Will you have me?'

'Yes!' Faith yelled. 'Yes, yes, yes!'

There was a round of applause from what Tom took to be the vast majority of the passengers in their vicinity. Wrapping his arms about Faith, he looked around feeling overjoyed. But then, as his gaze caught a young man standing on a seat near him, his phone pointed towards them, Tom's mouth fell open.

# 58

Mrs Caraleen McGuire had just finished preparing the vegetables for lunch. She was feeling down about her lot. She was forty-two years of age with no home of her own and no children. She was also living a lie.

She'd called herself Mrs and had worn her mother's wedding ring to get the job just over ten years ago. But she'd never been married or widowed. She pretended to be respectable when, in God's eyes, she was not. The Right Reverend Brendon Costello had persuaded her that there was no harm if they were discreet, and they had been. But she was deeply unhappy about the situation.

She twisted the wedding ring thoughtfully as she checked the timer to see if the chops were done. There was time to have a cup of tea before she laid the table. She was just about to put the kettle on when her phone gave the notification sound of an incoming message.

The short missive was from her dearest and closest friend. The only friend she'd dared confide in. *Check out the link!* Curious, Caraleen tapped the link address. It was to a YouTube clip named, *The Right Reverend Brendon Costello can put that in his pipe and smoke it!* She tapped to play.

The scene opened with a man in what looked like a train carriage shouting, 'We've found a priest!' She heard the sound of clapping and a man in black with a white dog collar appeared. She watched avidly as the dramatic story played out on screen.

Almost at the end of the clip, the priest said, 'I intend to marry you, Faith Goddard, and The Right Reverend

Brendon Costello can put that in his pipe and smoke it!'
The priest kissed the girl, presumably called Faith, and then she wound her arms around his neck. Then he asked, 'Will you have me?' Faith shouted, almost screamed, 'Yes!... Yes, yes, yes!'

Caraleen gripped the edge of her phone as though her fingers had gone into spasm. The footage had already had fifteen-thousand hits. What she couldn't get over was that the priest had *kissed* the woman. Smack on the lips. And he'd proposed to her. In front of all those witnesses. No hole-in-the-wall affair for them.

Why couldn't Brendon give up the Church like this priest had and propose to her? Why couldn't she have a happy ending to her love life? It was clear that the man on the train—who appeared strangely familiar—truly loved Faith, whereas Brendon did not truly love Caraleen. He couldn't. She realised that now.

She recalled the last time she'd seen the face of that man on the train. It had been inside the Bishop's study about six months ago. When she was packing for Brendon to see the Pope. She'd gleaned he'd committed a misdemeanour and was being banished from his parish. Was that because he'd fallen in love and intended to marry the woman on the train? Brendon had never shared the reason for the visit with her as Caraleen had expected him to. Now it was clear why. He hadn't wanted her to know. It served his purpose better to keep her in ignorance so that she wouldn't expect the same from him! The new understanding of the situation was bringing her to her senses.

Caraleen McGuire was a dedicated and dutiful housekeeper. That was why, in the face of adversity, she didn't crack up, she didn't succumb to the pain and anguish that gnawed away at her innards. She was so in control that she managed to complete the meal she'd planned and have it ready at one as usual so that the Fathers' schedules would not be wrecked. But she'd been clattering and banging the pans and had broken two plates. Well, who said she was an angel?

The food was on the table when elderly Father Deary, who had been given a room when the demands of his own parish had got too much, and The Right Reverend Brendon Costello walked in.

'What would this be now?' Brendon asked as he approached the table and then lifted the upturned dish on his plate.

'What does it look like?' Caraleen asked nonchalantly, but felt her eyes narrow.

'It's a pipe,' Brendon said. 'What's it doing here?'

The pipe had been her dad's and had become a useful prop. 'There's a link I emailed you. A video clip from YouTube. That will explain it to you.'

With a thoughtful expression, Brendon placed the pipe next to his plate.

'Are you not eating with us, Caraleen?' Father Deary asked.

Caraleen smiled sweetly. 'Haven't I already eaten?' she lied. 'Haven't I got cases to pack all of a sudden?'

'Would you be going somewhere?' Brendon sounded alarmed. 'Has something happened? Is someone ill?'

'Not at all,' Caraleen stated calmly. 'Quite the reverse. She's started to make a recovery.'

'Who would that be?' Father Deary asked.

'That would be me.'

Brendon was looking confused, his face purpling with restraint.

'I thought that you might like to have a quick look at the clip while you're eating.' She gestured towards the laptop on the sideboard. 'I'll be pressing play once you've said Grace.'

'I don't think—' Brendon began.

'Oh, I insist,' Caraleen said, walking over to the laptop.

After Brendon had made the sign of the cross and said Grace, Caraleen clicked on the play icon.

'I know him!' Brendon exclaimed. 'Father Thomas Sheridan. He's got an appointment to see me this afternoon.'

*That* was his name. Caraleen had forgotten it.

A few minutes later, they'd reached that part again: *... I intend to marry you, Faith Goddard, and The Right Reverend Brendon Costello can put that in his pipe and smoke it!*

Then the applause.

Then the doorbell rang.

'Excuse me.' Caraleen almost ran to the front of the house. She'd a fair idea of who it might be.

Caraleen found Father Thomas Sheridan and Faith on the doorstep. 'Come in, come in,' she said with forced brightness. 'Haven't we been expecting you? You must be Faith.'

'Yes... but...?'

'You're famous now, did you not know?'

Faith gave a nervous laugh. 'Famous? I hardly think so.'

'Sure you are. And Father Sheridan here. By tonight, you'll be world-famous, the pair of you.'

Father Sheridan smiled politely. 'I think you're mistaking us for—'

'No, no. There's no mistake. Now, come this way. His Excellency is having lunch.' Caraleen beckoned them to follow. 'Would you be wanting something to eat now?' She noticed Father Sheridan bite his lower lip. 'That you will. I'll fetch a couple of extra plates.' She always cooked plenty and what would it matter if Brendon only had one chop to eat instead of the usual two or three? The guests were welcome to her portion.

'Father Sheridan and Faith for you, Your Excellency,' Caraleen said as they walked into the dining room. 'They'll be having a bite to eat after that long train journey.'

'How do you know we came by train?' Father Sheridan asked. 'I'd intended to come by car.'

'The whole world knows you came by train,' Brendon said. 'And you can take your collar off now. There's no need to wait to throw it on my desk. Haven't I already got the message? The sooner you're gone from here, the better.'

'That's no way to talk to a man who dedicated so many years to the Church,' Faith said.

'And it's no way to kiss a man of the cloth, in clerical dress, with an audience of millions!' Brendon shouted. 'How dare you bring the Church into disrepute?'

'Audience of millions?' Tom said.

'You're on the Internet. Someone filmed you, you eejit.'

'Oh... I did see someone with a phone...'

Faith gasped, and her hand went to her mouth. 'I'm on the Internet? What if Mum and Dad see it before I get around to telling them I'm engaged?'

'Here you are.' Caraleen placed two extra settings on the table. 'Don't be shy about helping yourselves. There'll be plenty as I don't think anyone else is too hungry today.'

Brendon turned to glare at Faith. 'Thomas here has not been laicised. Only then, with special dispensation, is he allowed to marry. If he marries you outside the Catholic Church, the marriage will be invalid. You'll be living in sin.'

Faith's expression froze in shock. Caraleen's

stomach churned. If Faith would be sinning by sleeping with her husband, it meant she'd been sinning for years because of Brendon. They weren't married in any sense. Her showing devotion in serving the Lord by supporting a man of God... well, it was all rubbish Brendon had been spouting so he could get his own way.

He wasn't showing a shred of sympathy for the couple. What did he really think of her? A temptress? If she recalled correctly, he'd been the one to seek her out. It made Caraleen wonder now why the last housekeeper had left. Had she really had family commitments?

'We do things quietly when priests choose to leave the clerical life.' Brendon slammed his hand onto the table. 'We don't make a song and dance about it, and we certainly don't broadcast it to the world.'

'You can't be getting angry with him,' Father Deary reasoned. 'Matthew 7.3: *Why do you see the speck that is in your brother's eye, but do not notice the log that is in your own eye?*'

'I don't know what you mean,' Brendon blustered.

Caraleen felt the blow of her shame having been known about all along. 'If I can guess, Brendon, then I'm sure you can too.'

'The world might not know,' Father Deary said, 'but I know—I'm a poor sleeper—and God knows. I... I didn't say anything before because of my own past failings in that area.'

'Will you be thinking of marrying me now?' Caraleen asked Brendon—just to make sure. 'Even if the marriage would be invalid?' Then she'd have a ring that deserved to be on her finger—everyone who wasn't Catholic would respect it. And perhaps those sympathetic Catholic souls like Faith and Tom would too.

'... I...'

Caraleen nodded, fighting back tears. 'I'll be off to

start that packing.' She turned, unable to look any of them in the eye. She would stay with the friend who'd sent her the link. Until she found another position with accommodation. Housekeeping was all she'd known. She'd make a new life for herself.

# 59

It was the day after Boxing Day and the vicar of All Saints Church where Faith and Hope had been baptised had just pronounced Tom and Faith man and wife.

'You may kiss the bride,' the vicar said.

Tom tenderly cupped Faith's face in the palms of his hands, held her gaze until just before his lips touched hers and lingered long over the kiss. For a moment, she forgot they had an audience and wrapped her arms around his neck, bringing his light grey suit in firm contact with the white faux fur cape she wore over her white dress. The vicar coughed. The guests laughed, and she sprang away from Tom. What would her parents think?

Once they'd signed the register, they were back in the nave, beautifully decorated with Christmas wreaths, flowers and a large, twinkling tree. Mendelssohn's *Wedding March* began to play. They walked back along the aisle—with Saul, Tom's best man, and Hope, Faith's bridesmaid. Perdita, who had given birth to Posy, winked as Faith swept past as though to say you're next. Faith hoped so.

After the photographs, she and Tom were in the stretch limo, bedecked with white ribbons, travelling down Pembroke Road, then along Clifton Down. Judith was footing the bill for the whole shebang at The Mansion House and had generously offered the refurbished annexe at the side of her house to Faith and Tom rent-free. Edison was moving into the flat she'd shared with Hope, and Edison was letting his place as the stairs made it unsuitable for her long term.

At The Mansion House, some guests were already there. A few of these had declined to attend the ceremony as they'd claimed that their rabbi did not approve of them entering a Christian church. Some were Tom's priest friends who had feared the Bishop's wrath for witnessing a marriage that was not valid in the eyes of the Catholic Church. But the reception would be fine for all, as Judith had made sure that dietary observances for the Jewish guests would be respected. Faith's relations and friends, and the Irish contingent from Tom's father's side of the family, would soon be following them from the church.

A harpist played while Faith tucked into a fillet of salmon with basil and Parmigiano Reggiano crust, chargrilled Mediterranean vegetables and Parmentier potatoes; Tom had chosen roast duck drenched in a cherry and wine sauce with red cabbage and Dauphinoise potatoes.

'I bet everyone's pretty much still bursting after Christmas,' Faith said to Tom. 'We've still got the chocolate-covered strawberries to go. Do you think we'll be able to dance after all this food?'

'We'd better. However many tunes we dance to with the ceilidh band must be matched to the number of dances with the klezmer band. Otherwise, Mum might get upset.'

After dinner, in another room, the Irish ceilidh band struck up. John Legend's *All of Me* filled the room. It was what Faith had requested for her first dance with her husband.

'Did you refresh your skills with Luke?' she asked as they walked to the dance floor, revelling in the feel of her hand in her husband's. Physically, it felt the same, but emotionally, well, it was different. It *belonged* there.

For life.

'No need. I've invested in a second-hand mannequin to help me practise portrait photography, and I confess I've been dancing with her.'

Faith regarded him speculatively. 'Seriously?'

He shrugged and gave a weak smile. 'I didn't want to mess it up.'

At times, Tom infuriated her. 'Did you honestly think that you stepping on my toes would make me regret being married to you?'

'It was in deference to your toes that I didn't wish to put you through it. Especially in public, on the big day.'

'Did it not occur to you that I might have enjoyed practising with you before the so-called big day?'

'Oh.'

'Don't ever,' she warned, 'substitute a mannequin for me again.'

'Message received and understood.' Tom saluted. Then he held out his arms and she slid into them, happy to feel his body close to hers and his warm breath on her skin.

When Tom carried Faith over the threshold of their room in The Berkeley Square Hotel, she saw heart-shaped chocolates wrapped in red foil spread on the white duvet in the shape of a huge heart. He side-stepped their awaiting luggage and laid her gently on the edge of the divan.

'Did you arrange this?' Her voice was filled with delighted surprise.

He sat next to her, appearing smug.

'It's lovely.'

He reached into his pocket and drew out a small box. He kissed her. 'For you, my wonderful, beautiful wife.'

Opening it, she found a delicate silver chain with a

heart pendant glittering with what looked like a diamond. 'Thank you. It's lovely, so pretty.' She kissed him and then said, 'I have something for you, too.' She reached into her case, brought out a box and handed it to him. She'd spent a great deal of time searching for something he might like.

He opened the box.

'I thought that you might like to have a smarter timepiece for when you want to impress clients.'

He pointed to his wrist. 'You're saying this one is too scruffy?'

'I am. For certain occasions.' The watch face, casing and bracelet were all heavily scratched.

'Then I shall certainly keep your gift for best and, whenever I check the time when I'm wearing it, I shall think of you.' His lips met hers for a lengthy kiss.

Then she looked at Tom, and he looked at her.

'Well,' he murmured, 'now what?'

The wait for intimacy up to now had been interminable—Tom had been very firm in his decision for them to wait until after marriage, to stick to his personal beliefs and to honour her.But despite longing for this private time alone with him, the atmosphere had suddenly become awkward. He'd never seen her naked. Would he like what he saw? Would she be able to please him?

'What are you thinking?' he asked.

She bit her lip. 'I think I'm nervous.'

'I think I am too. I've spent plenty of time imagining, fantasising, how this would play out but now, I'm floundering. Perhaps you could help me—as you did in the cupboard?'

She wished they'd made love before now, without the pressure of it being their wedding night. 'I think a good place to start would be to help each other undress.'

She was wearing another balconette bra since the last one he'd seen had been such a hit. Like the other, it was white and lacy and revealed plenty of flesh. She turned her back to him. 'I wouldn't have been able to manage all the little buttons on my dress anyway.'

He seemed to be fumbling ineffectively with the fiddly fastenings. 'I'm having trouble getting them undone.'

'I think they might need tiny fingers.'

'I don't think that's the only problem.'

Faith twisted around to give him a questioning look.

'My hands are shaking too much.'

She held her right hand in the air. She couldn't hold it steady either. 'I think we're both very nervous. Take a deep breath and take your time. There's no rush.'

Why had someone designed a wedding dress that took the groom almost twenty minutes to undo? When Tom had begun, she'd been standing to make it easier for him. Then she'd sat on the edge of the bed, and he'd knelt behind her. By the time he was on the last buttons, the chocolate hearts had been swept into a pile on the easy chair, and she was lying on her stomach with him astride her thighs. It had been a long day and, now that she'd lain down, exhaustion overcame her.

He flopped down on the bed next to her when he'd finished freeing the last button. 'I was worried I'd tear it. The material's so delicate.' He smoothed her hair from her face. 'May I assist you out of your dress?'

'Mm.'

He took great care—and she helped him by rolling in whichever direction he needed her to so that he could free the material from her body.

As she felt at a disadvantage in her bra, knickers, suspenders and stockings, she decided to even things out by getting him down to his boxer shorts. Judging by the grin on his face, he seemed to be enjoying the process. It reminded her that she was the first woman, other than his mother, to have undressed him. There were no competing memories of other women she would have to worry about, and it made her feel more secure, less skittish, and desire spread through her body.

Tom struggled with the back fastening of her bra as she lay over him until, finally, she was free. Then he stared and stared and stared. What would he make of her lower half if his hypnotic reaction to her upper body was this intense?

'Let's get under the covers,' she said.

He pulled back the duvet and she bent her knees so that she could get her feet underneath and then she slid down. He joined her. She removed her suspenders and stockings and then tugged at his boxer shorts. He moved obligingly so that they slid down his legs. She helped him likewise with her knickers, and then they were kissing. He was touching her breast and a tsunami of desire overcame her. She'd waited so long for this moment, had yearned to feel his naked body against hers, and had imagined what it would feel like to have him inside her...

Faith's hand went downwards. *Oh.*

'I'm sorry, I don't know what's happened. I wanted tonight to be so special, so memorable.'

'It will be memorable,' she assured. 'I love you and we are spending our first night together as a married couple. We have many, many nights ahead of us. A lifetime of nights... and other times too.' She knew that Tom must be hurting right now and wanted to do everything she could to take his pain away.

'But not memorable in this way.' He groaned.

'It's called,' she said, in the utmost understanding tone, 'performance anxiety.' Hugging him, she kissed him gently. 'It's not a problem for me. But it will be if you practise on that mannequin.' Then a thought struck her. 'Please tell me you haven't already practised on the mannequin.'

He grinned. 'I could not be unfaithful to you, my love.'

'Just so long as you realise, it's me or the mannequin.'

'You'd win hands down every time,' Tom said. 'Now I'd like to find out what it feels like to spoon with a woman, hold her in my arms all night long.'

'By all means, after I've switched the entrance light off.' She swung her legs to the floor.

'Let me put on the bedside light so that you don't bump into something on your way back.'

She flicked the entrance switch and then hurried back to bed.

'I think,' Tom murmured, 'spooning might have to wait. I've never seen a completely naked woman before, and I find that I am...'

Under the duvet, she felt for him. '... coming back to life.'

His touch, tender and exploratory, inflamed her and she heard him moan under her ministrations. This time, there was no performance anxiety.

Later, Tom gave a happy sigh and very proudly said, 'We have consummated our marriage, I have just lost my virginity and I will be released from a clerical life. And I enjoyed what we did immensely.'

'Mm. Me too,' she said, kissing the dip below his throat. Her skin was still glowing in the aftermath of their lovemaking and she was already thinking about what the next time might be like. If this had been Tom's starting point...

Remembering what would happen when she and

Andy had made love, Faith thought she'd better get her question in before her husband fell asleep. 'Tom, what were those numbers you were muttering just now?'

'Oh, you heard?'

'Yes. It sounded like you were doing maths problems.'

He gave a shy laugh. 'As I said before, I wanted it to be a night to remember. I thought I might have a problem in... er... rushing things. So, I wanted to slow things down.'

'By doing sums?'

He rolled onto his back and put his hands over his face. There was enough light coming in around the curtains for Faith to see his outline but not enough to see his expression.

'Would you care to explain?' she asked.

'Remember the time we met in that shop? With a woman you mistook for my mother?'

Faith recalled it very clearly. 'Of course, I remember. It was one of the most embarrassing situations I've ever found myself in.'

'Well, I'd gone to the library in search of help... But found out that the library did not stock the... literature... I was looking for. The librarian was very helpful and... offered... to take me somewhere I could find the information I required. And I bought a book.'

It was a very odd librarian who offered to take people to a particular kind of shop to help them find a particular kind of book. Did Tom's acceptance of such unorthodox assistance make him odd as well? She didn't care but wondered what kind of book it was. Did it include pictures? 'A book?' She would very much like to see it.

'A book.'

Faith had been impressed by his performance, considering it had been his first tryst. His research explained why their love-making hadn't been over in just a few frantic seconds and how he'd considered her needs.

'Perhaps you could show your purchase to me sometime. And the maths? That was to do with advice from said publication?'

He cleared his throat, coughed and then cleared his throat again. 'Promise you won't tell anyone? Not even Hope?'

Faith found his hand and squeezed it. 'Promise.' But she couldn't promise not to laugh. If she bit her lip any harder, it would bleed. 'What kind of sums were they?' It was difficult to keep her voice steady.

'I started at 300 and kept subtracting in threes. It's tougher than you'd think, and it was sufficient to distract me enough to...'

It was no good. She couldn't hold it in any longer; she gave a full belly laugh. Then she sobered. She couldn't imagine Andy doing anything like that for her. 'That's so...' she giggled, 'sweet...' she giggled some more, 'and kind of you.' And she kissed him. And giggled some more.

'What were you doing in that shop? Perhaps I can have a chuckle too.'

Abruptly, Faith's mirth left her. 'How about an agreement? I never tell about your maths sums and you never ask about what I was doing in that shop?'

'Uh-uh. We should not start our married life having secrets. You've just had a good laugh at my expense. Now, it's my turn.'

Burying herself under the bedding, she spoke to Tom's chest. 'I was missing having sex. Gavin suggested I visited the shop and, although it seemed like a good idea at the time, I ended up chucking my purchase in a litter bin. That's all I wish to say on the matter, okay?'

'Okay. But unlike you, I haven't sniggered, and it's safe for you to show your face as I'm not going to either. Now let's do some spooning.'

'Do you snore?'

'Probably.'

'Badly?'

'Isn't this a question you should have asked before you said yes?'

'I only just thought of it.' Would she be back on the farm again this evening or on a runway listening to jet engines taking off?

'I don't recall anyone ever mentioning snoring to me, so I don't think you need worry about a sleepless night on that count... Hey, I've got a great idea to help us get to sleep.' Tom's chest was against her back as he moulded his body to her shape. It felt wonderfully comforting.

'Counting sheep?' she suggested.

'No, doing some sums. 300.'

'I think it's going to be fun married to you.'

'You like maths that much?'

'No. But I like how you deal with the embarrassment and turn it into a joke. 297.'

'What makes you think it's a joke? 294.'

'Isn't it a joke? 291.'

Tom kissed the back of her head. 'It is indeed a joke. 288.'

Faith was too drowsy to continue. Since Tom didn't nudge her for the next number, she guessed he was too. She drifted off to sleep.

# Epilogue

It was towards the end of January and the end of Faith's second week back at work after their honeymoon in Ireland. They'd stayed in a boutique hotel, twenty minutes' walk from the centre of Dublin, but had not ventured out to explore as much as Faith had expected. Tom's new hobby was her body, and he'd taken it up with a great passion. She'd dubbed his manhood Fido as she'd sometimes felt compelled to say, 'Down, boy'— Tom's newfound appetite for bed-related activities had surpassed her own.

Which was why she was rather thankful she was back at work; she needed the respite. Were all priests such voracious lovers once indulging in guilt-free sex? True, he had needed the training, but she wondered whether a strapping Welsh rugby team could have got in any more practice than Tom had achieved. And she was feeling off-colour now: a bit queasy.

Unsure whether to show Faith how much he loved her before he left for the office just after six that morning, Tom had decided to let her rest, hoping that she wouldn't feel too neglected.

Miraculously, he now had a respectable number of bookings and an influx of queries that had arrived during his time away, which promised even more work. That YouTube clip of him proposing to Faith on the train had done more for his photographic business—and his relationship with Judith—than his own efforts. Tom just hoped that the vagaries of modern trends would not swing demand for his expertise back the other way once the novelty of having an ex-priest photographer wore off.

Now that he had dealt with all his mail and deliveries, he could continue uploading edited photographs to his website. The sheer workload had, at first, distracted him, but now that it had reached a hiatus, Tom sat thinking of Faith and how much he loved her—and how much he was missing her. He took out his phone and started thumbing the screen: *Mrs Sheridan, I am really missing you. Fido is missing you too. Care to have lunch in my office? We could lock the door xx* He pressed send.

Faith texted back: *Out on calls. Fido needs to learn to stay in his kennel during office hours xx*

Tom laughed and replied: *His kennel can get very small when he's thinking of you xx*

Her reply was instant: *Take him on a brisk walk. Cold, fresh air should do the trick xx*

It was five now. Faith started the shutdown of her computer; she intended a quick getaway, longing to be with Tom—and to tell him her news. Hope was comatose on the sofa bed in the inner office, recovering from the ordeal of answering calls and emailing responses all morning—doing some of what Faith's job had been before she'd got promoted. Edison would take Hope home. His care for her couldn't be faulted.

Just then, Faith's mobile buzzed. Fishing it out of her bag, she saw that there was a text message from Tom. He'd texted her earlier in the day too, just after noon, but she'd been making calls in the community and hadn't wanted to go back to the office for lunch as she'd wanted to visit a pharmacy to buy a special test. Although it had been rather soon to be suspicious,

suspicious she'd been.

When she'd read the result on the stick, her first instinct had been to call Tom. But on reflection, she'd decided to wait, savour the knowledge for a while and choose her moment.

Smiling now, she opened the latest message.

*Mrs Sheridan, would you do me the honour of meeting me in the cupboard? Now?*

Her smile widened into a grin. *Mrs Sheridan would be honoured to meet you there.*

After routing calls to the switchboard, she turned the key softly in the lock of the office door so as not to disturb Hope and headed for the cupboard.

'Hello, Mrs Sheridan,' Tom whispered.

She shut the door behind her. 'Hello, Mr Sheridan. I'm afraid I might need that bucket.'

'Let me guide you.'

'Just pass it to me.'

'Are you all right?'

'I feel a bit sick. I'm not sure if it will get worse.'

'Are you ill? Would you like to go home?'

'No, I don't think I'm ill. I think it's something else...'

She heard Tom's clothing rustle faintly. 'Try this.'

Something small and rough was passed into her hand. 'What is it?'

'A Fruit Pastille. It might help. Dad gave me these when I got travel sick.'

Although sceptical, Faith popped the sweet in her mouth and chewed for a moment before swallowing the first sugary result. It did help and she put the bucket down.

'It seems that your years of celibacy have packed one hell of a punch in your sperm. I've done a pregnancy test...'

His hand touched her shoulder. '*What?*'

She put her arms around him. 'You, my love, are going to be a daddy.'

'Oh…!' Tom held her tight and his lips found hers. She kept her mouth shut as she didn't want to choke on the sweet.

She heard him sniff. 'Are you all right?'

'Mm. I love you so much. I'm so happy.'

'That makes two of us.' She kissed him. 'You know,' she said, pulling slightly away, 'we haven't discussed the issue of contraception, and I think that perhaps now is a good time.' She chewed what was left of the pastille. The nausea had abated.

'Isn't that trying to shut the door after the horse has bolted?' He nuzzled her neck.

'For nine months' hence.'

'You're worried that I'm so fertile, I'll give you a baby every year?' His lips skimmed her skin as he spoke.

'Something like that. But I don't see why you're taking all the credit for making a baby. My eggs have to be in good shape as well as your sperm. But for it to have happened this quickly, so easily…'

'I will leave the matter of numbers entirely in your hands. Because whatever you want, I'll run with. I'm over the moon to have even one child, considering that prospect had been completely out of the realms of possibility not so long ago.'

'That's a relief. I was concerned you'd want a whole flock.'

He nibbled her ear. 'I've got my flock: you, all your friends who are now my friends too, my mother, Miranda. Amazing what having Faith can do,' Tom murmured. And then he kissed her. Just like the first time in the cupboard.

Mari Jane Law lives in the UK and loves cats and chocolate. She also loves books, TV series and films that make her laugh. Through her writing, she discovered she could make other people laugh too. She is a member of the Romantic Novelists' Association's New Writers' Scheme and The Society of Authors.

Her Catholic upbringing gave her ideas for some great fictional characters in the Love & Mishaps quirky romantic comedy series. As a child, she was amused by Giovanni Guareschi's *Don Camillo* books. As an adult, she was entertained by *Father Ted*. In between, among other titles, there was Jon Cleary's *Peter's Pence* and Paul Burke's *Father Frank,* which nurtured her taste in Catholic-themed comedy.

She hopes those who buy or borrow her work have as much fun reading it as she had in writing it.

There will be more to follow in the Love & Mishaps series, so you can meet your favourite characters again, to see how they're doing, as well as enjoy new quirky romance stories – happy ending guaranteed!

If you enjoyed reading *Love in the Cupboard*, please consider leaving a comment on Amazon and Goodreads to help other readers decide whether this book is for them, and to help the author!

amzn.to/40YVBkr

Find out more at:
www.marijanelaw.com
Twitter: www.twitter.com/MariJaneLaw1
Facebook: www.facebook.com/marijane.law.1
Goodreads: https://tinyurl.com/566avtb6
Amazon author page: https://amzn.to/3lFWe2o
YouTube: www.tinyurl.com/2ryst3w9

Perdita Riley is facing the greatest dilemma of her life. Why had she taken Violet Freestone's advice on how to make herself look more alluring? It led her into the arms of a womaniser.

To cheer herself up, Perdita goes shopping, where an extraordinary encounter deposits her, literally, into the lap of Saul Hadley. She would like to stay there, but...

Will she find a way to deal with what has happened? Can she manage the complications of her growing attraction to Saul?

This hilarious situational romantic comedy will keep you gripped until the very end. Shortlisted for Choc Lit's 2019 Search for a Star competition

Paperback: ISBN-13: 978-1913410056
Paperback: ISBN-10: 1913410056
eBook: ASIN: B08772BTFZ
Buy it from Amazon: amzn.to/3KbgbbE

Printed in Great Britain
by Amazon